SKY LAKE LOST

LOST

Leigh Chandler

That would be my fault, too, since he visited Sky Lake for me. But that's not something you can ask a nurse.

The doctors sent David home with appointments for three different kinds of scans and no answers. We went back and forth for injections, medications, and blood transfusions, and I ran to the pharmacy so often that the cashier started to slip free candy bars into the prescription bags. I bought pint after pint of chocolate ice cream—David wouldn't eat anything else. I bargained and prayed. Late at night, when I knew no one would hear me, I cried until my eyes ached.

One by one, I threw my lake rocks away, thinking the sacrifice might remove the curse from my brother. They clattered lightly against pavement and landed soundlessly in grass and plopped gently into water.

They were small. Insubstantial. Just pebbles.

It felt like a bad dream. But I didn't wake up, no matter how wide I opened my burning, gritty eyes.

Bobby hired an acupuncturist, an energy healer, and a man who mixed a foul-smelling combination of herbs into a tea that made David gag. Months went by. Tense. Waiting.

David faded a little more every day while the doctors scratched their heads. He was perfectly healthy, and he was also dying, and no one could tell us why. But I didn't truly understand how bad things were until Bobby came home and told me to pack, because David had an appointment with Johnathan Everett in the morning, and we needed to be at the airport in an hour.

Even a kid knew you didn't go anywhere near Johnathan Everett unless you had no other choice.

3

GRACE

None of us slept on the overnight flight to Boston. Even David, who could hardly keep his eyes open anymore, buzzed with nervous energy. "Relax," Bobby said, patting David's skinny wrist as the plane rumbled a low warning in the background. "They have the best medical research facility in the country. It's totally above board. We're not getting involved in any of the... sketchy stuff."

David offered a tight smile and squeezed Bobby's hand. I pressed my own hands together, my last lake rock smooth and warm between them.

"The guy who got us the appointment—his mother was treated there. Experimental cancer drug that you can't get anywhere else. It worked."

Bobby sounded sure, but he was talking fast and avoiding our eyes. We all knew that Everett Research & Consulting swallowed most of the desperate people who went there for a miracle. "They have resources," Bobby said, hyping himself up as we helped David off the plane. When he took my suitcase out of the overhead bin, he slammed it down hard enough to make me jump. "And no red tape. It's what we need."

ERC sat deep in the woods of Western Massachusetts, not far from Sky Lake. I wished Bobby would just keep driving. But he followed the directions through a gray, abandoned town half-eaten by the woods and into a dreary world of warehouses and office parks.

The warning rumble was in our tires now—*mistake mistake mistake.*

Like Sky Lake, the place we finally pulled up to in our tiny white rental car did not feel ordinary. A small forest of block shaped buildings sat, heavy and menacing, in an unfriendly expanse of manicured lawn bordered by woods. The air crackled with energy, but it wasn't the welcoming, perfumed energy of Sky Lake. This place sucked us in like something hungry.

This was a place you could walk into and disappear.

Into the woods we go, I thought, the words dancing on a dark, whispering melody.

"My friend told us to go to building one," Bobby said. "They give tours of that building. There's nothing scary in there, I promise." Our collective knowledge of the horrors lurking in the other buildings hung in the car like a bad smell. "Come on," Bobby said.

Time slowed as Bobby got out of the car and opened David's door, like it recognized the threshold we stood on—*stay or go.*

Bobby jerked my door open. "Come on," he repeated. An order.

Bobby needed to believe this place held the answer. And, even though I knew it didn't, I couldn't do anything except follow them in. That's the thing about being a kid. It doesn't matter how much you know, no one listens to you.

I shivered, sweaty and cold inside a fleece jacket that used to be David's. We were going in, whether I liked it or not.

I listened. To Johnathan Everett's words—clear, calm, pragmatic—and the hum underneath them—greedy, grasping, sinister. Bobby's eyes glared warnings at me—*stay still, be quiet, don't screw this up*—as I slid from suspicion to certainty. The right decision wasn't *stay.* It was *go.* And time was pulling us now, fast and deep and far away from safety.

Even Bobby was scared when a woman in blue scrubs came into the comfortable public waiting room and said "Mr. Everett will see you personally. Come with me." But he tried not to show it. And so did I until the elevator opened.

The hallway was shiny and black, and it smelled like smoke. My grandmother would have called it a sign. I flattened myself against the back wall of the elevator and probably would have stayed there if not for David, reaching for my hand. He needed me.

"I never promise results," Johnathan Everett barked, pacing like a predator in a cage. He was tall and stern, with military posture and eyes that flashed with curiosity, intelligence, and power—too much to be contained behind the big wooden desk that took up half his office.

The office itself was ordinary enough—coat rack, candy dish, swirling marble floors—but I could feel the heavy, pressing darkness of the hallway outside. Standing behind David with my back against the door, I tried to summon the spongy surface of the homemade stage at Sky Lake. My safe place.

"My medical researchers are top notch, but they aren't here to ease your pain, or prolong your life, or even to put you out of your misery if it comes to that. ERC is a research organization, not a hospital, and our only interest is to get as much information as possible."

A melody built up in my throat, turning the volume down on the terrifying man who held David's life in his hands.

Johnathan Everett stopped pacing and blasted the full force of his stare on David. "But my people will get an answer. And if the answer comes in time, you might get those other things you're after."

I let the melody rise a little higher, into my mouth. It tasted like pine trees and lake water and the spicy-sweet smell of the roses.

Bobby cleared his throat. "We should… discuss it," he said, reaching for David, and my heart leaped. Bobby didn't want to stay. My mouth filled with roses, so real that I could crush their sweet, perfumed petals between my teeth.

But Johnathan Everett wasn't paying any attention to Bobby. He was sniffing the air. *The roses,* I thought, but they were already in the room. His eyes landed on me like a snake about to strike. The melody slid down my throat. Too late.

"Unusual." He drew the word out like it didn't have enough syllables, and I wished I could make myself invisible. "Your name?" he demanded.

I longed for the safety of the elevator. The rental car. The window seat on the plane. "Grace," I whispered. Even that felt like too much of myself to share with this dangerous person.

He made a note, then pressed a button on his desk to call the woman back. "Take them to the hospital wing," he ordered, and that was the end of the discussion. We were staying.

David reassured Bobby as the woman led us away. "This is good," he said, holding one of Bobby's big hands in both of his weak, bony ones. His voice shook. He knew we were in too deep, but he cared more about Bobby than he did about himself. "We're here now, and we're going to get to the bottom of this."

Bobby's head nodded, but his shoulders hung like the whole building squatted on top of him.

David tugged his hand. "It's going to be ok," he promised.

Trailing behind, I felt alone and forgotten. But David was right. We were here now. Prisoners. I heard it every time another heavy door clicked shut behind us.

Back then, with my child's understanding of the world, I thought Johnathan wanted to solve the puzzle of David's mysterious condition. Now, of course, I know better. If David and Bobby interviewed alone, they would have had a choice: Stay, knowing that any treatment was purely for research purposes, or leave.

We didn't get that choice.

Johnathan didn't let people go if he wanted to keep them.

And he wanted to keep *me*.

It's hard, even now, for me to describe ERC. Most of it looked like any other office building, as evidenced by the national sigh of disappointment when the press finally got in so many years later. People expected dungeons and torture machines and human skulls, and got old printers and filing cabinets and white tiles. But that's part of what made it so awful—the boring routine, punctuated by real horrors.

The public building that we entered that first day felt like a parlor in a fancy house—nice, but no one sits on the couches. The business of ERC happened in the back buildings and the basements, where you needed a keycard to get in or out. Those buildings held labs and storage closets and giant, walk-in freezers. Whole rooms housed machines that only one person knew how to use. Several floors stretched below ground, and people whispered about locked cells and cages and tanks. Huge screens presided over every room, and anyone who had been there longer than a few months didn't look at them.

I didn't know any of that until much later. I only knew how the place *felt*. And I still can't quite express it. When they asked me to describe it in an interview, I said it was like being inside a jellyfish. The poor reporter just sat there, blinking, until I changed the subject myself. But that's still the best description I can come up with. ERC was more like an organism than a place. You never knew if what you touched would be soft or stinging, or if you were going to get a breath of air or water, or what would be behind the next door you opened.

The hospital wing was white, bare, and antiseptic, with a soundtrack of beeping monitors and the occasional moan or scream of a patient. It looked like a hospital on TV. But it felt dark and damp in spite of the harsh lights. I wanted to open a window and stick my head out for air, but the windows didn't open. You could tell just by looking at them.

The panic I'd been managing like a little garden since David collapsed expanded, making my skin prickly and tight. I allowed the melody in my throat to swell into a low hum. Humming was my bad habit. It started after my grandmother died and before I felt comfortable in David and Bobby's apartment, and it irritated Bobby. But it made me feel safe and protected, feelings I desperately needed as my sneakers squeaked behind the wheelchair that held my brother. The music bloomed, pushing fear out of me like splinters.

My song blocked out the terrible hallway one sense at a time. Beeping became birdsong. The smell of rubbing alcohol faded, replaced by pine trees and dirt. The chill of air conditioning turned into a cool breeze. The glare of the lights eased, revealing green trees and blue sky and the glassy shimmer of water. The *slap slap slap* of my sneakers became the rhythmic lap of water against the dock. I felt lake mud between my toes. The tension in my muscles let go. *Home.*

"Keep up," Bobby barked, and his voice hit me like a bird flying into a window. He was half a hallway ahead already, walking briskly next to David's wheelchair while the woman pushed. David's head bounced in a slow, gentle way that reminded me of the rowboat on the lake. "Grace," Bobby called, louder this time. "I said keep up."

I heard Bobby's impatience with me in his voice, and I saw his impatience with the woman pushing the wheelchair in the twitch of his fingers by his sides. I wondered what advantage he thought he could gain by getting David to his room a minute faster. The melody called, and I wanted, more than anything, to sink back into its arms.

"I'm serious, Grace. You could get lost in here."

He didn't say *and I have more important things to worry about than you,* or *if you don't behave yourself, I'll send you away.* In hindsight, I know that's not what he meant—he was overwhelmed and grasping at whatever control he could. But it's what I heard. Bobby needed me to behave. Or else.

More importantly, David needed me to be right there with him, in the hospital, with the harsh light and hard floors and bad smells.

I swallowed, and the melody slipped down my throat. The birdsong turned back into beeping. The lights burned the trees away, and the floor hardened under my feet. The hospital smell filled my nostrils and burned my eyes, sharp and unnatural and real. Ahead of me, David's head bobbed, and I couldn't imagine the rowboat under him anymore, only the wheelchair.

I promised myself that I would stop daydreaming. David needed my full attention, just like he had always given me his full attention. But when I caught up, he grabbed my hand and smiled up at me. "I'll send him for coffee as soon as I'm settled," he whispered, forcing strength into his voice. "And you can bring the birds back."

4

GRACE

I lived in David's room because no one told me to go anywhere else. I slept on the chair by his bed, or on the floor when I needed to stretch my cramped legs. I talked to him, sang to him, coaxed bites of food into him, tried to make him laugh. I didn't let him see my hands trembling, like they wanted to shake themselves off and run away without me.

Doctors and nurses bustled in and out. They took blood, listened to his heart, and didn't make much eye contact, but when they did, I saw the same empty expression every time. Looking into their eyes made me cold all the way through.

The only person who seemed to care was the psychiatrist. Damia clicked her pen, tugged her hair, and shot constant, guilty looks at the camera in the corner of the room, like she'd done something wrong and hadn't gotten caught yet. But she also smiled sometimes, and even though they were sad smiles, they were real. She brought extra pillows and blankets from an empty room. She called me by my name—no one else even asked who I was—and gave me watery hot chocolate in paper cups. She instructed the kitchen to send double meal trays, even though David barely ate and we could get by on one. Mine came with an extra dessert.

Those tiny kindnesses meant more and more as my old life faded, replaced by the reality of David's failing body in that cold room. "Do you need anything?" she always asked before she left, her voice hesitating just enough to let me know I shouldn't ask for much. But the question mattered.

Bobby, who worked security for ERC to pay our way, visited David between shifts. I slunk into the hallway to give them privacy even though Bobby wouldn't have noticed if I stayed. David was the only thing in the world to him then. But the room closed around me like a cell when Bobby rushed in, wearing his security uniform and gulping a cup of coffee to stay awake.

We were only just starting to feel like a family when everything went wrong. Now we were just Grace and David, and Bobby and David. David couldn't be the bridge anymore.

At first, I waited right outside David's room during Bobby's visits, squeaking my too-tight sneakers on the slippery tiles. I was lonely and invisible in the hallway, but I didn't have to keep a brave face on for David. I could sulk or cry or make whispered deals with the universe. No one cared. But crying gets old, after a while. I ventured a little farther from the room every day, until I reached the end of the hospital hallway.

I expected something—an alarm, or an employee—to block the last door. A sign with two arrows identified the area I'd just come from as "Hospital, Protective Clothing Required" and the area beyond the door as "Authorized Employee Access Only." I put my hands flat against the door. No one stopped, me, so I pushed.

The door opened with a smooth, slow whoosh. *Not locked.* A gust of warm, coffee scented air hit me and I stepped into an entirely different place.

It was like a story, except that instead of a magic land, I emerged in an office with mauve carpet, pale blue walls, and shiny silver filing cabinets. A long desk held a big, old computer, a stack of yellow folders, and a pink mug full of pens. A fluffy faux-fur jacket hung over a chair, and a worn-out blue couch leaned in a corner like it was tired. Tears welled up, blinding me. It was the first soft thing I'd touched in months, and its lumpy embrace felt like heaven.

I don't know how long I slept, but I woke to the sound of gum snapping. "Finally!" a voice groaned, and I scrambled up, too disoriented to run for the door. *Caught.*

A teenager sat at the desk, sucking an extra-large iced coffee through a lipstick-smudged straw. "I thought you were dead. But then I held a mirror up to your face and it fogged, which meant you were breathing—I saw that trick in a movie once—so I figured you couldn't be dead. Although around here, that might not be a great bet, they're probably making zombies in the basement somewhere." She flipped her hair and rolled her eyes, like making zombies was just a silly thing grown-ups did sometimes. "I'm Janey," she said. "What's your name?"

I wiped drool off my chin, face flushing with embarrassment. "Grace," I mumbled. The word felt funny in my mouth. I'd only told two people at ERC my name—Johnathan, and Damia. I wondered which kind of person Janey would turn out to be.

"How old are you?" She leaned forward, bright with interest, and I could tell she had a lot more questions.

"Eleven. Almost twelve." As I said it, I realized that there wouldn't be a cake or a wish or David singing his own cheesy version of happy birthday to me this year. I would turn a year older and no one would notice.

"Well, gosh, don't cry," the girl said. "Twelve isn't so young. I'm only thirteen and a half." She bounced up from the desk and joined me on the couch, where she awkwardly patted my arm. "We can be friends. We kind of have to be. Everyone else here is ancient. Want some gum?" She held out a package of bubble gum. I hesitated—it felt risky to accept a gift. "Go ahead," she encouraged. "Take a few pieces. Chewing is a good distraction." Her bright eyes darkened for a split second, almost too quick for me to notice. "Also, it tastes like grape. Best flavor."

Janey was—is—Johnathan Everett's niece, and she'd been working in that office for three years when I met her. She went home at night to a mother who loved her, but Johnathan owned Janey just like he owned me, and we bonded the way prisoners do.

She still calls me her best friend. I call her my oldest friend, and if she notices the difference, she doesn't show it. Back then, she saved my life.

"Chin up," she said, withdrawing the gum and offering a tube of lip gloss. "You're gonna be ok."

Janey started leaving little offerings on the couch. A pile of warm blankets and a pillow. Snacks. Gossip magazines. My own tube of pink lip gloss. Bubble gum. Sometimes, a packed lunch from home that she said she didn't feel like eating, although I know she packed those lunches especially for me. I'd eat, and nap, and when I woke up, she'd be working her way through a pile of paper or typing something.

On my birthday, she brought a cupcake with a candle in it. "Can't light it," she apologized. "You never know what's floating around in the air. Last year, Susan from accounting sneaked a cigarette in the bathroom and it exploded. Burned her eyebrows right off." Janey raised her own eyebrows as high as she could, making them disappear under her bangs. "But you can pretend. Close your eyes, imagine it's on fire, and make a wish."

I wished for David to be healed, even though I knew he'd be better already if my wishes had any power at all. Janey said that was ok—the wishing mattered, all by itself, even in a place like ERC where good wishes never came true.

"You should take those with you," Janey said one day, waving at the pile of magazines accumulating by the couch. "I know it's not your thing, but it'll make you less… interesting." Her voice got quiet at the end of the sentence and her eyes darted to the camera in the corner of the room.

"Less interesting?" It had never occurred to me that I might be interesting in the first place.

"To *him*." She lowered her voice a little more, flipping through her own magazine as if she was completely engrossed. "If he thinks you're an airhead like me, he'll stop watching you so closely."

I opened my mouth to tell her she wasn't an airhead, but Janey's hair sat high in pigtails, her lips were working overtime to manage a large glob of purple bubble gum, and a spray of blue glitter framed her eyes. "Airhead" seemed like exactly what she was going for. "He's watching me?" I asked, instead.

"Yeah. He watches everyone when they first get here. But you've been here a while, and he still has your brother's room pinned on the screen in his office. The other ones rotate, but that room is always up there. And the camera's pointed at you."

I closed my eyes, trying to process this new information while some protective part of me shut it out. Screens, cameras, my face in Johnathan Everett's office. Suddenly, I could feel the burn of his eyes on the back of my neck.

"I don't know what he's looking at." Janey rolled her eyes and flipped her hair again. "He's a lot of things, but I don't think he's a creep, so it's a mystery why he'd be watching a kid all day. From what I can see, you just sit there and hold your brother's hand and sing."

On the surface, that's exactly what I did. I kept my voice quiet, my eyes down, and my melody simple. But I rarely stopped, and maybe that drew Johnathan's attention. Or maybe something else shined out of me when I sang to my brother.

I wouldn't know, because when I sang, David and I went somewhere else.

Under the influence of my voice, we spent long, lazy afternoons on the beach at Sky Lake, where David buried my feet in the stand and dared me to jump into the dark water. We stole gulps of icy winter air as we skated, scarves flying behind us like banners.

We stood together in the rose garden with snow and petals falling around us. Sometimes, David gathered armfuls of them for me. "My princess," he would say, joking but also not joking. We were in an enchanted place, after all. And David was as healthy and happy as a person can be in a patch of borrowed time due back at any moment.

We sat on the dock and kicked ripples into the cold blue water. We walked through the woods under the shimmering silver light of a full moon. We ate ice cream at the kitchen table. We talked.

It was real. And it also wasn't.

The water bit my feet, icy-cold. The air smelled of pine and spicy-sweet roses. But time passed strangely, reminding us that we were in an in-between place with its own rules. The weather changed, but the moon was always full. Sometimes, we escaped for seconds and came back to find a whole night gone, and other times we saw summer turn to fall and came back an hour after we left.

Although I didn't age physically there, I imagine that if you cut me open, you'd find more rings than there should be.

It was a trick. A spell. And it broke the moment my melody did, so I sang despite Janey's warning. I had to. It was the only thing I could give to David, and I gave it even after I started to break under the weight of his pain.

I didn't appreciate the extra time I had with him. I was too tired, too scared. It hurt too much. But after I lost him, I would have given everything for another minute.

"That is all you do, right? You just sit there and sing? There's nothing weird going on? Because my uncle has a sixth sense for weird." Janey snapped her gum and flipped a page, the actions so graceful that I wondered if she practiced them in front of a mirror. "He loves weird. He, like, seeks it out and locks it in cages in the basements." Her eyes darted up again, to the camera.

"Nothing weird." My voice shook as I tried not to imagine the cages.

Janey shrugged like we weren't talking about anything important. "Whatever," she said. "I'm just telling you what I saw. You do what you want with the information. But if I were you, I'd read one of these by his bed from now on." She flapped her magazine shut, sending a flurry of papers across the desk. "What harm could it do?"

I took the stack of magazines back to David's room and kept one open on my lap. But I didn't stop singing. I couldn't. Even if I wanted to stop, the music had a mind of its own, and if I closed my mouth, I think it would have forced its way out through my eyes and nose and ears. It would have torn me apart to get to him.

Years later, a vocal coach told me to imagine my voice as a liquid, and I thought of those endless days and nights by David's bed when my voice grew into a thing my body couldn't hold. I didn't have to imagine. Sometimes, I thought my voice didn't belong to me at all. That it just lived inside me, a creature desperate to escape.

One night, as David drifted in and out of a fitful sleep, he gripped my arm. I took a quick sip of water and opened my mouth to sing, but he shook his head. "No. We need to talk about this *here*."

He stopped for a breath. The melody was fighting to get out of me, and I swallowed hard to keep it down. He needed me to listen.

"Bobby will take you," he whispered, the words coming with effort, like the air wouldn't cooperate. "He loves you, Gracie, even if he doesn't know how to show it. He'll keep you safe."

He loves you. I didn't believe it, but I understood that David needed to believe it. "Ok," I said. "He won't have to, though. You're going to get better." The melody pressed hard, almost gagging me, and I clenched my teeth against it.

"Gracie," David whispered. "Let's not pretend."

My chest tightened until I wasn't sure I could take another breath.

"Bobby will take you. But if he doesn't... if he leaves you here... Go to Sky Lake. It's not far. You know how to find it. You'll be safe there." David stopped like a man at the end of a run, not a sentence. "The real Sky Lake," he added. "Not... wherever you take me."

I started to argue, but he shook his head so hard that I was afraid he'd hurt himself.

"You have to promise." He squeezed my wrist with more strength than I thought he had, and I felt the terrible sharpness of his bones against mine. "I need to know you understand."

I nodded. "The lake," I repeated, as my throat tried to close around the words. "I'll go to Sky Lake." I bargained with the sobs that threatened to burst out—*not here, where he can see you.* "But I won't have to, right, because Bobby will take me with him?" The question was the closest I ever came to acknowledging that David would die, and it hurt like a pill swallowed sideways.

"Of course he'll take you." David's eyes were closing. "You'll bury me at Sky Lake, together, and light my stone with your memories. I'll always be with you, Gracie, as long as my stone is lit. You know that."

I knew that. And it wasn't enough. I nodded, losing my fight with the tears.

He took a shuddering breath. "But if you're ever in trouble, you just go to the lake. Promise me."

I promised, and then I sang. Safe at Sky Lake, we sat together on the dock under a light rain that grew heavier until the water and sky became one thing with us in the middle. "We should go in," I said, nodding back toward the house, but David just sat with his face turned up to the clouds, smiling.

"No. This is perfect. Remember that, Gracie. Remember to notice all the times when it's perfect." He turned to me, his face shining with rain and joy, and I should have known that he didn't have much time left. But I stayed in denial to keep David with me a little while longer.

I didn't notice the shift from easing David's pain to prolonging it until Bobby took my small hands in his enormous ones, looked straight into my eyes, and said "Keep him with us while I'm at work, ok Gracie?"

I looked at David's trembling body, shrunken into the very center of the narrow bed, and thought, *that's the last thing I should be doing.*

But I took David's hands when Bobby let mine go, and the song came on its own.

The day I stopped singing to David, Bobby told me, again, to keep him with us. But I knew I could only give him more hours of suffering and Bobby another night of unheard prayers. It had to stop. I had to stop it.

I clamped my lips between my teeth and focused on the hard angles of my brother's hand in mine. Bone and skin. Too weak to hold his guitar. His breaths were coming in spurts—two fast ones, then a long silence, then a long, strangled gasp—and I wanted to take him away from it. But I knew I'd just be bringing him back to this bed.

The song fought to get out. But I fought harder, my teeth grinding together, my own breath hitching and stopping along with my brother's. By the time he stopped for good, my throat was raw and my mouth was coppery with blood.

Bobby came back to the silent monitors and threw himself on the flimsy metal bed. His weight crushed the fragile ribs that David didn't need anymore, and the bedframe screeched under him. A strangled moan filled the room. Then, he turned on me. "How could you?" he asked, and each word hit like a rock. "How could you let this happen?"

I hugged myself, caught between what I knew—it was wrong to keep David alive any longer—and the reality of my lifeless brother in the bed.

"He was in pain," I whispered. "I had to let him go." Tears spilled suddenly, hot on my hospital-cold cheeks.

"You could have kept him here." Bobby grabbed the bars on the sides of the bed and rattled them, shaking David's ruined body. "You let him go!"

He doesn't mean it, a voice said inside me. David's voice.

"He's gone. Gone gone gone. I didn't say goodbye." Bobby was talking to the ceiling now. To God. His big hands gripped handfuls of his own hair. Despair came off him in black, smoky waves.

He doesn't know what he's saying, the David-voice in my mind insisted. *He'll take you with him.*

But Bobby took off down the hall, so fast that I had to run.

"Bobby, wait." But he didn't stop.

David's voice whispered in my ear—*Bobby loves you. He'll keep you safe.* And then Bobby tuned around, and the pain in his eyes froze me. It was raw and wild and blinding. Worse, I realized, with dawning horror, than the pain I released David from.

I want to go back, I thought, not sure if I meant back in time or back to Sky Lake or just away from the grief, guilt, and rage in this hallway. "You can't leave him here," I begged, thinking it might be more persuasive than *you can't leave me here.*

"He's not there anymore." Bobby touched his keycard to the heavy front door, making it beep. "And I'm not responsible for you." His voice shook, and I know he regretted those words as soon as he came to his senses. But his rejection pinned me to the floor like a knife. He yanked the door open like it weighed nothing.

Run, the David-voice urged, but I was paralyzed. *You promised,* the David-voice reminded.

You lied, I thought back, hard. Bobby didn't love me. No one but David loved me, and he left me. A scream built in my chest and I held it back like the song. With my teeth.

Bobby hesitated in the doorway.

How different things would have been if I'd scurried out and found my way to Sky Lake. But I made *two* promises—that I'd go to Sky Lake, *and* that I'd bury David there. I wasn't leaving him behind.

He never would have left me. Not if he had a choice, anyway.

The practicalities of keeping my promise didn't hit me until I saw the nurses buzzing around David, taking whatever they could. He belonged to them—I couldn't just take him to Sky Lake.

He was a body. Not my brother. Not David.

I backed into a corner and blocked my ears against their sounds—vials clinking, scissors snipping, voices asking for towels, instruments, and containers like my brother was nothing but blood and hair and fingernails. They covered him with a shiny white sheet. They would wheel him away to take the rest of it. Eyes. Heart. Liver.

As they freed the brakes and pushed his bed out of the room, I wanted to crawl in beside him.

"You forgot something," I whispered, to the nurses but also to myself. David's voice was gone from my mind, his smile fading. I couldn't find the brother who laughed so hard he had coughing fits and dragged the piano into the dining room and lit up every stage he stood on—it was like the blank silent thing under the sheet replaced him.

I thought I knew what it felt like to be lonely. But, until that very moment in the room that used to be David's room, I'd never really been alone in my life.

Johnathan gave David back to me hours later in a small wooden box. Dozens of cold, empty eyes watched me walk to his neat, ice-cold office. They followed me out ten minutes later, David's box cradled like a baby and not a pile of ashes.

"What are your family's burial practices?" Johnathan asked. He leaned forward with such interest that I imagined his eyes leaving scorched trails behind. Later, when I knew him better, I understood that he asked all questions with that burning curiosity. Like every answer had the potential to amaze him. At the time, it made me feel so exposed that I checked to make sure my shirt was still buttoned. "I assume you follow some tradition?" he prodded. "Religious? Spiritual?"

I weighed my options. Janey said he had a sixth sense for weird, and anyone could feel the magic at Sky Lake. I didn't want him to put whatever made Sky Lake special into a cage in the basement. But this might be my only chance to get back there. "We have a cemetery at my grandmother's house," I confessed, choosing the second door.

"Ah!" His cheerful tone made me wonder if I had misjudged him. "That's local, yes?" He flipped through a file on his desk and nodded, satisfied with whatever he found there. "I will arrange for you to take him tomorrow." I dared, for just a second, to hope for kindness, but his expression closed with the file. "And then you will return here. Or, if you prefer, there are burial options on-site." He clasped his hands and waited for my decision.

On-site. *A bin in the basement*, I thought. *Or an incinerator.* "I'll take him home." I clasped my own hands to hide their trembling. "And I can stay there, too. With my grandmother." I held my breath.

Amusement lit Johnathan's unnaturally blue eyes. Cold, intense, *dangerous*. I chose the wrong door. "Grace." He sighed like he expected more from me. "You have no grandmother."

My tears made the room as watery as a fish tank. *Shark*, I thought. *Johnathan would be the shark.*

"And we'll have to work on your lying if you're going to be useful. Now run along and be ready to go first thing tomorrow."

I walked away on wobbly legs, gripping the box so tight that my fingers throbbed. I didn't want to be useful to Johnathan Everett. I wanted to go home.

I spent the night in David's room on the hard chair that didn't have a bed beside it anymore. The box sat heavily in my lap. A disconnected monitor held vigil with me, casting the shadow of a horror movie monster on the wall. An appropriate companion, I thought. I tried to sing, but the trick didn't work without David.

I was stuck. Physically, at ERC, and in a deeper, more painful way. I couldn't even escape in my mind.

Early the next morning, a man in a suit came to collect me as Johnathan promised. He gestured at the box in my lap and my bare feet. *Get your stuff and let's go.* I kicked my shoes out from under the chair. Taking my backpack would look suspicious, so I slipped a few small things into my pockets and stuffed my feet into my shoes.

Plans flew through my mind as I ran after the man. I could talk him into leaving me, or kick him in the knee and lock myself in the house, or hide in an animal's burrow deep in the woods. The best plan, the one I settled on, was to throw myself out of the car before we arrived. The man couldn't find Sky Lake without my help unless he had a handwritten map or a rock from the lake, and Johnathan didn't know about that. I just had to get close enough and then run.

I took my last pebble, just to be safe.

My plan crumbled when I found Damia in the back seat of the SUV with sad eyes and two paper cups. *Hot chocolate.* "Grace," she said, in a kind, motherly way, offering the hot drink. But she might as well have been holding a pair of handcuffs.

The man in the suit closed my door. The lock clicked. *Trapped.*

"I'm so sorry about your brother," she said. "But I'm glad I can help you bring him home." She squeezed my hand, and it made me feel claustrophobic. I wished she wouldn't touch me. "Does your family have any burial traditions I should know about? I'd like to help you make this as meaningful as possible."

I hadn't let myself think that far ahead. But we were going to Sky Lake, where we would get shovels from the shed, and we would use those shovels to dig a hole that I would put David in. That I would *leave* David in. I shook my head.

A parade of heavy clouds collected over the car as we got closer to Sky Lake. By the time we reached the last turn, it looked like thunderstorm weather. "Are you sure?" the man asked, when I ordered him to take a sharp right. "I can't see a damn thing."

"Just turn." I wished I could grab the wheel and turn it for him.

By the time we navigated all the way up the long, bumpy driveway, the clouds were so low and thick that it could have been midnight. Trees reached for me with their long fingers. The empty house loomed darkly, each window an eye. All the songs I sang to David sat in a hard clump in my throat.

The man muttered about the weather, urging us to hurry.

For a second, it felt like David would get out of the car with his backpack over one shoulder and race me to the house. But Damia emerged instead, zipping her coat against the cold breeze off the water and looking nervously up at the sky. "It was supposed to be sunny," she said.

Music swelled in my throat. The darkness reminded me of the weeks after my grandmother threw David out, when it rained every day and thick fog made the lake invisible. I was barely older than a baby, but I remember my little feet squishing ankle deep in mud and understanding that the earth and I were sad together.

Sky Lake was mourning my brother.

Worry crept past my grief. On a sunny day, Damia might not notice anything different about Sky Lake. In the dark, she couldn't miss it.

Damia followed me to the shed, worrying out loud about rain and wishing we brought umbrellas. I jiggled the rusty latch open, grabbed the shovels, and hurried up the path. The rose garden glowed with light that seemed to come straight from the ground. The lake was so full of reflected clouds that you could easily mistake down for up. Sticky tears dripped from the trees. I risked a glance at Damia. Her eyes were on her feet, not on the roses.

Much later, she confessed that she thought she was having a stroke and didn't want to scare me by saying anything about it. At the time, I hurried us through the flowers—yellow, orange, lavender, almost-black violet, shimmering white—as fast as I could with all my fingers crossed.

Past the rose garden, down a path lined on both sides by a low stone wall, we reached the cemetery. Smooth stones from the deepest part of the lake marked the graves. They were fuzzy with moss, and the most recent ones glowed with a soft, golden light. I found the ones that belonged to my grandparents, pulsing gently near the wall under the apple tree. At first, I couldn't find my mother's stone. Then I realized—nobody remembered her anymore. Her stone went out with David.

I plunged my shovel into the earth and shook my head when Damia tried to help. I wanted to do it myself, and I also needed to buy some time.

I must have terrified poor Damia when I jumped into the water, but I needed a stone from Sky Lake to mark David's grave and I knew she wouldn't let me get one. I kicked off my shoes, emptied my pockets in a hurry, and leaped from the big rock before I could think too much about the water itself, deep and full of clouds below me.

I hoped Damia wouldn't jump in. The lake could be tricky with things that didn't belong in it.

I had never been to the bottom of Sky Lake. Retrieving stones was a grown-up job, and I was not supposed to grow up for a long time. But it wasn't like I needed directions to the bottom of a lake. I was a good diver—straight as an arrow—and I felt free and weightless as I cut through the cold water.

Sky Lake loved me. It would keep me safe.

I hit the bottom suddenly, raising a gritty cloud. *You don't belong here*, my body screamed, and something outside me joined in. *You don't belong here.*

On my hands and knees under all that darkness, I felt small and weak. *Not safe.* My muscles cramped in the cold and my lungs shrieked for air as the water pressed down, heavy and indifferent.

But I couldn't leave without David's stone.

I grabbed frantic handfuls of slimy clay, decomposing leaves, and sharp things that might have been branches or bones. Not what I needed. For one terrible moment I thought I would come up empty handed, and then my elbow hit something hard and smooth and much too large to carry up through all that water. *David's stone.* I could feel the rhythm of his beautiful voice beating inside it.

I wrapped myself around the stone and pushed. For one, terrible moment I remained anchored to the floor of the lake, and then I was flying, flung up and up by a forceful current, the stone nearly weightless in my arms.

Not saving me, I thought.

Spitting me out.

I was breaking through the surface by the time Damia finished struggling with her fear and worked up the courage to go after me. "Grace!" she shouted, leaning precariously over the edge of the big rock, her voice high with panic. "Grace, are you alright? Are you in trouble? Do you need help?" I could practically hear her thoughts underneath. *Please don't need help. Please don't need help.*

"I'm fine." I hoisted myself and the rock out of the water that had almost swallowed me whole, arms stinging where I scraped them, lungs aching with the effort of holding my breath for so long. I shouldn't have been able to carry the stone, let alone swim with it, but I dropped it on the mound of dirt that covered my brother and rested my forehead against it.

"David," I whispered. "I did what I promised. Come back to me, please." Memories of my brother—the real, live brother who loved me—flooded in like a movie. His head shaking like a dog's as he popped up from the lake. His arms around me after a nightmare. His voice calling me Gracie.

The stone brightened, but I couldn't feel its warmth.

I pressed my hands into the dirt, forcing gratitude through my fingers. Begging the place I loved to love me back.

Damia hovered behind me, eyes bouncing from the stone to the ominous sky. "Are you ready to go, honey?" she asked, impatient but trying not to sound that way, and I reluctantly led her back the way we came. David's voice didn't follow, and the forest didn't open its arms. I was alone.

Grief threatened to topple me over, but fear kept me moving. What if I collapsed, and the carpet of soft petals didn't embrace me? I couldn't bear that. Not on top of the silence where David's voice used to be.

I just had to trust that my brother was at peace now. And that I would learn to live with the hole he left behind.

I did not consider the possibility of returning to the black SUV and the man in the suit and Johnathan Everett until we reached the yard. I assumed

Sky Lake would find a way to keep me. But we were almost there and it wasn't even raining. I calculated the distance to the house. The time it would take to break a window, because I didn't have time to find the key hidden in the garden. The time it would take to hide. If I hid well enough, they'd have to go for help, and they wouldn't find their way back without a stone or a handwritten map.

My last lake stone sat heavily in my pocket. I touched it, praying for a miracle.

Damia took my arm like it just occurred to her that I might run. The house—safety—stood just out of reach, windows glinting like it was trying to turn the lights on for me. "Please," I begged, remembering Damia's hand on my shoulder, her worried eyes, the blankets and pillows and hot drinks she brought me. She cared, at least a little bit. She could be persuaded. "Let me stay."

"I can't leave you here." She sounded sorry but she held my arm tight enough to hurt a little.

"You can, though. I can take care of myself. I… have a grandmother."

Damia shot a skeptical look at the abandoned house. A faint light blinked in the window of an upstairs bedroom. *Glow,* I thought, as hard as I could. *Make it look like somebody's home.* But the light didn't get any brighter.

"She's not here," I lied. "But she will be." The light sputtered out. A hello, and a goodbye. Sky Lake, I realized, was not going to save me.

"We both know that isn't true. You're a child, Grace, I can't leave you alone here."

"But you're going to bring me back to him?" *I'd rather fend for myself than be fed to a monster.*

Damia sighed like this was just the latest in a string of terrible, no-win decisions.

"Please. Just say I ran away. I'm fast."

"I can't. He would know." She closed her eyes. "He would punish me." Her voice trembled. Fear, I thought then. Shame, I know now. I shivered, and the cold wasn't coming from my wet clothes. It was coming from the house in front of me and the lake behind me and the rose garden in the woods. All cold and closed up. Pushing me out. "I'm not proud of myself," Damia said, so softly that I almost didn't hear her. "I wish I was... braver."

"You don't have to be brave. Just look the other way for a minute."

She shook her head. "He owns me, Grace."

"Can I go in the house at least? Just quickly? To get something?" *To lock myself in the basement and hide until you go away.* I shot a desperate, pleading look at the house, but the windows were blank. Glass and wood, not eyes.

"He'll take whatever you bring back." Damia's other hand gripped mine and her thumb rubbed gentle circles over my knuckles, the gesture at odds with her nails digging into my upper arm. "You can't get away from him. Not like this, anyway."

"Someone will come looking for me," I said. "He can't just... keep me."

Damia pressed her lips together and shook her head. "Oh honey, I wish that was true. He... erases people." She closed her eyes, like the admission hurt, and I wondered if she helped him erase people. But it didn't matter. I was a twelve-year-old orphan with spotty school attendance—I already didn't exist.

"Please," I whispered.

A breeze carried the rose garden to us, thick and sticky and achingly familiar. I leaned into it. *Love.* But it blew around us and away without running through my hair or sticking to my clothes. A wave of sadness squeezed me breathless.

Damia's grip loosened. "This place..." Her eyes were soft and dreamy from the roses. "There's something special here."

I nodded, seeing potential in her dreamy expression. Her eyes drifted to the house. I held my breath. She only had to believe in magic for a minute.

"You'll be safe in there?" she asked. "If I leave you?"

I nodded wildly, heart racing, but an impatient honk dragged Damia's attention away from the house and back to her responsibilities.

"Yes! Yes. I'll be safe, I promise," I said, although I wasn't sure anymore. Would I be safe at Sky Lake, if Sky Lake didn't want me anymore? But anything was better than going back to ERC. "Please just let me stay."

The honk blasted again. "Sweetheart," Damia said, "I wish I could..."

"You can," I insisted. "Just leave me here."

Another honk sounded, louder and longer, and Damia shook her head.

Decision made.

Spell broken.

My life, as I knew it, over.

The windows darkened another shade, their message clear and painful— keep out. I was leaving, whether I wanted to or not. As Damia pulled me to the car, I let my last pebble fall from my fingers.

"I'm sorry," Damia whispered, trying to wrap her coat around me as we sped away from the only place I ever felt at home. "I'm so sorry."

I slid as far away as I could get, hugging myself to keep warm and straining for one last glimpse of Sky Lake through the back window. In the yard, the dining room table stood like a monument to all the magical summers that I didn't know enough to treasure. The magical summers that were in my past now.

I was a plant yanked out by the roots. I couldn't imagine my future, and I wasn't sure I wanted to. And in the end, it didn't matter, because it didn't belong to me. My future—my life—belonged to Johnathan Everett.

5

GRACE

"Where do I go now?" I asked, following Damia back into ERC. I wanted to curl up right there. Close my eyes. Block my ears. Pretend none of this was happening. But damp jeans stuck to my legs, wet hair dripped down my neck, and Johnathan Everett waited somewhere in that building. I needed dry clothes and a place to hide.

Damia shoved the door closed with a grunt, moving like our trip put years on her.

"I don't think I'm supposed to go back to David's room," I prodded. *David's room.* My chest tightened. No more David.

"Johnathan didn't assign you a room yesterday?"

The irritation in Damia's voice pushed me back against the door and panicky tears stung my eyes—I was not Damia's responsibility, either.

"Of course he didn't," she grumbled. She was annoyed with Johnathan, not with me. I took a careful step toward her. "He wouldn't think of something like that, would he?" She went to a cabinet and selected a set of keys. "I don't know where he wants you, but if he had a preference, he should have set it up himself. You'll stay in the North Tower dorms. They're nicer."

We went to David's room first, where Damia sighed at my backpack. "Is that all you brought with you?"

I nodded. I could have described the rushed trip to ERC, the apartment in San Francisco where my clothes hung next to my brother's coats in the front closet, the old sneakers pinching my toes. But none of that mattered now. My ever-present tears started leaking out, hot and embarrassing.

I got the stone from the bottom of the lake, I reminded myself. *I'm a grownup.*

"Ok," Damia said, in a kinder voice. She looked more like the woman who brought me hot chocolate and less like the one who watched me stumble out of the lake. "I'll get you some things. Don't worry."

I felt grateful and angry at the same time. If she left me at Sky Lake, I wouldn't need anything.

We twisted and turned through the ERC maze until we arrived in a dim hallway lined with numbered doors. Damia unlocked number nine and waved me in. A bed with a gray comforter, a wooden desk, a chair, and a small chest of drawers crowded the tiny space. From the bed, I could touch the desk and open the drawers.

Damia flicked a switch, bathing my dreary new room in fluorescent light. "Bathrooms are at the ends of the hall. Cafeteria one floor down. You'll get a key card soon."

I unpacked, each item in my bag reminding me of David. Damia pulled an old receipt and a pen out of her purse and started making a shopping list. "I'll be back tomorrow with more clothes for you, ok?"

"Ok." I sat down next to my sad little wardrobe, crushed by the knowledge that David would never take me shopping for jeans at Goodwill or give me his old band T-shirts again.

"Do you need anything more tonight?"

My stomach grumbled, but I didn't think I could eat and Damia looked like she had places to be. "Can you... can you tell Janey where I am?" I asked. Janey would know what to do.

"Of course. First thing tomorrow, I promise."

I started humming as soon as Damia closed the door, but the melody was wrong—ordinary. Just a song. It came from my body, not from Sky Lake, and it couldn't take me anywhere.

Janey burst into my room at 8:30 the next morning in a cloud of strawberry vanilla body spray that made my eyes water. She slammed two enormous iced coffees on the desk, flung herself onto the bed, and wrapped her arms around me. "I'm so sorry," she said. "I looked for you yesterday but you were..." She stopped, her exuberant flow of sympathy gummed up by the awkward words she needed—*death, cemetery, ashes, burial.* "I don't know what to say," she admitted. I had a feeling Janey didn't often find herself without words.

I leaned into her fruity hug and we sat, Janey's chin tap-tap-tapping against the top of my head as she chewed her gum. Eventually, I reached for my coffee and she did the same. The sugar hit me, cold and energizing and familiar. *Normal,* I thought, and immediately felt guilty. David was dead. How could anything be normal?

"Are you going to be ok?" Janey asked in a serious voice that didn't match the glitter glinting all the way up to her eyebrows.

"I guess so?" I looked to her for confirmation. She had been at ERC for a long time, and she seemed fine. But Johnathan might care about his niece. He didn't care about me.

Worse than that, I was *interesting.*

She nodded firmly. "Yes. We'll take things one at a time and figure it all out. You just stick with me, ok?" She gave me another tight, strawberry squeeze that I struggled to breathe through. "We're in this together now, ok? I'm going to keep you safe no matter what."

We drank the candy flavored coffees and Janey promised to take me to the coffee shop as soon as I had "credentials" to go outside. "You're not going to be a prisoner," she said, her voice jittery with caffeine or uncertainty, I couldn't tell. "I bet you'll just work with me. Answer phones. File papers. It's not so bad. There's school, too. Not with a teacher, it's just on the computer and you can finish your lessons fast and play games. I'll show you."

She looked around the room as if noticing our surroundings for the first time. "And we'll fix this place up. We can have sleepovers! It'll be fun." My stomach growled, and she laughed. "Let's get you some food, and go from there."

In the cafeteria, Janey showed me what to eat—short list—and what to avoid—long list. "Stick with carbs," she advised. "And stuff in packages. Avoid anything wet." I obediently selected a blueberry muffin and a bag of chips while Janey filled a plate with cookies. "Not healthy, I know," she said. "But ever since they tried to make recycled chicken a thing, I steer clear of the hot food."

I decided I didn't want more details about that experiment. The cafeteria smelled like soup, nail polish, and burned hair and I couldn't imagine eating any of the mysterious brown things steaming on the buffet.

"The fries are fine, though. Except on Thursdays. Thursdays everything tastes like fish."

She led me through a sea of white plastic tables. "Always sit in the corner and face the room. Some of the scientists are creepy. I'll show you who to watch out for." She examined a chocolate chip cookie like it might have something other than chocolate in it before taking a cautious bite. "If you're alone, you'll want something to read, or headphones."

After breakfast, Janey showed me how to get from my room to her office and back again. "That's all you need to know for now," she said, but she still circled the important places on the map, and put angry red slashes through the ones I should stay away from.

There were a lot of things crossed out.

She bought me a pair of flip flops for the shower—"Don't ever go in there in bare feet, people are disgusting"—and we spent the afternoon in her office. "We'll just put you right to work," she said brightly, "and by the time my uncle remembers you, it'll look like you're all taken care of." She pushed a stack of paper over. "He'll think it was his idea." She did not sound convinced.

"What do I do with the papers?" I asked.

"Who the hell knows? They don't tell me anything. But the paper keeps coming, and the filing cabinets are full of folders, so I put the papers in the folders and label them and put them back in the cabinets. No one's ever going to check."

"But what if they do?" I remembered Damia, saying *he'll punish me*. It seemed important, in a place like this, not to mess things up.

"Easy, I'll just say someone told me to do it that way." Janey grinned, but it sat on the surface, like the glitter. We both knew nothing about ERC was "easy."

"And if they ask who told you?" I asked, determined to push something true out of her.

"Then I'll blame someone who's… gone." She lowered her eyes and tugged one of her pigtails. "No offense, Grace, but it's better not to ask a lot of questions around here."

Lying in bed that night, I hummed until my throat was raw, but reality held me like a vice. I couldn't escape to the Sky Lake in my mind. I couldn't even escape into sleep. When Damia collected me the next morning for "paperwork," I shuffled behind her, exhausted.

"Janey's been looking out for you?" Damia asked. "That's good. I bet you'll be working with her, in the office." Her voice rang with the same hopeful uncertainty that Janey's did, and I bit my lip to stop myself from asking what terrible alternatives they knew about and I didn't.

She took me to a small office where a pale young woman scanned my eyes, smeared my fingerprints on a purple notecard, and made me stand between two tall metal pillars that glowed red and then green when she pushed a button. She checked my height, weight, and temperature, drew three vials of blood, and gave me several injections.

I spoke when spoken to, Janey's warning about questions still on my mind.

After a long wait, the woman issued me a black badge with a thick red stripe. It said "Permission Required Beyond Doors."

"Are you serious?" Janey shrieked when she saw it. "That means you can't go outside. You can't go *anywhere*. You're a prisoner!"

Janey's office, once my sanctuary, closed in on me. There were walls and screens—no windows. No way out. My heart hammered, beating for freedom.

"I didn't mean it like that." Janey put a comforting hand on my shoulder. "I'm sure it's temporary. We don't usually have kids here." She rubbed my back as my heartbeat returned to normal. "I'll talk to him."

I thanked her, even though I knew she couldn't help me. The only place I wanted to go was Sky Lake—the real one, or the one in my mind—and no badge would get me there.

The screens came on for the first time during my second week of office work. They made a low buzzing noise. Quiet, at first, but quickly growing into a vibrating hum that came from everywhere, like the building was being carried off by bees.

Janey's office boasted a screen on each wall. We were surrounded.

"Oh *fuck*," Janey muttered, freezing halfway between desk and filing cabinet.

I didn't realize the gravity of the situation at first. Janey said *oh fuck* when her iced drink dripped a little puddle of condensation on the desk or her lipstick wore off too quickly. I searched for one of these disasters, but a fresh coffee sat on a folded napkin and her lipstick appeared intact. She walked back to the desk without any of her usual bounce.

"Fuck," she cursed, again, her face so white that her blush looked like paint. The overhead lights flickered as the screens brightened.

"What's wrong?" My heart pounded in my ears, competing with the bees, and sweat bloomed under my arms. I'd been waiting for something new and awful to happen since David died. This seemed like it.

Janey's eyes drifted up for divine guidance, and her hands gripped the edge of the desk so hard that I expected a fake nail to pop off.

"Janey," I said. The buzz sharpened—more like a saw than a bee—and Janey flinched. "Tell me."

She rubbed her face with both hands, spreading glitter down her cheeks. "Oh Grace." She blew a long breath into her hands.

Pens rattled in their cups and my chair vibrated underneath me. Maybe they were going to take me to a cage in the basement. "Just tell me, Janey."

Janey took a deep breath and sent her eyes to the heavens again. I could feel the buzz in my teeth. "This is going to be bad," she said, pushing her shoulders back and raising her chin bravely. "Very bad. You think you know what I mean, but you don't. This is the worst thing you've ever seen."

At first, I felt giddy with relief. This was something happening to all of us. Not something happening to me, specifically. But Janey's distress brought me back into the room.

Her eyes flicked to the nearest screen, then back to me. She swallowed hard. "If you're smart, you won't look. I looked the first time and..."

She sucked her lips in and shook her head against the memory, then pushed a magazine across the desk. On the cover, a teenage model with sparkly makeup like Janey's struck a pose in a tight red dress. "If you read it backwards, it keeps your brain busier," she said. And then, in the saddest voice I've ever heard in my life, "You *will* get used to this. You won't think so, today." Her voice broke and she blinked fast. "It's amazing, the things a person can get used to."

A little nugget of wisdom between snaps of bubble gum.

Janey scooted her chair over and motioned for me to do the same. I slid as close as I could get, leaning into the comforting fruity smell of her as the screens brightened. She wrapped her arm around me. "Don't look," she reminded.

But I couldn't help it. The screen flashed and changed, becoming a window into a bright white room with rounded walls. In the center, a naked woman tried to cover herself with an awkward arrangement of arms and hands and long hair as the camera zoomed in. She shook from fear or cold or both and the camera got so close that I could see the goosebumps on her pink skin, like raw chicken against the bright white. Her fingernails dug red craters into her bare chest and shoulders.

"What's happening to her?" I asked, unable to look away from the terror on the screen. I thought of David, and his pain, and how I sang him away from it. I wanted to sing for that woman, but the melody was gone.

Janey shook her head and tipped her head. Still finding no answers on the ceiling, she turned to me. "Hopefully, someone loves her enough to spring for the sharp knife, and it will be over quickly."

I won't tell that woman's story, or anyone else's specific story. I never have, because I worry that someone will recognize a person they lost. A detail—hair color, eye color, a last word that meant nothing to me—could be the thing that identifies a mother, father, daughter, husband. It's one thing to know your loved one went badly. It's another to know exactly how badly.

All I'll say about that woman is that no one had the money for the knife.

Reluctantly, Janey explained that everyone at ERC received a series of injections. I received them—vaccine boosters, the doctor said. But one came in a blue vial and burned going in. If you asked about it, the doctor mumbled "measles" or "blood fever" and jabbed you before you had time to argue.

Most of us didn't even ask. We knew our bodies didn't belong to us.

The blue vial contained a substance called Nacium. It did us no harm, unless we received a second drug, contained in blood-red pellets loaded into the guns carried by all the security personnel in the facility. If you did something bad enough, or outlived your usefulness, or got too close to someone Johnathan wanted to punish, you got the red pellet.

And went into the white room.

And the screens switched on.

Victims didn't die from the red pellet. They went crazy with pain, and Johnathan offered the only way out. It was up to us, the viewers, to pay for it. The more lethal the item, the more it cost. On a good day, the menu might include a knife, a gun, a long rope, and a shard of glass. On a bad day, it might include a teddy bear, a butter knife, a brick, and a basketball.

Over the years, a woman killed herself with a toothbrush, a man ended his life with a single orange balloon, and a girl hacked her veins open with a plastic fork.

Johnathan appreciated persistence and creativity.

When the screens finally switched off that night, Janey gave me the same practical advice she received from her mother when she started working at ERC. Stay under the radar. Don't get attached to anyone. And if you do get attached, keep enough money set aside to buy the sharp knife.

She looked away when she said it because we both knew the truth—we were attached to each other, and that, more than the locked doors and the cages in the basement, put Johnathan Everett in control.

He owned me.

I lingered at the long row of sinks in the dorm bathroom that night, examining my eyes. It amazed me that I could still look like myself when I felt so different.

I lost David. I lost Sky Lake.

I saw a woman die.

Now that I knew about the injection, it burned in my veins like a threat. How long, I wondered, until Johnathan realized I wasn't interesting anymore? Once he knew that the magic had gone out of my voice, he'd have no reason not to put me in the white room.

What if he thought I was holding the magic back, and he put Janey in the white room, instead? My mouth went sour. *She's his niece*, I told myself. *He wouldn't hurt her to punish me. I'm not that important.* And yet I couldn't shake the memory of his eyes drilling into me in his office. He wanted something from me, and I didn't have it anymore.

I pressed tight fists against the cold edge of the sink. Many heavy, locked doors stood between me and the outside world, and the ID around my neck didn't give me the right to walk through any of them. I was trapped, at the mercy of a man who killed people for sport. I wished I had forced Bobby to take me with him, no matter how much he hated me. I wished I had found a way to stay at Sky Lake.

If Damia jumped in after me, she would have drowned. I could have escaped. The idea swelled inside me, not quite a wish—yet. But the wish hulked in the distance. *David would be ashamed of me*, I thought. And then, with urgency that seemed to come from somewhere outside of myself, *I have to get away before this place turns me into a monster.*

Looking into my own haunted eyes that night, I was afraid of the right things. But I could not have imagined how Johnathan Everett would transform me—for better and for worse.

6

GRACE

There's nothing new to say about Johnathan Everett. Speculating about him was a full-time job for a lot of people even before his arrest. They say he kept a pair of elephants, a real live dinosaur, and an angel in the basement. I can't vouch for the angel or the dinosaur, but we've all seen pictures of the elephants being led into the sun for the first time.

I saw it on a t-shirt once. That was a weird moment.

Johnathan loomed invisibly over my first few months of captivity, communicating through a typed schedule delivered to my room on Monday mornings. It said "Subject 437G" on top, and split my days into two-hour blocks of testing in different labs.

Johnathan's researchers studied everything. In one hallway, someone would be contacting aliens, someone plotting to overthrow a government, someone curing cancer. I remember a computer programmer with a limp and a twitchy eye who wanted to create a god. He came out of his office once a day to buy twinkies and diet soda in the cafeteria, and I don't think he ever managed to birth a deity. But Johnathan demanded monthly reports from him, and took them just as seriously as all the others.

From Johnathan's perspective, any of those mad scientists might make him a million dollars. Even the ones studying me.

ERC gave the world good things—lifesaving medications, groundbreaking discoveries, ice cream made out of broccoli. But it also produced new weapons, perfected several dangerous methods of mind control, and damaged the actual sun, because Johnathan liked results and didn't care about consequences.

He didn't really *experience* consequences. Investigations of ERC died early, uneventful deaths, because Johnathan knew something incriminating about everyone who mattered. He had a knack for finding people, like me, who wouldn't be missed if they disappeared. But most of us came to ERC on our own. Desperate people looking for miracles. Brilliant people looking for no-questions-asked funding. In the end, we were all trapped, even the ones who were allowed to leave.

Locking someone up isn't the only way to trap them.

Look at me—I traveled all over the world.

For months, I bounced from one lab to another. A tall, apologetic man scanned my head while asking questions about geography and US presidents. A broad-shouldered doctor who looked like his arms were going to burst out of his lab coat made me run on a treadmill until I collapsed. On my thirteenth birthday, a tiny woman with unblinking green eyes poked me with needles attached to a screeching sphere. I sang into at least thirty different machines and one large cage of mice.

After the first few weeks, the mood around me changed. Researchers rushed through my tests, shifty and nervous. Johnathan thought I had something special, and no one wanted to be the one to tell him that I didn't. They tossed me like a hot potato.

Eventually, he noticed.

"Hook her up to every monitor small enough to hide under her clothes and put her on stage," he ordered, bursting into a lab where I was tossing shapes into buckets while an itchy cap of electrodes transmitted information to a computer behind me. I hadn't seen him since the day he gave David back to me, and his sudden appearance sent a tremor of fear through my belly.

I was deeply tired of being studied at that point. The researchers treated me like an object, not a person, and I felt increasingly irritated with their demands for my cooperation. I was trying as hard as I could. I just didn't have any information to give them.

The only bright spots in my schedule were my visits to Janey's office and my daily sessions with Kit, the one researcher who actually wanted to work with me. Kit made me guess what she was thinking, or whether it was raining outside, or what someone in the next room was doing, and she seemed happy to see me every day even though I failed all her tests.

The other researchers acted like I was being intentionally difficult.

"Stage?" The bald scientist unlucky enough to be in charge of me backed away from Johnathan, sweating visibly. I longed to be at Janey's desk or huddled in Kit's tiny office. They would know what to do with an instruction like "put her on a stage." This man was going to get us both in trouble.

"Useless," Johnathan snapped. He dismissed the terrified scientist with a flick of one hand and motioned for me to follow. "You," he said, ushering me down the dark hallway to his office, "are holding out on me." He sounded more interested than angry, so I didn't argue with him. I knew that his curiosity kept me upstairs, instead of in a cage in one of the basements, and I needed to maintain it at the right level. If he got bored, he'd feed me to the lions. If he got too interested, he might crack my head open to see how it worked.

It *didn't* work. That was the problem. Reflexively, I searched for the melody, but found only my own empty throat.

Johnathan made phone calls while I lingered by the door of his office, next to a crystal bowl full of dusty hard candy. "Excellent!" he proclaimed, at the end of the last call. "She'll be there." He turned to me. "You go on at seven. One song, your choice, but I'd choose a crowd pleaser because they

can be rough over there. Your name is Sarah and you're eighteen years old."
He narrowed his gaze. "Don't worry, they'll make you up, you'll be
believable."

He gave no further instructions. Just pressed a button and someone took
me away, like a meal being returned to the kitchen.

Makeup happened in a room that looked like something out of a horror
movie, with silicone heads lining the walls and fake body parts on every
surface. A jar of glass eyeballs stood between two piles of arms. A tray of
fingernails in several different colors balanced on a clear tub filled with blond
hair. I almost tripped over a box of noses.

"What are you here for?" a short, round woman in a green dress asked
me. When I told her I needed to look eighteen, she laughed. "I could do
that in my sleep." She moved a patch of hairy skin off a chair. "Sit here,
sweetie, and I'll fix you right up." She mumbled as she worked—"good bone
structure," "pretty eyes, so dark." I felt like a doll being dressed by a little
girl.

While the woman painted my face, the bald scientist stuck electrodes on
my chest, back, upper arms, and thighs. He didn't explain their purpose, but
I knew—Johnathan thought I had some kind of power related to my singing,
and he wanted to measure it in front of a crowd.

I could have told him it wouldn't work.

When she finished, the makeup artist spun me around to face the mirror.
A different girl looked back. I touched my face and she batted my hand
away. "No!" she barked. "You want to touch, we need prosthetics. This
looks good, but it's all smoke and mirrors."

She might as well have been telling me my future.

That night, a big man in a black suit prodded me into a tiny karaoke bar.
"Your name is Sarah," he reminded me, his breath hot and wet in my ear.
"When they call you, you go up there and sing one song."

"What song should I sing?" I never sang in front of anyone except David. I only knew the songs he liked, and it felt like a betrayal to sing those songs in this dark room that smelled like failure.

"I don't give a shit. Boss said one song. *Don't try anything.*"

I chose "Wish You Were Here," by Pink Floyd. It was one of David's favorites, and I thought if any song could summon him into the room and make those electrodes do something interesting, that one could. "Forgive me," I whispered, as my shaking legs carried me onto the stage. It was wrong to show Johnathan Everett what I could do—I felt it in my bones. But if I didn't give him something, he would kill me. I felt that, too.

I planted my feet firmly, took a deep breath, and tried to welcome the attention of a crowd that wanted me to make a fool of myself. The electrodes scratched my chest and back. The microphone smelled of other people's breath. I could feel the man in the suit glaring at me.

I can do this, I thought, releasing the first notes into the room. I heard my voice, amplified through the microphone, reverberating in the small space. There was more mystery in it than I remembered. Less sweetness. It was worth listening to, with or without the magic.

I am singing for my life, I thought. And then, a quieter thought—*I have always been singing for my life. Singing is my life.*

My fear and hopelessness fell away, chased by the joy of freeing my voice. It grew, strong and powerful and not entirely my own, and something started to shift. The crowd, so close a moment before, receded like a wave. My voice rose over the tinny music from the speakers until there was only me, singing with a cool breeze on my face and the low, rumbling hum of the forest somewhere in the distance. Sweat and spilled drinks became faint traces of pine and roses.

I sucked the music in greedily. Into my feet and legs and hips and belly. Into my chest, where it spun and swelled into something bigger than I could hold. Into the place between my eyes, where it settled, a burning ember that would take me home if I followed it. The harsh spotlight softened. I could almost see David in front of me, strumming his guitar.

How I wish you were here, I sang, and I meant it from the bottom of my heart.

The crowd rustled. We weren't at Sky Lake, but we weren't in the dark little bar, either. I could feel them, hovering halfway to a dream as the forest of my childhood flickered just out of reach. I grasped at it with my voice, my hands, my toes, but it kept me at arm's length as the crowd leaned in—frozen travelers warming themselves at a fire.

I pushed everything I had into the song, willing the forest floor to become solid underneath me. I was almost there.

And then it ended, a sudden, sharp split in the world. The ghost of Sky Lake fell away, the bar smells rushed in. The room looked and sounded and felt as ugly as it did when I arrived. Uglier, maybe, because I had something to compare it to.

But the people were different. They reached, eyes shining, mouths open in wonder. They had never been to Sky Lake, and so they didn't know that I failed. That we didn't even make it halfway there.

They only knew that I took them *somewhere.*

I did. I took them somewhere. I smelled the roses.

As I stood alone in the last shimmering echoes of the song, I *knew.* My voice still knew the way to Sky Lake, even if I'd forgotten how to follow it. The magic was inside me somewhere, and I would cling to it, no matter how hard Johnathan Everett tried to take it away.

Johnathan called me into his office first thing the next morning. He smiled when I entered, and invited me to sit instead of leaving me by the door. Both good signs, I thought, although he had the demeanor of a spider inviting a fly to lunch. "You are a puzzle," he said, flipping through a report on his desk.

I wasn't sure if he meant a good puzzle, that you lose a whole rainy day working on, or a bad puzzle, that you sweep off the table in a fit of rage when the last piece turns out to be missing.

He waited, like I might confess if he subjected me to enough silence.

"I don't know what you're looking for," I admitted, finally. "If I did, I'd tell you."

It was a lie. I knew what he was looking for—the thing that made the bar smell faintly of roses and the crowd light up from the inside.

"We'll figure it out," he said, as if we were solving a fun mystery together. "You gave me some data last night. But not enough of it. You'll go back tonight. Same song. Be in the makeup room at five."

For weeks, I spent my days half listening to Janey's stories while my tongue rubbed grooves into the song I would sing later. My lips formed the words as I slipped papers into yellow folders. I hummed under my breath as we walked to the cafeteria. The music, more than food or water or sleep, kept me going.

I still couldn't escape to Sky Lake when I hummed—that power went away with David. Sky Lake only came to me on stage, and only as a ghost. A feeling, a smell, a sound floating on the wind—never a solid place I could see or touch. Always just ahead, out of reach and not reaching back for me.

I chased it, testing the limits of my growing voice. Looking for the magic note that would carry me home. Singing in circles around the place I loved. But Sky Lake remained as closed to me as it was the night I buried David.

David said the magic of Sky Lake ran through my veins. But I wasn't the little girl who danced in the rose garden and soaked up the moon like a sponge. I was a girl who saw her brother die. Who *let* her brother die. A girl who wasn't loved enough to be rescued or brave enough to run away. A girl who took orders from a monster.

Maybe, I didn't deserve the real thing. And so, I held onto my ghost.

Night after night my voice poured out of me, cool and soothing. It grew higher and lower and *deeper*—a living thing that moved in more dimensions than I did. It dusted the audience with the light of the roses, filled my nose with the deep, earthy smell of the forest, and made everyone in the room long for something they couldn't define, because they'd never been to Sky

Lake. My hands caressed the microphone like a friend and I pressed my feet into the stage, willing them to grow roots and keep me there.

For a few, beautiful minutes, I was almost home, in a crowd of people who wanted to go there with me.

At some point, I stopped worrying about being sent to the basements, and started worrying that Johnathan might stop sending me to the stage. Staying alive, staying upstairs, staying out of the white room—it wasn't enough anymore. I wanted more. I wanted to sing. Sky Lake might not be running through my veins anymore, but its music did, and I needed to let it out as much as I needed to breathe.

And I could only do it if Johnathan Everett allowed me to.

I'd been performing for a month when Johnathan called me back into his office. I went reluctantly, feet scraping the tiles, arms dragging heavily by my sides. I could feel bad news coming.

Johnathan sat pensively behind his desk. Fingers steepled, brow creased. Curious or angry or both. "We're not getting useful data," he said, as soon as I sat down.

Fear prickled down my spine.

"Not to worry," he added brightly, slapping the desk like a man with a good idea that might hurt a little. "I have one more thing to try." He leaned forward, hand still flat on the desk. "But if you're holding something back, this is your last chance to come clean."

Last chance. The words sent a feverish shiver through me. I sang my heart out every night, but Johnathan didn't want music—he wanted something else. I shook my head as his eyes burned a path around my face, searching for the lie. I wasn't holding anything back. I gave it all, every night, and it wasn't enough.

That night, they didn't put the electrodes on me. They put them on three people in the audience.

I spent the next day in knots, stomach churning as I waited to learn my fate. If Johnathan didn't have the information he wanted now, I wouldn't be singing again. I would be trapped. My voice would be trapped. I could feel it, getting ready to rip me apart from the inside. But if he *did* have the information he wanted, I shuddered to think of what would happen next.

When Johnathan summoned me, I tried not to get my hopes up. If a month of data didn't answer his questions, one night of data probably wouldn't make the difference. He was done with me. I was done singing. End of story. But I found him in front of his desk, practically vibrating with energy. He didn't look like someone who was giving up.

He gestured for me to follow him.

To the makeup room.

I was singing, after all.

"Two songs tonight," he ordered, as the round makeup lady painted my face. "I'm taking you myself."

At the bar, he sent the driver away and offered me his arm. "Shall we?" When I didn't take it, he shrugged off his jacket and patted his pockets dramatically to demonstrate that he held no weapons. "You're not in any danger."

I didn't agree with him and I didn't trust him, but I took his arm and let him lead me inside.

"Show me what you've got, kiddo," he said shooing me toward the stage. He sounded almost encouraging. But his words hung in the air behind me— a threatening, irresistible challenge. I wanted his approval, and I wished I didn't, and I had to get up on that stage and sing for him either way.

I forgot Johnathan as soon as the music wrapped its arms around me. His opinion didn't matter anymore, and neither did his data. There was only me, and the melody, and my audience like a colorful school of fish below. I felt light and giddy, the way you feel after a big laugh or a bite of really good chocolate. Perfectly content and still desperate for more.

The first song ended, the second one started, and the crowd cheered when they realized I wasn't going anywhere.

They wanted more, and I could give it to them.

I was the *only* person who could give this to them.

A startling jolt radiated out from my chest, hot and electric. My voice swelled—it was too big to hold, and I felt it burst out of my mouth but also my eyes and ears and the top of my head. Sparks rained down my arms and shot up my neck. I was a lightning bolt, and one wrong move would set the room on fire.

I wasn't following orders anymore—I was, for now at least, the most powerful person in the room.

The fish shimmered. I spun my voice around them and they whirled, faster and faster until they were just bright streaks below me. All around me. A whirlpool of color between me and the world. Between me and Johnathan Everett.

I closed my eyes and reached for Sky Lake, but my moment of triumph didn't bring it any closer. When the music stopped, the fish fell away, and I crashed with them. Back into my life. Pounding heart. Headache. Constant, low-level sense of dread. And Johnathan Everett at my side already, hands clasped behind his back.

The power was gone.

"Impressive," he commented.

My face flushed with pride and then shame. I did want to impress him, after all. To show him what I could do. To be more than an experiment.

To know that I didn't imagine what just happened on stage.

Johnathan made the guard take us to a drive through for burgers and milkshakes instead of going straight back to ERC. "Surprised?" he asked, raising an eyebrow as I hesitated in the doorway of his office with the greasy takeout bags in my arms. I didn't answer, but I didn't need to. He laughed. A real laugh, not a hungry-spider laugh. "Go ahead, spread it out on the table and sit down. Relax. You worked hard tonight."

I couldn't imagine relaxing there, but I sat.

"Do you like singing, Grace?" he asked, settling next to me. I wanted to scoot over, but didn't want to be rude. I remembered David telling me to listen to my gut. To never put myself in danger for the sake of politeness. *I'm already in danger*, I thought. *It can't get worse.* Except that at ERC, it seemed like things could always get worse.

I nodded, keeping my eyes down.

"That's good." He sipped his milkshake—double chocolate—thoughtfully. I imagined him as a cloth napkin kind of guy, but he seemed perfectly at home eating junk food out of a paper bag. He was a mystery, too. "I think you could do something with it," he said, carefully, pausing to gauge my reaction.

I held my breath. What did he find when he measured the audience?

"I think I—we—could make a lot of money with your voice." Relief flowed through me. I was not a science experiment. I was a *singer.* "I can help you," he offered, "if you're willing to put some effort in."

This time, I didn't hesitate. I was willing to do anything, if it meant I could keep singing.

A band materialized the very next morning, along with a practice space and a list of songs that Johnathan expected me to add to. "I want you to sing words that mean something to you. Don't be shy." He fixed me with a hard look. "I'm serious about that. My research didn't tell me much, but I know for a fact that you only have impact on an audience if you feel something. Choose songs you like. And start writing your own. You need to sing from your heart."

I bobbed my head obediently, but I was pretty sure singing from my heart wasn't something I could do in response to an order.

The band, plucked from the relative safety of various ERC labs, deeply resented me. I didn't blame them. They were anonymous before. I put targets on them. "Your first show is next week," Johnathan announced, and they glared daggers at me while promising to be ready. Johnathan Everett's attention was dangerous, and I'd dragged them right into the spotlight.

I felt terrible. But what could I do? If Johnathan wanted me to wrangle this group of moderately talented misfits into a band, I had to. For all of our sakes. In hindsight, I should have worked harder to win their affection, but Johnathan's commands, deadlines, and unspoken consequences put us in an impossible position. Someone had to take charge. I couldn't have known, then, that I was dooming myself to years of loneliness and reluctant collaboration.

I was a teenager. I couldn't see past tomorrow.

The first show went badly. My throat was tight and strained with nerves, and the clashing performances of my bandmates kept me firmly anchored in the bar. Our second attempt went a little better—I smelled the roses, even though I couldn't see their light. But the third night, when I shook with the knowledge that our days must be numbered, something shifted. I opened my mouth to sing, and my voice came out hot and liquid. I could feel it, burning between my eyes and shooting goosebumps down my arms.

A familiar jolt—tingling and electric, so strong that I had to brace myself—radiated out from my chest. The band came together around me, and I felt the rhythmic pull of the music. Out of my body. Out of my mind. I raised my arms over my head. *I'm in charge*, I thought. The current reached my fingertips. *Johnathan Everett doesn't own me right now.* Sparks burst out, crackling in my supercharged, too-big-for-my-body voice. Spilling out of me and rushing through the room.

Rushing into all those strangers.

It settled on their shoulders. Flowed into open mouths and noses. Made them glow like the cemetery stones at Sky Lake—the glow of someone loved, remembered, treasured. *I'm doing this to them*, I thought, fear and excitement battling in my belly as the song stormed out of me. Something—water flowing, or birds singing—sounded in the distance. Far away. But not gone.

At the end of the show, every eye in the room shined bright and hopeful, full of such optimism that I wished I could follow someone home, just to see what happened next.

I was doing something to them. Doing something *for* them. I was powerful, in a way Johnathan Everett couldn't measure. He could have the money—all of it, if he wanted. But he couldn't have the thing that made the audience shimmer. The thing they took with them in their shining eyes. The thing they left behind, sparkling in their footprints like a light dusting of snow. That belonged to me.

Foolishly, I thought I could control it.

Johnathan called me to the public building for a meeting the morning after our fourth show. Janey said nothing scary happened over there, but Johnathan didn't seem to be full of *good* surprises. I felt like I was walking to my execution. My legs were rubbery. My knees kept trying to bend the wrong way. Every part of my body wanted to turn me around, but Johnathan summoned me. I didn't have a choice.

Every time I started to get comfortable, everything changed.

The public building was modern and bright, with windows overlooking the lawn, soft music drifting out of invisible speakers, and friendly employees who, as far as I could tell, didn't wonder what lurked behind and underneath their offices.

It felt like a different world.

A woman with a clipboard met me in the lobby and took me to a crowded, glass-walled conference room. She pulled out my chair and offered coffee in a low voice intended only for me while the meeting continued around us. I scanned my surroundings, alert for danger, but potted plants, mugs full of pens, and a small screen displaying a power point presentation communicated the benign purpose of the room.

The group sat stiffly around a long oval table like stylish soldiers, taking no notice of me. Only Johnathan looked up when I entered. "Please stand," he ordered, as soon as I got settled, and waved me toward the head of the table so everyone could see me. "This is our star," he announced, a satisfied, cat-like smile twitching the corners of his mouth. The younger members of the team nodded eagerly while the older ones looked me up and down. Measuring.

"Can she do anything?" someone asked, and Johnathan glared his answer. If he wanted a star, he got a star, talent notwithstanding. The questioner retreated like an animal into a hole. I slouched, embarrassed. I *could* do something, and it was amazing. But standing there, in front of those people, I felt like nothing at all.

"How old is she?" someone else asked.

Johnathan raised an eyebrow in my direction, like a co-conspirator. We both knew I would be as old as he wanted me to be. He dismissed the question with a flick of one hand and introduced me to the team—manager, agent, publicist, assistants. Slowly, it dawned on me—he really intended to make me famous.

I stood next to a potted plant, conspicuous, trying not to shake visibly as they assessed me. Eyes, hair, body. I felt their comments like tweezers, picking me apart.

I wished he sent me to the makeup room first, or had me sing instead of making me stand there like a lost child. But Johnathan liked to negotiate the way other people like sugar or sex—in all its forms, and for its own sake. He presented me as a vanity project and everyone took crappy deals, thinking they'd win more by making a powerful man happy.

It didn't matter—even the crappy deals produced an obscene amount of money—but Johnathan liked winning even more than he liked money. And I was part of his game.

Over the next few weeks, he transformed me—colored contact lenses, hair extensions, a new wardrobe. It was all too tight or too short or too bright, but no one asked me. They just told me to stop tugging at my skirts.

"New me" took shape slowly, then all at once. She had long, red hair with just enough caramel undertones to look natural. Her eyes were a surreal, lollipop shade of blue. Her eyelashes were long and her fingernails were perfect ovals and she wore lipstick all the time. Even the shape of her face looked different from mine, and I wondered if the round makeup lady would follow me everywhere with her brushes.

I loved it.

It's a shallow thing to admit. But I was thirteen years old. Every cell in my body screamed for transformation, and everyone who loved me was gone. I would have given anything to be someone else, and I got to skip straight past "awkward teenager" and become a beautiful stranger on the verge of fame. I felt, for while at least, like I won the lottery.

I didn't, of course, because you don't actually get to skip things. Teenage insecurity plodded behind me, waiting for its moment. And its moments came, now and then, and then all at once when everything fell apart.

At the time, though, I only saw my new reflection in the mirror and the exciting future Johnathan painted for me.

He hired an army of coaches to turn me into the thing he imagined. I learned to talk differently, walk differently, sip a coffee differently. The music teachers he hired pushed me to be more than raw talent and tight dresses, and he prioritized those lessons in my schedule even when his goals might have been better served by other things.

I practiced until my vocal exercises started joining me in my dreams. I followed the scales higher and higher and lower and lower thinking, *maybe this is how I'll find my way home.* But home kept its distance.

Maybe, I thought, late at night when I couldn't get away from myself, *it doesn't recognize me anymore.*

7

GRACE

Johnathan could manufacture a person from scratch as easily as he could erase one, but the creation of my new identity hit an unexpected snag. I needed a name, and he shot down suggestions like a father choosing the perfect name for his only child.

Alice Knox. Victoria Robertson. Olivia Jacobs. Sara Duke. Charlie London. They blended together, rattled off by a young woman in a black suit with shiny dark hair pinned into a bun that pulled her eyes back. We'd been running in circles for weeks. I wasn't even listening anymore.

"Charlie London." Johnathan seized the last name on the list, repeating it thoughtfully while the room held its breath. "Charlie. Yes. That's it." He smiled a satisfied, uncomplicated smile. "Last name needs to be one syllable, though."

The team scrambled through their notes and started firing off one syllable last names—*Brooks, Grey, Ford, Lane, Grove, Ross, Rose.*

"I like Lane, Ross, and Rose, in that order. Run them through the database to make sure there aren't any notable matches. Serial killers.

Actresses. Etcetera." He stood, signaling the end of the late-night meeting. Problem solved.

"No," I said, my voice rising over the rustle of the team gathering their papers.

The air went still. Nobody said no to him. Normally, I wouldn't have said it, but we were meeting after a show at a tiny bar where I could have made the audience carry me away if I'd been a little braver. Power still tingled in my fingertips, making me reckless. Everything I touched sparked.

"I like my name," I said, boldly. *You can't tell me who I am.* "I don't want a new one."

My mother named me Grace, and I didn't have anything else from her.

"Well, you can't keep it," he barked. Then, to the team, "If none of those check out, bring more options for the last name in the morning."

The shuffle of papers began again, but slowly. Everyone wanted to see what happened next.

I held my ground. "No." The tingle receded, up my arms, abandoning me. *No one says no to him.*

Johnathan cocked his head like a wolf regarding a very interesting trapped rabbit. "*No,*" he repeated, rolling the word around in his mouth. The group froze again. "We're done here," he snapped, gesturing impatiently at the door. "You can all go. *Now.*" Then, to me, "You stay where you are."

I waited, still feeling dangerously defiant, while the team filed out and Johnathan slowly poured himself a cup of coffee. He sat down across from me, also slowly, each deliberate movement designed to increase the tension.

"Grace," he said, once the silence was thick enough to cut, "is thirteen years old. Almost fourteen. Very young." He took a long sip of coffee, then returned to the coffee bar and poured me one, adding extra cream and sugar. Johnathan didn't pour coffee for other people, and I couldn't decide if he meant it as a kindness or a threat. "She goes to middle school." He sat and leaned forward, gesturing for me to drink. "Is that what you want to be doing? Algebra homework? Student council? College applications?"

He sat back, hands clasped over his stomach, one eyebrow up. Waiting, not for my answer, but for my realization.

I didn't want to go to middle school. I wanted to *sing*.

The truth knocked all the air out of me.

"I thought as much." He smiled with what looked like genuine amusement, although something predatory lurked underneath. "You have ambition. That's a good thing. Don't apologize for it." He sipped, made a face, and got up for more sugar. "I can't let you keep your name," he said, regretfully. "Just like I can't bring your brother back."

Tears pricked my eyes. *David*. What would he think, if he saw me now?

"But I can make you who you really are."

I can make you who you really are. What a thing to offer a teenager. The last of my power fizzled out—a lie. Johnathan still held all the cards. But he waited, hopeful, wanting my agreement even though he didn't need it.

"Fine," I said, like a woman making a decision, even though I felt like a child backed into a corner. "My name is Charlotte, then. Not Charlie. And we keep London." I could at least imagine my mother naming me that.

"Have it your way. But they'll shorten it to Charlie. You just wait and see." He sounded certain, but not triumphant. Like he wished he could give me something better.

It was only later, telling the story to Janey, that I realized what a risk I'd taken over a name that wasn't any more "mine" than my fake eyes and fake hair and fake walk. "Holy shit," she said, shaking her head like I'd narrowly avoided death right in front of her. "I don't know if I should be impressed or furious with you. No one gets away with talking back to him, Grace. Don't take any more risks like that, ok?"

I agreed, but I didn't regret pushing my limits with him. Johnathan knew I could make him rich, and he knew he couldn't force the magic out of me, and that was something. Not much, but something.

8

CHARLOTTE

While Johnathan and his team transformed me into Charlotte London, Damia managed the day-to-day life of thirteen-year-old Grace. She bought me new shoes and pajamas. She told me where to go and when. She made sure I was eating real food, and not just blueberry muffins. But she never truly relaxed with me, and our therapy sessions went nowhere. I would drink hot chocolate in her office, but I wouldn't tell my feelings to someone who was afraid of me.

In the middle of one of our sessions, the hum of the building slowed, then stopped, and the lights went out. Power outages happened when someone's project drew too much electricity, but there were safeguards on top of safeguards to keep anyone—or anything—from getting out. I'd been at ERC long enough by then to know the locks still worked, so I just waited in the dark.

"That place," Damia said, rushing the words out before the lights came back on. "It's different, isn't it?" She shot a pointed look at the camera in the corner of the room. The little red light was out.

Damia already saw the rose garden and the glowing stones. She watched me dive into the deepest part of the lake and swim back up with a rock bigger than my head. Lying to her seemed pointless and insulting. "Yes," I whispered. The word scratched my throat. Sky Lake—lost to me now.

"I couldn't find it when I tried to go back." She confessed this with a mixture of curiosity and guilt, hands twisting a pen hard enough that I thought it might break. She had the freedom to go back, and I didn't, and this truth stood between us like a wall. "I drove and drove," she said, voice cracking. "Circles." She released the pen and traced a spiral on the desk with one finger, eyes lowered.

I nodded. Of course she couldn't find her way to Sky Lake. She didn't have a pebble or a hand drawn map. I remembered the sound my last pebble made, clattering onto the driveway. I wondered if it glowed among the ordinary pebbles. If it longed to go back to the edge of the lake.

"If I left you there, you would have been safe." Even in the dark, I could see grief painting shadows on her face. She would do anything, I realized, to go back and make another decision.

Damia wasn't afraid of me. She was *guilty*. A feeling I knew.

"You couldn't leave me," I said. "The driver wouldn't have let you." I pulled a loose thread on the sleeve of my shirt and it slid out easily, unraveling the way my lie would if she asked too many questions. She could have made the driver go for help, and if he did that, they never would have found their way back. Doubt nagged at me, though, as I remembered the light flickering in the window. Sky Lake didn't want me.

She let out a slow breath. "I didn't try to make him," she said, instead of *I'm sorry.*

"Johnathan would have hurt both of you," I said, instead of *I forgive you.*

She nodded, her regret so heavy that I thought she'd sink right through the floor and end up with the monsters in the basement. The truth was, I didn't want to be safe at Sky Lake anymore. Not when I could sing instead. The ugly secret made me burn with shame, but Damia couldn't see my red cheeks in the dark.

"Can I trust you?" I asked, and grabbed a page from her stack of notes as soon as she said yes. Squinting in the dark, I drew an irregular oval in the center, winding roads snaking out until they reached the highway. In the oval, I wrote "Sky Lake." The letters glowed like the roses, brightening when she reached for them.

Lit for her, not for me.

I blinked back tears. "This will lead you there, as long as you keep it safe. Don't spill anything on it or let the ink smudge, though, or it won't work anymore."

Damia took the map carefully, holding it between two fingers, eyebrows knit with questions. It was not a plausible story. "It won't work anymore," she repeated, "if I spill something on it." Her eyes bounced from the map to me, and back again.

"Someday, you might be able to help someone else," I said. She nodded slowly, like a sleepwalker. "Someone else can be safe there," I clarified, because I couldn't tell if she understood me.

"A safehouse." She said the word like it felt good in her mouth. Like it could save *her.*

"Yes." It felt right in a way that nothing had felt right since David got sick. Sky Lake couldn't protect me—wouldn't protect me—but it could protect someone else. *See?* I asked, pushing the thought out to David. *I'm keeping my promise. Sort of.*

"Thank you, Grace." She held the map reverently in both hands, tears making her eyes shine in the dark. "Thank you for trusting me with this."

"Be careful, though," I warned, as the lights flashed back to life. "Everything is... different there."

Different. Careful. Such inadequate words, but what words could describe the place where I grew up, with its impossible beauty and peculiar dangers?

The roses, to start with. They grew abundantly in every color except red, glowing more or less depending on weather, moonlight, and soil conditions. But sometimes, they blazed like a fire. I touched one—pale yellow, kissed with orange as if someone dipped it in paint—on a night like that and it left a blister that smelled like smoke and rose petals for days. I still have the scar.

And the roses weren't the only hazard I should have warned Damia away from. There was the old well, hidden in a tangle of weeds just waiting to lure an unsuspecting person with its orange and jasmine perfume on a full moon night. The hot springs, much deeper than they looked, with caves and tunnels that would let you in but not out. The lake, dark and deep and powerful.

In hindsight, David and I should have fenced a lot of things off, but we never thought about anyone else living there. Sitting in Damia's office, the map between us, I still didn't want to think about it. I wanted Sky Lake for myself.

That's what I should have told her. That the stars would rush into her lungs with her first breath of lake air. That the trees would watch her walk to the house like an adoring crowd. That magic rumbled in the earth there like thunder.

I should have told her that Sky Lake could grow roots inside you and make you feel incomplete anywhere else, then disappear and never let you find your way back. I should have told her it could break your heart.

But the lights came back on and made all of it—the warnings, the map, my decision to share Sky Lake—feel far away and improbable. Damia slid the map into a drawer, and I spent the rest of our session not telling her my feelings. Because I didn't trust her, not really. After David left me by accident and Bobby left me on purpose and Johnathan made that woman kill herself for everyone to see, I didn't trust anyone.

9

CHARLOTTE

After months of preparation, I felt ready to go in that way you can only feel ready when you're too young to know better. "When am I leaving?" I asked, every time I saw Damia, but she only told me not to rush. "I'm not rushing," I snapped one day, exasperated, twirling a stack of silver bangles around my wrist. "I'm just ready to get out of here."

"Of course you are." She looked out the window longingly, dreaming of whatever life she left behind. I realized she probably felt ready to get out, too. "Soon," she promised, but her eyes were cloudy with worry.

The days blurred together in a haze of lessons, practice, and more clothes than I could imagine myself ever wearing. My life smelled like nail polish and hairspray, not roses. The air rang with orders and criticism and the echo of my own voice in empty rehearsal rooms, not birds. I didn't feel the rush of people riding on my voice. I was a child dressed up like a woman, singing to an unfamiliar reflection, my future a question mark in sand.

I wasn't Grace anymore. But I wasn't Charlotte London, either.

Janey offered iced coffee and lip gloss and bubble-gum optimism. She wanted to sit in on my makeup sessions and borrow my clothes. She wondered if Johanthan would let her visit me on tour. "Italy, maybe," she'd daydream, sprawled on the fluffy pink rug she insisted on putting in my room. "Or someplace tropical, with a nice beach." She twirled her hair and sighed, thinking of seashells and bikinis and cute guys on surfboards. She always saw the bright side, and from her perspective, my new life sparkled.

Kit, the one researcher who still worked with me regularly, became my refuge as I disappeared and Charlotte London charged in to take my place. I walked into her office lost and confused every afternoon, and walked out feeling, if not hopeful, then at least understood.

Kit couldn't have been older than forty—she had a son my age—but the streaks of white in her hair and the voluminous skirts obscuring her legs turned her into a wise witch from a story. She worked in a converted storage closet that smelled like bleach and Earl Grey tea. It was crowded and dark, but it didn't feel that way—Kit was so bright and expansive that her space felt that way, too.

Most of the closet was occupied by a large black box that hummed quietly and emitted slow pulses of light. In theory, the pulses changed with psychic activity, measured through clips that she attached to my fingers. In practice, they stayed as steady as a heartbeat because, in Kit's words, I was "decidedly below average."

"You see nothing?" she asked, concentrating on the card in front of her and then on me, trying to beam the idea of a red circle or blue square or black triangle into my mind.

I saw a chocolate glazed donut. My personal trainer had me on a strict diet, and all I could think of was food.

"Try again." She flipped a new card. "Just relax and let it come to you."

I relaxed, but the donut remained. My stomach growled.

Kit tucked the cards back into their box, laughing, and we moved on to the fun part of the session, where she shuffled her tarot cards while we talked and drank tea. The cards were large, worn at the edges from constant use, with a swirling white and gold pattern on the back. A second, identical set sat in the middle of the table. I never touched it—I preferred to watch Kit. Her graceful, efficient movements, combined with the spooky light from her machine, were hypnotic.

"I have to do this," she told me, when I marveled over her skill with the cards. "Otherwise, I bite my nails. Filthy habit."

Kit wasn't like the other researchers, who kept their heads down and barely said a word. She spoke in a musical French accent overlaid with a British one, and always seemed to be on the verge of laughing. She didn't treat me like a child, the way Damia did, or like an adult, the way my coaches and teachers did. She just treated me like a person—valuable in my own right, not as a performer or a project or an experiment—and I did my best to deserve her friendship.

She looked forward to being home with her son for Thanksgiving, Christmas, Easter, the summer—her goal changed with the season. "Poor thing," she said, squeezing a carved stone pendant so tightly that I could feel its imprint on my own palm. "He's like you. Teenager. Musician." She released the stone and massaged her hand. "His band is good." She punctuated the sentence with a firm nod—*proud*, I thought, and felt a pang of jealousy. "But his father…. My ex… Classically trained pianist!" She rolled her eyes. "Calls it noise. They are at war. I need to be home for his birthday." She said the last bit wistfully. Johnathan didn't let people go home for birthday parties, and we both knew it.

When I asked Kit how she ended up at ERC, she sighed. "There aren't many chances for someone like me." She gave the machine an affectionate pat. "He was interested. I was blind. Ironic, yes?" An edge of bitterness crept into her voice and shook her hands, sending a card flying out of the deck. It landed between us with a heavy slap.

I'd never seen that happen before—Kit always had full control over her cards—and it felt important. Weighted. A *before-and-after* moment, enhanced by the machine's insistent murmur and rhythmic lighting.

Kit froze, hand hanging in the air over the card. I held my breath. I didn't necessarily believe in tarot cards, but I believed in Kit, and I imagined the image transforming underneath her fingers—bad news to good.

Her face, tense with anticipation, softened into a smile as she turned it over. "Of course," she cried, nodding conversationally at the card. "Where is my mind?"

She held it out to me. *The Wheel of Fortune.* "There are no accidents," she explained, her usual brightness back, although her eyes were shiny and I wondered if she might be smiling for my sake. "No mistakes. I am here for reasons." She banged her fist on the table. Certain. Or trying to be certain.

"No mistakes?" I asked. I thought of David dying. Of Bobby, blaming me and walking away. Of Kit's son, missing his mother.

Of me, selling my soul to Johnathan Everett.

Kit shook her head solemnly. "No accidents, no mistakes, no beginnings, no endings," she chanted. She reached for the teapot and refilled my cup. "Bad things happen. Of course. You know better than most, little one." She sighed, and I felt seen in a way that I only felt—that I have only ever felt—in Kit's storage closet. "But we don't know the whole story. If we could zoom out…" Her eyes drifted to her machine. "We'd see it all. The whole picture. And it would be *perfect.*" The machine's light cast a slow shadow across her cheek, like a caress.

I thought of David, on the dock, with water above and below. *Remember to notice all the times that it is perfect, Gracie.* I wanted to believe he was speaking to me through Kit, and everything would fit together someday. But my life felt more like a smashed window than a puzzle.

She shuffled the cards back together. "You are here, which means the message is for both of us. Our destinies, they are entwined." She looked into my eyes, searching. "Someday, it will be clear."

"Are you sure?" I asked, my voice high and young, more like Grace than Charlotte. I couldn't think of a good reason for my brother to be dead or for lovely Kit to be trapped in a storage closet, an ocean away from her son. Part of me didn't want there to be a reason.

But I liked the idea of Kit's life and mine tangled up somehow.

"It's the one thing I am sure of, little one." Her serious expression dissolved in a sparkle of mischief. "Enough philosophy. You stay here. I'm getting us a whole plate of donuts."

Kit always knew exactly what I needed.

Once, I offered to sing for Kit, hoping she could make sense of what happened to people when they heard my voice. But she shook her head firmly. "No," she said. "You sang for me, and my machine did not respond. There is no reason to repeat the experiment."

When I opened my mouth to correct her—I never sang for Kit's machine—she pressed her lips together and silently pushed one of her cards across the table.

Two swords crossed over each other in an "X".

10

KIT

I gave Grace so many tasks.

Tell me if the man in the other room is standing or lying down.
Use your inner eye to open this box, what's inside?
Make the light blink faster.
What am I thinking, what am I thinking, now what am I thinking?

And then I teased her for her lack of talent.

If only I could sit with her now. Share a pot of tea and the truth and have a good laugh together. But she was a child. Too young for the truth, although we laughed plenty and I poured enough tea into her little body to fill that lake she couldn't let go of.

"Really, Grace," I said one day, "I've never seen anyone get them *all* wrong."

She usually went along with me, eager to get to the part of the session where we drank tea and talked about other things. But that day, my criticism hurt. I could see it all over her pretty little face. It was easy to forget that she was still a baby behind all that makeup they made her wear. "What is it, little one?"

I knew I shouldn't call her that. She was Charlotte London now, and we were meant to treat her as the adult she would soon pretend to be. But she was fourteen years old. Barely a teenager.

She shrugged, her standard response. I used to think she didn't want to talk, but over our time together I had learned the language of her shoulders. The high shrug that meant she didn't know the answer. The low one that meant the very idea of explaining made her tired. The loose, boneless one I'd been seeing more and more lately. The one that said *why bother, no one cares what I think anyway.*

"Come on, tell me. Why does it bother you not to guess my thoughts today?"

"It doesn't," she sighed, and that much I believed. Grace did not care about her psychic development. If she did... well, I wonder sometimes what would have become of her. "I'm just tired of being bad at things."

I wanted to gather her up in my arms and rock her. But that was what I needed. Not what Grace needed. I took a breath to steady my voice. "And what do you feel like you're bad at?" I kept my eyes on my cards, shuffling steadily. She talked more when I didn't look at her.

"This?" She gestured up and down her body. "I don't know how to be Charlotte London. I thought I did, but now I'm not sure."

She paused, but she wasn't done, so I kept shuffling, pulling cards so she wouldn't feel too much of my attention on her.

"They made me record the songs I wrote," she said, eyes stormy. I would not have liked to be the reason for that dark look. "But they weren't my songs anymore. Someone changed them. Made them simple and boring so the band Johnathan found in the basement can play them... Even the words. I don't know why they'd change the words. My words were better."

I knew why he changed the words—to test the limits of her influence—but I kept that to myself. I did not want to make her frightened of her own voice.

"I told him I could play the complicated parts and he said no. He hired all those teachers for me and now he's not letting me do what I learned." Fire burned in her eyes, and I was glad to see it. She would need that fire. "He won't even let me have David's guitar. He put it in the basement." The fire faded, extinguished by grief, and I thought, *that is also good. That is how she will stay human.*

"I didn't think it would be like this," she said, her despair too big for her little body. "I thought I was going to get out and sing and I'd be happy. But I've been stuck here for months and they won't even let me sing my own songs." She paused for a long time, but I knew she wasn't finished. "And I'm scared," she said. "Of what he'll do to me if… if I can't do this. If I fail."

I waited a few beats to make sure she was done. Grace took her time between thoughts, an admirable trait her coaches seemed determined to train out of her. "First of all," I said, when I was sure she didn't have more to tell me, "you won't fail." My cards gave me plenty to worry about when I asked about her future, but there was no failure in it. "And he won't hurt you."

I paused, debating the wisdom of sharing too much. Information could empower, but it could also endanger. She was still young and impulsive underneath the adult façade. I slid a card out of my deck. *The World.* One cycle complete, another one starting. *Ready or not.*

"He needs money," I explained. "It costs a fortune to run this place. To stay out of trouble. He made some bad bets." I went back to shuffling. "He needs you more than you need him. Remember that."

Her eyes widened, and I couldn't tell if this knowledge made her feel better or worse. "He'll get it another way if he has to," I told her. "Don't think you can defeat him with failure. I'm only saying that he is invested in your success. You will be safe."

She swallowed hard. Safety and security, wrapped in an unimaginable burden. I could see it settling on her expressive little shoulders. Holding her down.

I pulled another card. *The Page of Cups.* I smiled, lifted by his youth and exuberance. *Art, music, emotion, inspiration.* All the things she needed to hang onto. "I'm sorry to hear that Johnathan changed your songs," I said. "It must be discouraging." She visibly relaxed, and I wondered how long it had been since anyone bothered to validate her feelings. "I hate that he did that to you."

"Me too." She sounded like a little mouse. Helpless.

"There are things he can't take from you, though." I sent a silent prayer into the universe. *Let what I am about to say be true.* "Simple music has a big impact if you perform it from the deepest part of yourself. Only you control that. He can change the words and the notes, but it is *your* voice."

A hint of a smile twitched the corners of her mouth.

"No matter how much of your songs he changed, he left something that belongs to you. Find it, and sing from *there.*" I placed my hand over my own heart, and she did the same, her hand tentative but steady. "From your heart."

Her heart was good. I just hoped it was good enough to overwhelm whatever experiments Johnathan planned to do with her music.

"Ok. I can do that."

I refilled her half empty teacup. "You said you don't know how to be someone else. Can I suggest something?" She nodded eagerly, so open and trusting that it hurt to look at her. "You are very young. No one, not even you, knows who you are or who you will be. Take what you like and leave the rest, and you will become yourself."

She considered this for a moment, then rewarded me with a real, unguarded smile, like the sun coming up. I had never seen it before, and its beauty made me speechless for a moment. "You will bloom like a flower," I told her, happy tears stinging my eyes. She would. I could see it.

Her smile wobbled and fell away. "I wish I could have David's guitar," she said, in the same small, choked voice that we all used to talk about the things Johnathan took from us.

"Your brother's guitar will wait for you," I promised, seeing it so clearly and suddenly that it must have come from beyond. In my vision she held the guitar in a dark room. She was lost and brokenhearted and teetering on the edge of something unimaginably wonderful, and I wished I could push that picture from my mind into hers. "But for now, you have a better instrument."

"Yeah, I know," she grumbled. "My voice." She slumped over her tea.

"No." I grabbed her limp little hand so she would look at me. "I'm not talking about your beautiful voice, although you do have that." She dipped a finger into her tea and stirred, eyes fixed on the little whirlpool of leaves. "I'm talking about the *audience*. No one will ever play that instrument the way you do, trust me."

She didn't say anything, but I saw the seed take root in her mind. And in the end, all you can ever give another person is a seed.

I never told Grace the truth.

I regret it, even though I know there are no mistakes—only time, playing tricks. But I still wish she knew that she never failed at anything I asked her to do.

There was no man in the other room.

The box had a false bottom, and I switched things in and out while her eyes were closed.

I never turned on my machine, only the pulsing light, and I never focused on the cards, I just thought about donuts until it was time for us to have our tea.

11

CHARLOTTE

Johnathan came to my room early on a Wednesday morning. He knocked, and when I answered he said "Good morning, Charlotte," in a light, friendly voice that I'd never heard before. My panic must have been obvious, because he added, "You're not in any trouble. But I'd like you to come with me."

I replayed my last few days, looking for some transgression bad enough to warrant a red pellet.

"This is entirely voluntary," he assured me. "I'm going to see something, and I think it might interest you. But you are free to decline the invitation if you're afraid to follow me into the basements." His eyes twinkled with the challenge. Cold, not warm.

I clung to my door with both hands, caught between two bad options—defy Johnathan Everett, or follow him into the basement. "I'm not afraid," I said, but my eyes flicked involuntarily to the nearest screen. Of course I was afraid.

Johnathan followed my gaze. When his eyes settled on the screen he closed them, briefly, before turning his attention back to me. "Not everything we do here is like that," he said, his voice soft and missing its usual crackle of danger. "That's what I'd like to show you." He pushed past me and jiggled the screen, testing its attachment to the wall. "There's no reason for this to be in here. I'll have it removed later." He returned to the hallway, oddly respectful of my personal space, and clapped the dust off his hands. "We can bring Janey along, if it would make you more comfortable," he offered, but I was already pulling my shoes on, curiosity overcoming fear.

Johnathan led me out of the dorms and into the tunnel that linked the North Tower to building number three, the only building with basement access. Johnathan didn't even need to stop or swipe a key card—the doors opened automatically. *It must be nice,* I thought, *to just walk through a door.*

The tunnel was long and wide, with bright lights, blue and white tiled walls, and a water-stained cement floor. Heavy doors at each end, manned by guards, prevented unauthorized entry. "This tunnel," Johnathan explained, throwing his arms wide to encompass it, "was built to withstand a nuclear blast. Between this and the bomb shelter in the basement, there's room for every single person who works at this facility, and enough supplies to last a full year."

He pointed out blast and radiation resistant features as we walked, and I felt like a character in a fairy tale whose curiosity might be rewarded or punished, depending on the moral of the story. I tried to look interested, but not too interested.

"Apocalypse survival is not an interest of yours," he commented, as we neared the second set of doors. "Noted. It is an obsession of mine, but that's a hazard around here. It seems like every other person who walks in has some kind of alarming government secret to share."

I tried not to react, but felt my eyes widen.

"They're mostly crackpots," he said. "But not all of them." He thanked the guard as the second set of doors opened for us. "What are your interests, Charlotte?"

"My interests?" The question startled me. What on earth could he want with my interests?

"Music, obviously. I've seen the work you're putting into your lessons. Most people with your innate talent would be less motivated to learn and improve, which makes me think your capacity for learning is higher than average. And, if there is one thing I am in a position to indulge, it is intellectual curiosity."

That answered my question. In this story, curiosity would be rewarded.

"Your favorite subject in school. Why don't we start there?"

David was just as likely to keep me home or bring me to band practice or devise an elaborate scavenger hunt around the city as he was to get up early and drag me to school. I rarely spent three days in a row in a classroom. Fearing that I would be caught if I lied, I confessed.

"Well then. You have no idea what your interests are, do you? I will send books to your room." He muttered subjects and titles as we walked. "History and science, to start with. Then psychology. Do you read fiction, Charlotte? I find that no one here is interested in literature. Another hazard, I suppose, of this place. I'm surrounded by number crunchers. But you are a poet, Charlotte, aren't you? That's right. We'll start with *poetry*."

As Johnathan rambled, he reminded me of Janey, and the similarity sent a chill through me. I still don't know if my discomfort came from the idea that she might have some of his evil in her, or that he might have some of her goodness in him.

The doors parted to reveal an elevator big enough to park two cars in. "There is a freight elevator also, accessed from the outside," he said. "For really large items. But this is the main entrance and exit." He selected "Sub-floor Three." It was labeled "Environment, Conservation & Food Science." I scanned the other floors quickly, before the screen switched to a countdown. Sub-floor One said "Medical Research, Genetics, & Volatile Substances. Sub-floor Two said "Weather, Geology, & Zoology. The remaining floors were simply labelled "Restricted."

"We'll stop by Food Science on our way out. I have a guy working on cauliflower chocolate. In theory, it remains nutritionally and calorically a vegetable, while offering the flavor of dark chocolate and a smooth, firm texture, similar to fudge. It was still about forty percent cauliflower the last time I tried it, but one of these days he's going to get it right."

He winked like we were sharing a joke, but I cringed at the idea of a man giving up his life for a cruciferous chocolate bar.

"The lemons were really something. They tasted just like lemonade. You could peel one and eat it like an orange. And surprisingly low sugar content, which is very marketable. Unfortunately, they caused a painful facial rash in one out of twenty testers. Perfectly acceptable odds in a drug, but a food... well, we don't want a list of side effects on our fruit salads, do we?"

I shook my head. This seemed like something we could safely agree on.

"You want to stay off the first floor—nothing but communicable diseases and explosions. They've worn out the sprinkler system twice, and we had a close call with a hemorrhagic fever last year that required a full overhaul of the quarantine exit procedures. But there are some interesting things on two. I have a guy with the most amazing collection of fossils. Things you couldn't dream up. Some very... unusual... creatures trapped in amber. He swears he has a mermaid, but I doubt it."

He assessed me for a moment and then nodded sharply, filing my interest away. I collected fossilized shells at Sky Lake. I kept them, with my other treasures, in a wooden box with an owl carved on it, and I wondered if that box was waiting for me on the antique desk in the room that used to be mine.

"And the weather research has some interesting applications. Did you know that a hurricane can be stoked like a fire? A tornado provoked with sound waves? Such destructive power, and yet totally untraceable. Fascinating stuff. Should be quite profitable, too."

He assessed me again, and I tried my best to keep my expression neutral.

"Strong sense of ethics," he commented. "Not to fear. While I can produce a tornado on demand, I cannot control its size or path, which reduces its value considerably. Even foreign governments are reluctant to pay for an uncontrollable tornado."

We reached our floor and he ushered me out of the elevator ahead of him. Sub-Floor Three was brightly lit and smelled a little bit like a garden center— dirt, fertilizer, and growing things—with an undertone of sea water and burned plastic.

A warning voice in the back of my mind told me I shouldn't be there. But I shook off my fear. *An adventure*, I thought, and a thrill ran through me.

"These vents are attached to a filtration system that maintains the levels of positive and negative ions that you'd find in a natural environment, and the light adjusts as the day goes on. You'd be surprised how hard it is to keep people healthy and sane underground. For a while, we were losing three a month to suicide alone." He said this casually, as if it was nothing more than a pesky staffing issue. To him, I suppose it *was* a staffing issue.

I shivered, adventures forgotten. It was not safe to be in the basement with Johnathan Everett. But it wasn't safe to be upstairs in my room, either.

When we reached the end of the hallway, he gestured at a sign pointing us toward "Conservation" and fell into step beside me. "You're going to like this," he said.

I did like it.

But I've learned not to talk about it. We love complicated villains in movies, but in real life, we prefer our bad guys simple. Everyone wants to hear about the red pellets and the manufactured tornadoes and people kept away from their families for years.

They want the monster.

No one wants to hear about the day Johnathan Everett took me to the basement to watch hundreds of extinct butterflies emerge for their first flights while a scientist with a long black braid looked on like a proud parent.

She gave up everything for those bugs, but in that moment, I could see that she didn't regret a single thing. And I could see something else, even more surprising—that her joy was only rivaled by Johnathan Everett's.

Maybe he was only savoring a win. Maybe he had already sold those butterflies to the highest bidder. But I never stopped seeing him through the lens of that moment, when we stood together in a storm of impossible wings and I wished, more than anything, that I could bring him to Sky Lake and show him the roses.

12

CHARLOTTE

"You're leaving soon, yes?" Kit asked one day as I walked in.

I'd been busy for months, practicing, recording, and learning to be Charlotte London. I learned her voice, her walk, her facial expressions. I learned to hold a fork like Charlotte, sip a drink like Charlotte, open a door like Charlotte. I learned to be alone in a room as Charlotte, instead of myself.

I've been told to reframe that—I wasn't *learning* to be Charlotte London; I was *creating* Charlotte London—but it didn't feel that way at the time. It felt like I was being created by Johnathan Everett, all-powerful god of ERC.

The thing that kept me going was the promise that soon, I'd been on stage again. A month or two of small shows while the team built up some buzz around my hastily produced album, and then a tour. A whole year, if I was lucky, singing to an audience every night.

I felt tight. Wound up. Ready to spring.

"Yes, but only for a month this time," I said. A whole month of *stages*. As nervous as I felt about being Charlotte London, I couldn't deny how much I wanted to be in front of an audience again. How much I wanted to feel them reacting to me. How much I wanted to smell the roses.

Kit shook her head. "No. That's what they think, but no. A year." She spread her cards out and plucked one, which she held up triumphantly. *The Chariot*. My blank expression earned an affectionate eye roll. Still below average. "Success," she said. "Beyond your wildest dreams. And all because of *you*. Not *him*." She grinned proudly. "Next time I see you, you'll be fifteen years old. And a *star*."

I blushed, embarrassed. I wanted to be a star, in the sense that I wanted to sing and I wanted people to hear me sing, but the process seemed to have very little to do with me and everything to do with Johnathan's power and connections. The songs we recorded were not the ones I wrote. The finished voice not exactly mine. And Charlotte London, built from scratch, seemed to have very little in common with me. No matter how many times I practiced her smile, her laugh, and her walk, I thought people would see through it in a minute.

"Don't worry," she said, reading my mind or my face, I could never tell. "Once you're out there, you'll be in charge." She gathered up her cards. "Can I ask you a favor?"

"Anything."

"Sign this for my son." She tapped a piece of paper with one long red fingernail. "So I can give him something."

Her voice cracked, and I wanted to comfort her, but what could I say? We both knew she probably wasn't going home. I scraped my chair back from the table to put space between me and the thing she wanted me to sign. I felt hot in the small, stuffy room. Embarrassed. "He doesn't want my autograph," I mumbled, because the talented, free-spirited musician Kit described intimidated me. He sounded a world away from whatever they were turning me into.

Kit laughed merrily. "Time," she said, "is such an incredible trick, isn't it?" She tapped the table with her fingernails, thoughtfully.

"Even if I get famous, he might not like my music."

"He will *love* you," she said. "I know it." She pushed the paper and a black permanent marker toward me. "And if he doesn't, I'll just sell it." Her eyes twinkled merrily. She was too sentimental to sell anything I gave her, and we both knew it.

I took the marker but rejected the paper. Instead, I reached for the extra set of tarot cards in the center of the table. They scattered everywhere when I tried to shuffle them—new and slippery—and I spread them, picture side up, over the table. I plucked the Eight of Swords, drawn to its blindfolded, tied up lady. But I couldn't choose that one. It looked like a cry for help.

The Emperor, then The Magician surfaced like threats—Johnathan Everett, in charge, pulling my strings. I buried them.

Finally, I fished out the High Priestess, with her flowing robes and distant stare. She was wise, like Kit. Like I wanted to be. On the back, over the white and gold swirls, I wrote "Your mom rocks. Love, Charlotte London" in the loopy script that I had been practicing in a sketchbook Johnathan gave me.

Kit beamed. "He's going to love this." Then, more seriously, "I love this. I only wish you could give it to him yourself. And sign it, *Grace*."

If only she knew how that small acknowledgement fed me. If only I understood how her heart must have been breaking for her lost son.

She stood and wrapped me in a tight hug. "You take care of yourself, ok sweetie?" She started to say something else but stopped herself. There wasn't anything else to say. Whatever she wanted to promise would have been a lie.

"Ok," I said. "You too."

It happened just like Kit predicted. I left for a month, and stayed away for a year. And along the way, Charlotte London stopped being a costume and became a suit of armor. As Charlotte, I could light up a stadium. And as myself, I could fade right into the wall. Both of those talents were useful, for different reasons.

I was only supposed to play small shows while Johnathan's team figured out how to make me famous, but my admirers quickly got ahead of them.

They waited to catch a glimpse of me—of Charlotte—everywhere I went. But I didn't take the attention too seriously at first. Johnathan's team created everything around me, and I assumed they were responsible for most of the starry-eyed fans outside my hotels.

A rude tabloid reporter changed everything. I was on my way out of a restaurant, surrounded by people who worked for Johnathan. I wasn't supposed to talk unless he gave me something to say, so I just smiled Charlotte's flirty half-smile. And then one of the guys—a reporter with a messy beard and a neon yellow shirt—yelled "Why don't you talk? Who's pulling your strings, girl?" and I thought *no way would anyone Johnathan hired say something like that.*

They were there for *me.*

I was in charge. Just like Kit said I would be.

"I talk." I rewarded him with a real smile. "When someone asks a good question." He laughed, and I laughed, and the assistant who kept a tight grip on my elbow let go because it suddenly looked all wrong. Power flooded through me, as hot and electric as it was on stage.

When Johnathan called a few hours later, the assistant put him on speaker and waited to see what kind of trouble I'd get into. But he was pleased. "People want to hear from her," he snapped. "Since she can hold her own with the press, I'd say we're ready to take the training wheels off."

"Abuse this privilege, and you go back to saying what I tell you to say," he warned, but he wanted me to succeed as much as I wanted to keep my new freedom. I suppose it was self-interest—I needed to be a real woman with a personality in order to make him the kind of money he needed. But at the time, I felt like we were on the same team. And in a way, we were. Both of us depended on the success of Charlotte London.

Johnathan scrambled to book bigger venues, dollar signs in his eyes, and he carefully reviewed every show to find the key to my power. He wanted to use me as a weapon, distill me into a bottle, breathe me in and take over the world, but he couldn't. My voice, like his tornado, was not a thing he could control.

It wasn't a thing I could fully control, either. People loved me—I made them glow, and we'll fall for anyone who shows us beauty in the mirror—but part of me preferred the grudging indifference of my band. They never forgot that I thrust them into Johnathan Everett's terrifying spotlight, and they avoided me like an extension of him. My fans, on the other hand, wanted to tear my voice out of my body and keep it for themselves.

Though their hunger came from love, it was a heavy burden.

But I still couldn't get enough of that rush—hundreds of strangers loving, wanting *needing* what I had to give them, while I floated in a cloud that smelled like Sky Lake.

For a long time, it was worth every single thing I traded for it.

When I returned to ERC, I found everything the way I left it. Janey, blowing bubbles behind a stack of yellow folders. Kit, interpreting the pulses of her strange machine. But sadness made Kit's office dark and stuffy. As crowded as a closet, when she used to keep it so neat. It smelled like the grease she used to oil her machine and the extra chair—my chair—was piled with laundry.

I burst in, full of stories, desperate for her approval. I was a different person—Charlotte London, for real—and I needed her to *see* me in that way that only Kit could. To look inside me and tell me I was good. Real. But she was working, her whole head inside the tangled guts of the machine, and she greeted me without stopping. "Grace," she said, voice muffled by the metal box. "How are you, sweetie?"

She was subdued. Distracted. Tools clinking steadily as she half-listened to my answers. I turned up the volume—voice, gestures, Charlotte London's charm—but Kit remained in another world.

She was clawing her way through the inner workings of her machine like home waited on the other side. If I'd looked closer, I would have seen her hope dimming a little more every day. But my selfish teenage brain only saw the way her eyes failed to light for me, and the rejection hit me right in the chest—a punch landing on a half-healed bruise.

I turned into someone else, and Kit didn't love me anymore.

Maybe, I thought, Kit *shouldn't* love me anymore.

I pushed that thought away, and pushed Kit away with it. She didn't want to test me, so I didn't go to her office—simple. We weren't friends. It was always a transaction, and she didn't need anything else from me.

I should have made her talk. I should have brought her tea and listened. I should have sat on the laundry chair in the stuffy closet and been quiet with her. But she was the closest thing I'd ever had to a mother, and I don't think I wanted to know how much she longed to leave me and go back to her real son.

I didn't know how to be there for someone else.

I lost myself in work, instead. Writing, arguing with Johnathan about my butchered lyrics, ranting to Janey when I lost the arguments. Recording. Rehearsing in empty rooms, with only Charlotte's reflection to keep me company.

Johnathan pushed me through three dizzying months before throwing me back out, and this time, he didn't take chances. I wore Charlie's makeup and contacts and expressions from the time I woke up to the time I fell into bed. I was never alone, and yet I found myself lonelier than I thought I could ever be.

Johnathan Everett wanted my power, but if he couldn't have it, he would wring every penny he could out of my fame.

I was a teenager, living the life of a superstar, and I am told that it would be more unusual for someone in my position *not* to be self-centered. But it weighs on me. I wish I said goodbye to Kit before I left for my second tour. I wish I sent a letter, or at least a postcard, to let her know how much I missed her. But I pushed Kit out of my mind until I returned from my second year away to find a storage closet where her office used to be.

I knew before I knocked on the door—you can feel the difference between an occupied place and an empty one—but I still couldn't make sense of what I saw inside. Mops where there should have been a table. A stack of orange buckets where her cot used to lean against the wall. Three industrial sized jugs of bleach, dripping, their smell so strong I couldn't take a breath.

I rubbed my eyes. I retraced my steps and walked back. But the only evidence that Kit ever worked there were four deep grooves in the floor, left by the legs of the table that held her machine.

I sank to my knees right there in the hallway and cried, hoping she made it home to her son but knowing she didn't. I pressed my hands into the tiles, half expecting them to light up with my memories of her. They didn't. Without Kit, the place had no life in it at all.

I didn't ask what happened. Like I said, it's one thing to know someone you love came to a bad end. It's another thing to know exactly *how*.

13

KIT

I don't believe in mistakes. I never have. But when Johnathan said, "You're right, it is cruel of me to keep you from your son. I'll bring him here for a visit," I felt like I'd made a very bad mistake. One that could cost me everything.

"Oh no," I said, even though it was already too late. "That isn't necessary. I'll just continue my work. Focus on the machine." The words poured out in a pointless, unstoppable gush. I shouldn't have gone near Johnathan in the state I was in—desperate, depressed, longing for home so badly that my hands shook. I knew this, and yet I walked into his office asking for things.

Love made me weak and stupid. Made me hope. Made me put a target on the back of the person I loved most in the world.

Johnathan smiled like a cartoon lizard contemplating a tasty bug. "Don't be silly. I completely agree that you've been kept from your child for far too long. And a visit with someone you love can be *very* motivating." He consulted the calendar on his desk. "I suppose he goes to school, so this would be a summer visit. Plenty of time to plan."

"He's so busy, though. Sports and activities. And he's in a band, there are four of them and they're quite good. He'd be heartbroken to miss practice." I could not let Johnathan have my son.

"Well, we can't have that," Johnathan agreed. "I'll bring all of them. I bet I can set up an audition somewhere. I'm a great patron of the arts, you know." He nodded at the magazine on his desk. Little Grace smiled up from the cover, wearing somebody else's face. It made my stomach turn.

He winked, and then he dismissed me, and I don't know how I made it back to my little office before my legs gave out. I wanted my baby so badly that I delivered him into the hands of the monster.

I spent months working and pacing, unable to sit still but afraid to go far from my machine in case I thought of something. I had to make it work before Johnathan got his hands on my son, but of course that kind of urgency stifles creativity. So, I worked and walked and worried and accomplished nothing.

Grace came and went in a blur of hair extensions and little-girl enthusiasm and I hardly saw her. All I could think of was my Nic, and how easily I could save him by asking her to sing to my machine.

I was glad when she left again. When she was safely away from me.

Nic arrived on a Wednesday—Johnathan sent a woman to bring me to the public building a few hours before his plane landed. I didn't want to go with her, but she looked at my tiny room with an expression of disgust and pity that I never wanted to see on my son's face.

She took me to a big, bright office with a wooden desk and a plush pink chair that didn't suit me at all. A separate table held my machine. Abstract art covered the walls, and a framed photograph of Nic smiled up from the desk.

I don't know why that photo felt like such an intrusion when, at that very moment, Johnathan had control over my actual son, but the sight of it knotted my stomach. It was a recent picture—he hardly even looked like himself anymore. Grief threatened to release the tears I'd been holding in all day, and I took out my cards, comforted by their familiar weight in my hands. I didn't dare pluck one from the deck.

Nic bounded in like an overconfident dog, trailed by Thomas, James, and Ben. I smiled through the pain as his eyes roamed over the art, the desk, the pretty view from the window, and the picture of himself. He looked impressed, and I felt something close to gratitude, because at least my boy wouldn't worry about me. "Nice office," he said, and hugged me like we saw each other every day.

He had to be cool in front of his friends, who lined up obediently for their own hugs. Following Nic, their star.

My first impression of him—of them—was *big*. They were so big. Not grown up. No, they were still boys, but their arms and legs and egos didn't know it. They were all awkward movement and cheap cologne and noise, a hurricane of hormones and attitude and hair gel in this office that didn't belong to me. Thomas, bless him, seemed to be trying to grow a mustache. I remembered him with cookie crumbs on his face, and pressed my hands on the desk to stifle the impulse to wipe his mouth with a napkin.

Nic, though.

He was beautiful.

He was always beautiful, and not just to me. He was an old soul, with dark eyes and an inner light so bright that his crib glowed when I woke up to feed him. *Look*, it said, *this one is special*. And he absorbed the attention like a plant in the sunshine, his charm and charisma and talent quickly outgrowing the marks I made on his bedroom doorway every year.

I often wondered how I produced such a marvel. He would be something amazing, I knew, and he would pull the rest of the boys along like the tail of a comet.

And this marvel stood in my office, showing off for his friends, somehow a head taller than his mother, and I could see his future blinking in and out like static on an old television. He was in terrible danger, because of me.

Little Grace's future blinked the same way. So bright and so uncertain. I would have given anything, in that moment, for the chance to put a knife in Johnathan Everett's heart.

I drank in everything as Nic strutted around my office. His shiny dark hair, desperately in need of a cut. His body, moving with confidence he hadn't grown into yet. I memorized him the way I memorized his brand-new face when they first put him in my arms. What else could I do? It was all so completely out of my control.

The morning after Nic's visit, I stayed in my closet-office, trying to make my machine work. I felt like a woman calling for help in a dream—everything moved too fast and not fast enough, all at once. My intuition sparked and fired, giving me busywork and worries and nothing I could use.

I am ashamed to admit it, but if little Grace had been at ERC that day, I would have let her sing to my machine. And she would have done it, because she trusted me, and then what would have become of her?

I thanked the universe for keeping her away even as I cursed myself for not letting her sing when I had the chance. Her safety, or Nic's. An impossible choice.

When I couldn't take it anymore, I wrapped myself in a soft black shawl and headed out for a walk. My mind always worked better in movement. But my brain ran in the same pointless circles my feet had been carrying me in for years. *No way out.* Not for me. And now, because I was stupid and careless, not for Nic, either.

I didn't realize how far I'd walked until I noticed the mirrored black tiles of the top floor of Building Three under my feet, and heard Johnathan's voice booming from his office. "Where are they?" he bellowed. "Tell me right this minute. Four teenagers do not just disappear."

Where are they. Four teenagers. Disappear.

I closed my eyes, savoring every word. He didn't have my beautiful boy, or his beautiful friends. Nic's future flickered back under the fluorescent lights, strong and bright. He would write his music and sing his songs and have a wonderful life. He would be loved and admired and he would make a difference. I felt it so keenly that it brought tears to my eyes.

But if Johnathan didn't have Nic, who did?

The door of the office—black glass, with antique brass handles that belonged on a haunted mansion—was propped open. Johnathan stood behind the desk, fists clenched, chest straining at the buttons of his neatly tailored suit. A superhero gone bad.

A figure cowered at his feet. *Damia.*

"I don't know," she wailed. "I took them to the hotel. Just like you told me to." Her eyes darted wildly around the room, on fire with fear. Terror made her posture stiff and unnatural, but something else wasn't right. Smudged mascara. Yesterday's clothes, wrinkled. Hair scraped back, unwashed. Her shoulders weren't just shaking, but convulsing—she couldn't stand up if she tried.

She didn't lose them. She took them somewhere.

With a pang of sadness, I remembered the grief that filled me every time I saw Damia's lovely potential wasting away. I always knew it was important to help her keep her humanity, and this was why. She was always going to save my boy.

I took a deep breath, gathering my strength. *There are no mistakes.* I pulled that certainty tight as I stepped into the doorway.

A bouquet on a low table smelled like cheap perfume, thick enough to make me cough. Damia's eyes flicked frantically down the hall—*go away.* She was brave. Willing to accept the consequences of her actions. But she didn't look like a woman with a plan, which meant she and Nic were both in danger. I had to do something.

Johnathan raised his hand. He would not hit her himself, he would only threaten, but someone would hit her, and she would do whatever it took to avoid the red pellet. She would talk, and Johnathan would probably kill her anyway. She and Nic would both be lost.

Johnathan's hand lowered. Slowly. Making as much of a point on the way down as it did on the way up.

"You *will* tell me. You've seen this happen and you know how it works. There is no reason to draw it out." He unbuttoned his coat. Casual. Bored. Human beings were his playthings, and like a spoiled child with too many toys, he tired of them. "Where did you take them?"

Feeling both inside and outside of time, I dragged my eyes away from Damia. She needed my help—she and Nic both needed my help—but a message flew around me like a trapped bird. I needed to catch it and write it down.

For my little Grace.

I ran, as fast as my shaking legs could carry me, down the black hallway, into the cold cement stairwell, and across the tunnel to my closet office. The little room, with its dull gray paint, cracked tile floor, and perpetually musty odor greeted me like a hug. It felt safe and familiar and I thought *if only I could stay here.* The walls weren't closing in anymore, they were a refuge. The air wasn't stuffy, it was warm and it was *mine.* I worked and ate and slept in this office and Nic was safe. I was safe. And I had no idea how wonderful it was.

My machine sat on the table, pulsing gently. *I'll never make you work,* I thought, and regret rolled through me. I poured my soul into that machine. I gave up my family for it. And I never even made it blink. Such a waste. I ran a hand over its smooth surface, silently begging it to respond, just this once. "I'm so sorry," I whispered. "I let us both down."

Leaving the machine felt like abandoning a loyal dog, but I had no choice. My life's work would be consigned to a bin somewhere in the basements. That was a fact, and I could live with it as long as I saved Nic—my real life's work.

But first, I had to leave a message for my little Grace

I was about to leave her alone in a big world where everybody wanted something from her, and I'd been too distracted by my own fear to give her a hug goodbye. My heart and stomach clenched—grief, guilt, love. Things I didn't have time to make right. But I could leave her a message.

I pulled out my cards, feeling their soft, worn edges against my palms. Warm and comforting. I sat at my little table and closed my eyes. It felt extravagant to meditate now, but there were no shortcuts. I had to take my deep breaths and listen with the ears inside my ears. It didn't work any other way.

I sank back, savoring the muffled quiet of my office. *How I failed to appreciate you,* I thought. *Your solid walls. Your locking door. The privacy you gave me.* I shuffled, summoning Charlie's face into my mind. *You need something from me, little one, what is it?* I shuffled some more, cards slipping between my fingers like a liquid. *What message can I leave, so you don't waste a moment of your precious life?*

I let my intention grow, like a vine, connecting me to the earth and the sky. I would take the top three cards, write the first message that came to mind when I saw each of them, and trust that I left Grace exactly what she needed. Because what else could I do?

I shuffled, and shuffled, and shuffled, and I didn't stop until I *knew.*

I peeled the three cards slowly. They were heavier, brighter, and more meaningful than I remembered. Each one a little universe of knowledge between my fingers. I placed them face up—no time for theatrics. The last three cards I would ever see.

The Ace of Wands.
The Four of Swords.
The Lovers.

The Ace radiated life, its green, growing branch raised to the sky. The four was a well of stillness with its peaceful tomb. And the lovers, lost in each other, blessed by a thousand angels. I smiled down at them, relieved and grateful. Little Grace was going to be *fine.* I caressed each card, then closed my eyes and took another breath. It was important, I knew, to only write the words Grace needed.

Intuition guided my hand as I wrote my last note to Grace, and I hid it as best I could. With any luck, Damia would find it and pass it on. *She will*, I told myself. *At the right time.* But I hesitated. It is hard to truly believe there are no mistakes when you are leaving the world with so much unfinished business. I picked up the framed picture of Nic that I stole from the other, nicer office that wasn't mine. I stared at it for a long moment—too long, the clock was ticking—and then kissed the glass. I hope he felt it, wherever he was.

"I don't know where they are," Damia sobbed, as I raced back down the black hallway toward Johnathan's office. She was still on the floor, crouched low against the ice cream swirls of marble. "I brought them to their audition, and then to the hotel, like you told me to. They were excited about room service. There's no reason they would have left."

"One. More. Chance," Johnathan growled. He sat, one foot propped on his knee, head tipped back. Tired of the show. Which meant he was almost done playing with her. Damia didn't have much time.

"I told you everything I know," she moaned.

"Fine." He waved her words away like smoke—a distasteful irritant polluting his air—and stamped his raised foot back down on the floor. "You want to do this the hard way? We can do it the hard way. It makes no difference to me." He reached for the phone, slowly, every movement a threat as Damia huddled on the cold stone floor. His long fingers wrapped around the receiver. He held it like a weapon.

Damia's future flickered just like Nic's and Grace's had, and I was overwhelmed by the certainty that I could not let it go out. She had more to do.

I pushed out a long, slow breath. *No mistakes*, I told myself, and stepped forward. "Did you think I'd let you have my son?" I asked, flicking a hand dismissively at Damia. "You left them at a hotel. It wasn't even a challenge."

Damia shook her head, panic-stricken, as he turned on me. His eyes were so cold I could feel them on my skin but I refused to tremble for him. I stood straight and tried to beam my thoughts into Damia's mind. *You did well. You were brave.* I couldn't tell if she received anything, but kept pushing the thoughts forward the way I saw little Grace push her voice into her dying brother. *Take care of them. Please, take care of them.*

Satisfied that Damia understood as much as she could, I turned my attention to Johnthan. "Torture me all you want. I'll never tell you where I hid him."

He covered the space between us in two steps, putting his eyes inches from mine. I could feel his breath on my cheek. Minty and ice cold. "You *will* tell me."

I felt like laughing. I would never tell him where to find Nic. I couldn't, because I didn't know. It was *perfect.*

14

CHARLOTTE

Early in my second tour, Johnathan appeared at my hotel without warning. We took up half the floor, and fear rippled from one end to the other when the news filtered through—*the boss is here.*

My keepers scurried away like rats. I knew what this meant—he was there for me—but I still rejoiced in the freedom to pace up and down the soft carpeted hallway by myself. I couldn't stand it—the tension, the constant desire to move with nowhere to go. After the novelty of the first tour, this one just felt like a different kind of prison.

Johnathan's unexpected visit was, if nothing else, new and interesting.

I could hear him arguing with my head of security, a man called Mack with meaty hands and a caveman's forehead. "She's a teenager," Johnathan said, his voice full of contempt. "You can't possibly be having this much trouble with her." I flattened myself against the wall outside the room, between a four-foot-tall vase of fake lilies and a fire extinguisher.

"She's like a wild animal," Mack complained, in a high voice that always made it hard for me to take him seriously. "Turn your back for ten seconds and she'll be gone."

"You're saying she's escaped from you?" Johnathan's voice rose falsely—mocking. I couldn't see them, but I knew he was circling. Toying with poor Mack, who really did have his hands full with me. "A sixteen-year-old girl who weighs a hundred pounds soaking wet has escaped from you?" I didn't like Mack, but worry squeezed my stomach anyway.

"No, of course not. We would have reported an escape attempt. But I can see it in her eyes."

"In her eyes?" Johnathan repeated. When he started repeating your last few words, it meant he almost had you where he wanted you. I tried to send a warning to caveman Mack. *Stop talking. Back away. Be glad I'm the worst thing you have to deal with.*

"Look, I know my team can outrun her," Mack said. "But if she bolts, she'll get hurt. It's not something you normally have to worry about in this business. Usually, they *want* you to protect them."

Protect me. I almost laughed out loud and gave away my hiding place. Everyone I needed to be protected from was in my inner circle.

"Her fans… they're crazed. Feral. Like nothing I've ever seen. She needs to understand how much danger she's in if she tries to get away. And I don't think she understands danger at all."

"I'll keep that in mind," Johnathan said, coldly. He was done with Mack. "You can go."

I edged closer to the vase, into the dusty plastic smell of the lilies. Mack huffed, my very presence outside Johnathan's suite proving his point. I didn't understand danger at all. He drew a finger across his throat—*you're in trouble now, little girl.*

"Charlotte," Johnathan called, and Mack raised an I-told-you-so eyebrow. I cringed. It was stupid to spy, and even more stupid to get caught. "You heard all that, I take it?"

I slunk into the doorway, not sure if I'd be more in trouble for eavesdropping or for lying about it.

"In," he ordered, and I took a reluctant step.

"Is it true? You're a wild animal, waiting for your chance to run into the woods and be free?"

He pressed his lips together, suppressing a smile. His hands were open and relaxed by his sides, his jacket limp on the back of the couch. He didn't look angry. But I didn't trust the twinkle in his eye, or the smile that tugged the corners of my own mouth as he repeated Mack's description of me. Johnathan's moods changed quickly.

I shook my head. Not an animal, although I spent much of my time caged like one.

He sat and motioned for me to join him on the couch. "I don't bite," he promised, which was true, and also not at all comforting. He didn't *need* to bite. I bypassed the couch and settled on the very edge of a stiff blue chair across from him.

"Still afraid of me, I see." Between us, an extravagant bouquet of flowers exploded out of a vase, and he leaned over it to get a better look at me. "He's right, you know. If you run into a crowd, they will rip your clothes off." He sounded both fascinated and sorry.

"I know." I flattened my hands against my thighs to stop myself from fidgeting. I knew I couldn't run into a crowd. I might be able to escape as Grace, but never as Charlotte. And they kept me dressed up like Charlotte all the time. They watched me, all the time.

"The price of fame," he said, thoughtfully, plucking a garish red rose from the bouquet and spinning it between his fingers. Petals, loose and overripe, fell into his lap. "And also, I remind you, the deal you made." His eyes turned cold and flat. "You are here because you wanted to be famous, Charlotte. Don't forget that."

I clenched my fists, nails biting into my palms. *The deal I made.* As if I really had a choice—I was between a hungry bear and the edge of a cliff. And I didn't want to be famous, not really. I only wanted to sing. A distinction that only mattered to me.

"I don't want you to be unhappy," he said, after a few minutes of tense silence. "I'd like to come to an understanding."

"What kind of understanding?" *What terrible bargain would I accept from him this time?*

"The kind where your head of security doesn't call you a wild animal, to start." He shook his head, almost smiling again. Part of him, I thought, liked the description. "Believe it or not, I don't want to treat you like a prisoner."

"So, you want me to *be* a prisoner, but you don't want to have to treat me like one."

He pinched the bridge of his nose like an exhausted parent answering a toddler's tenth "why" question in a row. "I don't want to do this *to* you, Charlotte. I want us to do this together." His eyes rose to the ceiling—so much like Janey—and then returned to me. "But it's your choice."

And there it was. The threat. Bear or cliff.

He plucked the last few petals off the rose slowly, then clapped his hands and stood. "For now, you'll put this on and come with me." He poured a wig and a hooded jacket out of a soft blue bag. "Time to stretch your legs, Charlotte. We're going out."

Johnathan took me to a restaurant on the roof of another hotel, where we sat so close to the edge that the view made me dizzy. He ordered champagne—at sixteen years old, my first taste of alcohol—and we shared a smooth, rich slice of chocolate cake with bitter sips of espresso for dessert. Stars sparkled over us and the city sparkled below us and under any other circumstances, it would have felt magical. But I was a rabbit eating dinner with a wolf.

He ordered half the menu, flirted with the waitress, and treated me with affection and interest. It felt surreal, after our conversation at the hotel. Like he was two completely different people, and I had no way of knowing which one was real.

He didn't try to intimidate me. There were no hard questions. No veiled threats. He asked me about the tour and seemed eager for my impressions of the cities I'd performed in. It bothered him to hear how little I'd seen.

"They just keep you in the hotel room?" he asked. "No wonder you want to escape."

He was angry with them—my captivity was not a thing he blamed himself for.

"I'll speak to someone about your schedule," he promised, signing his name on the check with a flourish and helping me into my coat. I felt unsteady from the height and the champagne and clung to the arm he offered, trying not to feel grateful. It wasn't right for him to take things away from me and get credit for giving them back.

We walked to the hotel together, and the cold, dark walk felt more decadent than the cake. I went ahead, arms swinging, the cool night wrapped around me like a hug. I pretended that I was free. That I was making a choice.

But I didn't even consider making a run for it.

Johnathan kept his promise. After that night, someone always took me to see the sights when I arrived in a new place. We usually visited things you'd find on a postcard, and pictures of me smiling too hard in front of tourist attractions ended up everywhere. I was photographed riding roller coasters, eating ice cream, posing with statues.

But sometimes, we went somewhere surprising. A dim café for a tiny, exquisite cup of coffee. A scenic overlook that required a long, bumpy ride to nowhere. An unremarkable neighborhood where tree branches reached over the streets like an awning. Those were the places Johnathan asked me about when I saw him next, because those were the places that meant something to him—the ones he wanted to share with me.

I spent many afternoons strolling around obscure museums and sitting in hole-in-the-wall restaurants, looking for whatever made a place special to him. Once, it was a painting of a woman with haunting blue eyes and hair that floated around her like she was underwater. Once, it was the way the light came through the stained-glass windows of an empty church at sunset. Once, it was a raspberry tart so delicious that it made the world dissolve around me. It was always unexpected and simple and, somehow, transcendent.

I hoarded these moments like prizes, never able to shake the desire to impress him. To see through his eyes. To recapture the moment when the butterflies lit him up with wonder.

It was a game, and to this day I'm not sure if we were both playing it, or if only I was, and I can't tell you which haunts me more—that it might have been a genuine bid for connection, or just an elaborate manipulation.

I believe Johnathan meant it when he said he didn't want me to be unhappy, but it takes more than sightseeing to make a life. I was supervised like a toddler, and the restrictions felt more intolerable as my fame grew.

I wanted to make choices. I wanted to spend a few of my waking hours wearing my own face. Every time Johnathan covered a new song in red slashes I wanted to scream—let me have my words, at least. But I could only make the best of his changes and punch the firm, anonymous hotel pillows. Nothing belonged to me.

But I was getting older. Seventeen years old, which made the fictional Charlotte London a twenty-one-year-old woman. Johnathan had to start letting her off her leash.

Suddenly, I had *opportunities*.

This dawned on me in the middle of a radio interview. I was in a cramped room that smelled like burned coffee with a DJ who couldn't have been more than five feet tall, the only immediate threat to my safety one man outside with a red pellet gun. The sun wasn't up. He dozed off as soon as he sat down. If I decided to make an announcement *right now*, he would not be able to stop me. The world would know who I was before he woke all the way up.

I could have it all. My career *and* my freedom.

The realization buzzed so loudly in my ears that I strained to hear the DJ. I was Charlotte London, beloved star. The world would not sit back and allow Johnathan Everett to hold me hostage. I sat, paralyzed, in front of a microphone that suddenly blazed with possibility.

It could be my ticket out. I touched it, and my fingertips tingled. But a flicker of misplaced loyalty held me back. *It will ruin him*, a voice whispered, and I hated how it pulled me. How it brought me back to the butterflies.

I shook the guilt away and silently chanted my decision all the way back to the hotel—I would demand my freedom as soon as the time was right.

But I'd missed my chance. I just didn't know it yet.

I started searching for my moment. I analyzed the circumstances of every interview. The escape routes from every room. The attentiveness of the guards and the devotion of every crowd. I woke up with purpose.

On the phone with Janey, I tried to keep the hope out of my voice. I didn't want her to worry about me, or worse, let something slip to Johnathan. But that meant I told her less and less. Late one morning, lying on a cloudlike bed with an uneaten breakfast tray next to me, I ran out of luck.

"Is everything ok?" she asked, worry curling around the words. "You sound… restless. Like you might do something… impulsive."

"I'm fine," I lied, nervously picking the leaves off an underripe strawberry. I regretted the three cups of coffee racing through me. "I'm just so busy."

It didn't sound convincing, even to me, and Janey knew me too well to be fooled. She pressed. I avoided. Finally, she took a shaky breath and lowered her voice. "Don't try to get away right now, ok?"

We were never so direct with each other, knowing our calls weren't private, and the words sent a chill through me. I glanced at my congealing bowl of oatmeal—healthy, ordered without my input—and clenched my teeth against a wave of nausea. Something was wrong.

"I'm serious, Grace. I need you to be careful."

"I'm always careful," I said. I hated lying to my friend, but it wasn't a lie. I was very carefully planning my escape.

"Careful was the wrong word," she whispered, urgently. "I need you to be *good*."

I laughed, the sound harsh and false in my own ears. "Ok mom, I'll be good," I quipped, but it didn't feel funny. It felt wrong, the idea that obeying Johnathan Everett was good. Getting away from Johnathan was good. And, once I got away, he couldn't hurt me. Janey didn't have anything to worry about.

Janey sucked in another long, slow breath, and I could practically see her eyes climbing to the ceiling for the guidance she never seemed to find there. "I'm not joking around," she said, so quietly that I had to press the phone hard against my ear. "One of those guys with the guns..." She stifled a sob. "He sits outside my office now."

My stomach dropped. Janey, supervised by a guard with a red pellet gun, just like me. *Because* of me.

Johnathan didn't *need* to punish me, because he could hurt her.

"I'm scared," she whispered.

"No," I said, crushing the sticky remains of the berry against a plate. "You're ok. I'll keep you safe."

And, just like that, Johnathan Everett had me by the throat again.

15

CHARLOTTE

I heard Nicolas Bell's voice for the first time at Charlotte London's twenty-third birthday party. In reality, I was still a teenager, pretending to have a sophisticated good time in a sleek new club that flashed with lights and smelled like alcohol and perfume. Johnathan kept a wall of people between me and the public whenever he could, and they flowed around me in a whirling dance of drinks and chatter. Soft, but impenetrable.

Suddenly, a voice cut through the noisy fog of my party. *His* voice. I felt it as much as I heard it, rushing around me like water. *Soul shine eyes, bright fireflies...Wrap me in your arms, your night sky...I'm spinning, lost, you're everything...just not mine...*

Spinning, lost—*Yes*, I thought, *that's me.*

The words were thick and shiny, riding on the most expressive voice I'd ever heard. It shifted—smooth, rough, soft, hard—a thousand emotions on a breath. The crowd turned to smoke, insubstantial compared to his voice.

A warm, tingling rush brought every inch of my skin to life, relaxing my shoulders, unclenching my hands, and releasing the tight fist of tension in my forehead. I smelled pine trees and roses and felt the gentle nudge of the breeze off the lake. But I wasn't floating away. I was grounded. Anchored by the voice of this mysterious stranger.

I wasn't listening to the song. I was inhaling it. I couldn't wrap my mind around the sensation, but I didn't have to—he was singing to my heart.

Someone turned the volume up, and I lifted with it, toes pushing me toward the sound. *I know you*, I thought, although I only knew people Johnathan wanted me to know, and Johnathan wouldn't want me to know someone like this. Someone who sang from his soul, directly into mine.

And then the music stopped, pulling reality down on me—heavy makeup, itchy wig, a hundred expensive perfumes waging war. It was unbearable after those delicious moments of freedom.

But it didn't wash his voice away completely. Nothing, I know now, would ever wash his voice away.

"Who was that?" I asked, gesturing up and around to indicate the music, praying somebody other than me was paying attention. I needed to hear it again. I needed to hear *him* again, even though it made no sense.

A blonde woman in a suffocating fur coat said his name, and the name of the song—*Witch*.

I stood perfectly still in the spin of the party, clinging to his last notes. For the first time in a very long time, I wasn't lonely or scared and I didn't want to run away from myself. I was whole. Held. I couldn't bear to let that feeling go. But he was gone, his beautiful voice chased out by the relentless beat of the dance music.

Johnathan never restricted my access to music, art, or literature. He sent me to see movies and museum exhibits. He arranged collaborations with artists I admired. He didn't know much about how my power worked, but he knew it only worked when I was inspired, and he worked hard to keep me that way.

So, nothing stopped me from greedily consuming every note Nicolas Bell ever recorded the moment I returned to my room that night.

At first, I balanced my desire to hear him against the risk. I knew what could happen to people who got tangled with Johnathan. Janey lived under constant threat. Kit was gone. Nothing good could come of getting mixed up with me, and I didn't want to do anything that might pull Nicolas Bell into my life.

But I couldn't resist him. I absorbed him through my ears, my eyes, even my skin as his voice bounced off the walls of one hotel room after another. I couldn't get enough of him. His hair flying like weather as he exploded across a stage. His voice, layered and uncontainable. His eyes, smoldering with something I recognized but couldn't explain.

I drank him in. A sliver of light coming into my cell.

Nicolas Bell and his band, Light/Black, were famous enough to make music for a living, but not so famous that I'd ever see his face on someone's shirt in the wild. I could listen to him every day without seeing anything that contradicted the personality I'd built for him in my mind.

From a distance, Nicolas Bell was perfect, and as close to "mine" as anything could be. A fantasy that gave me just enough nourishment to keep me going.

It's an embarrassing admission, but I was so young, living such an unnatural life, and I couldn't help it. I fell in love with Nicolas Bell, a stranger across an ocean.

And Johnathan didn't know.

I had a *secret*.

It was half an idea. Nothing more than a seed. But I kept it safe and warm and one day, it sprouted.

I had just received a fancy new MP3 player from Johnathan—a gift to recognize another award nomination. I didn't care about the award. If anything, I was ashamed to be rewarded for my butchered songs, forced to stand on stages with people who really fought to be there. But Johnathan was a gift giver. A good one, although that's another thing no one wants to hear about him.

He always included a handwritten note with his gifts, addressed to Charlotte although he was right—the world had shortened it to Charlie by then. The note he sent with the MP3 player said, "Please accept this in appreciation of all your hours of travel (not your favorite, I know!). Enjoy the gift of distraction and inspiration until you return. I took the liberty of loading it with a few things I've been enjoying lately, would love to hear your thoughts and recommendations. Be well. J.E."

I traced the words with one finger. I knew the fancy silver pen he wrote it with. I could see his satisfied smile when he thought of just the right message. I poked these images for sore spots, but I felt numb. I had a hard time reconciling the version of Johnathan I knew—the one who watched the butterflies—with Kit's storage closet full of mops.

That night, his initials didn't even stir me. They couldn't. I had Nicolas Bell's beautiful voice in my ears, making me feel alive and whole. Making me crave freedom. It didn't matter what version of Johnathan Everett I believed in—they all used me like a puppet.

I might have tossed the little box away or given it to an assistant. Punished Johnathan with indifference. How different things would have been. But I opened it and found the little gadget. It could hold many thousands of songs.

Songs, yes. But also, anything else I wanted to store on it. Information. Evidence. The truth.

The sliver of light became a door.

I fell asleep that night with Nicolas Bell's voice in my ears and hope curled up in bed beside me.

As soon as I returned to ERC, I started gathering evidence. Johnathan cared about keeping people and information inside, but I already *was* inside, and had access to more than he probably realized. I could take any file I wanted from Janey's computer.

Or maybe he knew, and just never thought I would betray him.

Over the years, my understanding of ERC grew. I knew exactly what to take, and could do it in seconds. The little music player quickly became obsolete, replaced by a smartphone that Johnathan had full control over, but he never thought to take the old gadget. I hoarded enough evidence to put him away ten times, a hundred times, a thousand times.

The information felt like a talisman protecting me—my ticket out. But I believed in it a little less every day. People failed to take him down so many times that I stopped following the news. Janey would mention a new investigation and I'd change the subject, because I already knew how the story ended—careers destroyed, secrets buried, Johnathan behind his desk with a smug look on his face.

The stolen evidence became a bomb in my pocket, and I was the one who would die if something set it off.

Small acts of disobedience kept me sane. I wrote lyrics just for Johnathan, scouring the books and songs he shared with me for perfect barbs that only he would recognize. I found poetic ways to complain about my treatment. I strayed closer and closer to the edge in interviews, making him hold his breath. But none of it made me feel better for more than a few minutes at a time. I couldn't win my freedom—I could only beg for it.

And then, freedom stopped being something I could hope for at all.

It happened late on a Friday night at a trendy restaurant where I sat with people paid to be my "friends." A woman with an annoying laugh and a very tight black dress whispered in my ear. A man masquerading as her date wore a transparent raincoat, even though it wasn't raining. A giraffe-like model asked for a salad of "mostly radishes" and laughed loudly at everything. They kept my wine glass full and pretended to find me charming and I did my best not to look obviously bored, in case someone snapped a picture.

A day in the life of the amazing Charlie London.

Next to our table, a stylish fish tank flashed with unnatural green light. Through it, I watched a green, underwater version of the kitchen. The fish and the kitchen staff seemed similarly anxious, twitching and flitting and moving too fast for the confines of their environments. I could relate to that.

I didn't hear the scuffle at the door, and only realized we needed to get out when raincoat-guy lifted me from my seat. "What's happening?" I asked, and that's when I saw the man struggling toward us, slowed, but not stopped, by two bouncers twice his size.

His eyes were wide and bloodshot and his legs kept pumping as they yanked him off the floor. I had never seen anyone look at another person with such hatred.

Safe in the back seat of the car, I demanded an explanation. I knew the man's fury must have something to do with Johnathan Everett. *What if*, I thought, hopefully, *the truth is coming out? What if that man knows Johnathan owns me?* Fear and excitement mixed with the wine, making me tense. I gripped the handle of the child-locked door so hard that my fingers hurt.

"Oh honey," the model said, patting my knee. "That's what happens when you're really famous. The crazies come out of the woodwork."

If I had aimed for a smaller kind of fame, I might have used it to slip out of my chains. *Maybe.* But it all became moot, because I became the kind of famous that required blacked-out car windows and teams of bodyguards and private planes. By the time I was twenty and Charlotte twenty-five, people loved me so much that they wanted to rip my arms off my body, my hair off my head, my eyes out of my face.

Sometimes, standing between security guards, a crazed crowd reaching for me, I felt like they *knew*. Like they could see the cracks in my mask and wanted to tear the costume off the imposter. Because I wasn't Charlotte. And I wasn't Grace anymore, either.

I was a prisoner in a big, beautiful cage—with or without Johnathan Everett. When he offered me fame or middle school, I walked right into the trap—Johnathan got everything he wanted, and I got everything I thought I wanted when I was thirteen years old.

16

CHARLOTTE

My mother died before I was old enough to make memories, and David never spoke of my father although he must have known something—he was thirteen when I was born. He didn't know his own father, either, but treasured a photo of our mother standing next to the most likely culprit—a skinny boy in an ill-fitting suit escorting her to prom. My brother painted a lovely picture of our mother, and I was happy enough to have it, but I wonder what he would have said when I got old enough for the truth.

Instead, I kept the imaginary mother he described and the imaginary fathers I invented for myself, until Johnathan Everett gave me a second set of parents.

Living parents were a risky choice that everyone tried to talk him out of. I remember the meeting where he made the final decision. I was practicing my non-verbals—that's what they called things like how Charlotte London sat in a chair and drank coffee and glared when someone said something she didn't like—so no one except my body language coach was paying attention to me.

"Parents are an enormous liability," one of the lawyers insisted, pushing his chair back from the long conference table. "She's a kid—we can build her from scratch. But two adults?"

He must be new, I thought, slowly dragging one eyebrow up. The body language coach nodded encouragement. The lawyer's chair slid fast on well-oiled wheels, and I imagined him flying though the tinted floor-to-ceiling windows and tumbling onto the lawn below.

"I can handle their history," Johnathan said, in the low voice he used right before he fired someone.

I dropped the eyebrow and forced a glint of interest into Charlie's candy-colored eyes—she would not be afraid for the lawyer. I felt the icy-sharp poke of a headache behind them.

"And if... when... she gets really famous? They'll stay in character all the time?"

"Yes." Like a door slamming, or a rock dropped in deep water—firm and final. From Johnathan's perspective, this was just another thing he could force a person to do. He locked eyes with me—with Charlie—his expression unreadable. "I don't want her to be an orphan," he said, and I remember thinking that I didn't want to be an orphan, either, but there wasn't anything Johnathan Everett could do about it.

I'd found the limits of his power.

Johnathan chose a tall, bearded man from the security team to be my father. He had red hair and a blinding smile and the security guys called him Hawk, but he became Jake London for me. He was warm and kind and visited often, especially during those first few years when I was a child living a grown-up life. He asked questions and listened for the truth underneath my answers. He was a good dad.

He had a daughter who he never expected to see again, and the role must have stirred up his pain, but I was too wrapped up in myself to ask about his life. I suppose I didn't want to know—when he came to my shows he beamed with pride, and I wanted to believe in it.

But if Jake was a gift, then Clara—my "mother"—was the price I paid for him. Clara was all sharp edges and cold grace, without a maternal bone in her body. She shattered any illusions I had that Johnathan gave me parents as a kindness.

And, worse, she was a groupie—one of the many women who devoted themselves to winning Johnathan's love. They gave me the creeps.

Jake and Clara lived together, working ordinary jobs and acting parental when our paths crossed. It wasn't a bad life, but from Clara's perspective, every inch of distance from Johnathan was torture. As I got more famous, their house turned into a mansion and their jobs gave way to hobbies and expensive vacations. But Clara saw me as a punishment—living proof of Johnathan's rejection. She hated me.

I didn't care for her, either. Every time I accepted one of her quick, sharp hugs, my heart ached for Kit, whose breath-stealing squeezes used to hold me together. I was growing into someone Kit wouldn't even know, and I longed to go back and change things—have the conversations I couldn't face then, repair our friendship, say goodbye.

I hated Clara for making me want things I couldn't have.

Since I still had to act like a dutiful daughter, I made the cracks show, arranging for our frostiest moments to happen in public and letting the press say everything I couldn't. My fans hated her.

Clara took more blame than she deserved when the truth came out, but I could say that about almost everyone who participated in the lie that was Charlotte London. No one left ERC whole. That's not how it worked.

If Clara tolerated me, I would have spent holidays and breaks with my parents. Instead, I bounced between hotels and my little room in the North Tower, living out of a hot pink suitcase that made everything smell like plastic. Years blended into a single, melted lump of time. I frequently had to remind myself of my own age, counting five years up to find Charlie's.

On the road, I kept myself going with coffee and sugar and pills that I didn't ask questions about. My nights were sleepless and lonely, punctuated by elevators beeping and the occasional jolt of a slammed door. They wouldn't give me sleeping pills back then—Johnathan refused to let me do anything to mute my senses—so my mind raced while my body begged for rest.

Waiting for sleep, I wrote lyrics, pen scratching words I'd never sing over the creamy pages of my journals. I tried, and failed, to meditate, practice yoga, and pray. I would have done anything to get away from myself during those endless hours, but my body, with its heavy limbs and fuzzy head, held me tight.

Exhaustion took its toll. Dark rings formed under Charlie's bright eye makeup, and I had trouble remembering things—I lived in fear of forgetting my backstory in the middle of an interview or the words to a song during a show. After a while, I couldn't do anything at night except lie there, limp as a doll, listening to the hum of another unfamiliar place.

So, I watched Nicolas Bell.

I wasn't supposed to have a phone in my room at night, but the assistant tasked with confiscating it stopped bothering after a while. A lot of my rules loosened that way—why take my phone, when any call for help I managed to make would be perceived as a celebrity breakdown?

But the phone, at least, gave me a window to look out of.

When I typed the magic words—Nicolas Bell, Light/Black—he sprang to life and I leaned close, pushing my earbuds deep. His voice felt like medicine pumped directly into my brain, as intense and captivating as it was the first time I heard him. He glowed, sparked, blazed—a fire in human form. *Like the rose garden, or a rock from the lake,* I'd think sometimes, eyes burning from the glare of the screen and the glow that surrounded Nicolas Bell.

I felt like I knew him. Like we were attached to the same set of strings.

But my crush had bloomed into something else by then. I didn't just want to know him. I wanted to *be* like him. It nagged at me—Nicolas Bell wouldn't like me any more than I liked myself.

When I sang, my soul flew out of its prison and soared, and my fans soared with me. People left my shows brave and limitless and shining with possibility. They told me as much, in their letters, but I didn't need letters to see what I did to a room.

But it was shallow. Empty. A trick of the light. I sang in circles, reaching for a moment of relief from the bone-deep ache of abandonment I carried all the time. Reaching for Sky Lake. Trying to get out of my body for an hour.

Nicolas Bell, though. He would have ripped the pain out of his chest and turned it into music. He would have shown them the abandonment. The grief. His despair would have sparkled when he held it up to the light, because he sang from his heart, his soul, his *body*.

It was like the music pulled more of him onto the stage. He ran and jumped and played. He absorbed the adoration of a crowd like a plant in the sun. People watched me perform and saw a magic trick, but I watched him and saw one. His charisma was built-in, natural, *real*. He was himself.

And I was… Charlie London, made-up person. I got to do what I loved every day, but my circumstances hung over me like knives and the truth lurked inside, rotting. I was afraid to let anyone see me. After the makeup came off and the contact lenses went into their little pot by the sink, I couldn't even stand to see myself.

I think most people probably feel like that, at one time or another, but I didn't have anyone to confide in. So, I studied Nicolas Bell under the covers at night, love and jealousy competing for my heart. I wanted to breathe his energy through the screen.

Over the years, I noticed more and more tension in his performances. The teasing that seemed playful in the earlier shows looked stiff and aggressive. I noticed a hint of challenge in his bright eyes, like he wanted to prove the crowd was there for *him*. I wondered if other people could see these things, or just me. Maybe just me, because no one expected him to break up the band, and I saw it coming a mile away. I'd been following his side projects for years, and I could see the gap widening an inch at a time until he couldn't cross it anymore.

He was harder to find after that, because he didn't get as much press solo as he did with Light/Black. But I still couldn't stop looking for him. He was a magnet, pulling me nowhere.

My life rumbled on, big and heavy and controlled by someone way up front. I alternated between round-the-clock work and long, boring stretches in my little room in the North Tower of ERC.

When I lived at ERC, I was called Sarah. I wore a short black wig and a thing in my mouth that tasted of rubber and changed the shape of my face, because Johnathan didn't want anyone to recognize Charlie London as one of his hostages. He pretended it was for my sake, to keep me from being mobbed. But I knew the truth. *Hope,* he told me once, *is as necessary for peak human performance as air and food and water.*

If people knew someone like me couldn't escape from him, they'd lose hope for themselves.

In theory, I was supposed to write music while I stayed there, but I couldn't think with Janey's worried eyes on me and the screens hanging ominously in every room but mine. So, I walked, and I always ended up in the same place—Kit's storage closet.

It was empty. Hollow. Full of mops. I didn't open the door, because I couldn't bear to see them where Kit should be. I stood outside and imagined my old friend shuffling cards while a more innocent version of me sipped Earl Grey in the warm light of her attention. Sometimes, I talked to her, but usually I just stood there, lights glaring down as the air conditioning numbed my fingers. It wasn't a nice hallway. But once, it had been my refuge.

I couldn't forgive Kit for abandoning me, and I couldn't forgive myself for not saying goodbye, and I couldn't stop poking the bruise.

I left chocolate glazed donuts outside her door like offerings. I'd seen people sentenced to a week in the basement for dropping a gum wrapper, but Johnathan never said a word to me about them. Maybe he didn't notice. Or maybe, he knew that Kit's room was a grave to me.

It always comes back to that. Maybe, he cared.

He appeared every few days with distractions to keep me occupied. It was safer than leaving me alone to plot my escape, but I also think he genuinely liked my company—I saw the way he brightened whenever I walked into his office on my own. ERC was a lonely place, and Johnathan was all by himself at the top. I was probably the closest thing he had to an equal.

He ushered me into the enormous basement elevator at least once a week to show me something he thought I'd like. He arranged for special meals— ten gourmet courses on the roof at ERC, a dessert buffet in the ballroom of a grand house. But he'd also chase a good taco truck for miles.

Once, he rented out a roller-skating rink, and I spun in wild circles with Janey for hours while he did paperwork in a full suit under the flashing purple spotlights. I'd never roller skated before, and I'll never forget it—the freedom of flying across that slippery expanse. Wind blowing my hair back. Air thick with the smell of popcorn. Janey's hand, sticky with cotton candy, in mine.

In a moment of exuberant courage, I asked him to join us. Janey's mouth fell open—blue, from the candy—and her eyes got very round. It was a ridiculous idea, Johnathan Everett on roller skates, but I knew another side of him. The side that ate greasy tacos off a paper plate next to a construction site.

He refused. I think he understood that our fun that day didn't belong to him.

Usually, it was just the two of us when we went out. He took me on long drives in his fast silver car, to see Christmas lights, to the movies. He passed interesting books on when he finished reading them. He let me pick the music in the car. But it wasn't easy, being with Johnathan. Our conversation was a dance. Him, trying to get inside my head with questions and long, observant silences. Me, trying not to learn things that would make me hate him. We took turns leading.

Sometimes, he asked me what I needed, and I begged for my freedom, or Janey's safety. But it closed him up. We'd spend the rest of the dinner or the drive in silence, his eyes coldly fixed on his dish or the road, his attention withdrawn. And I didn't want to be alone. So, I started asking for things he would give me. A nicer assistant, more control over my wardrobe, a week someplace warm. Lying in bed at night I made my mental wish list. Like letters to Santa.

The way I saw it, if I was going to be trapped, I might as well stretch my legs, enjoy a meal, or see the endangered butterflies. But it was more than that. I wanted to sit across the table from someone who cared about my real thoughts, and not Charlie's charming, made-up ones. Someone who *knew* me.

Even Janey, at that point, believed most of what she read about Charlie in her magazines.

I know how that sounds. When I go out now and see an angry little mob waving "Not A Hero" signs, part of me wants to grab one and join them. They're right. I didn't have to cooperate, I chose to. But it's easy to look at a single moment of someone's life and say *you should have been fighting harder.*

Not going to dinner with him wouldn't have saved anyone.

But my role weighed on me. Some weeks, the screens went on, or someone I knew disappeared, or Janey's eyes were swollen from crying underneath her glitter, and I hated Johnathan Everett so much that it took my breath away.

He was a monster. And I was his pet. His useful, complicit pet. A monster in my own right.

But the human mind protects itself from ideas like that, and mine always brought me back to the safehouse at Sky Lake. My rebellion. People were being protected, because of me. *Instead* of me. I was fighting.

Sometimes, I dreamed of it—the big old house looming over me, the lake sparkling beyond it, my feet rooted to the driveway by my cumbersome dream body. I wanted to throw myself into the water or run to the rose garden. I wanted to crawl up the front steps and fall, exhausted, through the front door. But I was heavy and helpless and couldn't do anything but stand there and look.

It would have been torture, except that it was always the right season, and the right time of day, and I could see signs of life—lights in the windows, cars parked outside, jackets draped over the old wooden dining chairs in the yard. *Real*, I told myself, although I couldn't smell the roses and the air felt as heavy and still as my body.

For a long time, those dreams made me believe that the map I gave Damia worked, and I was helping people. But they also broke my heart—Sky Lake was bright and alive and safe, just like I remembered. But it still didn't want me back.

On day three of another stay in the North Tower, Janey appeared at my door with a bottle of wine and an overnight bag. "Sleepover!" she announced, like we were still kids, and I closed my eyes against her relentless sunshine. It had been an especially grueling four months.

"I said, sleepover!" she repeated, louder.

Exhausted from constant travel and a performance schedule that no rational person would have agreed to, I barely managed a smile. I felt tired and empty. And Janey still bounced and grinned and flipped her hair like a fifteen-year-old.

"Come on," she nudged. "It'll be fun. Like old times."

Old times. Like we were regular people, with a regular childhood behind us. "Not tonight," I said.

Janey wedged herself in my doorway. "We haven't hung out in ages," she complained. "You're always away. Please." She held the bottle up, like I might not have noticed it. "You're finally twenty-one in Grace years, not just

Charlie years. We have to celebrate! We'll drink wine and eat candy and talk about boys."

That offer would have sounded great six months before. Even three months before. But I couldn't stretch a smile across my face and pretend anymore. Janey was still the same person she was when I met her, and I didn't even recognize myself. It wasn't fair.

"We're not kids anymore, Janey," I snapped, clenching my fists so hard that I could feel the skin straining across my knuckles. "Alcohol and sugar and gossip aren't going to fix this." I tore the itchy wig off my head and whipped it onto the floor, like it was personally responsible for everything I didn't like about my life. Cool air rushed over my scalp. Relief.

I stood like an observer, watching my own meltdown, wishing I could do something to stop it. I'd regret hurting Janey's feelings. But the wig was crumpled and the words were pouring out of me. "What 'boys' do you even want to talk about? The ones they make me go out on one date with, just for the photo op? Or the ones who send letters? I heard a guy mailed a finger last week, that's a thing we could discuss."

Janey took a sharp breath, trying not to cry. Those things must have seemed so exciting to her. She spent all her time in that building, filing the same papers in the same yellow folders, living through me. And I wouldn't even share a bottle of wine and a little gossip. It wasn't her fault that she always made the best of things. That she accepted our situation more easily than I did.

That her life hung like a weight around my neck.

"You could just say you're too tired, like a normal person. I'll come back when you've had some rest. With coffee, maybe." Two fat tears oozed out in spite of her efforts, each one sparkling with the green glitter that framed her eyes, and she became fourteen years old in front of me. Standing outside the same door with two sugary iced coffees, saving my life. I wished I could suck the words back in.

She nudged the wig with her toe, eyes darting up and down the hall to make sure no one else could see my uncovered head. Anger bubbled over the guilt. "You should put that on," she whispered. "We don't want anyone to recognize you."

I wondered, as she walked away with the bottle of wine clutched to her chest like a baby, who she meant by "we." Was it Janey and me? Or Janey and Johnathan? Or did she consider herself such a part of ERC that she didn't think about it at all?

I found a note from Johnathan pinned to my door the next morning. He never left notes. He knocked and waited, like an old-fashioned gentleman caller. *See me in my office* felt ominous.

I crushed it—a tiny, satisfying act of defiance—and went to face the music.

"There has been a change of plans." He spoke without looking up from his papers. "You'll fly to Los Angeles tonight."

"I don't understand." I dropped into one of his slippery leather chairs, miles away from the girl who used to cower in the doorway. "I'm supposed to have some time off. I *need* some time off." I relaxed back, cocooned in the sweet warm smell of his office—vanilla, woodsmoke, extra strong mints. *In a minute*, I thought, *he'll snap out of it. Invite me to dinner. Give me a stack of books.*

He slowly flipped a page before raising his eyes over a pair of reading glasses. It startled me—his piercing eyes behind the square wire frames. Horror crawled up the back of my neck. I had been Charlotte London long enough for the all-powerful Johnathan Everett's eyes to fail him.

He went on, unaware of the existential crisis brewing in my belly. "The schedule we've been imposing on you is unreasonable." He pushed his papers away and raked his fingers through his hair—*thinning*, I realized, wondering when that happened. "And your life is… limited. I've tried to personally provide enrichment, but I realize it isn't enough."

He gave me a long, penetrating look, like he wanted to climb inside my head, and I fought to keep my feelings off my face. *Enrichment.* Like I was a caged parrot, or a gifted preschooler. It stung far more than I wanted to admit.

"You're a grown woman. You need more," he said, caught, as always, in the gap between what I needed and what he needed. "It is a difficult situation."

A flash of anger dissolved my hurt feelings. It was not a difficult situation. "You could let me go," I said, made bold by the old-man glasses and the shine of his scalp.

"Charlotte," he warned. "Don't test me."

I had been testing him ever since he allowed me to choose my own name. I knew his taste in movies, which slice of cake he would choose from any menu, how much he loved a well written love story. He acted like a *person* with me. I didn't trust him, but he couldn't silence me with a look, either.

"If it's the money," I said, "just leave me enough to take care of myself." I winced, regretting the word "money" as soon as it came out of my mouth. It was a sore subject—siphoning Charlotte London's funds to ERC wasn't easy, and a lot of it sat in accounts he couldn't touch.

He whipped the glasses off and pressed his hands against the desk. "You know it isn't that simple."

My heart was pounding and I could feel sweat trickling down my back, but I called Charlie's charm to the surface. He didn't say no. All was not lost. I held out harmless, empty hands. "You're right. But--"

Johnathan rose abruptly, making me small in the low, soft chair—a trapped rabbit again. "I apologize if I gave you the impression that this is a negotiation," he said, coldly. "My niece asked me to reconsider your situation, and with her input, I've decided to give you a more normal living environment. I trust that you won't take advantage of my generosity. But if you do, please remember that your actions will have consequences, just like anyone else's."

You aren't different. You aren't special. You are disposable.

"Do you understand?" he asked, towering over me.

I gripped the seat of the chair, its solid, animal weight comforting as I forced my head to bob—*yes, I understand, please don't eat me.*

"Good," he said, settling back in his chair. The air conditioning hummed to life and blew a gust of cold air down my shirt. "From now on, you will not return to ERC between tours. Los Angeles is a temporary arrangement, but we can discuss a more permanent solution if all goes well there."

It wasn't freedom, but it was close, and I knew I should be thrilled. But my eyes throbbed with tears—happy and sad ones, all mixed up. A promising new life ahead. Another home, casting me out. I bit my tongue to keep them in.

He returned order to his desk—papers, glasses, pen—and indicated the door with a short, curt nod.

Dismissed.

I bit down again, grounded by the bright stab of teeth into soft flesh. My future was a question mark again. An exciting, hopeful question mark, but still terrifying.

I stood on rubbery legs, dizzy, grabbing at details. The vase of yellow roses on his table. The many-armed shadow of his antique coat rack. The bright bowl of hard candy by the door, with the dull brown honey lozenges I liked mixed in. They formed a lifeline back to the elevator, where I could let the tears out.

And then pack my pink suitcase and fly away to Los Angeles.

Underneath the pain, I felt light, fizzy bubbles. No more North Tower dorm, with its smelly cafeteria and hard, narrow bed. No more screens on the walls, threatening to break my heart at any moment. I took a shaky breath and pointed my feet toward the roses, then the coat rack. One thing at a time, like Janey always said.

Just as I reached the candy dish, he said my name in his other voice. The one that invited me for ice cream on hot days and sang along with the radio in the car. "You are, of course, always welcome and encouraged to visit."

The pain flowed out so fast that I expected to see a puddle of it glistening on the black mirrored tiles of the hallway. Not rejected. Not cast out.

"Thank you," I whispered, and he didn't answer, but his nod of acknowledgement had the weight of the whole world in it. *Understanding*, I thought. *Regret. Maybe, affection.*

But we see what we want to see. I've been told by many brilliant people that Johnathan Everett never said a word that wasn't a manipulation, and I have no reason to think I know better. But when he invited me to visit, I didn't hear anything except hope in his voice.

All I know for sure is that I thanked him, he nodded, and when Los Angeles appeared below me that night like a handful of jewels thrown by a giant, I greeted it with a smile.

17

CHARLOTTE

Johnathan gave me two, glorious weeks of rest in a rented house with an amazing view and a yard full of sweet-smelling orange trees. I drifted from the kitchen, where I brewed pots of honey-sweet mint tea that reminded me of my brother, to the yard, where I dragged a patio chair under my favorite orange tree. I stared up at the bright, heavy fruit for hours while my tired body healed in the sun and bees buzzed lazily around me. Only the distant roar of traffic reminded me that I wasn't at Sky Lake.

But the vacation ended, making way for a strict schedule of appearances and social engagements. Sometimes, I thought I preferred the North Tower. There, at least, I was mostly left alone. And I didn't particularly like Los Angeles, with its slow traffic and monotonous weather and beautiful people.

And then, I met Chris.

I would love to cover Los Angeles in a paragraph, as a brief, beautiful, uncomplicated adventure. But that would be dishonest, and also pointless. I hope my story will undo some of the damage to his reputation, because I feel terrible about what happened to him when the truth about me came out.

He was—*is*—a good guy. And very talented. And all anyone remembers about him is me.

Before Chris, I had been on plenty of staged dates, always under the threatening eyes of a few of Johanthan's people. I'd see a guy once, maybe twice. He got some publicity, and I got the appearance of a normal social life. It was a simple transaction—nothing personal. But my conspicuous lack of attachments fueled rumors, and Johnathan only liked rumors when he started them himself.

"You're going to be seeing an actor named Chris Wolf," my new assistant told me at the end of my first month in Los Angeles. Everyone else— security, housekeepers, cook—came and went in shifts, but Candy remained no more than one room away from me at all times. She looked like a Barbie doll, with bleach-blonde hair, an impossibly small waist, and high heels that made me hold my breath when she walked down steps. But any illusions about her competence or loyalties evaporated on day two, when she casually allowed the butt of one of the famous red pellet guns to peek out of the sleek pink purse she carried everywhere.

"Seeing?" I asked, exhausted by the idea of it. The smiling, the small talk, the carefully timed kiss in good lighting. I was under the orange tree, head tipped back, my folding lounge chair tipping precariously with it. I didn't want to move.

"Yes," Candy snapped, bouncing on her toes to avoid sinking in the grass. "You'll meet at a party tonight. Go out tomorrow. Have dinner twice next week. He'll come back to yours after dinner for the first time the week after that, you'll enjoy a weekend getaway in the mountains, and then he'll move in here." She spoke in the clipped, efficient voice of a TV news anchor, eyes glued to a purple clipboard. "He'll stay in the guest room, obviously," she added, like this could be my only possible objection.

I tipped forward, righting the chair and squinting up at Candy. "Meet at a party? Go on vacation together? Move in here? That's ridiculous."

She glanced at me with a mixture of pity and irritation before returning to the clipboard like she had more important things to do than reason with a spoiled pop star.

"I'm serious." I waved to get her attention, but she remained focused on her papers. "How am I supposed to keep up this Charlie London charade with a boyfriend who lives here? My *eyes* aren't even real." I wished an orange would fall on her perfect head. "It's one thing to make small talk over dinner. A relationship is... another level."

It was hard enough to be Charlotte for the cameras. If I had to do it twenty-four hours a day, I thought I might actually go insane.

"I'm sorry. I wasn't clear," Candy said, speaking slowly, like I wasn't smart enough to keep up. She glanced impatiently back at the house, a more suitable environment for her footwear. "You don't have to worry about playing a part in private. He's one of ours."

One of ours. I wondered if he'd have a gun, too.

I didn't want to go to the party. I dreaded the noise, the crowd, the conversations where I lied about everything and it didn't matter, because we were all lying. I wanted to stay in my bedroom, which seemed to exist outside of Candy's jurisdiction, with my guitar and a notebook and write something true that I'd never be allowed to sing.

But it didn't matter what I wanted.

After a brief power struggle about my outfit—Candy favored sky-high heels for everyone, not just herself—I followed her out to the car and into a dark, crowded bar. Someone put a martini glass full of something blue in my hand. Someone pulled me into the center of a lively group hired by Johnathan Everett to make me look popular without letting me mingle. They expected very little– *drink, smile, stay where we put you.* A woman wearing an elegant black dress and combat boots talked to me, never stopping for a response.

The rumble of conversation blended with the heavy beat of the music and I tried to relax into it, but I could feel the noise in my teeth. The room was too hot. The drink was too strong. Someone near me ate garlic for dinner. I wanted fresh air.

And then Chris arrived. Conversations quieted. The woman in the combat boots gave me one last pat on the arm and scurried away. Johnathan clearly communicated the purpose of this scene—Chris was supposed to be the star.

Tall, with broad shoulders, a strong jaw, and blue eyes, he *looked* like a star. If he'd been blond, he would have been a perfect match for Candy. But he had dark hair and his eyes, while bright, were very serious. *They definitely gave him a gun*, I thought.

He swept through the crowd, as tall and sculpted as a cartoon prince in a Disney movie, and I clenched my fists behind my back. Chris was full of himself. Chris was not my type. Chris had some nerve, walking into my life like he owned the place. I forced my lips into a smile and Charlotte London to the surface. Behind me, my fingernails bit into my palms.

Chris didn't bother with a handshake or a hello. He pulled me to him, a possessive hand on the small of my back before we'd been introduced, his ceder-and-sage cologne surrounding me like a manly forcefield. My skin prickled with irritation and I tried to step back, but there was nowhere to go. The crowd had formed a wall behind me.

"I know you don't want to do this," he whispered, his mouth so close to my ear that I could feel the moisture in his breath. I resisted the urge to step on his toes. He was rude and presumptuous and he deserved to be put in his place. Then, loud enough for the people around us to hear, "Charlie, take a walk with me."

The crowd parted, letting us out.

Letting us out.

We burst through a door and into cool, dark air that smelled of the ocean, and if anyone followed, they gave us so much space that I didn't notice. I took deep breaths, swinging my arms and savoring the emptiness around me.

No little pod of hangers on. No security guys pretending to protect me when they were really holding me hostage. No clinging assistants. I'm sure someone was there, but I felt free.

Chris let me enjoy that feeling for three full blocks before he said a word.

"I'm not a fan of those parties, either," he said, when he finally spoke, and I fell back to earth. I was not alone. I was with Chris, the impertinent new boyfriend who grabbed me before he said hello. But his party persona was gone. He walked a few steps back, hands clasped behind him, shoulders rounded—this muscled, mountain of a person trying to take up less space. Trying not to intimidate me, I realized, and felt my own shoulders relax. He was playing a part. Just like me. "But this isn't so bad, is it?" he asked, eyes glinting playfully in the dark.

I slowed, and he shortened his steps, maintaining the distance between us. Around me, the neighborhood made nighttime sounds—wind rustling through trees, the occasional bark of a dog, the hum of the freeway mixing with the roar of waves in the distance. Sounds that didn't want anything from me. It was the farthest thing I could imagine from "bad."

Chris could have forced me to play along, but he didn't. He let me enjoy the cool air and the starry sky and the delicious quiet of the dark streets without asking for anything in return.

And, in return, I gave him a chance.

"It isn't," I agreed, stopping to let him catch up. "It's wonderful, actually."

He fell into step beside me, and we walked. Simple. Perfect. For a long time, I imagined that night—the salty air, the cool breeze, the simple comfort of being with someone who understood—when I wanted to escape from the moment I was in.

I used Chris.

It looks so ugly, in writing, but it's the truth.

The moment he led me out of that party and no one followed us, I knew—Johnathan Everett trusted him, and he could give me my freedom, if he wanted to.

If I *made* him want to.

It was half an idea. A whisper in the back of my mind. But it got louder every time we went for a walk, or out to dinner, or took off for a weekend all by ourselves. It buzzed between our palms when he held my hand and hammered in my chest when we hugged.

Charlotte London could charm him. Shift his loyalties.

Make him love her.

After all those nights on stage, I thought I knew what I was doing. But it's a different thing, up close.

"So, Charlotte London," Chris said, as soon as I arrived at the tiny café where I was supposed to meet him for our first real date. "What's your story?" He raised one eyebrow. I wondered if he, like me, had been trained to do that, or if it was natural.

I sat down across from him at a table so small that our noses practically touched. I'd been nervous about this lunch, but his appearance disarmed me—he looked like an adult in a child's seat. "My real story, or the one I'm allowed to tell you?" I asked, taking a chance.

He smiled—a slow, whole-face smile that made me believe the expressive eyebrows were natural—and leaned in, resting his elbows on the tiny table. It reminded me of the way Johnthan sometimes smiled when I surprised him in a good way, except that there was nothing threatening underneath. "I like made-up stories," Chris said. "But I'm not in the mood for one. Tell me something true, Charlotte London."

Charlotte, not Charlie.

The fist of tension that sat between my eyes all the time loosened. He wanted to know something real. But I wasn't prepared to tell him anything real. No one ever chose that door. I scrolled through my memory for something true but not too revealing.

After a long, silent moment contemplating the sandwich someone ordered for me before I arrived, I settled on a safe confession. "I hate tomatoes," I said. Light. Harmless. Maybe cute.

He absorbed this information like it mattered. "Tomatoes," he repeated, picking up a salt shaker and turning it thoughtfully. It looked miniature in his hands. "Slimy. Cold. Little seeds. A lot not to like." He placed the salt down gently and picked up the pepper, still thinking. Suddenly, his eyes filled with compassion. "And the people who work for you don't even know you well enough to leave them off your sandwich," he said.

I felt like he found the wet little ball of loneliness inside me and dropped it on my plate, and I was grateful for Charlotte's thick makeup—he wouldn't see me blushing. But my face burned. I felt exposed. I caught a glimpse of our waitress out of the corner of my eye, and had the irrational urge to mop my feelings off the table. As if he sensed this, Chris turned his attention to his iced tea, slowly pouring a packet of sugar over the ice cubes.

I couldn't look weak in front of this man I hardly knew—just because he called me Charlotte and wanted to know something real didn't mean I should trust him. He worked for Johnathan. I forced myself to look him in the eye. "Exactly," I said, with Charlotte's false confidence. "What about you? Tell me something true."

I gave him my best Charlotte London sparkle, but I still felt naked underneath.

He leaned in, like he was about to tell me a very big secret, both eyebrows climbing, eyes glinting with mischief. "I," he said, removing the top slice of bread from my sandwich, "absolutely love tomatoes."

He plucked one off and ate it, and that's the picture that ended up in all the magazines. Our heads close over the table, laughing. Nothing to hint at the moments before or after, when it wasn't so simple.

Our first kiss was scheduled for the end of that date—my stomach dropped when I saw it on Candy's clipboard, the intimate word underlined in bold, business-red—but Chris was too good to end our forced date with a forced kiss, and Candy didn't have the authority over him that she had over me. She backed off and ordered us, in her no-nonsense way, to be "affectionate" in public. She left the details up to us.

Up to Chris, really, because I didn't know the first thing about affection—people only touched me to fix my hair or make me stay still—and it came naturally to Chris. He talked with his hands and hugged with the exuberance of a golden retriever. His strong arms felt safe, even though I knew they really belonged to Johnathan Everett.

Our "relationship" proceeded slowly and steadily, one staged date at a time. But Chris had a shocking amount of freedom. Almost every time I saw him, he whispered, "want to break the rules?" and my heart jumped—free and joyful even though he'd bring me back to Candy at the end of it. And then heavy with shame, because he planned such wonderful surprises for me, and all I could think about was using him to get away.

Selfish, part of me scolded. *Practical,* another snapped. And, underneath, the constant drumbeat of survival against my back.

I would have been crazy *not* to look at Chris and think *escape.* Or, maybe, I would just have been a better person than I was.

In the meantime, Chris and I had a surprising amount of fun. We spent a memorable morning in a dusty antique shop, sifting through cluttered shelves in comfortable silence until we each found a treasure—a statue of a lion for Chris, the Leo; carved stone earrings shaped like roses for me. We rode the Ferris Wheel at the Santa Monica Pier. We sneaked out for ice cream cones and gave ourselves headaches racing to finish before they dripped all over us. Sometimes, I forgot that I was required to go out with him.

But, as much as I enjoyed his company, I couldn't see anything beyond his relentlessly kind and fun-loving exterior. He was an actor, after all, playing a part just like me. And he had inside information. I always wondered how much of his thoughtfulness came from his heart, and how much was just Johnathan, whispering in his ear.

Maybe Chris and I were becoming friends. Or maybe I was falling for a trick. So hard to tell the difference.

One night, Chris took me to the observatory to see the rough silver skin of the moon up close. Even the urgent beat of my escape plans couldn't compete with the jasmine-scented evening and the universe, as close as the city lights below us. It took my breath away.

I don't know what made it happen—the full moon, the perfumed air, the sense of quiet awe that the place inspired in me—but I leaned into the telescope, cool metal against my brow, and suddenly splashed knee deep into Sky Lake. For a split second, sharp icy water lapped my legs. Moonlight soaked me from above. I smelled the earthy-sweet scent of the sleeping forest.

And then, just as fast, I slammed back into myself, pressed against the telescope with Chris's cheek scratching mine and his big warm arm draped lightly at my waist. No water. Ordinary moonlight.

But I could still feel Sky Lake racing through me.

"How did you know?" I asked, as we flew back down the winding road in his fast little car. It was a personal, revealing question that I should have swallowed—he didn't know anything, he just took a girl to see the stars. But I was warm and wrapped up in wonder in the dark, and I couldn't hold it back.

Chris just smiled and shrugged. "Seemed like something you'd be into," he said, like it was no big deal.

And maybe it wasn't—he had no way of knowing that my moment with the moon brought me closer to Sky Lake than I'd been since the night I buried David. But when I hugged Chris goodnight, I meant it.

Eventually, Candy started to notice the incomplete items on her checklist—*first kiss, move in together*—and scheduled the kiss with the precision of a general preparing for war, right down to the thin white dress I would wear and the most flattering camera angles.

I told myself I should be grateful to her for pushing things forward. If I wanted Chris to defy Johnathan and help me, he needed to be enchanted, devoted, desperate to pick me up and carry me away, like the crowds I sang to. A kiss, I thought, with a melody in my throat and fire between my eyes, would make him forget who he worked for.

It was a solid plan. And it felt a little uglier every day, until I couldn't stand to look at myself in the mirror or Chris in the eyes.

"Make it look good," Candy ordered as I left the house that night, but she'd done all the work. I only had to show up and pucker my lips.

I expected dinner to be awkward, but it wasn't. Chris entertained me with his Hollywood stories and laughter settled the butterflies in my stomach. Soft lighting and low music and the murmur of other couples enjoying each other's company lulled me until I could almost imagine myself on a real date. One that would naturally end in a kiss. But Chris talked fast and almost knocked his wine glass over twice. *Nervous*, I thought, and a sickening wave of guilt washed over me. Chris *wanted* to kiss me.

He touched my elbow across the table, and a shiver ran up my arm. *Maybe*, I thought, hopefully, *I want to kiss him*. But then the cool breeze from the opening door cut through my thin dress and disappointment rounded me over my plate. The shiver had nothing to do with Chris's fingers on my elbow.

He wanted to kiss me, and I only wanted to win him.

I didn't *want* to be a bad witch plotting to put a spell on a nice man, but that's exactly what I felt like.

Chris grabbed a mint and fumbled with the wrapper as we walked out of the restaurant. *You shouldn't kiss him if you aren't sure*, a wise, far-away voice whispered. But that voice didn't know what was best for me anymore

Chris shoved the wrapper deep into his pocket and shuffled us to our mark—a glaring streetlight near a dumpster. The butterflies raged like a storm in my belly. Chris's Disney-prince face loomed over me, smile wobbling, eyes full of questions. A breeze thick with garbage and the rattle of the restaurant's exhaust fan enveloped us.

The fan's grating, metal-against-metal sound vibrated in my skull and I could feel the rotten-fruit smell of the dumpster on my skin. This was not a kiss Chris would choose. He would kiss me in a lovely, ordinary moment—in the kitchen or under the orange tree. Just the two of us. He would be grinning, or laughing, and he would sweep me into his arms like a doll.

A fly buzzed between us, full and lazy, so close that I could see his filthy little legs. Beyond the fly, Chris's handsome face, eyebrows quirked like question marks, body starting to lean out of the spotlight. His hand, damp and tentative, pressed the zipper of my dress into my back. I craved home—soft clothes and fresh air and Chris's easy, relaxed arm around me.

I didn't know if I wanted to kiss Chris, but I was sure I didn't want to kiss him like this.

I didn't want to be a woman who would trick a man into loving her, and then use it against him.

If he said *Charlotte, let's just go home*, I'd let him pull me away from the dumpster. I'd be the good witch, who chooses not to trick the nice man, even though she could.

The one who risks her only chance at freedom.

The idea squeezed like ropes around my middle, cutting off my breath so fast that it made a little noise in my throat. If I let Chris take me home before the kiss, I might never be free.

He shifted toward the waiting car. I held my ground.

I'd never kissed anyone with music in my throat. The idea of it—a real person, loving me with the intensity that brewed, red-hot and feral, below me when I performed—made my skin prickle with fear.

You don't have to decide now, the wise little voice counseled, calm and soothing. I could wait. Kiss him tomorrow, under the orange tree, where bees buzzed and the sweet citrus air already smelled like magic. He would like that better, and it was all the same to me.

I hesitated, Chris's sweaty hand soaking my dress, the fan rattling warnings, taking shallow breaths of rotten air. Caught between doing the right thing and doing the thing that might set me free. But what was my choice, really? Johnathan would never give me anything more than a fake life. I had to take the chance. Now, before I lost my nerve.

A kiss would make Chris *mine*.

A terrible thing to do, when I wasn't even sure I wanted him, and some part of me—the part that still remembered what it felt like to stand in Sky Lake under a full moon—knew I deserved to be near the dumpster when I did it.

Chris wasn't tugging toward the car anymore, but uncertainty creased his forehead as I raised up on my toes and decided for both of us. *Let's get this over with*, I silently urged, *before I change my mind*. But Chris just cupped my cheek, eyes glued to mine, half-smiling.

Banishing the flies and summoning the orange tree.

I wished he wouldn't.

The moment stretched—slow, romantic, intimate. Everything I didn't want. His eyes explored my face, leaving a hot red blush in their wake. Candy wouldn't like that in the pictures. I bounced on my toes. I wasn't tall enough to kiss Chris without his cooperation.

Finally, when we were movie-kiss perfect in every way except my burning, beet-red face, he closed his eyes.

Bent his head.

Paused, giving the kiss more weight than I could hold.

His minty breath met mine and panic gripped my throat—if this didn't work, what would I do? But the kiss was proceeding, with or without me. Chris's lips brushed mine, the touch so quick that I might have missed it if every nerve in my body wasn't at full attention. *Focus*, I told myself, but the sensation drowned out thought. He pulled back for another excruciating moment of eye contact, then leaned in again. Another gentle touch, like a paintbrush skimming a statue.

And then, he stayed.

Warmth slid down my throat like a shot of bourbon—a hot, comforting shock—and settled in my belly. It was a sweet kiss, but fire glowed underneath, promising more in private. My body wanted to let him pull away. Take my hand. Lead me to the car. Finish this alone, away from the dumpster and the photographers and my scheming mind.

But bodies want short-term things, and I wrenched control away from it—away from Chris, whose lips were making me forget what mattered. I wrapped my arms around his neck.

"Let's go home," he whispered in my ear, but his arms were wrapping around me, lifting me. Only my toes scratched the gritty sidewalk. I'd already won the argument. "I mean it," he whispered, but he didn't, because he found my lips again before I could answer.

I didn't know how to take charge of a kiss, so I parted my lips and invited his tongue in, hoping that was the right thing. He grabbed a handful of my thin white dress and a handful of my hair.

My body winced away from the roughness of his hands—*too much, slow down*.

My mind said, *now*.

I imagined a melody, brewing it in my chest until I hovered just a breath away from singing, then pulled it into my throat. Without the rattle of the fan and our heavy breathing, he might have heard me. I followed the music away from my lips and hips and hands. Away from the dumpster and the flies. Away from the photographer crouched in the bushes. A familiar, liquid glow filled the place behind my eyes. I smelled roses in the distance. I started to relax—I knew this feeling. I loved this feeling.

But something wasn't right. The glow grew into a fire, burning so hot it brought tears to my eyes. The roses were cloying and artificial, like perfume and plastic with something dead underneath. My audience tumbled awkwardly in my arms, instead of floating peacefully below me.

I knew I'd made a mistake just before I felt the jolt.

It was a sudden explosion that came from everywhere, like a car crash. It would have knocked us both down if I didn't have a split second to brace for impact. But it wasn't just physical, and I couldn't shield myself from the gush of emotion that followed. Desire, fast and grasping. Loss, heavy and wet. Forcing themselves into my nose and ears. Prying my lips open. Pressing insistently against my eyelids.

There was no air. Only desperate, consuming need—for love, for connection, for *more*.

I grappled with the melody, but it wouldn't release us. Chris's muscles clenched—arms, abs, thighs, all reacting to me like a lightning strike—but I was afraid to let go. He hung on like he'd fall otherwise. His heart beat a desperate *thump thump thump* against mine.

My throat was practically closed, but the melody didn't need my throat anymore.

I moaned, hoping one sound would cancel out another, but the melody fed on it. My boundaries blurred. I was losing myself. I was going to lose us both.

I didn't realize, until that moment, how carefully I controlled myself on stage—how I inhabited Charlotte London and suppressed my own emotions. Of course it would be different here, in a puddle of conflicted feelings with a man who was, at the very least, my friend.

The melody spun like the peel of an apple, endless, with bright, cutting edges. I couldn't find the end of it, and Chris was all tangled up. In the melody. In me. His feelings were sinking roots wherever they could, and mine were fighting like caged things to meet them.

Panic gripped me, ice cold and paralyzing.

Singing requires air. The words rose like a gift, leftover from a long-ago lesson. Without air, I couldn't make a sound.

I exhaled until my lungs screamed. Until I was dizzy and lightheaded, my throat full of blades. The melody clawed at me, but finally spun back into my chest, razor sharp and angry against my ribs. I squeezed my eyes shut, clenched my fists, and pressed down.

It shattered in a blinding burst of pain.

The air smelled like garbage. A fly buzzed somewhere to my right. Chris's arms held me up, his ragged breath warm on my neck. I was limp and exhausted and wanted to bury my face in his chest and sleep, but his eyes were glassy. Shocked. I sucked in a breath and shook him. "Come on," I croaked, and stumbled toward the waiting car, lips burning, head swimming, fear tunneling my vision.

What had I done?

Squeaky leather stuck to my thighs as I slid across the back seat, pushing Chris ahead of me. His eyes were blank, his expression dazed, his body visibly shaking. *I did this to him*, I thought, brain scrambling to rewind five minutes or wake up. I could have hurt him. I probably did. "Chris?" I asked, willing the light back into his eyes. "You ok?"

His feelings reached across the space between us, seeking the connection I created—and broke—so casually. But color was gradually returning to his face.

"You're ok," I said, wishing words could make it true.

His eyes flicked back on. Puzzled. Hurt. *It didn't work*, I thought, but my disappointment was eclipsed by the terrible risk I took.

Chris opened his mouth like he expected words to bubble out, then closed it. I gave him a water bottle and a reassuring smile and stayed on the other side of the car, where his feelings couldn't grab me. I didn't know what to say. There wasn't anything to say.

I'm dangerous, I thought, fear running rough fingers down my aching ribs. *And I can't control it.*

Chris went straight to the guest room. He didn't look at me or say anything, and any doubt I had about whether I made a mistake thumped up the steps with him.

When his door opened hours later, I dashed into the hall and tried to take it all back. "I'm sorry," I said. "Fake kissing isn't something I have a lot of experience with. Can we forget it happened?"

"No," he said, simply, eyes searching for something. Answers. Feelings. "I don't think it works like that."

He was right. It doesn't work like that.

The kiss followed us for months. It was a shadow behind the car as we drove into the mountains for our little getaways. A ghost floating on our late-night walks. It crouched under the table when we ate dinner and bumped into us as we made coffee in the morning.

After a while, I stopped minding it. It encouraged us to talk to each other. Made us brave enough to share a secret or two. Insulated us from the reality of our situation, for a while. I think we both started looking forward to the days Candy marked on our calendar with a red dot. "PDA days," she called them, when we had to give the press a little glimpse of passion in a restaurant booth or through a car window.

I didn't even think about music during those kisses. I just examined my reactions.

My body responded, but what about my heart? It was hard to tell, under the circumstances.

18

CHARLOTTE

"Just a few small shows," Candy said, in her most condescending voice. "Small," she repeated. She held her thumb and forefinger an inch apart to demonstrate.

"Yes, Candy, I get it." I also knew that nothing I said would convince Candy that the size of the room had nothing to do with how much work a performance was for me. But, if Johnathan's team wanted me to do *a few small shows*, I'd have to do them, like it or not.

It had been almost a year with no mention of going back out on tour. Persuaded by Chris, who had even more influence than I hoped, Johnathan set me up at a real studio with real musicians to record a new album. I chose my own clothes most days. Made my own grocery lists. Chris taught me to make pancakes and promised driving lessons, pending Johnathan's approval. I wanted to stay in this little bubble of "normal" as long as I could.

A few small shows signaled the beginning of the end. I could feel it. Johnathan didn't make money if I wasn't on tour.

"Please update my calendar so I know where I'm going and when," I said, because "update my schedule" was the only thing I could order Candy to do.

"You have a driver," she huffed, rolling her eyes. But she typed a new schedule, so I considered it a win.

When Candy said "small" she meant it. I couldn't imagine why Johnathan would book me at the tiny downtown venue Candy typed into my schedule. The last time I sang in a room that size, Johnathan still thought he could get what he wanted through sensors stuck to my chest. I didn't like the idea of being so close. So exposed.

After the kiss, I didn't trust myself with people.

In the car on the way there, Chris held my hand and assured me that I'd be great. "I'll be in back, right in the center," he promised. "Just look for me." He squeezed my hand, and I squeezed back, examining my feelings. Cared for. Reassured. He hugged me goodbye, and I hugged him back. But wanting to hug him and being in love with him weren't the same thing. At least, I didn't think they were.

Feeling cared for and *being* cared for weren't the same thing.

I waited in a dim corner, feet squeaking on the sticky floor, a vague hum drifting in from the crowd just a few feet away, until someone said "ready when you are." As if I had a choice. I walked out with my fake confidence, feeling bright and artificial. Charlotte London was a cartoon in a black-and-white movie in that room. Even the band behind me was fake—Johnathan didn't need to send the usual guys for just one show when he could hire similar looking local replacements for an evening.

It was a tiny, dark pit of a room, with pipes crisscrossing the ceiling and a chaotic bar in the back. Across one wall, people crowded around a table buying shirts. Behind me, a splash of color lit a big screen. I didn't have a fancy stage set or a big light show—I didn't need it. I had my voice.

But my voice wasn't calibrated for such an intimate performance, and I felt trouble rising as soon as I opened my mouth. Power in a stadium was something else in a setting like this, with the ceiling and walls and audience so close. I told myself that's all it was as the first notes exploded out of me. Fireworks that grew into bombs.

I thought, *too much*, but the sound was already beyond me, filling the room. I wished the sprinklers would come on and wash it out of the air before anyone breathed it in.

This place couldn't hold me.

I could make an audience happy or sad. I could sing about love and send them searching for a hand to hold. I could send them home brimming with joy and freedom and power. But I couldn't take them where I wanted to take them. I could only take them along with me. And the control that always came so naturally on stage abandoned me that night—I couldn't get ahold of myself. I was the first car of the rollercoaster, dragging the others over the edge, praying we'd stay on the track.

I powered through the first two songs, searching for calm spots in the tornado my voice stirred around me. By the time I reached the third one— a love song that never felt like mine after Johnathan's team butchered it—I had wrestled a few inches of composure back. But two lines in, it started to slip again.

And this time, we were definitely at the *drop*.

I squeezed the microphone with both hands, fingers going numb as the sharp edges of the song tore through my throat. *A love song shouldn't feel like this*, I thought, gripped with real fear, focusing on my feet to ground myself. What if everyone in the room felt my pain? But the people in front of me were caught up in each other, drawn to the beauty around them, full of love. I could feel it—love, throbbing like a toothache under the booming pain of each note. I couldn't even hear my voice over the moan of my heart, reaching into the room for something to hold onto.

And then, suddenly, it all changed.

A breeze rustled my hair. Bird song erupted around me. *Home.*

I didn't trust it, at first, but I couldn't deny the smell of pine, roses, and lake water filling the air. Wrapping around me like a blanket. I was on the beach, barefoot in cold sand. Ahead of me, the lake shimmered. Inviting. Behind me, the house watched like a proud parent. Love rose up from the ground and shined down from the sky and poured out of my mouth—the magic of the dark forest, cool and thick and soothing in my raw throat.

I felt cherished. Understood. At home. Like I felt at the observatory, looking at the moon, except that this time, Sky Lake stayed.

Is this how I make them feel, I wondered, marveling at the miracle of it. And then I thought, *Chris*. I couldn't see him, but as my heart banged against my ribs, determined to get out of my chest and find the source of this feeling, I knew he must be there.

My heart reached out and found something. *Someone.* It had to be Chris. I held on, forgetting my feet. I didn't need them.

The ride smoothed out after that song. The crowd turned back toward me, flushed and rosy with love, eyes soft and dreamy. The air above them glowed faintly, like the roses at Sky Lake, and I focused on keeping the energy at that level. But I was on fire, heart pounding painfully, chasing something without knowing what. *Chris*, I told myself. *It has to be Chris.*

I ran like a criminal fleeing the scene after the last song. I brushed past grabbing hands and ignored shouted questions and felt grateful, for once, that Johnathan's people didn't let anyone near me. I ducked into the car and collapsed against Chris. "You were great," he gushed. Then, face crumpling with worry, "you ok?"

My breathing was shallow, my body drained and wilted from the effort of controlling my voice. I had a headache and a sore throat and my strange experience on stage already seemed like something that happened to someone else. "Just tired," I said, leaning into him, and he wrapped an arm around me. I felt safe. Cherished, even.

But my heart was still trying to crack through my ribs and go somewhere else.

The next night, Chris came into my room with a bag of disguises. "Wig," he ordered. "Maybe the nose." I scrunched my real nose. "It'll be worth it," he promised.

We took off in his fast little car and I thought, for a split second, that we might be running away together—leaving it all behind, just the two of us. The thought thrilled and terrified me. An escape attempt had to be discussed. Planned. But Chris pulled up to a small music venue.

He led me into a dark, crowded room even smaller than the one I sang in the night before. It smelled sticky—spilled beer and a hundred different shampoos. I heard a rumble of voices, the shriek of a microphone, someone tuning a guitar. I rarely got to see live shows—no one wanted to be responsible for keeping me safe in a crowd—and it was thrilling.

"I heard you love this band." Chris pointed up at the stage.

I followed his finger and gasped. The backdrop said "Light/Black." "Are you serious?" I asked, unable to believe what I was seeing.

"Something special," he said. "For your birthday."

Only Johnathan knew my real birthday. I woke up to flowers that morning—twenty-three perfect violet roses—and a card promising a surprise later, signed JE. This, I realized, must be the surprise. A gift from Johnathan, not from Chris.

Part of me felt loved. Remembered.

Another, disappointed. Controlled.

"Do you like it?" Chris asked, anxiously, and I decided to let this be ours. It was my birthday, and Johnathan wasn't there.

The band walked on stage late, looking like they'd just been in a fight. Nic clenched his fists and paced. The others kept their distance, tense and wary. They played right through the first three songs, like no one trusted themselves to talk, before Nic said a half-hearted hello to Los Angeles. The second guitarist, who wasn't one of the original members, stomped off stage and didn't come back.

What I remember about that show, though, isn't the anger ricocheting across the stage, or the resentful slump of Nic's shoulders, or the way they rushed through the last few songs. I remember Nic, singing like his life depended on it. Like the song could lead him somewhere better. It reminded me of those impossible days with David, when my song tethered us to the imaginary Sky Lake.

Nic sang like he needed the song to breathe. And I felt, for an hour, like I could breathe, too.

As we waited for the car after the show, Chris apologized. "The singer is amazing," he said. "I see why you like them. But that performance was disappointing, I'm sorry. It wasn't what I hoped"

I squeezed his hand and assured him that I loved it. I did love it. How could I not? All those people around us, none of them belonging to Johnathan Everett. Nicolas Bell, so close, his voice real and raw and *right there*, his beautiful eyes roaming over the room, over *me*.

But I didn't want to love those things, because they weren't things I could keep.

I wanted to love Chris, who was mine, at least for a while. I wanted it to be Chris who made me feel like I was knee-deep in Sky Lake on a full moon night, lit up with that impossible energy. I wanted my heart to bang on my ribs for him.

I wanted to believe it hard enough, and make it true.

So, I didn't let myself think about Nic, who looked right into my soul when he sang "Witch." I didn't think about him as we drove home or took off our coats or walked upstairs, skipping the creaky step. I didn't think of him as I led Chris to my room, instead of the guest room.

I woke up the next morning with Chris's arms around me, so tight that I couldn't get out of bed. It was probably a mistake. But I didn't let myself think about that, either.

19

NIC

It all fell apart in Los Angeles.

I arrived with a pretty girl on my arm as the lead singer of a successful band, and left alone, my future blank. Worse than blank. Shredded.

I should have known I couldn't half-ass my life forever, but I'd been hanging by a thread for so long that I thought I could stay there. I was too smooth for consequences. But something about the sunshine and air pollution and beautiful people made everyone crave a commitment from me.

We shouldn't have been in Los Angeles to begin with. We were tired and burned out and a small show like that, in a place where we didn't really have a fan base, wasn't worth the trip. But the money was too good to pass up, so we packed our bags and our grievances and went ahead with it.

I should have known better. If something looks too good to be true, it probably is. And mystery money always brings bad luck.

That's something my mother would have said, and she was usually right.

First, Thomas sat me down on behalf of the band. I'm sure the others couldn't talk to me without exploding, but he didn't say that. He just said,

"Let's grab a beer," and I heard the rest of it rumbling underneath. The arguments that happened without me. Thomas, the peacemaker, getting stuck with the hard conversation.

I followed him to the hotel restaurant, where my leather jacket and beat-up boots looked all wrong—I belonged someplace where people still smoked indoors, and the sleek bar belonged on a spaceship. "You have to make a choice, man," Thomas sighed, in that earnest way of his, shifting a bottle from hand to hand without drinking. He hadn't changed since we were eight years old. Open, honest, and kind. I respected this, and found it deeply annoying—no one should have that much character.

"You've been half-in for a while now, and it's not working. We need you *all* in." He raked his fingers through his hair—still long, starting to thin on top—and lowered his eyes. He didn't want to be the one saying this.

I waited a few beats, fingers drumming the shiny blue surface of the bar, some kind of repetitive, electronic music droning in my ears. "It's not that simple," I said, when I realized I would not be rescued from this moment. It was that simple, actually. He was right—by the time I agreed to that ridiculous show in Los Angeles, where maybe two hundred people had ever heard of us, I wasn't even pretending to give Light/Black my full attention. But he didn't understand. None of them understood.

"Explain it, then. I can't help you if you won't *talk* to me."

The way he phrased it—I can't *help* you—hit me like a knife in the gut. My oldest friend's future hung on my decision, and he still just wanted to help me make the right one. But how could I explain that I wanted to be more than "Nicolas Bell, lead singer of Light/Black" to a guy who would give a limb to trade places with me?

They would *all* trade places with me. From their perspective, I won the lottery.

We all sang when we started. I might have had a little more actual talent, but any one of them could have closed the gap. It didn't matter, though, because I had the other thing. That undefinable quality that makes strangers throw themselves at you. My mother called it my "glow." More like ego, if you asked me. But you could just look at us, goofy fifteen-year-old kids lined up against a wall, and see it.

I could see it, shimmering around my eyes, oozing out of my pores, staining everything I touched. I thought it would destroy us, until the money flowed in and the crowds started yelling their names, too. But being the star isn't as fun as it looks when you're fifteen.

"I want to help," Thomas insisted, his fist strangling the bottle. He did want to help me. But, for his own sake, he needed me to choose the band. Thomas, the natural diplomat, would feel a conflict like that all the way down to his toes. I wished I wasn't the reason he felt that way.

"I know you do," I said, my eyes drawn, again, to his hair. Long and straggly, scalp showing through on top. A perfect example of something he could get away with, and I couldn't. The rest of them could take chances, make mistakes, forget the words. Hell, they could *not even show up* and it would be fine—someone else could fill in. But I had to look cool, sound cool, act cool, otherwise Light/Black wasn't cool.

God, did I hate being cool.

"So, talk to me," Thomas begged.

I couldn't talk to him without sounding like an asshole. He would give anything to be the pretty one, the charming one, the one the girls wanted *first*. But I was bored. Unsatisfied. I couldn't spend the rest of my life doing the same old shit, and the rest of the band *loved* the same old shit. Clung to it. Worshipped it.

But it went deeper than that. I woke up in the middle of the night in a cold sweat sometimes, grabbing at the air, scared that I'd used all my music up. If I didn't make a change, I was afraid that nightmare might come true.

"You have a lot going on," Thomas said, releasing the bottle and dropping his hands heavily on the bar. "We get that. But we have Light/Black. This is *it* for us. And if you're not all in, we have to figure some things out."

Guilt squeezed my chest. What could they do, without me? But I was angry, too. I shouldn't have to feel guilty about living my life. They wanted to keep me in a box we built when we were teenagers, and I couldn't breathe in there.

"Nic? I'm serious about this. You have to make a decision."

He has no leverage here, I thought. *There's no way they can replace me.* I didn't like the voice in my own head—calculating and strategic, someone we all would have hated when we started out—but maybe that's what growing up sounded like. "I don't think it has to be such a black and white decision," I said.

Black and white. Light/Black. My mother would have said this painful moment was written into my life story when we named the band.

Thomas went back to tossing the bottle between his hands. "I get it, man, I really do. You know I want you to be happy."

I believed him—he wanted me to be happy—but his disappointment stuck to me. I needed to make a decision. And no matter what I decided, someone wasn't getting what they wanted. Hell, I didn't even know what I wanted.

Not even twenty-four hours later, Tess started asking for promises. We had just ordered drinks, and I wished mine would get to the table faster. Based on her grim expression, I was going to need it.

We'd been together for two years by then. A good two years, from my perspective, but she wanted more than half of my bed and a ticket to wherever I was going next. I didn't blame her, but it still irritated me. Tess had always been so gentle about the future. It was, if I was being totally honest, one of the things I liked best about her.

"We don't have to get married." The words rushed out like she thought I might walk away if she didn't clarify. "I don't care about that. It's just a piece of paper. But I love you, and I need to know that you see this as a long-term thing."

I poured a little pile of salt in my appetizer dish. It was a fancy restaurant pretending to be a beachside dive—sawdust on the floor, waves right outside the windows, wine list like an encyclopedia—and I expected her to be impressed.

Grateful, if I was being totally honest.

Tess tugged a dark curl and I watched it stretch and spring back into place. Like Tess. Flexible.

"We've been together for two years," I said, finally, pushing the salt into shapes with my thumb. We were only twenty-four, and it seemed perfectly reasonable not to have the future figured out. "Seems pretty long term to me." The nautical décor—nets draped on the walls, lobster cages piled in a corner—suddenly felt ominous.

"I'm not sure what 'together' means to you." She was calm but determined, her hands flat on the table, her big brown eyes on me as she took a slow, controlled, about-to-plunge breath. "Do you love me, Nic? Really love me? Like, the forever kind of love?"

The forever kind of love. My stomach dropped. "How can you ask that?" I shined my best smile at her, trusting my charm to do the heavy lifting. A week before, it would have. "You know how I feel about you. Of course I love you." I brushed the salt off my hands and reached for hers.

Tess shook her head, tears threatening, and swept out of the restaurant without glancing back just as the waiter arrived with our drinks. I drank both of them in stunned silence, scuffing my feet on the sawdusty floor, a hungry seagull peering in the window, my life almost unraveled.

I bought roses. She got her own hotel room.

All in. Long term thing. Forever.

I could feel my time running out. A razor blade on a fraying string.

When Tess knocked on my door the next day with tickets to see Charlie London at a small venue downtown, I thought we were ok. She was wearing the pink dress I liked, a necklace I gave her, and a small, hopeful smile. A peace offering. It had to be, because I loved Charlie London, not Tess. She teased me about it all the time.

I should have been relieved that the fight was over, but I just felt like a jerk. Tess deserved more.

Her hands were fists around the tickets. "What do you think?" she asked, eyes eager, voice trembling, eyes big and worried. I was about to open my arms to her. And then she gave me that shaky little smile again, holding the tickets out with the reverence of a fairy-tale girl who just spent her last coin on a spell, and I saw the truth.

Tess believed the stories.

Something inside me shouted *seriously, Tess?* But guilt and affection overwhelmed my annoyance. A lot of people believed the stories about Charlie London.

People said that if you were close to the stage when Charlie sang a love song, you'd fall for whoever you were with. Charlie got blamed for more happy marriages and disastrous one-night-stands than anyone else on earth, probably. But she got blamed for all kinds of impulsive decisions—ending relationships, quitting jobs, running away from home. It was just a myth, built up because Charlie's voice was so special you couldn't help wanting it to be more.

But Tess believed. The tickets weren't a peace offering, they were a calculated move.

"Well?" she asked, anxiously. "Will you go with me?"

She threw her arms around me when I said yes, and I hoped her trick would work—then I'd finally be able to give someone what they wanted.

Tess clung to me as we stood in line, waiting for the doors to open. She knew this was our last chance, and she didn't want to lose me. I didn't want to lose her, either, but her grip felt tight and stifling. I was restless before we got in the door.

I insisted on standing in the back. I needed to focus on Tess, and I wouldn't have a chance if I was close enough to make eye contact with Charlie London. I'd had a crush on her since I was a teenager, and the idea of her actual eyes on me made me itchy. I needed to focus on repairing my relationship with my actual girlfriend.

"Don't you want to go closer?" Tess tugged my arm, leading me toward the stage. "You'll hardly be able to see her from back here."

I put my arms around Tess. "I don't want to see anybody but you." I pulled her close, breathing in the coconut smell of her shampoo. I didn't mean it, but I *wanted* to mean it. I wanted Tess and the band to be enough. On paper, they *were* enough, and I couldn't even identify what more I was looking for. *I* was the problem.

She grinned and settled in front of me, just the right height for my chin to rest on the top of her head. Standing in that dark room, surrounded by strangers, feeling the press of Tess's slight weight against my body, I thought, *maybe this could be it.* I could love Tess. I could commit myself to Light/Black. I could decide not to need anything more.

And then, Charlie started to sing.

Tess was right. I could hardly see her. At least, not the way I wanted to.

I wanted to see every movement of her lips, every blink, every twitch. I wanted to see her eyelashes and her fingernails and the color of her eyes close up. I wanted to feel her elbows and knees and the lines on the palms of her hands. I wanted her voice in my ear, just for me.

My eyes filled with tears, and I was not a crying kind of guy. But I felt like she was *home*, and I was stuck outside. My skin burned.

Charlie finished one song and started another. Her hands were clamped around the microphone, her eyes down. But it didn't matter—her voice filled the stage. The room. I imagined a crowd outside, pressed against the side of the building, listening.

And me, inside, feeling just as far away from her.

It took every ounce of strength I had to keep my arms around Tess, my chin resting on the top of her head. I broke out in a cold, feverish sweat. Every cell in my body screamed at me to move. To push forward. To climb up on the stage and throw myself in the arms of a total stranger.

Insanity, obviously. I clung to Tess and tried to breathe.

By the time Charlie started the third song—a love song that I'd never been crazy about—my heart was pounding so hard that I thought it would bounce over the crowd and land like a bloody offering at her feet. My shirt was soaked, sticking to my back, wet under the arms. I couldn't get a full breath.

Tess melted closer and I resisted the urge to push her away. I needed movement and air and space. I needed Charlie, so close, pulling me with her voice. When her eyes fixed on the back of the room, it didn't matter that I knew she couldn't see me. She was looking for someone. Looking for me. She had to be.

Tess swayed to the music, oblivious, as my feet tried to break away and run for the stage without me.

And then it ended, and Charlie bolted with a wild look in her eyes, and I felt every tendon in my body snap. *Disconnected.* The crowd came out of its trance, ready to do whatever people did after a Charlie London show—get tattoos, join the circus—but I didn't want to move from the spot where I heard her voice.

I shuffled out, weak, like I'd been turned inside out and shoved back together in a hurry. Organs out of place, nerves not wired right. My head floated, my hands swung like weights, my feet dragged. It wasn't about Charlie London—it couldn't be. I didn't even know her. It was about me. But it still felt deeply wrong to walk out, holding Tess's hand, leaving Charlie behind. My fingers around Tess's felt like they belonged to someone else.

"Well?" Tess asked. "Did you love it?"

I knew what she was really asking. Did I love *her.* And I couldn't say yes, at least not the way she wanted me to. I didn't want to be *all in* and I wasn't ready for a *long-term thing* and *forever* sounded like a prison sentence.

I left a Charlie London show, broke up with my girlfriend, and quit my band. The irony is not lost on me.

20

CHARLOTTE

Johnathan didn't call or visit while I lived in Los Angeles. He acknowledged my twenty-third birthday with the violet roses and the Light/Black show, and my twenty-fourth birthday with a thick gold necklace recovered from a shipwreck. But he never called or surprised me with a disguise and a day out. He was the mastermind behind everything in my life, from my relationship with Chris to what kind of coffee I drank in the morning, and I felt like he didn't exist anymore.

He sent a bottle of champagne for the release of the new album, and I scoured his note for hidden meaning—*Charlotte, congratulations on another triumph. J.E.* Brief. Impersonal. It made me cold, but I shook it off. Reframed it as a gift—the normal life I wanted so badly, free from his supervision.

"The boss is happy with the pictures," Chris said one morning, casually, and the bubble popped. The coffee pot was gurgling. Onions and tomatoes caramelized together on the stove. Chris kissed me good morning and pushed a carton of eggs into my hands. A normal Sunday, except for me, frozen halfway to the coffee pot.

"You talked to him?" I asked, blindsided.

Chris turned the stove down and gave me his full attention. "He checks in every week." Then, in his calm I've-had-a-lot-of-therapy voice, "That bothers you."

I felt betrayed, and I couldn't tell who betrayed me—Chris or Johnathan. They were the men in my life, and I didn't spend much time thinking about their relationship independent of me. But it was a ridiculous way to feel, so I grabbed a bowl and smacked an egg on the rim. The shell shattered and I focused on fishing out the pieces.

Chris came around to my side of the counter and sat on a high stool, trying for eye contact. He was older—Charlie, after all, was supposed to be twenty-nine by then—and he had the maturity to sit down and talk about feelings. I didn't, so I smacked another egg and busied myself cleaning the goo that dripped down the side of the bowl.

"It bothers me, too." He sighed, and I could practically feel the warmth of his empathy on my shoulder. "But it could work for us." He expertly cracked the last two eggs, one per hand, and pushed the bowl away. "He likes the way this is going. We could stay together. Get married. Have a couple of kids, even."

He said it like a shopping list—no big deal. Marriage and kids and happily-ever-after. I stared mutely at my slimy fingers, wishing I still had the bowl because whisking the eggs would give me something to do with my hands. When I risked a look at Chris, his face was wide open and smiling. Full of affection but still, somehow, betraying nothing.

I tried to imagine it—Chris in a suit, me in a big white dress. A family that I could *keep*. It made me breathless and dizzy. *Hungry*, I decided. *I'm just hungry*. But the image stayed, like a perfect scene inside a snow globe. Safe on a high shelf, where no one can shake it.

Chris jumped up and stood behind me, wrapping his arms around my waist. I smelled the ceder in his aftershave. The rosemary he chopped for the omelets. "Weddings and kids are great publicity," he said brightly, planting a clumsy kiss near my ear. "Just think about it, ok?"

Great publicity. The words settled in the pit of my stomach as I leaned back, letting my body shape itself into his. Was that all he wanted from me? Publicity, like all the others? The question crouched on the back of my tongue.

I didn't ask. In the end, it didn't matter—even if Johnathan let me have a future with Chris, I'd always be waiting for him to take it away. He'd never give me a happily-ever-after.

Still, it nagged me as we cleaned up the breakfast dishes—did I want the happily-ever-after? Would I step inside that snow globe if I could?

My tangled feelings made me restless and hungry for assurances. *Do you love me, is any of this real?* But I wasn't brave enough for those questions, so I fell back on the one that had been screaming inside me since the first time I saw Chris.

Will you help me get away?

"It's just us now," I said, as we contemplated the calm, black ocean at the end of our walk. "No supervision. We could run." We were away together, with minimal security and no set plans. The timing was perfect. I'd been watching for the right moment for two years, and this was it.

Waves lapped hypnotically and a light breeze tugged at the hood of my sweatshirt, freeing a few strands of hair so they tickled my face. The air smelled like salt and possibilities. I had taken my shoes off, and my feet were buried in cold, dry sand, but I felt light. Ready to run. I let a melody rise inside me, humming underneath the wind and water and traffic in the distance, my heart reaching for his for the first time since our first, disastrous kiss.

Next to me, Chris was silent, but I could feel him inside the melody. Reaching. I waited one beat, then two, and the melody began to spiral. But a wall was coming down between us, thick and dark, like the huge metal front doors that closed when I arrived at ERC.

The wall crashed down. I was alone inside the music. Chris wasn't reaching anymore—not with his heart, anyway—and I let the melody fall into the sand. "Or you could let me go," I suggested, tears rising at the thought of Chris letting me go, instead of coming with me.

Chris's hand closed around my upper arm. Tight and bruising. Unfamiliar, although I knew it was the same hand that stroked my cheek before a kiss and massaged the knots out of my shoulders. His eyes were hard. Dark. Serious. The playful exterior I loved but never quite believed in, gone.

Not real.

My heart cracked open in a sharp, surprising way as he pulled me off the beach. He didn't say a word, and that made it worse. His "no" was physical, like we never meant more than that to each other. I swallowed sobs as we flew through the sand and onto the street.

I couldn't really run away, not like this, without taking steps to protect Janey. But I still wanted Chris to say yes. To choose me. And, for all my scheming and manipulation, in the end it only mattered because I cared about him.

Chris rushed me back to our hotel. I was carrying my shoes and I had to run to keep up with his long legs, but I didn't ask him to stop. I couldn't. My throat felt swollen shut and I couldn't hear anything over the roar inside me—heart breaking, breath heaving, brain shouting truths I didn't want to hear. He didn't love me, none of it was real.

He looked down at me once, as we waited for the elevator, and the ice in his eyes answered all my questions.

I wished I left things the way they were.

Chris signaled for the security guard to stay in the room with me while he took a shower, and I sat on the edge of the bed with my shattered heart—a wet, messy thing that would start to smell if someone didn't clean it up. The guard kept his eyes on the door, and I kept mine on the window, hoping he couldn't see my feelings staining the carpet. Steam billowed out of the bathroom for a long time.

Chris slept on the couch that night, and I curled up in the big empty bed, arms crossed protectively over my heart. We barely spoke until we returned to the Los Angeles house.

"I think it's better if we keep this professional from now on," he said, in a quiet, strained voice, and I called him a jackass because it seemed like the only way to reclaim my dignity, and Candy, who had just come in to update our schedules, decided a dramatic breakup would be great publicity.

"Go," she ordered. "Make sure someone sees you checking into a hotel. Start the rumors." He did as she said, and, for once, I was grateful that Candy was in charge. With Chris gone, I could cry.

Except that I couldn't. Chris was the one who cared about my feelings. Without him, what was the point?

Someone wrote a script for our final fight, which took place in an airport lounge a week later. Chris stuck to it. I did not, and if I had any remaining doubts about my feelings for him, that fight put them to rest. I couldn't have sliced him open with words the way I did if I didn't love him.

If we didn't love each other.

Later, in a rare moment of approval, Candy called my performance "epic."

The press had a field day with our breakup. But nothing compared to the headlines after the truth about Charlotte London came out.

Actor Chris Wolf Held Charlie London Hostage.
The Real Story Behind That Breakup Fight.
Chris Wolf Sold His Soul For Fame.
Chris Wolf, Man or Monster?
Inside Chris Wolf's Twisted Fantasy.

It was brutal, and I saw the coverage so long after-the-fact that I couldn't set the record straight. But it probably doesn't matter. Everyone thought they knew my life better than I did back then, and they wouldn't have believed me. Much later, I pulled Chris's file from the ERC archive—unethical, but I think I can be forgiven that small lapse—and while it wouldn't be right for me to share its contents, I will say that Chris didn't belong to himself any more than I did, and he was protecting us both in the only way he knew how.

One of my biggest regrets is that we turned on each other, but Johnathan had a way of making people do that. It's how he built his empire.

21

CHARLOTTE

Breaking up with Chris won me almost a year of rest while the press burned itself out on the drama. I spent most of it relaxing at nice resorts where someone could get a good bikini shot every few days. I lay for long, punishing stretches in the sun, pushing my feelings out through my pores until I couldn't stand it and then letting the ocean rinse me clean. I was gritty with sand and salt and a stylist had to come every week to touch up my sun-bleached hair.

I kept waiting for Johnathan to call me back, but I think he knew my heart was truly broken, and I needed some time.

Eventually, though, he sent the plane to fetch me. Normal life required supervision. When I lost Chris, I lost my privileges.

I dragged my "vacation" out a little longer with the obligatory breakup album, recorded in the dismal ERC studio with a new set of resentful basement musicians. The atmosphere at ERC felt even more dense and stifling than I remembered, but I blamed it on my long stretch of freedom.

I told myself that the halls were always silent and thick with worry, that the researchers always kept their eyes on their feet, that Janey always jumped at the slightest sound, but it was clear that things had changed for the worse while I was away. Every time I opened the door to leave my little room in the North Tower, I instinctively took a deep breath and held it.

No one would tell me what was wrong. But I saw their eyes flick to the screens when I asked.

Johnathan avoided me. No dinners. No special outings. No visits to the labs to see something incredible. I didn't know the extent of it at the time, but the wheels were coming off—money drying up, influence waning. And Johnathan was ruling ERC with an iron fist to compensate.

I think, although I'll never know for sure, that he was ashamed to show me that side of himself.

The financial problems, however, were no secret. They were etched around the hollow eyes of his researchers, working day and night to produce a profitable miracle. Johnathan had to jump through hoops to get my royalties into ERC's bank account, and my long vacation wasn't helping matters. I knew it was only a matter of time before his financial concerns outweighed his sympathy.

A tour would bring him an easy fortune. Plug the holes in the boat, for a while. Keep the power flowing to those terrible screens.

"Enough," he said one day, marching into my room in the North Tower with ice in his eyes and a thick folder gripped tightly in one hand. The other one flexed, like it wanted to hit something. "You've had plenty of rest, and the album is done. It's time to get back out there."

I pulled my shoulders back, determined not to look weak although every muscle in my body wanted to drop me on the bed. He thrust the folder into my hands.

"Just business this time," he said, softening slightly, and I let out a breath I didn't know I was holding. At least there wouldn't be another Chris. But his words echoed in my mind. His business, funded by my voice. I didn't have a choice, but that didn't make the lives any lighter on my conscience.

According to the schedule inside the folder, I'd be performing almost nonstop for three years. Just looking at it made me tired. But I didn't argue. No one would listen to me. And I fully expected to collapse from exhaustion long before I reached the last show.

"Fine," I said, and started throwing my clothes back into the pink suitcase. As I crossed dates off the list, new ones appeared like magic, so I stopped thinking beyond the next show. I saved all my energy for the stage, kept Charlie wrapped around me like a cloak, and locked my feelings away.

The world wanted everything from Charlie, but nothing from me, so I let them have her. They could rip every thought out of her head and every feeling out of her heart if they wanted to.

They couldn't touch her. She wasn't real.

My countdown started three days after my twenty-eighth birthday. I was already on edge—a conversation with Janey had been interrupted by the nightmare buzz of the screens, and I knew better than to believe her muttered "false alarm." Things at ERC were getting worse. I could hear it in her voice. I could feel it grating against my bones as I walked out on stage. It sat like a rock in my stomach when I opened yet another gift from Johnathan.

My successes, funding his crimes.

The ticking—faint but impossible to ignore—was waiting in my hotel room. I was already jittery, and the steady tap sawed on my frayed nerves as I peeled tight jeans off my legs and freed my hair from a handful of pins. *Maybe*, I thought, *I've finally cracked up.* But an imaginary sound is just as irritating as a real one.

The room was full of mirrors, every wall reflecting my tired eyes, and the noise felt magnified. *Tick tick tick.* Steady. Not coming from anywhere in particular. I untangled my headphones, desperate to replace the sound with Nicolas Bell's voice. But the tick broke right through the music.

It wasn't in the room—not exactly. And it wasn't in my head, either.

Warning, I thought, cold creeping down the back of my neck. I searched for clocks. Turned the television on and then off again. Searched the smooth, modern hotel room for hiding places. Nothing. But the ticking followed me from the bed to the bright white bathroom to the tall doors that led out to the balcony.

The balcony, where a guard should have been slumped in a folding chair or leaning against the door.

I blinked, hard, sure I must be missing something. He was always there.

I pressed my hand flat against the door, numb with shock. I was completely alone.

Two guards always watched my room. One outside, to prevent me from escaping. And another on my balcony, to prevent me from jumping. I had just said goodnight to the guard at the door, who seemed far too young to be holding a woman hostage. And I was looking at my balcony, bare except for a round metal table and the wind, moaning mournfully twenty-seven floors up.

No guard.

I opened the balcony door slowly, body keeping time with the warning beat, emotions tumbling over each other. Cool air that smelled like city—cars, food, sewer—quickly overpowered the powdery, lavender-lemon smell of my room. My head swam with possibilities—no way down, but no one stopping me, either. I took a deep, cold breath.

And then it hit me—a sudden, blinding, bee-sting shock that made me sag against the door.

I was worth as much to Johnathan dead as I was alive.

And he wanted me to know it.

I should have been terrified—my body knew it, cold and thrumming with adrenaline. But as the wind howled around me on the empty balcony, all I felt was hurt.

A stronger person might have faced her own mortality with a renewed commitment to escape, but I spent each night leaning over a different drop, my body vibrating with the desire to tip just a little more. Just enough to take the decision out of my hands and replace the *tick tick tick* with a final whoosh of air.

I didn't want to die, but sometimes, it seemed like the only way to make an impact.

I struggled to sound upbeat for Janey. It should have been easy—I stopped confiding in her long before—but I craved the comfort of our old, easy friendship. I wanted her to babble about fashion and debate the merits of bubble gum flavors. I wanted her to tell me, like she used to, that everything was going to be ok. But she had secrets of her own.

Hope rushed in, as soft and soothing as a drug, when she finally told me the truth—ERC was under investigation, and this one wasn't going away like they usually did. It had been going on for over a year.

Johnathan was occupied with something more important than my security arrangements.

I seized the information like a life raft, reimagining all those empty balconies as nothing more than an accident. An oversight. Evidence, maybe, that Johnathan trusted me more than I thought. I was grateful that I never found the courage to jump.

And then I heard the familiar tone of Janey's famous eyeroll.

"Her name's Mallory Harmon and she's set herself up in the office park down the street," Janey said, dismissively. I could see her, flicking her hair and shaking her head just like she did the first day I met her, joking about zombies in the basement. "It looks like a custom print shop, but it's actually a bunch of FBI agents trying to figure out who's coming and going from here. Johnathan sent them a letter, inviting them into the parking lot for a better view."

I clutched the phone tightly, heart sinking.

"He said he'd have lunch delivered," she added, giggling, and I doubled over, hugging myself. This investigation, like the others, was nothing more than an inconvenience. And Janey thought the whole thing was *funny*. "They turned the offer down, obviously. So, he sent pizza to the print shop."

She laughed—a tight, scornful sound that tied my stomach in a knot—at the cleverness of this move. I squeezed my eyes shut, trying to summon memories of the bubbly teenage Janey who saved my life. That girl wasn't impressed with anything Johnathan did. She would have been plotting ways to get a message out. That Janey laughed from her soul—big and bright and real.

"It sucks, though," she sighed, slurping her iced coffee. "We're on even tighter leashes than usual. I have to get my coffee in the cafeteria."

Cafeteria coffee—the ultimate insult. My fingers twitched, itching to break something. "Doesn't it bother you?" I asked.

"Doesn't what bother me?"

"All of it. Don't you wish you could do something?"

"Charlie," she said merrily, like I'd made a very good but inappropriate joke. "Don't be silly." She put a little more emphasis on "silly" than it deserved, to let me know I was on the verge of getting us both in trouble, and a flash of anger sizzled through me, raising my heart rate and tensing my muscles. All these years staying out of trouble, and what had I accomplished? No one was coming to save me, and it was too late for me to save myself. I was in too deep, just like everyone else who got sucked into ERC.

Except that I wasn't in ERC. I was out in the world. If anyone could do something, it should be me, and I'd let so many chances pass me by. My heart slowed, becoming a steady drumbeat in my chest. Trying to push me up another hill.

"I'll talk to you soon," Janey promised, in a voice that belonged to someone I didn't know, and I thought, *will you?* Because no one at ERC was safe. The thing I tried not to think about—that I could go back and find her desk as lifeless as Kit's closet—barreled through my denial. It would break my heart for this to be our last conversation. But she hung up while I was still struggling to force words past the hard lump of regret in my throat.

I slid down the wall, fists clenched against my chest, legs too tired to hold me. I wanted—needed—to do something, but I was just swimming in circles. Why, I wondered, dropping my head between my knees and sinking into myself, couldn't I just stop kicking?

If not for that call, I might have turned away from the opportunity that knocked on my door a few weeks later. But Janey's laugh haunted me—a constant reminder of what she had become. What we were both probably becoming. I would have jumped at any chance to defy Johnathan, even if that chance came from my nemesis—Clara.

She appeared unexpectedly. Charlotte London would turn thirty-four in just a few days—people were already speculating about what cosmetic procedures I must be getting in order to look so young—and Clara often brought a gift near Charlie's birthday. But I was far from home that week, and it surprised me that Johnathan would make her go to the trouble of an in-person visit.

She was alone, clutching the gift so tightly that silver wrapping paper puckered around her fingers. I forced myself to smile, although she was the last person I felt like spending the morning with, and opened my arms for the obligatory public hug. Clara leaned in and squeezed so tight that I felt the pointy pinch of her ribs. She smelled like baby powder and hand sanitizer. When I tried to let go, she held on. *That's strange*, I thought, as I untangled myself and ushered her into the suite. Usually, she tried to hug me without touching.

Inside my suite, I dropped the pretense of affection and expected her to do the same. If Johnathan told her to be photographed delivering a birthday gift, she would arrive loudly with an elaborately wrapped box, hug me hello, and then sit, pinched and disapproving, on my couch for exactly an hour. I intended to retreat to the bedroom and leave her to it.

But as soon as the door closed, she fell to her knees, fingers sinking into the plush pink carpet. It startled me so badly that I dropped the gift.

"Help. Please," Clara begged. The box bounced lightly. Her gifts, unlike Jake's, were just for show. "He's going to let me die." She spoke in the quick, right-to-the-point way that we all did when Johnathan wasn't listening.

No words wasted. But I'd never heard Clara talk like that. My skin tingled—danger. Clara would report on me in a minute, and I suspected a trap.

"Please," she whispered, the word warm and wet, like she tore it out of her belly. *It would kill her to ask me for help*, I thought, and took a step back, disgust and compassion vying for control of my body. I didn't like Clara, and she didn't like me, and no good could come from getting mixed up in whatever this was. If Clara got herself in trouble, she could get herself out.

But then she looked up, lips trembling, and I saw the truth all over her face. Hollow eyes, smudged so purple that concealer only emphasized it. Clammy skin shining through a thick layer of powder. Sharp bones poking through her cheeks. I remembered her ribs, cutting like knives when she hugged me.

She was sick, and she was at Johnathan's mercy.

My mouth went dry and my pulse thudded at my temples. Johnathan *had* no mercy. Which meant Clara was at *my* mercy, and I resented her for putting me in that position. For putting me in *his* position.

A sudden wave of dizziness forced me onto the couch. Pink, like the rug. Not the place for a conversation like this. Clara sank down beside me, as light as a bird but surrounded by misery so thick that I felt it thunk onto the cushion.

My mind flashed to the sad, heavy silence that hung around Kit the last few times I saw her. I didn't listen to Kit, and I lost her. Clara was still here. I could be better this time. But something held me back—Clara didn't deserve my help.

Clara's story came out between sobs as she hunched on the couch, a tissue clutched in one hand, the other a tight fist in her lap. She had cancer, and Johnathan thought the tragedy of a mother's death would be good for my image. "He's waiting until it's too late," she wailed, heartbreak and terror making her voice thin. I knew how deeply his coldness must have hurt her. "I just can't believe he's going to let me die."

She grabbed my hands, the soggy tissue squishing between our fingers, and searched my face for some confirmation of her safety—of his love. My skin crawled. I remembered all the times I searched for the same thing. All the times I convinced myself that I'd found it. What if the only difference between Clara and me was twenty years?

The difference, I thought, steadying myself, *is that I will help her. I'll defy him. I'll do something good, even if it gets me in trouble.* She collapsed into my arms. *I'll help her even though she doesn't deserve it*, I decided, *because that's who I want to be.*

"Where do you want to go for treatment?" I asked.

"I told you, he won't treat me." She yanked her hair, pulling like she could get the pain out that way. "I begged him …"

I shook my head, hard, to silence her. "I can't force Johnathan to treat you." Impatience made my voice meaner than I meant for it to be, but we didn't have much time before someone interrupted us. "But I can back him into a corner so he has to let you get treatment somewhere else. What's the best place where you live?"

That night, in a packed stadium, I announced the sad news of my mother's cancer diagnosis. The unusually personal confession drew a warm swell of sympathy from the crowd, and I let it build until the comforting heat pressed against my skin. Somewhere, Johnathan was watching. Furious—I could feel it. And I was about to make him even angrier.

I braced myself and played my hand—a heartfelt thank you to the wonderful doctors at the Courage Cancer Center in New York City for the lifesaving care they were providing. "She's going to be ok," I said, covering my fear with one of Charlie's big smiles, real tears shining in my eyes. "But she'd really appreciate some good energy from all of you!"

The crowd was with Charlie. And if they were with Charlie, then they were with Clara. Which meant Johnathan Everett had no choice—he had to let her live.

Because of me.

That small victory fed me for a few days, but dread soon overpowered triumph and I jumped every time a knock sounded at my door. Eventually, I knew, it would be Johnathan. With consequences.

I was back in Los Angeles when he finally appeared, wearing a fedora and a fake moustache. The whole city was haunted by my ill-fated relationship with Chris, and even his anger would have been a welcome distraction. But Johnathan didn't even mention Clara. "We're going out," he announced. Not smiling. But not scowling, either. I wavered between relief and fear, unable to read his mood.

"What am I wearing?" I asked, looking for the bag he always carried my costume in. I should have known something wasn't right when he told me I could go as Charlie.

Heads turned as we walked through the hotel lobby. People pointed and snapped photos, and I thought, for a second, that this might be the moment he got too careless. Could a moustache really conceal his identity? But it did, of course. The tabloids called him "Charlie's Mystery Man."

When the car dropped us outside a dive bar, I started to feel uneasy. Johnathan didn't go to places like that. A charming hole-in-the-wall restaurant in a foreign country, yes, but this was a place where no one had a plan for the evening beyond "get drunk." I couldn't even imagine him there. Under normal circumstances, he wouldn't want Charlie to be seen there.

I realized, too late, how odd it was for him to come all the way to Los Angeles when I visited Clara in the hospital in New York—just a couple of hours from ERC—every two weeks. He was up to something. But I couldn't do anything except walk in, half a step ahead of him, his hand possessively resting on my lower back.

He pulled my chair out and ordered gin martinis. The table was sticky, rough with gouged initials and crude drawings. The room smelled like spilled drinks. Clouds of cigarette smoke blew in every time the door opened. Johnathan's manners were too sophisticated, and our waitress raised her eyebrows while I tried to keep my face in the shadows.

We sipped in silence until the screech of a microphone cut through the din of drunken conversation. I hadn't noticed the little stage in the corner of the room, and my first thought was *oh shit, I can't sing in here.* Ever since that show in Los Angeles, I avoided small performances at all costs. Even in a stadium I was starting to feel too big, too powerful, too close to the edge, and was taking more and more pills Johnathan didn't know about to keep myself sleepy and numb and *safe.* Singing here, in front of Johnathan, was out of the question.

A man fiddled with the microphone, and I saw a young woman waiting next to him. *The singer.* Relief rushed through me. I didn't have to sing in this little room, in front of Johnathan. And then it hit me—she had to sing in front of him. And he was examining her with the same predatory interest I remembered from our first few meetings. Gin sloshed in my belly, sour and acidic.

The girl took her place at the microphone. She was young and beautiful, but Johnathan didn't care about that. As long as nothing interesting came out of her mouth, he'd lose interest and she'd be safe. But if she could do what I could do, then she was in trouble.

I felt sick, waiting for her to sing. Praying for something—anything—to stop her from singing.

"Is she... like me?" I asked, unable to withstand the suspenseful silence. He wanted to tell me. I could see it in his fingers, drumming impatiently on the defaced table, and his eyes, flicking back to me every few seconds. It was better to know. To get it over with.

"Like you?" he asked, pinning me in place with his eyes. "What are you like, Charlotte?" His voice, sharp as a blade, made me flinch, and he waited. Still hoping he could scare an answer out of me. "She might be," he said, finally.

"What are you going to do to her?" I stuttered over the words, afraid for my sake as much as for the girl's. If she was like me, then I was even more disposable than I thought.

"I haven't decided."

On stage, the girl adjusted the microphone. Fiddled with her guitar strap. Cleared her throat. I prayed for a miracle. Fire alarms. Or an earthquake.

Johnathan sighed and leaned back, hands clasped over a rounder belly than I remembered. "I would prefer to leave this disgusting place," he said. "Take you to dinner. Put all this behind us."

The girl was tuning the guitar. She didn't look like she could do what I could do. But neither did I, until I opened my mouth. I nodded, although I couldn't imagine eating a meal with him. "I'd like that, too," I said.

He gave me a long, hard look, peeling me back in layers. "We have an understanding," he said.

We did. I understood that Johnathan Everett could take me out as Charlie London, with nothing but a fake moustache hiding his face, and nothing would happen to him—I couldn't escape. And, even if I did, he'd find someone else. Someone would suffer in my place.

I nodded. I understood. I only had bad options. And the best one was the one where he took me to dinner.

I took his arm and we walked into an evening that would have felt exhilarating an hour ago. His mind was already on the restaurant—an old favorite that he was eager to share with me. He was glad I hadn't finished my drink, because the wine list was incredible. We'd get the chocolate cake, he promised, pushing the heavy oak door open and ushering me inside.

White tablecloths. Piano music. Johnathan's eyes, soft in candlelight, full of questions just for me. Another world.

Alone in the brief bubble of privacy offered by the ladies' room, I closed my eyes and made myself think about all the vulnerable people Johnathan captured while I turned my voice into money for him.

I saved Clara. Maybe I saved the girl at the bar. But they were grains of sand. Meaningless. The nice lady in the makeup room should have given me horns and fangs and glowing yellow eyes along with Charlie's hair extensions and push up bra all those years ago, because I was a monster, just like him.

Even if Damia pushed a thousand people through our safe house at Sky Lake, it wouldn't be enough to balance the scales. I was still doing more harm than good. And I always would be.

22

CHARLOTTE

The night I decided to end everything was hot and sticky and so still that I could hear my heartbeat. The empty balcony beckoned with the barest hint of a breeze and I thought *this is as good a night as any.*

I knew that I would never get away from Johnathan, and the longer I made money for him, the more damage I would do in the world. The fact that the money would keep coming after I was gone made me wish I'd had the courage to end things sooner, but didn't dampen my resolve. Doing something actively had to be worse than doing it passively.

I dressed in jeans, sneakers, and a black hoodie, the hood up, the drawstrings tight at my neck. I didn't know exactly how it worked when a person jumped from that height, but I hoped my clothing choices would minimize the mess. I took off my jewelry and removed Charlie's contacts, so no one would have to do it afterwards.

That's how I know I meant to kill myself. You don't think of those details if you're just being dramatic.

I left a note and three neatly packed bags. I didn't have much to give away, but I wanted Janey and Damia to have a few sentimental things. One of the girls who worked for me coveted a coat and a pair of leather boots that would look better on her, anyway. I hoped someone would destroy my songwriting journals, though I had little hope of that. Johnathan would do whatever made him the most money, no matter what my note said.

I slipped the little drive that held my evidence in my pocket, cushioned inside a sock. I'd just have to hope it survived, and that someone got to it before he did.

In the months after Johnathan stopped posting a guard on my balconies, I'd considered my mortality in many beautiful places. I thought about jumping while gazing into an impossibly blue ocean studded with small, rocky islands. I considered it over a glittering cityscape that twinkled like the window display in a jewelry store. I almost leaped from a balcony that overlooked green hills rippling all the way to the horizon.

This balcony, by contrast, presided over an empty, cement courtyard. Beyond it, I could see a few trees and the lights of a freeway. It wasn't pretty, but it was practical, with no parked cars to destroy or pedestrians who might unwittingly join me on my journey to the next world.

Next world. I shivered in spite of the humidity. I couldn't imagine I'd be heading anywhere good.

I gripped the railing and looked down at my hands. I flexed one, then the other, appreciating their easy movement. I ran my thumb over the callouses on my fingertips. I remembered when David taught me to play his guitar, and wondered what he'd think of where my "gift" got me.

He'd be proud, I decided, and horrified.

I sent my awareness to my feet and scanned all the way up to the top of my head. It felt like the right thing to do—to give my body my full attention before I took everything away from it. I swung one leg over the railing, and paused, half in and half out. For all my planning—the note, the bags, the outfit selected for its ability to hold my body together—I hadn't considered *how* I would jump.

There were so many options. I could stand and leap, arms outstretched, face turned to the stars until gravity took over. I could dive and hit the end head-on. I could sit and slide gently over the edge, the way I used to slip off the dock into the lake on a hot day.

The leap appealed to me the most, because it would feel good at first, but there was no joy in this decision. Even the relief I expected didn't come. I was consumed by the roaring injustice of living such a big, dream-come-true life, and still doing so much damage in the world that the only responsible thing was to jump.

Inside, a jumbled playlist of my favorite songs played on shuffle, because I didn't want the world to know what song Charlie London killed herself to. I swung my other leg over and sat, gripping the railing tightly, heart racing as the distance to the ground became real. I hadn't been allowed to make many decisions in my life, and I wouldn't let the wind take this one out of my hands. A moment of quiet contemplation, followed by a gentle push off the edge, seemed like the most dignified and respectful way to go.

A song ended, and another one started. I took a deep, slow breath. I wanted to appreciate it, because I wouldn't get many more of them, but it hurt. I slid forward, sweaty hands still tight on the railing. And then, like a hand reaching over the railing, Nicolas Bell's voice wrapped around me.

Soul shine eyes, bright fireflies...Wrap me in your arms, your night sky...I'm spinning, lost, you're everything...just not mine...

I tried to focus—block him out—but his voice would not be ignored. The part of me that wanted to survive gripped the railing so hard that it hurt. The part of me that packed the bags fought to loosen my fingers. A familiar smell drifted—roses and pine—carried by the voice of a stranger who had no idea how much he meant to me.

Now, I thought, but my hands were frozen in place, my body leaning back, not forward. I closed my eyes and tried to fight it, but Nic's voice pressed like a physical thing, holding me up.

For a long time, I hovered there, in-between, held by a man I never met and the sweet, humid air. In or out. Stay or leave. I couldn't decide. And then it came to me—the magnitude of what I was about to do. Because I wasn't just killing myself. I was about to kill Charlie London.

Grief swelled in my throat for this imaginary woman. I thought of the headlines and shook with a sudden, startling sob. Her voice meant so much to so many strangers.

Slowly, I tipped into the safety of the balcony. *No good options.*

I hung there, knees over the railing like a kid hanging from monkey bars, arms folded like a corpse, hair pooling on the balcony floor, until the song ended and I lowered myself, trembling, onto the dirty tiles.

Not tonight, I thought. *Not like this. There has to be another way.*

But there was no other way. There was only my voice pouring into the world, and money pouring into the ERC bank account, night after night. Nothing changed. I despaired of anything ever changing. I barely ate and didn't sleep. When I took off Charlie's makeup, I saw a ghost in the mirror.

I turned thirty at a hotel in New York during one of my obligatory visits to Clara. Charlie was already thirty-five, so it hardly felt like a milestone, but I still woke with the weight of another year on my shoulders. Thirty felt like a big deal, and not in a good way. I pulled the blanket over my head and tried to go back to sleep.

Go back to my twenties, when I could pretend my life hadn't really started yet.

Johnathan sent his usual lovely gift—an aquamarine ring that shined like a perfect pool of water. It winked up at me like we knew each other. Later, when I read my file, I learned that Chris was supposed to propose with that ring on a beach in Hawaii. If there are parallel universes, I hope there's one where he slipped it on my finger and we lived happily ever after. But I received the ring, along with a bouquet of exquisite white roses, on the real thirtieth birthday no one but Johnathan knew about.

I felt miserable that day—head spinning, skin too tight, a dizzying headache tumbling inside my skull. *Something's wrong, something's wrong, something's wrong,* the headache drummed, no matter how hard I tried to ignore it. My head did not want to be thirty or a prisoner or in New York, visiting Clara.

I stayed under the covers until my assistant arrived with the birthday present. She was excited because I often passed gifts on to my employees, and the black velvet box meant something sparkly and expensive. When I said my head hurt too much to get out of bed, she repeated "you have a present" as if presents were a known cure for headaches.

I barely had the strength to sit up, but she pressed the roses into my arms anyway. They were snow white, with a shimmer that reminded me of the ones that bloomed at Sky Lake, and they smelled expensive. I knew one of Johnathan's researchers worked hard to create such a miracle, but the heavy scent made my skull shrink around my throbbing brain. I pushed them back into the assistant's arms and she thrust the gift at me before I could fall back into my pillows.

I fumbled with the envelope, fingers clumsy with pain, and squinted at Johnathan's blurred message—*Charlotte, I saw this and thought of you*, it said, and his large, bold writing felt like an anchor in the spinning room.

I untied a smooth purple ribbon and flipped the box open, intending to admire its contents and go back to sleep. But the stone hit my eyes, cold and refreshing, making me forget how sick I felt. The assistant leaned in, eyes wide, mouth open like a hungry bird.

I held the stone up to the light, where it reflected like a pool on a sunny day. *I saw this and thought of you.* What, I wondered, could I possibly have in common with this beautiful thing? I slipped it on my finger—a perfect fit, of course—and lay back, letting it beam its soothing blue light into my aching head. Like ice numbing a burn. Maybe, it would knock the headache down enough to let me sleep away my birthday.

But the headache wasn't gone, just regrouping. It clawed its way back, from the base of my skull to my forehead, while the stone tossed sunshine around the room. I wasn't getting off that easily. But it wasn't the same—

the drum was beating a different message. I closed my eyes and sank back, listening.

Go back go back go back, it chanted, and the painful, insistent beat came as a relief. An order I could follow. My body moved without me, feet finding shoes, shoulders shrugging into a light coat. I would go back—ERC was only a couple of hours away—and then, maybe, I'd feel better.

"I need four Advil," I told the assistant, who doled out my pills like a nurse. "And a car for the day."

The driver assumed Johnathan summoned me—why else would I go there?—and didn't ask questions or call ahead. I sagged against the window, taking shallow breaths of the artificially pine-freshened air as my headache grew like an uncontrollable weed inside my head. It spread leaves over my face, bloomed extravagantly in my sinuses, and dug deep, sending jolts of nervy pain down my neck. It burst in my eyes—tiny black explosions that blinded me—and then brought the word back in searing color. I clenched my teeth, every pothole agony.

Outside, the world rushed by. We were so close to Sky Lake, and I longed for it in a way I hadn't in a long time. I wanted to suck in a big breath of lake air. Dip my aching head in the hot springs. But even if I could have made the car drive that way, I didn't have a handwritten map or a rock from the lake. The road would stretch out forever, twisting and turning and keeping me away. Because who was I kidding? I didn't have the magic of my childhood home running through me anymore. Not after everything I'd done. Sky Lake couldn't possibly want me back, and I couldn't bear to face its rejection again.

In the end, it didn't matter where I wanted to go. Every light turned green before we reached it. Pedestrians didn't cross in front of us. Slow drivers got out of our way. Even the silent driver commented on our good fortune as a traffic jam broke up like mist. It was as if fate itself flew behind the car, pushing us to our destination. Sky Lake might as well have been a thousand miles away.

Go back go back go back, the headache drummed. Like I could make us go faster. And then, as we turned into the driveway, it shifted again—*too late too late too late*. I threw myself out of the car before it came to a complete stop, driven by the rhythmic warning.

The front doors opened readily when I swiped my card—gone were my days of limited access—and I headed straight to Johnathan's office. I was operating on instinct more than thought at that point, following the headache's instructions, or my own intuition, or the first symptom of a psychotic break.

My head hurt so much that I needed to run one hand along the wall to walk in a straight line, and I almost changed course and went to the hospital, instead. How different all our lives would have been if I made that decision. But I got in the elevator and pushed the button for his floor, a nervous hum joining the drumbeat in my skull.

I had a good enough excuse to be there—I wanted to say thank you for the flowers and the ring, and he always encouraged me to visit. But I hadn't seen him since that night at the bar, when he threatened to take the girl. I was afraid.

His voice slammed into my aching head as soon as the elevator doors slid open. "Don't you dare argue with me!" he shouted. Even from the elevator, I could hear the curl of his lips and see the fire in his eyes and feel his unfortunate challenger regretting whatever brave thing they'd done. "Don't you dare!" he repeated, and doors rattled up and down the hallway. "You can't help her. The decision is *made*."

He banged something—his hand on a table, or his foot on the floor— and I flinched. Another nauseating wave of pain crashed over me, blocking everything else out. My legs wobbled. I seriously considered sitting down in the elevator and waiting for someone to find me. But a terrified whimper drifted down the hall. Someone needed help.

"Do you want to join her?" he asked. "Because that's what happens next, if you don't back the hell off."

His voice boomed, explosive and uncontrolled. I couldn't remember ever hearing him like this. Angry, yes, he was often angry. But he never lost control. He normally spoke as if cursing was beneath him.

"Answer me!" he ordered, high and sharp. Demanding answers, when the man I knew would sit back and let silence do the work. Fear shot through me, raising goosebumps on my arms and urging me to run.

The whimper echoed through the hallway. Tugged me out of the elevator. Took my hand like a child and led me down the hall.

Just short of the doorway I paused, my headache screeching so loudly that I wondered if other people could hear it. I didn't feel well enough to deal with whatever was inside that room. *You can still turn around*, the headache wailed. *You can go back.* But my feet slid forward, pushed by the same mysterious force that turned all the traffic lights green.

Pushed by the sound of someone in trouble and the crushing weight of my guilt.

Trembling from a combination of terror, pain, and exhaustion, I entered Johnathan Everett's office for the last time.

The candy bowl sat on a low table by the door, full of my favorite honey lozenges. The coat rack hulked in the corner, holding Johnathan's suit jacket and the fedora he wore in Los Angeles. His heavy, imposing desk took up half the room.

And Janey kneeled in front of it, hands clasped so earnestly that I imagined her at an altar, and not on that swirling marble floor. She was only wearing one shoe, and I could see her heel through a hole in in her sock. As pink and smooth as a baby's. Johnathan loomed over her, eyes flashing, fists clenched. A thunderstorm come to life.

"I'm sorry," Janey sobbed. "I'm sorry. Please." She huddled, shoulders round, head bowed, rocking back and forth in a futile attempt to soothe herself. Her hair stuck up, half in its ponytail, like he dragged her in by it, and my stomach flipped. He never hurt anyone directly. And yet I could practically see the shape of his fist in her hair. "I should have minded my business," she moaned, her voice gurgling and wet. "I *will* mind my business."

I hesitated in the doorway, Janey crumpled on the floor, an enormous bouquet of shimmering white roses on Johnathan's desk. *Just like mine*, I thought, except they didn't remind me of the roses at Sky Lake anymore. Their unnatural perfume stung my eyes and throat, too sweet and too spicy and too strong. *Funeral flowers*, the headache whispered.

"Please. I'll just go back to my office." She started to raise her head, but cringed back like a dog when Johnathan opened his mouth to spit another threat. I stepped forward before he could, heart racing, hands slick with sweat. I didn't have a plan. But I couldn't let him keep her there on the floor, begging for her life.

He turned and expressions flew across his face—anger, surprise, embarrassment. His mouth snapped shut. Janey yelped.

Adrenaline, cold and steadying, rushed through me just in time. "What the hell is going on?" I asked, suppressing the part of me that knew I was disposable.

Johnathan straightened, eyebrows rising to conceal the angry creases in his forehead, fists cracking open with visible effort. He was trying to show his better side, to pull his rage in and hide it, and this gave me a little room to breathe. I still had some power. I could fix this, maybe. "Charlotte," he said, his voice rough. "I was not expecting you."

Emboldened by his embarrassment and my birthday flowers on his desk, I stood tall and looked him in the eyes. "Do I need an invitation?" I asked, buying time. Janey spun on her knees, mouth open in a silent, horrified scream, eyes round. Her alarm at my presence told me everything I needed to know about the seriousness of the situation.

"Of course not." Johnathan said, trying for a smile but only managing a grimace. He brushed his hands on his thighs. "You never need an invitation." He turned his attention back to Janey. "Out," he ordered, jabbing a finger at the door.

Ten seconds before, this would have sent her scurrying gratefully into the hall. But she found her courage, or maybe she couldn't make herself abandon me. "Damia." She scrambled to her feet and pointed urgently to the nearest screen. "She's hiding, but as soon as they find her..."

A second too late, Johnathan silenced his niece with a slap. She spun into me, clutching her jaw, too shocked to make a sound, and my arms closed around her automatically. My eyes never left Johnathan, trembling, red with rage but also shame. I had never seen him hit anyone. I had certainly never seen him ashamed. Whatever Damia did, she must be in very bad trouble.

Janey pressed her snotty face into my chest and I patted her back robotically, wishing she'd leave. I couldn't protect us both. "Damia," she gurgled into me, her breath hitching too violently for sentences. "If they find her. Red pellet."

Johnathan made a low, animal sound. A warning. But I held his gaze like an equal. "No," I said. "Not Damia." Begging, I knew, would get me nowhere. "She's been a good, loyal... employee." The word tasted bad—none of us were employees, we were hostages—but he didn't like to see us, or himself, like that. "Whatever she did, it doesn't cancel that out. It doesn't justify..." All of our eyes went to the screen.

"You have no idea what she did," he said, in that rough voice, like he was choking on it. His fists clenched and unclenched by his sides, the gesture at once threatening and deeply distressed. He was in pain, and incredibly dangerous because of it, and every cell in my body wanted me out of that room. But something deeper kept me there. Made me long to wrap my arms around him, in spite of everything.

"I know she doesn't deserve to die for it," I said, gently.

"You know no such thing!" In a sudden explosion of movement, he swept the vase off his desk. It burst—glass, water, thorns, petals. Janey shrieked. "Your beloved Damia made a deal with the investigator. Harmon." He grabbed at his hair, eyes wide and wild. "She agreed to be an *informant*. She put together a file. She tried to destroy me." His tipped his head back like a better explanation waited on the ceiling, the gesture so like Janey that it brought tears to my eyes. "She betrayed me," he said, his voice soft now. Weak. "She betrayed us."

He held out his hands, palms up. A man in a puddle of broken glass and rose petals, begging me to understand. And I *did* understand. I could just see Damia, shining with meaning and purpose as she put that file together. And I could also see the pain—the betrayal—in Johnathan's eyes, as real as the water pooling around his shoes.

My heart broke for both of them, as much as I wished it wouldn't.

"I'm sorry." He took a step toward me and stopped, hands out, eyes pleading. Genuinely regretful. "There's nothing else to be done," he said.

He meant it. He really was sorry. There was no game, no lie, no manipulation, and that scared me more than any threat—I couldn't save her by reasoning with him. In his mind, he truly had no choice.

He thought he was just like the rest of us. Only bad options.

I took a heavy breath, feeling Janey's damp, sniveling weight in my arms, smelling the unbearable perfume of the ruined roses, wishing I could think of something else. But there wasn't anything else. We were all doomed—Damia, Janey, me. It was too late. I wasn't going to save anybody today.

But that didn't mean I had to let him win.

Janey quaked in my arms, her whole body arguing with our situation, but I felt calm. Peaceful, even. The headache was fading. In its place, like something left by the tide—clarity.

Johnathan Everett could hold me captive. Take my money. Kill me, even, if he wanted to. But he didn't own me.

I remembered the day, so long ago, when he told me he didn't want to treat me like a prisoner. I played along—I was a child, what else could I do? But I wouldn't go along anymore. I wouldn't roll over and forgive him.

I could *take* something from him. I could make him bleed right along with us.

Once made, the weight of my decision fell away, leaving my body light enough to do the only thing I had the power to do.

I *ran*.

I headed for the stairs, because Johnathan could stop the elevators with a button but the stairwells didn't lock remotely. Down I raced, two steps at a time, my feet slapping hard against the cement. I lost a shoe and kicked off the other one. I dropped my purse and my coat. I threw myself forward, thinking only of the next step.

I knew what would happen. Someone would grab me, or cut me off, or shoot me. But I wanted to be running when my time ran out.

Somehow, I made it to the lobby. To the front door. *Out* the front door.

I heard Janey scream, and felt fingers lightly brush my shoulder, but they were too slow. No one expected me to throw myself outside, and so no one moved fast enough to stop me from doing it.

I heard the *beep-beep-beep-beep* of my keycard triggering the lock. I felt the weight of the door as I shouldered it open. I saw the impossible brightness of an early spring day, fresh and green, the sky so blue it hurt my eyes. I flew into that sky, thinking it would be the last thing I saw. I was moving fast, on my own terms, with Johnathan behind me and not a step ahead. I couldn't have chosen a better set of last moments. I only regretted Janey at the front door, watching.

I've replayed that moment a thousand times—the sky stretching forever, the smell of wet grass in my nose, my hair tangling in the wind as I hurtled down the steps.

Johnathan's voice, ragged and desperate, pulling me like gravity.

Don't shoot.

I'm almost sure I heard it. *Almost.*

But it was all in motion by then. The red pellets flying through the air. My body flying toward the woods. The whole world going still as *before* turned into *after*.

At first, I only felt stings. Left shoulder. Right hip. Two pellets weren't good, I knew that, but I was still moving, and that seemed like a good sign. And then it came. Pain, tearing like teeth. I focused on running—one foot in front of the other—and breathing. But my lungs stuttered and gasped, looking for a way around the fire raging in my muscles.

I didn't expect the pain to be so bad, so quickly—the people in the white room always had time. But I was running, and my blood must have pumped the poison through me in a hurry. Electrifying stabs tore through me, riding a relentless, agonizing wave. I felt my bones crunching. My muscles ripping. My skin coming off in strips.

The pain felt like it had always been there, and always would be.

The sky burst in a blinding blast of white, swallowing everything. A disorienting, internal roar blocked the birds and the wind and Janey's screams. Something ripped at my skin and something else squeezed, so tight I expected to pop like a balloon.

And yet, my body kept moving, trying to get away from itself.

I stumbled into the thin strip of trees between the lawn and the road, feet crunching on pine cones, branches whipping my face. I could hear the pain screaming inside me. I could taste it—bloody, rotten, sour. Gagging me.

It was unbearable.

But it didn't stop me. If anything, it made me faster, and luck or fate or divine intervention sent my body in a straight line toward the road while I cowered inside it, consumed. I was the horse and the pain was the whip and the road was *right there.*

I broke through the trees with enough of myself left to keep going, and my body turned right instead of left. A miracle.

I ran, nothing but pain and pounding feet, and no one followed. No more shots. No hands, grabbing. No shouts and no screams and no brakes screeching behind me. My mind should have been gone before I reached the road, and I don't think Johnathan wanted to see me like that. He thought I'd lose myself in the woods.

Maybe he wasn't thinking at all.

But my body turned right. And kept running. And less than a mile away, Mallory Harmon was waiting for Damia.

She burst out of the print shop, flanked by two armed men in cargo pants and black T-shirts, as I stumbled into the parking lot. I remember being relieved when I saw the guns—they could put me out of my misery. I lurched toward her, arms out, drowning as she processed the horror in front of her. Charlie London. It must have seemed absurd. But Mallory didn't waste time wondering why I was there. "My name's Mallory," she said. "And I'm going to get you some help, ok?"

Her voice was far away and I struggled toward it, sure I must be dreaming. She gripped my arms, steadying me. Her hands were warm and firm, her eyes full of compassion. I thought *real* and then I thought *gun* and then some small part of me that was still human remembered what I had in my pocket.

I gripped it with slow, clumsy fingers. I'd stopped adding information to my little device years before, because there wasn't any point. But I kept it. I carried it everywhere. I wrapped it in a sock the night I almost killed myself. And here I was, finally, close enough to give it to someone he didn't own.

I *did* it.

But his voice echoed around me, ordering them not to shoot. I saw his shoes in the puddle of roses and smelled the minty-smoke smell of his office. If I did this, it would ruin him. I couldn't take it back.

No, I told myself, tearing free from the memories as my hand closed around the unassuming plastic square. It felt huge, my senses turning surreal as pain overloaded my nerves. Or, maybe, I was feeling what was really there—Johnathan Everett's downfall.

I thrust it at Mallory before I could remember his eyes, climbing to the ceiling for guidance. Regarding me across a restaurant table with that burning curiosity. Lighting up in a tempest of butterfly wings.

"That's everything you need," I tried to say, but the words tumbled and rolled, slipping hopelessly out of reach. I was losing myself, but it was ok. If Mallory hurried, she might save Damia.

I got *out*, and that meant something, even if it was the last thing I'd do.

Inside the print shop, someone dropped me onto a couch and applied pressure to my wounds. Someone said "She's burning up," and people came from every direction with cold things—ice packs, frozen meals, rolls of toilet paper soaked in water. Someone tipped the contents of a first aid kit onto the floor and someone pulled off my shoes while I fought them. I needed my shoes. I might have to run again.

Mallory shouted orders from another room. Men and woman dressed like a movie SWAT team ran toward Mallory's voice.

I tried to get up, but people held me down. I shook the ice packs off, and people piled them back on. I was frozen, teeth chattering. I couldn't understand why they wanted to make me colder. The pain held me, giant hands that wouldn't let go as I tried to explain to all these well-meaning strangers that they couldn't help me. They could only put me out of my misery or let me do it myself.

The words hung just beyond me, taunting, replaced by the wail of an animal. Only names emerged from the sound, each one a prayer.

Janey.

Damia.

Johnathan.

Bobby.

I didn't care who came, as long as they knew enough not to try to save me.

And yet, I lived.

"We're going to take good care of you." Mallory's hands cupped my face and for one, beautiful moment, I thought she might know something I didn't. But the pain grabbed me and shook me and I knew—she was wrong, no one could help. "The ambulance is here." She pulled one of my caretakers down so I could look into his eyes, too. "This is Jeremy. He's going to stay with you. Do you understand me?"

I tried to nod. Tried to speak. Tried to free an arm and grab the gun at her waist.

"You did it," she said. "You took Johnathan Everett down. I'm not going to let him get away, I promise." That part, I believed.

In the ambulance, I used my teeth to hold my lips closed, afraid of the way my noise would echo in that metal box. Blood filled my mouth. Someone put an oxygen mask on me and it hurt. Someone expressed concern about my pulse. Someone—Jeremy, maybe?— took my hand and squeezed, sending fresh waves of agony up my arm. *Stop helping me,* I thought. *I don't want to live like this.* Underneath, an uglier wish—*let me go, so the headlines say 'Charlie London dies a hero.'*

The paramedics pushed me into the chaos of an emergency room, already busy with accidents and heart attacks and old people with the flu. I wanted to tell them to help someone who could still be helped, but a scream forced itself out, and then another, and I remember wishing someone would make that woman be quiet.

None of you can help me, I shrieked, but all that came out was that horrible, animal wail.

"We're going to cut these clothes off you," a nurse said, and I heard the snip-snip-snip of scissors efficiently freeing me from my favorite pair of jeans.

"You're going to feel a pinch," another one said, and new pain tore through me as she placed an IV.

"This will help the pain," she promised, but it didn't.

Nothing did, for months.

23

NIC

"Hey, man, you hear about Charlie London?"

I was still half asleep when I answered the phone, thick shades drawn so it could have been noon or the middle of the night for all I knew—it didn't matter much, when I slept. No one relied on me for anything.

Thomas's voice floated into my ear like a ghost. "Nic?" he asked. "You there?"

I wondered if I might still be dreaming—Thomas hadn't called in ages, and I didn't blame him. I wouldn't have wanted much to do with me, either, after I broke up the band and blew up our lives. I squeezed the phone. In a dream, it would crunch or squish or disappear, but it felt real.

"Yeah," I croaked, still swimming up from sleep. "I'm here."

"Crazy story," he said. "Isn't it? About Charlie London?"

Charlie London. My heart sped up at the sound of her name and I kicked my way out of the tangled blankets. I sat up. Her voice was another ghost in my life, drifting in to poke the teenage crush that never quite went away. I fumbled for the lamp next to the bed, remembering how she sang me inside out in that dark club. But no, I hadn't heard anything about her, and Thomas's question made my stomach hurt.

I knew it wasn't going to be good news. In the last video I saw of Charlie, she looked pale and thin, sick with the kind of long-term exhaustion that makeup can't hide. I'd seen a version of it in the mirror, in the last days of Light/Black, but never that bad. She'd been dimming for a couple of years—her deterioration played out in real-time all over the internet—and I saw it all because I couldn't stop searching for her.

I wanted to reach through the screen and pull her out of whatever she was stuck in. But, of course, I couldn't. And she just kept fading. An overdose or a suicide didn't seem out of the question.

Grief totally out of proportion to my non-existent relationship with her seized me. *No*, I wanted to say. *I haven't heard. Please don't tell me.* I wanted Charlie alive and well, at least in my imagination. It felt important.

The light clicked on, bringing my bedroom into focus. Rumpled blankets. Single dresser. Dusty guitar standing in the corner. An empty beer bottle on the nightstand. *Pathetic.* I wanted to go back to sleep.

"Nic?" Thomas asked.

I hadn't spoken to Thomas, James, or Ben in more than six months. Before that, we'd been in touch off and on, but mostly off, for years. The final break in our communication felt inevitable. We didn't have anything in common but the past, and that rope won't hold forever.

They thought I was a selfish shit who broke up the band. I thought they were selfish shits who held me back. We were all wrong and all right and by the time I realized it didn't matter, we'd been mad at each other too long to untangle it.

I always thought there'd be a moment when it felt right to call and put it all behind us, but the moment never came. It hurt too much to be sorry for a real mistake. I could only be the bigger person if I was also the more *successful* person. And, by all reasonable measurements, I wasn't—I left to do bigger and better things, but the writer's block that chased me out of Light/Black followed.

I thought I was the whole show, but I never wrote a single thing alone that measured up to what we did together. People came to see me because of who I *used* to be. After all those years feeling like my friends were riding on my coattails, I ended up doing the same damn thing. Me on stage, all alone. Light/Black lurking behind me like my more attractive older brother.

"Yeah, I'm here." I padded into the kitchen and opened the refrigerator—moldy pizza, curdled milk. A notebook, as empty as the fridge, waited on the coffee table, brand new pen laid across it. I bought them with good intentions, but I swear that pen gave me a look in the checkout line—judgmental. I hadn't been able to write anything new in almost a year. My last attempt ended with three pages of crap basically stolen from old Light/Black albums. I wasn't even trying anymore.

I didn't believe in karma, but anyone who did would say I had it coming.

Thomas's voice on the phone, full of concern, put an uncomfortable spotlight on my bad behavior. He was my best friend, and I threw that away because the alternative—swallowing my pride, picking up the phone, and apologizing—would have hurt my ego. And Thomas—good, kind, humble Thomas—put it all aside because something happened to a girl I used to like. It was pretty clear who was the better person.

Thomas never minded holding up both sides of a conversation, and he launched into the story. "It's nuts, isn't it? About Charlie? Who would have guessed, right?" He fired the questions quickly, not giving me a chance to stop him.

I didn't want the bad news. I wanted to keep the Charlie in my mind. The one on that little stage, singing her heart out to me. "I mean, it kind of makes sense," he said. "When you think about it. That's how your mom must have gotten her autograph. Geeze, remember that? We thought she was such a rockstar, getting Charlie London to sign a tarot card for you. It seems like a hundred years ago."

He trailed off and went quiet, and I could feel the weight of his memories. I forgot, sometimes, that she mothered all of us—especially Thomas, because his parents were crap—and they didn't get to mourn her. They had to support me. The star, even before we were famous. Guilt chewed on my empty stomach. Here we were—Thomas, grieving my mother, while I grieved a pop star I never met. Typical.

"It got me thinking about your mom," he said. "About that whole time. The trip and the auditions and all of us in that crazy old house…" He paused again, remembering. "We were so *young*," he said. "And you were so in love with her back then, remember? Charlie? And then I saw her all over the news this morning and I had to call you."

I sank down on the couch—hard and too short to stretch out on—and grabbed the remote, triggering a coffee table avalanche of unopened mail. I didn't want to click the TV on and make this real. But Thomas was still talking. I might as well pull the Band-Aid off.

I closed my eyes, preparing myself. Charlie London was a stranger. Bad things happened to strangers all the time, and it didn't affect me. This shouldn't be any different.

But it was. I could feel it, squeezing my heart like a water balloon.

I opened my eyes, blinded for a few, merciful moments by the light of the television. But the headlines scrolling across the bottom of the screen were slow and patient and they burned a hole straight through me as they came into focus.

Charlie London Hospitalized; Condition Unknown.
Johnathan Everett in Custody.
Ten Celebrities Who Probably Knew the Truth About Charlie London.
Charlie London Takes Down the Most Powerful Man on Earth.

My mind tried to make sense of the bedraggled line of people filing out of the huge facility where I visited my mother all those years ago, but it was impossible. They were stunned, blinking in the sunlight, clutching disorganized bundles of belongings like they didn't have time to pack. A woman tipped under the weight of a huge bird cage. A man cradled a large, silver ball close to his chest. Another man led three monkeys on leashes. A girl who couldn't have been more than eighteen dragged a cart laden with flowers, a carpet of trampled petals in her wake.

They looked like people fleeing a circus, not a research facility, and the nightmare strangeness of the scene lifted the hair on the back of my neck. I wanted to turn off the television. Erase them. Go back to sleep and tell myself it was all a dream. But the reporter was talking, and I needed to know what happened to Charlie.

The reporter explained that ERC was under the control of law enforcement pending a full inventory of its contents, and Johnathan Everett was in custody at a secure military facility as the charges against him mounted. Murder. Terrorism. Treason. The list went on and on, and I didn't care about any of it. I cared about Charlie.

"Your mom only showed us the nice bits of that place," Thomas said, voice shaking. "It was a horror show in there." Then, like he suddenly realized who he was talking to, "I mean, I'm sure it wasn't so bad where she worked. Her office looked nice, remember? She had windows and a soft chair and an assistant. And she seemed happy. And you can't believe everything they say on TV...."

"It's ok." My voice felt rough from sleep and emotion and lack of use and I didn't even know what I was talking about yet. The reporter shifted gears, flashing a picture of some actor who helped hold Charlie hostage, and I wanted to scream at her because that guy didn't matter, *Charlie* mattered. Was she ok?

Maybe I didn't want to know. Based on the tone of the reporting, nothing good was coming out of those buildings.

A picture of Charlie, arms raised to an adoring crowd, filled the screen. She always looked surprised—like a regular person who suddenly received a standing ovation. She covered it with a big smile and a sparkle that struck me as practiced, but the surprise was real. The idea that someone so famous could go through life constantly amazed by the attention charmed and fascinated me. I leaned in, trying to see through the glitter.

The picture transitioned to a video of Charlie signing autographs somewhere. She turned to the camera, laughing, and I tipped forward. She was vibrant and alive. Not fading yet. I let myself fall into her eyes.

And then, the reporter said "poisoned."

Poisoned. Charlie London.

The reporter kept shooting words past Charlie's smile—*condition unknown, more information as soon as we have it*. They hit me like spitballs. Annoying, insignificant. Not good enough. I needed to *know*.

"No," Thomas said. "It's not ok. None of it is."

He took a deep breath and let it out slowly, and I tore myself away from Charlie. I always knew my mother was lying about her situation at ERC, so I had years to come to terms with what happened to her. Poor Thomas was doing it all at once, right now. He needed me. And, for once, I was going to be there. "It looks like they shut the whole thing down," I offered. "He won't be able to hurt anyone else. That's good."

"I guess." Thomas sounded unconvinced. "Charlie, though."

Charlie. If she died to save the whole world from Johnathan Everett it still wouldn't feel like a fair trade. An old version of me, the boy who loved a pop star he never met, cried out for vengeance. How could anyone do this to her?

"It could have been us, you know." Thomas's voice shivered with the excitement of a near miss. "He could have kept *us* prisoner for all this time. We didn't realize it, but he had us."

I changed the channel, hoping for more information about Charlie, finding only speculation.

"I'm serious," Thomas insisted. "He could have kept us."

I forced myself to stop clicking the remote. Thomas was right. We were in Johnathan Everett's clutches, just like Charlie. My mother paid the price back then—her life, for mine—and I didn't feel like I'd lived up to her sacrifice. "He could have," I agreed, even though I knew she never would have allowed it. "I wonder if that would have been so terrible, though. We would have stayed together." The words rushed out before I could stop them, like they'd been waiting for a chance to bypass my pride, and I felt their impact in the silence that followed.

"Yeah," Thomas said, eventually. "I guess that's true. I guess that wouldn't be so bad. If we stayed together." He paused for another deep breath. "But we all would have had to do things differently for that to happen. Not just you."

"I don't know about that. I was an arrogant jerk."

"Yeah," he agreed. "You were. But we were lazy. We didn't understand why you'd want anything more than money and girls back then. We should have tried to understand."

"My mom would have said it worked out like it did for a reason."

"She would have." Thomas laughed, and I joined him, but it felt forced. I didn't know what else to say. It was a miracle that I opened my mouth once and the right thing came out. One more word, I thought, and I'd ruin it.

On the screen, a reporter gave an update on Charlie's injuries. "I'm being told that, at present, there is no antidote to the poison." Fear tightened my chest, and I reminded myself that Charlie London had nothing to do with me. "Reports indicate that the poison itself is not deadly, but no one has ever survived the pain it inflicts for more than fifteen hours. Doctors are racing to save her, but the prognosis is not good. As we speak, supporters are gathering outside the hospital where she is being treated..."

The camera panned over a crowd, rippling with signs and flowers and teddy bears. People waved and cried and sang, and I felt the totally irrational desire to be in the middle of it. Guilt—my favorite chaser—followed. Of course I wanted to be in that crowd, supporting someone I never met. So much easier than cleaning up my own life. I clicked the television off before I could decide to buy a plane ticket and write *Charlie, I love you* on a posterboard.

The phone beeped with another call.

"I have to get this. Can we talk later? Maybe meet up? It's been way too long." Then, realizing this was not the time to hold back, "I miss you."

"I'd like that," Thomas said. "I miss you too. How about if I call you tomorrow?"

My own reflection stared back from the dark TV screen, all stubble and shadows and smudged regret. "That would be good," I said, grateful that he hadn't left the next call up to me.

I rubbed the sand out of my eyes, thinking about tomorrow for the first time in a while.

I called Thomas back thirty minutes later. I like to think I would have done it even if he hadn't reached out to me first. But I probably would have packed up and left and never even considered that anyone else deserved to know what was going on, even though Bobby saved all of us, not just me. But Thomas did reach out first.

I hit redial, hand shaking so hard that it took three tries, as soon as I hung up with the nurse.

Thomas sounded so happy to hear my voice that I considered not breaking the news at all. But that's what the old me would have done— avoided the hard conversation—and I didn't want to be the old me anymore. "The call... was about Bobby," I said, pulling the words out with effort. The room was spinning. "He's in the hospital. He... tried to kill himself." My stomach burned, sour and acidic, as I said it. "I have to go. Can you tell..." Their names stuck in my throat. "Tell... everyone?" My pride wouldn't let me ask for what I really wanted—for my oldest friends to face this horror with me.

Thomas was quiet for a beat too long—as shocked as I was—but he recovered quickly. "On it. What hospital?"

A long-lost memory surfaced of Thomas calmly helping me home with a broken wrist when we were eight years old. My parents weren't there, so he gave me an ice pack and knocked on the neighbor's door, and I remember thinking that he seemed so much older than the rest of us. I clung to that memory as I wrestled a suitcase out of the closet.

"You ok to travel on your own?" he asked. Calm and practical and ready to act.

"Yeah, I'm good." I threw clothes into the suitcase as I talked.

"We'll see you there."

The next afternoon, I sat in a grim beige room with Thomas, James, and Ben. It smelled like stale coffee and somebody's oniony breakfast burrito. A fan whistled over a soft rock station. If hell had a waiting room, this would be it.

James and Ben came for Bobby, not for me, and they made sure I knew it. I could feel their anger in the air like weather. Ben's teeth were clenched so hard that I could see the tension in his cheeks, and James practically growled when I asked if anybody wanted coffee. Thomas sat between us, the smiling, reliable bridge. He talked to them, then to me, then to them again, giving the illusion of a larger conversation while we didn't acknowledge each other.

I never thought about how much weight I put on him, making him the peacemaker.

Bobby tried to kill himself. The sentence repeated on a loop, making no sense. Bobby was a superhero—strong and brave, never complaining, always there for us. I couldn't imagine him even thinking of ending his own life, never mind actually trying to do it.

I would have been waiting for him to walk in and say "gotcha," except that he wasn't a joker. He took everything, especially me, so seriously.

A television in the corner quietly recapped the Charlie London situation, which still eclipsed all other news. I wished I could turn it off. I didn't want to hear any more about her injuries, her pain, her low odds of survival. "We are well past the fifteen-hour mark," a reporter announced, "and her condition is currently listed as serious but stable. A hospital spokesperson declined to provide more information…"

My therapist would say it was easier for me to feel the impact of Charlie's situation than Bobby's, but it was more than that. The connection I felt when I first heard Charlie's voice on the radio never went away, it just faded into the background, roaring back when a new album came out or I saw her on television or couldn't resist googling her again. She was just feet away from me at that show in Los Angeles the night I broke up with Tess. Learning the truth about her life filled me with regret, almost like I could have done something for her if I'd known.

Of course I couldn't have. We were both just kids. But the helpless feeling remained, making me restless. *I wish I could do something for her now*, I thought. Another irrational thought, because why would Charlie London want anything from me? *Bobby*, I reminded myself. *I'm here to help Bobby.* But Bobby wouldn't even see me.

I walked to the other end of our little row of plastic chairs and dropped into the last one, next to James. He was a slouched ball of stress—arms folded, legs hooked underneath him—and my arrival made him spring open and closed like a startled turtle. He probably rehearsed what he'd say to me in a thousand different places, and this wasn't one of them. "I was an idiot," I said. "An asshole. I'm sorry." This, at least, I could do something about.

"Hey," Thomas interrupted. "We don't have to do this now. We're all here to support Bobby. The other stuff isn't important."

"Yeah, we do have to do this." I tried to give Thomas a reassuring look, but based on his reaction, it wasn't convincing. "And it's not your job to smooth things over for me. I fucked up, and I'm going to take responsibility for it, and then you can say whatever you have to say. It's not like there's anything else to do in here."

Nothing else to do except think, and I'd done enough of that already. Even a fight would be better than soft rock and the maddening creak of the fan.

"You weren't the only one who fucked up." Thomas glared at James and Ben like a mother prodding children to apologize. They glared at their feet, playing their parts so perfectly that I would have laughed under better circumstances. "Come on. We shot down every new idea he had. We weren't perfect." They shrugged, but didn't disagree. "We all have things to apologize for."

I wished I had trusted Thomas to take charge of things back then, when his diplomacy might have kept us together.

In the end, no one had as much to say as they thought they did. We all wished we'd done things differently. We were all worried about Bobby. None of us knew what to do next. We couldn't change the past, but the conversation took some of the chill out of the air.

Thomas and I switched places—a symbolic gesture that he undertook with the solemn dignity of a priest—and we were sipping coffee in relatively peaceful silence when a crowd of men in hazmat suits led two enormous elephants out of one of the ERC buildings. They came through a loading door, four men per elephant.

"That's not something you see every day," James commented, tipping his head to one side.

"Poor things." Thomas leaned forward like he wanted to reach through the screen and give the animals a hug.

"You think there's a whole zoo in there?" Ben asked. "Monkeys and birds and lions and stuff?"

And I laughed, cracked wide open by the absurdity of it. There wasn't anyone on earth I'd rather be witnessing this moment with. No one alive, anyway.

We waited all day for Bobby to decide to see us, and I felt my mother's ghost flitting from me to James to Thomas to Ben, fussing with our hair and worrying. They felt her, too. I could see it in the way Thomas rubbed his face, like a mosquito was biting him, and the way Ben shook his head every so often.

I wondered, for the thousandth time, what made her so unsettled. "We're together again, mom," I said, when I found a little privacy in the bathroom. "You can relax." But she didn't relax. She *never* relaxed. I could feel her buzzing around me, breathing down my neck, smoothing my wrinkled shirt. Wanting me to do something but never saying *what*.

And the things I thought she wanted from me—commit, break up, stay, leave—never turned out to be the right things.

Part of me didn't want to get it right. Because then she'd rest, and I'd be alone.

Two weeks later, I was installed on the hard white couch in Bobby's minimalist condo, supervising his recovery while he tried his best not to recover. James and Ben flew home two days after Bobby left the hospital, our truce delicate but holding, and Thomas stayed, getting a room in an extended stay motel near Bobby's place and trying to give me breaks. But I wouldn't leave him alone with Bobby. The guy barely ate, and didn't seem to sleep. He avoided eye contact, spoke only when he absolutely had to, and never smiled. I didn't have any illusions about being able to prevent him from killing himself—he could still probably pick me up and throw me across a room—but I didn't want Thomas to be the one who found him if it happened.

I wouldn't risk burdening my friend with anything else.

Gradually, though, Bobby started eating the meals I brought him and smiling at the jokes Thomas made. He stopped arguing every time we had to go back to the hospital for a follow-up or a therapy session. His skin, which looked so pale in the hospital that I asked a doctor if he might need a blood transfusion, started to get some color. He stopped looking disappointed to wake up. He still had bad days, when eating a bowl of oatmeal in bed was too much effort for him, but they were fewer and farther between. My back, tied in knots from stress and sleeping on the couch, started to relax.

The caution that kept our conversations light for the first few weeks slid away as Bobby's eyes brightened. He tried to kill himself—to leave us, permanently—and I wanted to know why. When he didn't answer I just asked again. And again, in different ways. I needed to know—how else could I make sure he wouldn't do it again?

But I also had selfish reasons. I'd neglected Bobby just like I neglected everyone else in my life, and I wanted confirmation that his breakdown wasn't my fault. I ran over our last, rushed conversation a thousand times— would I have known he was in trouble, if I wasn't so self-absorbed? My feelings—guilt, fear, anger—demanded more and more attention.

I pushed him, and he pushed back.

"I can't tell you why I did it," he said, for the tenth time in one morning. Then, rethinking his words, "I *won't* tell you. Is that clearer? I don't *want* to tell you. I don't want you to know. That's not going to change. You can accept it, or you can leave, but we're not having this conversation again. I am an adult, and I am entitled to some privacy." Then, softening, "I know this was hard for you, and I'm sorry. I should never have done it. I'm glad they found me in time. It was stupid." He gripped my shoulders in his big hands and squeezed. "The stupidest thing I've ever done. And it had nothing to do with you, ok?"

I couldn't decide if that made me feel better or worse. He regretted it now, but that might change. It had nothing to do with me, but that meant I couldn't fix it. But if Bobby didn't want to talk, I couldn't make him. We watched the news and rented action movies. We took turns cleaning the bathroom, making grilled cheese sandwiches, and choosing pizza toppings.

At some point, I started to lose track of who was the patient, and who was the nurse.

"You have to get out of here." Thomas stood in the middle of the stuffy condo with one hand on his hip and the other on the top of his head, surveying our mess of pizza boxes like a disappointed parent. "He needs some space. You need some air. Go for a drive or something, just for the afternoon. I'll stay."

Bobby nodded encouragement, eager to be free of my constant observation. Thomas held out the keys to his rental car.

"Fine." It had been days since I left the tiny condo. I did need some air. "I'll bring dinner back."

I didn't know where I was headed until the highway spit me out on a long, twisting, tree-lined road. I laughed at myself. This wasn't what Thomas meant when he encouraged me to go for a drive. He wanted me to get out of my head, not go looking for my mother's grave. But the lake house drew me like a magnet. It was messed up, when I thought about it, that no one had visited her since we were teenagers.

The fact that our last attempt to get there ended with the psychiatrist in tears on the side of this very road at three o'clock in the morning seemed like a minor detail. I had a good sense of direction. I would find it.

I drove and drove and drove, following the signs and landmarks I remembered. I stopped at a gas station, then a diner, then a tiny bakery that I remembered going to when we stayed there all those years ago, for directions. Everyone rattled off the same list of quaintly named country roads in the same order, like they rehearsed it. But they all looked sympathetic while they did it, like they knew I'd never get there.

I returned to Bobby's condo late that night, without dinner. I'd been driving in circles for hours, prodded by stubbornness and my mother, who flitted around the car like a trapped bee. I was moving toward something, for once. But I still wasn't getting anywhere.

After that, I searched for the lake every day. It felt like the missing puzzle piece, and I couldn't let it go. There was a sense of magic there that seeped into me, and into every song I wrote for a long time after we left. But it ran out. I wanted to find the place where I buried my mother, but I was looking for something more than a grave. I had never felt as inspired as I did in that place, and I wanted that version of myself back. The one who could do anything. I wanted to find the place where I buried *that*.

I rented my own car and set off early every morning, before Bobby woke up. Inevitably, I returned late in the afternoon or evening, no closer to finding it. One country road looked like all the others. The GPS couldn't seem to tell them apart any better than I could, constantly recalculating and encouraging ill-advised U-turns. Physical maps only led me to the edge of the place I remembered, never to the center.

I couldn't find the lake, but I dreamed of it, and the dreams were deep and real, like falling into to another world. I woke up feeling like I'd *been* there.

It always started in the driveway—old trees reaching over me, rutted dirt road under my feet. I could feel the breeze off the lake and almost taste the sweet, pine-and-roses smell of the forest. But the air changed as I got closer to the house. Thicker and... wrong, somehow. By the time I could see the front door I hung, limp as a puppet. Suspended in something I couldn't see.

The dream swallowed me, and all I could do was wait for it to spit me back out.

The house looked just like I remembered, white with faded green shutters, surrounded by overgrown bushes, the huge antique dining table presiding over the yard like it expected company. I'd hang there for a while, watching. There'd be squirrels. Birds. A storm coming in over the lake. But usually, I only got a glimpse before Bobby's couch sucked me back.

Once, though, I pushed through the glue that held me in the driveway. I always tried, but this time, when I pressed, the air felt soft. Overripe. Ready to burst. And it did, like a bubble popping. Whatever was keeping me out let go and sent me sprawling on the grass. I lay there for a minute, breathing the fresh dirt smell of it. And then I scrambled up as fast as my clumsy dream-body would let me, because who knew how much time I had?

I maneuvered myself up the path, straight for the cemetery beyond the rose garden. I wanted to kneel in front of my mother's stone before I fell back into my body. Put my hands on its sun-warmed surface and be with her, for a minute.

The idea of her in the ground made me second guess the whole plan. But I was nearly there. And I owed her this.

The cemetery stretched out in front of me, bordered by low stone walls. Vines climbed over the stones, and roses—refugees from the garden— peeked out around them. It was friendly. Welcoming.

And then night crashed down around me, bringing a disorienting swirl of fog with it.

Nightmare, I thought, as shadows turned vines into snakes, but nothing else changed. I took a tentative step forward.

The stones glowed in the dark—gentle pulses lighting the weeds—but I couldn't find the one that belonged to my mother. I knelt where it should be, two hands on the soft, unblemished earth. It had to be there. This was my dream, after all. But I couldn't find it.

I sat back on my heels, hot with frustration and the effort of moving inside the dream. I imagined the stone. Willed it to appear. But I was alone with nothing but dead strangers to keep me company.

I pushed myself up, heavy and awkward. I could still feel the dampness seeping into my sneakers, see the fog around my ankles, but I could feel the dream starting to slip.

And then I heard a voice, in the darkness, calling.

I turned, the effort almost pulling me awake. There was a woman through the trees, crying out in a distant, musical voice. She moved slowly, like a person underwater. Like me, stuck in the driveway. But she wasn't like me. She glowed with the roses behind her. Radiant, like they were.

She raised her arm—liquid and graceful. I tried to raise mine, but it wouldn't cooperate. Our eyes snapped together like two halves of a whole, and my heart flipped. I would have known her anywhere.

She took a step toward me, but it was too late. I could feel the dream swelling around us—a bubble again, about to break. My ears rang. My vision blurred. The air turned thick and strangling. And then, I was gone. Yanked back into my body before I could respond to her.

I woke up with my sheets in knots and her name in my mouth—*Charlie*.

It felt right for her to be there. The girl I wanted but would never have, in the place I searched for and couldn't find.

Once, just as the sun set, I'm certain I caught a glimpse of the long, winding driveway that led to the lake. I saw it for less than a second, out of the corner of my eye, but I felt its vibration in my bones. I covered the same half mile stretch of road ten, fifteen, then twenty times, but I didn't even see a break in the trees.

It was like the place never existed at all.

24

CHARLOTTE

Four hours and several pain medications after I destroyed ERC and ended my life as I knew it, a grim young doctor appeared above me. I registered him as a serious face, floating—I had little awareness of anything beyond my own body, and even that was starting to blur into the room beyond it. "We can't do anything about the pain," he said, calm and matter-of-fact.

A murmur rose. Other people, but I couldn't make my eyes focus on them. The doctor was talking to them, not to me. A scream built inside me, straining against my skin. The doctor wasn't talking to me. No one was talking to me. I was not making decisions here.

I tried to let the scream out, but it turned into a choked gurgle. I couldn't scream. I reached for my throat, frantic—what happened to my voice?—but someone grabbed my arms. Held me down.

"This is a very unusual toxin," the doctor said, ignoring my thrashing body. Panic turned to horror. He was talking about me like a case in a book, not a real woman in a bed. He didn't care about me. "It interacts with the nervous system in a novel way," he droned.

I couldn't breathe. I was suffocating. No one was going to help me. I clawed at the bed.

"I ordered restraints from psych. For now, all we can do is keep her heart beating and prevent her from killing herself."

I tried to tell him *no, that's not what I want*, but I still couldn't do anything except gurgle. I bit down to make the noise stop.

Another murmur—agreement—and then his head receded. In its place, gray ceiling tiles.

"See if you can keep her from biting her tongue," the doctor added. "Her mouth looks like raw meat."

Over the next few days, I tried sliding out of my restraints slowly, like a snake shedding its skin. I tried wrenching myself out violently. I slammed my head over and over, always just an inch or two away from the metal railing at the top of the bed. I rasped and gurgled, trying to push the pain out in the sound, and trapped the noise inside, thinking I might explode if I held onto it long enough.

I chewed my lips and tongue and dug my fingernails into my palms, because new pain might free me, for a moment, from the old pain. I bargained with the pain, argued with it, begged it to let me go. I cursed Johnathan for doing this to me, Bobby for leaving me, Damia for getting caught.

Nothing changed. I was locked inside myself, in agony.

Through it all, my heart beat strong and steady, helped by a cocktail of medication that kept me alive without doing anything to make my situation more bearable. I yanked my IV one way and then the other, hoping to dislodge the needle, but the nurses fixed it. They jabbed me over and over, using up my veins and sending new waves of pain through my tortured body. They tightened my restraints.

At some point, they figured out how to keep me still. But my mind and heart and nerves remained wide awake. Trapped.

If they released me from the restraints, I would have clawed my wrists open with my fingernails.

I tried to do it from inside the restraints.

But the pain was more than happy to wrestle with me, if that's what I wanted. I couldn't reason with it or tire it out and there was no way around it. I could only help it break me.

My nails digging into my palms triggered infections that made my body rage with fever. My clenched jaw cracked two molars. My heart thudded so hard that I could feel it shrinking and weakening in my chest.

Lost inside the fever, I heard a doctor say "we might have to amputate." He said it like he was ordering food in a restaurant or commenting on the weather. Just a thing he had to do, sometimes. That's when I knew—they were not going to let me die. They would cut the rotten bits out and drag whatever was left of me back to life, whether I liked it or not.

The only choice I had was fight, or surrender. And if I fought, I would lose myself a piece at a time.

So, I swallowed the hoarse little voice screaming that it shouldn't be like this. It *was* like this. I couldn't resist my way out.

I could have resisted my way out, actually. My heart was failing by then. If I struggled for a few more days, it would have been all over. But I couldn't stand the pain anymore, and so I tried the only thing I hadn't tried yet. I let it have me.

I think I'm supposed to say things improved when I stopped fighting, but they didn't—it was just different. When I fought, the pain fought back as an army. When I gave in, it became my whole world. I wasn't in pain anymore. I *was* pain.

I floated in a dark, endless well, and every day I tried to sink a little deeper, searching for that illusive spot with water cold enough to numb me, or dark enough to hide me, or still enough to give me a moment of peace.

Even now I have nightmares where I'm back inside it. In the dreams I float inside a womb made out of teeth, being eaten alive, forever.

Around me, the hospital went on. Strangers poked, prodded, and tested. They cleaned me, changed my clothes, changed my sheets. I was lucid enough to know these things were happening, but not lucid enough to be embarrassed by my vulnerability. My body and its needs belonged more to the hospital staff than to me.

Sometimes, the nurses talked to each other as they worked, sharing gossip and commiserating over difficult children and disappointing relationships. They comforted me. They described what they were doing, just in case I could hear them.

I understood less and less of it as I sank deeper into the well.

I smelled rubbing alcohol, bleach, perfume, coffee, fabric softener, mint. I heard myself moaning, my voice hoarse and broken, stripped of the power it once had. Shoes squeaked on the tile, reminding me of those early days in the hospital with David. Monitors beeped along with the vague, comforting hum of classical music. Needles pinched, blood pressure cuffs squeezed, hospital blankets scratched my raw skin. At some point, I heard the snip of scissors cutting my hair. I felt the scrape of a nail file. There were hands, gently rubbing lavender scented lotion into my feet. I smelled the familiar, chemical odor of nail polish.

Sometimes, I recognized a voice or a face. I saw Janey, snapping her gum and reading a magazine and worrying about me, but I also saw Kit, shuffling her cards and pouring tea that I couldn't drink. I heard Jake's voice, big and comforting and warm, telling me I would be ok, but I also heard Clara, raging at me for locking Johnathan up.

On my hardest days, my desperate brain conjured Nicolas Bell, who sat next to my bed and sang to me. Always that one song—*Witch*—the first one I heard. It was the only thing I found truly comforting. Sometimes, as he sang, I felt Sky Lake in the distance. Roses, pine, *refuge*. But I couldn't get there, and he wasn't real.

None of them were real, and it was just as well—Johnathan's face loomed over me often enough to make me hope I imagined everything.

My heart failed, slowly at first, then faster. It started with small palpitations that produced a stuttering beep from a machine and a burning flash in my chest. The stutters turned into long, gasping silences and then dizzying lurches that brought nurses running two or three times a day. Soon, my struggling heart felt like a fish in my chest, wriggling, flapping, and thrashing for air.

It's almost over, I thought, and I was glad.

And then, someone changed the music.

Janey told me, later, that the soothing classical playlist my nurses chose made my room feel like a funeral and she couldn't stand it anymore. Since it clearly wasn't helping me, she decided to put on something I enjoyed. She never said it, but I know she thought I was dying, and she wanted me to hear my favorite music at the end.

She hooked my phone up to a speaker and put the playlist labelled "favorites" on shuffle, just like the night I almost jumped off my balcony.

At that point, the pain turned everything into a soup of useless information. Voices had a distorted, underwater quality that I couldn't follow. Music collapsed into static. Even my hallucinations had lost their shape. The people who visited my bed melted into puddles, dissolved into flocks of birds, shrieked through their eyes—they didn't even pretend to be real anymore.

My life, such as it was, had shattered into a dream.

A nightmare.

But Nicolas Bell cut through it.

At first, I only registered the clarity of his voice. Nothing had been clear in so long that this alone was a revelation. It felt like I'd just shaken water out of my ears. The relief made my heart flop and roll dramatically, setting off all the monitors. *This is it,* I thought, and let myself fall into the song—a slow, graceful, flying drop—as I waited for the clatter of the medical team around my bed. They would try to save me, but I didn't think they could, this time. I was almost *free*.

The beeping faded, and the pain faded with it. The end, I realized, was going to be peaceful. Tears flooded my eyes and spilled down the sides of my face, into my ears. Peace. Finally.

I drifted with the song. It would all be over soon.

And then, something changed.

Like a boat pushed onto the beach, I stopped drifting. Underneath me, a soft, uneven surface. Around me, my body. Arms and legs and hips. Belly. Chest. Neck Head. None of them shaped like pain anymore.

For a moment, I couldn't make sense of myself.

Outside of my shocking new body, I smelled pine trees and dirt and roses. A cool breeze tickled my face. In the distance, birds sang. Nic's voice joined them, far away and haunting.

Cautiously, I eased my heavy eyes open. Green trees and blue sky hung over me, vibrant and alive and impossible. I wiggled my toes, scrunched my eyebrows, and opened and closed my mouth. Carefully, I raised one arm a few inches, and then the other. My body cooperated, strong and flexible, no tubes or needles or restraints holding me down.

I took a deep, satisfying breath that smelled like Sky Lake on a hot summer day.

When I worked up the courage to roll over, a golden blanket of pine needles greeted me.

This isn't real, I thought, but when I pushed myself up, the needles stuck to my hands. I crouched in the ground that couldn't be underneath me, squinting at the golden coating on my palms.

Sticky. Scratchy.

Shimmering.

Almost real, but not quite.

I stood, savoring the press of bare feet into soft ground. How long had it been since I stood? Did I care what was real, when I could walk on my own two feet? I touched the rough bark of a tree, and when it felt real, I pressed my hand into it until I felt pain.

Healthy pain.

The kind that stops when you stop pushing.

Ahead of me, through the trees, I saw sunlight glinting off the water. I was *home*. In a place I never thought I'd see again.

No one goes through life rejoicing because they don't have a headache or a sprained ankle or a sore back. But when you're in pain, your whole life is pain. And when it goes away, everything shines brighter for a while. I spun, taking in the woods, the sky, the water in the distance, needing nothing more than that moment.

And then the pain sucked me back into my body. Back into the hospital bed. Back into the well. One minute, I was spinning in the woods, face raised to the sun, and the next I was sweaty and convulsing against my restraints, pain white hot and blinding and *new*, now that I'd experienced a moment of relief.

I would have thought Sky Lake was a dream, if not for the smell of roses, clinging to me so strongly that one of the nurses commented on it as she changed my soaked sheets.

After the pain took me back, I wished I had done more during my brief reprieve. I should have run straight to the water, where I could sink my toes into the mud like I did as a little girl. I should have touched the smooth counters of the old familiar kitchen, checked for David's chocolate ice cream in the freezer. I should have played the piano. I should have buried myself in rose petals.

I should have called for David, who might have been there, waiting for me.

But I was overcome by the miracle, and then it was over.

The second time I opened my eyes to find sky and trees above me, I wasted no time. I ran straight to the lake, bare feet crunching through dry leaves and kicking up sand and finally settling on the damp pebbles at the edge of the water.

The pebbles shined like jewels on a bed of caramel colored sand. They were too bright. Too clean. All the same size. But the lake stretched out in front of me, golden under a mellow sunset, and my eyes drank in the light like they were thirsty.

Home. Almost.

I think I knew, even then, that I was not home. That this was only an in-between place.

A fantasy, and fantasy always comes with a price.

I shuffled into soft, sucking mud, then slimy clay. As a little girl, I felt the lake in my bones. It spoke to me. This water didn't speak. But it was cold and refreshing and it made me weightless.

Hip deep, I slid into a swim, arms out, feet up, belly open to the cold. It felt like pool water—clear and sterile—not the living soup of a lake. But I was smooth and silent and graceful—almost a fish—and I let myself believe that the water would heal me, or at least keep me. It didn't breathe like the real Sky Lake. It couldn't wrap its murky fingers around me. But, somewhere deep, I was still the little girl who brought David's ashes home all those years ago.

Like her, I believed Sky Lake would save me, even when I could feel it spitting me back into a body chained to a bed.

I fought to stay in the lake, splashing and struggling and finally, desperately, diving as deep as I could. But I couldn't escape from myself. The cold water fell away as Nicolas Bell's voice faded, making way for a song with no magic in it at all.

The pain took me back every time, but it couldn't keep me anymore, and that changed everything. At least once every two hours, sometimes more often, Nicolas Bell's voice burst into my room and gave me my freedom.

Gave me something like freedom, anyway. The lake house in my mind was an exquisitely constructed snow globe, just like the one I sang David to when he was dying. The birds chirped a little too beautifully. The sun shined a little too bright. When it rained, the drops were fat and reflective—carved crystal. Perfect leaves fell from evenly distributed branches, and the moon hung full and low more often than not.

It wasn't real. The real Sky Lake didn't want me back.

But this false place let me walk. It let me run and dance and shout. Cold made me shiver, heat made me sweat. It hurt to stub my toe. I could drink a cup of coffee on the dock while the sun rose. I could read the books on the shelves and fry eggs on the stove and put new sheets on the bed.

The only thing I couldn't do, no matter how hard I tried, was sing.

The music stuck in my throat, a strangling lump that made me cough. It knew the place wasn't real. That *I* wasn't real.

It wouldn't waste itself where no one could hear it. And I thought that might be just as well—where had singing ever gotten me, really?

No matter how loud I yelled, or how far I walked, I never found another living thing in that place. I heard birdsong, crickets, and the shuffle of small animals in the brush, but never saw them. At night, the eerie voices of coyotes rose over the lake, and the hoot of an owl sounded outside my window, but I never even saw a butterfly or a mosquito. I smelled trees in the woods and roses in the rose garden, but if I leaned in to smell a specific flower, it released the same earth-pine-water-rose scent that permeated everything.

When I stood in front of a mirror, or over the lake, a woman-shaped disturbance looked back, like a faded impressionist painting.

It didn't bother me at first. I spent whole days baking in the sun on the sandy beach by the lake. I sat on the dock through thunderstorms, soaked and not caring because I left my real body somewhere else. I walked through the woods in the swirling fog like a ghost, my feet just vague shapes in the haze. I slept in the rose garden, the light of a full moon draped over me like a blanket. I floated on my back in the lake and soaked in the hot springs and played David's piano until my fingers ached.

I looked for him, endlessly, even though I knew he couldn't be there.

But it got lonely, after a while. All my earlier visits were with David, and I could end them by ending my song. Now, I drifted from the lake to the forest to the house alone, at the mercy of whatever unknowable rules governed time there. Sometimes, I only spent a few stolen minutes. Sometimes, I spent a day, or a week. Once, I saw the snow melt and the first flowers of spring bloom, and I wondered if I had died and entered some kind of personal eternity.

I stared at my vague reflection, willing my own eyes to come into focus, until I couldn't remember what I looked like. I walked toward the street, but the driveway continued like a giant, wooded treadmill. I climbed to the top of a big rock and screamed until my voice gave out. I felt lost. Tired. Alone.

I left the pain behind, but brought everything else with me. The guilt. The loneliness. The fear. The thing I really wanted to get away from—myself.

One night, I stood in the rose garden, bathed in the soft glow of the flowers, and saw a shape through the trees. My eyes had been playing tricks on me—faces in clouds, shadowy figures in doorways—but this was more than movement out of the corner of my eye or a rippled reflection in the lake. This was a man, pacing the perimeter of the cemetery like he lost something there.

Tall. Slim. Wearing a dark jacket and boots and standing feet from David's glowing stone—it had to be him.

I called out, heart hammering in my ears. I couldn't see his face through the fog, but who else would haunt Sky Lake with me? "David!" My voice flowed—a long, howling note that felt like breathing after being underwater.

David was *right there*.

Right where I left him.

Joy nearly knocked me down, unfamiliar after the pain of the hospital and the dull contentment of this imaginary place. But I kept my eyes on David. I followed his instructions—*if you're ever in trouble, go to Sky Lake*—and he found me. After all this time.

I tried to run, but the air was thick and sticky-sweet with roses—it wouldn't let me. I waved, and my arm swayed like seaweed in a gentle current. "David?" I asked. "I'm over here!"

It was almost a song. But it still sounded hollow in my ears—no forest in it, no earth. Uncertainty shivered through me, and the note fell apart. Was any of this real?

"David?"

I might as well have been trapped in a jar of honey—I couldn't get to him. *No*, I thought, forcing my body forward. *I can't lose him again.* I took one step, then two, each such an effort that I didn't think I could manage another. But then I imagined my brother's arms—strong and healthy—wrapping around me, and propelled myself forward.

The fog swirled, slow and liquid. For a second, I saw my brother—the cheerful tilt of his head, the relaxed presence he carried everywhere, the dance of affection in his eyes when they fell on me. He was *right there*.

And then I saw the truth.

Not David.

The fog still blurred his face, but I could see enough to know it did not belong to David. The face was square where David's was a diamond. It had dark eyebrows and a thick shadow of stubble—David couldn't even grow a goatee.

Grief clawed at my chest. I was losing him. Again.

Like my pain broke the spell keeping him there, the stranger in the cemetery began to flicker. He would disappear, like the cloud faces and shadow people. He probably wasn't here at all. But my heart stretched toward him even as the rest of my body went limp with despair.

He wasn't David. And yet, I *knew* him—a stranger, but also familiar. Recognition tugged me forward, fighting the syrupy air.

I tried to shout—*who are you*—but the rose-sweetened air swallowed the words before they left my lips. I was stuck, my heart reaching through my ribs like a vine. And he was turning to smoke. Feet, then legs, then, torso. Dissolving into the fog.

I struggled to move, but it was no use—even if I could run, I wouldn't reach him in time. His mouth, open in a silent scream, was the last thing to unravel.

I was alone.

Sky Lake wasn't saving me. It was just a different kind of prison.

I sank into rose petals so perfect they could have been piped on a cake, broken by the realization that I only had two choices—return to my ruined body, or be alone forever.

Pain there, or pain here.

No good options.

As if the magic couldn't work until I *wanted* to return to the world, my body began to heal. Every time Nic's voice took me away, a little more of me came back. The machines beeped less and less. The hushed voices of my caretakers grew louder, less respectful.

And then, one day, the pain let me go.

I became aware of it gradually, not processing it as the absence of pain as much as the presence of everything the pain covered up. Hunger and thirst, two sensations I hadn't felt in months. The warmth of the bed. The pressure of the restraints. The many horrors of my physical body—needles, tubes, the crushing weakness in my muscles.

I wanted to go back to Sky Lake.

But Sky Lake wasn't real, at least not the one I'd been hiding in. My dry mouth was real. My raw throat was real. My wrists, tied to the bed, were *real*.

Questions rushed in like water filling a cave. How long had I been there? Was Damia alive? What happened to Janey? I remembered seeing them

232 • LEIGH CHANDLER

both in my room, but I remembered so many things that couldn't have happened. Was Johnathan in jail somewhere, or had he blackmailed his way out of this?

Who was I, now that everyone knew the truth about Charlotte London?

Urgent beeping announced my rising blood pressure, and a nurse rushed in. She said something comforting and changed the IV bag without noticing anything different about me, and as much as I wanted to be untied, I was afraid. What if she said she couldn't release me? That Johnathan was still in charge, and I was a prisoner? What if I moved, and the pain came back?

The nurse talked to me without waiting for answers. "I'll get Janey," she said, smoothing my hair back with a cool hand. "She'll sit with you for a while."

One question answered.

Janey arrived in her familiar cloud of cheap perfume, talking on the phone. "Yes," she shouted. "I mean, no. I mean, that's off the record, don't publish that."

Don't publish that. An interview. Janey would not be giving an interview if Johanthan was free. He would never let her talk to the press. Some of the pressure on my chest eased. Janey was fine, and I was probably not a prisoner.

"Right," she said, and I could hear her eyes rolling. "But I wasn't involved in that. I answered phones and filed papers. It was an *office job.*" She blew out a loud, frustrated breath. "I mean, we all knew he was doing... other things. But I certainly didn't know anything about terrorism or treason or... what did you say? War crimes? That seems like a stretch, but ok, war crimes, whatever you say. That was very much not my job."

War crimes. Relief flowed through me. Johnathan could not possibly be in charge of anything. He wasn't waiting outside to punish me. I was safe.

Grief followed, sharp and unexpected.

He wasn't waiting outside. He was *gone*. I couldn't imagine the world without him—myself, without him.

Janey paused for another question. "No," she said. "Definitely not. I was never afraid for my own life. He was my uncle, and he cared about family, in… his way. He wouldn't hurt me."

He wouldn't hurt me.

My vision, already blurred by whatever flowed through the IV, narrowed until I could only see a pinprick of ceiling tile. I clung to my first, comforting thought—*why is Janey lying to protect Johnathan?*—but I knew Janey, and she didn't sound like she was lying.

"Nonono," she said, tripping over the words, "I don't mean that. I wasn't there voluntarily. None of us could just get up and walk out. But I had… privileges, I guess? Like, if I messed up, I was going to get a lecture, not a bullet, you know?"

Anger filled me, hot and stinging. I remembered Janey's voice on the phone all those years ago, terrified, begging me to be good because he would kill her if I escaped—*lies.*

And then I remembered the red pellets hitting me as I ran, and pain bloomed in my chest. I messed up, and I got the bullet, not the lecture. I tried to remember Johnathan's voice, telling them not to shoot. But I couldn't quite summon it. Was it real, or just more of the same wishful thinking?

I heard the thunk of Janey's iced coffee hitting the table next to my bed. Smelled her strawberry perfume. Heard the familiar snap of her gum. All exactly like I remembered. I turned my head just enough to see her eyes, dark and sunken but still painted three shades of sparkle.

The same girl who saved my life when we were just kids, trapped together in a nightmare. We'd been through so much.

She looked exhausted. Thin. Held together with bubble gum and lip gloss. And she was still in the nightmare, with me.

My heart squeezed. *Janey.*

I wanted to scream at her. To hurt her. To beg for an explanation—any explanation—that would go back in time and make our friendship real. But she hung up the phone and turned her attention to me with a brave, heartbreaking smile, a bottle of lotion in one hand and a nail file in the other, and the anger balled up in my throat.

She helped Johnathan hold me hostage.

She rubbed my feet with lavender oil every day for months.

I was furious with her. I was overjoyed to see her. I couldn't pull those feelings apart. As Janey rubbed the circulation back into one of my limp, restrained hands, all the fight went out of me. She stayed—that had to count for something.

Oh, how I wanted it to count for something.

I blinked, hard, hoping she'd recognize the movement as more than my usual struggle to escape the pain.

All the blood drained from her face. "Grace? Charlie? Charlotte?" Her voice rose with hope and panic on each name. "Are you really there? Can you see me?" She held my face in her lavender hands, nothing but love and worry in her eyes.

I blinked again, harder, and rattled the restraints, wishing I had a clearer way to communicate *get this fucking tube out of my throat* because I couldn't stand it for one more second.

"Ohmygod," she shrieked, mushing the words together. Then, turning toward the door but not leaving my side, "Help! Help! Someone *get in here!*"

I could always rely on Janey to make a scene. And that was all I needed from her. The rest could wait.

Damia arrived at noon three days after I officially regained consciousness. I say "officially" because I was never truly unconscious, unless you count the time I spent at Sky Lake, when I was conscious somewhere else. But the nurses and doctors who cared for me were from the real world, not ERC. They didn't want to think they'd been torturing me. For them, I pretended my memories were hazy and the pain completely gone.

I pretended to be glad they saved my life.

It seemed like the least I could do, considering all the trouble I caused. No one would tell me much at that point, but I could hear the noise outside, where crowds gathered early every morning and stayed until the police sent them home at night. Their shouts were just a vague roar, but I could feel the emotion underneath. Like the crowds I sang to, except that I wasn't singing. I was lying in a bed, and the people outside were not under my control.

Whatever I was had taken on a life of its own while I slept.

When I first woke up, Janey insisted that the shades couldn't be raised, just like she insisted the television didn't work and her phone had no internet access, but I was soon strong enough to shuffle from bed to window on my own.

I had to see the crowd. Reveal the monster, and take away its power.

I was blinded by flashes as soon as I pulled the drapes aside. It honestly didn't occur to me that my face would be splashed all over the tabloids—the hospital room felt a million miles away from the outside world—until that moment, and I should have closed the curtains. But I was still too detached from my body to protect it from a camera.

I felt hot and lightheaded as I took in the sea of people. They stretched all the way to the street—later, I would learn that I'd been moved to different hospitals twice during my recovery, but the chaos followed me. Reporters lined a police-enforced corridor that led to the front door.

Fans clutching flowers, stuffed animals, and "Get well" banners clustered together. Some were praying. Others swayed together—singing, maybe, or listening to Charlie sing. As I became visible in the window, they pointed and waved. But I hardly saw them, my eyes drawn to the protestors. Angry. Marching. Holding signs that said things like "Bring her out," "Make her talk," "Not a hero," and "Too little, too late."

I leaned on the windowsill, absorbing every word.

A roar went up from the crowd—*Charlie, Charlie, Charlie.* So loud, now, that I could hear the desperate howl of love underneath it. I wanted to cover my ears, but I couldn't. I was a statue in the window.

When I woke up, I wondered who I was now that everyone knew the real story of Charlotte London. Looking outside, I had my answer. I was still Charlotte London. If anything, the truth made her bigger.

Larger than life, because she wasn't real. The hero and the villain— Charlie London could be whoever you wanted her to be.

A light rap sounded on the open door. I ignored it. I didn't feel like company. I pressed my forehead against the window. *Too little, too late.* They were right.

"Grace."

The name pulled me out of the protest. I had been Charlie longer than I'd been Grace at that point, and it felt like seeing something I used to own in a thrift store, or on the side of the road—mine but not anymore. Part of me longed to reclaim it, but I knew it didn't fit any better than *Charlie, Charlie, Charlie.*

Footsteps crossed the room—light and tentative, like the knock—and a hand reached around me to close the curtains.

"Grace," she repeated, and I turned my head slowly, because movement made me spin.

Damia.

Her face was pale, her nails bitten so low that it hurt to look at them, but she was alive. She didn't get a red pellet or go in the white room. It wasn't too late, after all.

My body couldn't decide if it wanted to laugh or scream or fall against Damia and cry. If she hadn't put her arms around me, I would have collapsed in a boneless heap on the floor.

"Let's get you back to bed," she said, hooking a foot around the leg of my walker to bring it closer. I resisted the thing—it made me feel like an old lady—but I let her drape me over it while a voice in the back of my mind reminded me that I'd wasted almost half of my life already.

"You're a hero," she said, giving the window a hard look, like she could erase what I'd just seen.

"Hero, huh?" I searched for a joke to ease my discomfort, but the drugs made my head too fuzzy. "They forgot my cape," I offered, lamely. Behind me, the festive protest sound of the crowd rose and fell, and Damia pulled the curtains tighter. "A cape would be nice, actually. The back of this gown is drafty as hell."

Damia laughed—a sudden, surprised sound—and I felt unreasonably proud of myself. Everyone was so serious, and it irritated me. I didn't want to comfort other people.

Damia put one hand on my back and the other on my elbow, gently guiding me back to bed. "You saved my life. So yes, as far as I'm concerned, you are a hero."

Whatever opened up in me when I saw Damia alive and well snapped shut. *Hero.* The last thing I felt like. I started to tell the truth—that I didn't save her life, or at least I wasn't trying to—but shame closed my throat around the words. The truth was, I never thought I *could* save her life. I only thought I could punish Johnathan for killing her, which made it a suicide, not a rescue. But her eyes shined when she called me a hero. She needed to believe a better story.

"How are you feeling?" she asked.

I slid back into bed, keeping my head as level as possible. I hoped the dizziness would go away when they finished weaning me off the pain killers, but the doctors wouldn't make promises. No one knew what kind of long-term effects the poison would have, because no one ever survived the poison before. "You really want to know?" My voice was scratchy and weak, a constant reminder that I might never sing again. I wasn't sure I wanted to, but I didn't want the choice taken away from me.

Damia nodded, leaning forward but not touching me. "I really want to know," she confirmed. "The ugly truth." She waited, patient and interested. Not pushing, but not backing away, either.

"I feel like shit," I said, and it didn't sound as brave in the room as it did in my head.

Damia smiled sympathetically. "That's to be expected. You've been through an unimaginable thing. Your body..." She pressed her lips together to stop the stream of platitudes. "You've heard this a few times, I take it?"

I blushed, realizing that I must have visibly reacted to the pep talk. I couldn't help it. It was like I woke up with a face that didn't know how to be in the world with other people anymore.

"No one here has any idea what you've gone through," Damia said. "But everyone wants to tell you what to do and how to feel. Is that right?"

Tears stung my eyes and my body softened into the lumpy sculpture of pillows Janey built to make the hospital bed more comfortable. Damia was exactly right, and hearing it was better medicine than anything the nurses gave me. She would have been a really good therapist if Johnathan hadn't gotten his claws into her.

I nodded cautiously, blinking the tears back. I didn't want to cry.

"Ok. We don't have to talk about your body. Not my specialty, anyway. How are you *feeling*?" This time, she touched her chest meaningfully on the word "feeling."

I touched my own chest, which flared a warning. If I opened that box, I was afraid I wouldn't be able to close it. "Like shit," I said. I didn't have a word for how I felt. And if I did, I wasn't sure I'd want to say it out loud, where someone else could hear it.

"Also expected. Tell me more."

I searched for something I could share, for her sake more than mine. But I didn't have it in me. I was pretending too much already. "Look, I know you want to help," I said, feeling like a kid again, sitting in Damia's office, trying not to talk about my feelings. "But I don't need a shrink."

"Ok," she said, unfazed by my rudeness. "That's fair. What do you need?" Then, before I could answer, "Actually, forget what you need. What do you want? You're free now. You get to call the shots."

That idea—that I was free to choose what came next—landed harder than any of the signs outside the window. For all my dreaming, I never thought about what happened after I escaped. I didn't know how to choose things. My future was a yawning abyss, as horrifying as my past. More, maybe. I leaned back and closed my eyes. "I'm tired," I said, because I didn't know how to explain.

Damia accepted my answer with her usual understanding. "I'll be back tomorrow, same time," she promised, scribbling her number on a piece of paper. "If you think of anything you need, text me. Or make a list, and I'll get it from you tomorrow."

Every day at noon, Damia arrived with something I didn't think I needed. Pastries from a great bakery near her apartment. Fresh fruit, because the hospital cafeteria tended toward the pre-cut, underripe variety. Good coffee with real cream and extra sugar. Stacks of novels. Warm socks. Soft clothes. Fast food hamburgers and milkshakes and peanut butter cookies.

She talked to my doctors, took careful notes, and kept track of all the information I couldn't be bothered with. She made me do my physical therapy exercises and moved me to a room that didn't overlook the crowd. She brought in a hairdresser to fix the roughly chopped mess on my head.

She dragged me out of bed and walked me, expanding my territory a little bit every day until we made it all the way to a quiet, private courtyard. There were ornamental trees, planters full of flowers, and birds pecking at crumbs. Compared to my room, it was a different world. We sat on a bench, soaking up sunshine, and it was *good*.

I should have known that everything was about to change.

I turned my face to the sky, where puffy clouds floated like cartoons. *Real clouds, in a real sky*, I thought, taking greedy breaths of fresh air.

Next to me, Damia shifted nervously, twisting a tissue. "Grace," she said. "I need to tell you something."

I don't know what made her choose that moment—my improved health, the weight of the secret. Maybe the breeze blew the truth out of her. But she couldn't hold it back anymore. "I spilled coffee on the map," she confessed. "And then one day... I couldn't find my way back to the lake. I drove and drove and it just... wasn't there anymore." She leaned, elbows on her knees, tissue coming apart in her fingers. "I kept trying. For weeks."

The words were hot and suffocating and I wanted them to stop, but she just kept talking. Explaining in circles while my world crumpled into a new shape—the past, the future, the ground underneath me shifting. Our safehouse kept me going for so long. And it was just another lie.

I wrapped my arms around myself and pressed until I felt hot needles of pain in my belly. Physical pain, that I could control.

Damia squeezed the wet remains of the tissue between clasped hands. "I've kept trying, since ERC collapsed. But it isn't there."

I bit down on my tongue and focused on the pain as tears welled up. "When... did it happen?" I asked.

"A long time ago. You were away on your second tour." She sounded as sad as I felt, hunched on the bench with her head bowed. She took a shaky breath. "I'm sorry, Grace. You told me it was important not to damage the map... You said I couldn't find my way back without it... I should have believed you."

I remembered the afternoon she helped me bury David. The thick black clouds, the glow of the roses, the cold bite of the water as I pushed myself down and down to retrieve the enormous stone. She saw all that, but she still didn't believe me when I explained the magic to her. And now the map was gone. I didn't realize, until that very moment, how much I counted on the map—to save others, yes, but also to be waiting for me when I was ready to go back.

Because without it, I'd never find Sky Lake again, either.

"I should have believed you." She forced herself to look at me, eyes so deep with sadness that I couldn't burden her with my own. She should have believed me. But she didn't. And here we were.

"It wasn't very believable," I said. "I should have told you to get a pebble from the lake. I don't know why I didn't." *I should have told you to take a pebble for me, too. To take handfuls of them.*

"You were a child." Her voice cracked.

I was a child. And she couldn't help me, even though she wanted to. Damia had her own past at ERC, longer and deeper than mine, weighing on her. We sat in silence for a while, lost in memories neither one of us wanted to revisit.

"So... the house... it wasn't a safehouse after all?" I asked, my voice faint, tears threatening to cut it off completely.

"No! It was. It was a safehouse." Damia squeezed my hand. "Once. It did so much good. And then I spilled coffee on the map and never found my way back." She forced a smile, but looked as close to tears as I felt. "I can tell you about it. About the people we helped."

Once. It helped once. Better than nothing, but nowhere near the debt I owed. And now, Sky Lake was lost forever. My teeth clenched, sending waves of pain into my skull, but I didn't try to relax. I deserved the pain.

"I think it might help you move forward," Damia said.

But I didn't want to hear about one good thing, when I needed thousands of them to balance the harm I'd done. And I couldn't even imagine what "forward" looked like from here. "Maybe some other time," I said. "I'm getting tired." My go-to excuse for avoiding conversations I didn't feel like having.

"Grace, you have to face your past at some point." She kept her hand on mine and I squirmed, not strong enough to pull away if she really wanted to keep me there. "I want to help you process this."

Anger flared at her words. My past wasn't a thing that could be "processed." "Still don't need a shrink," I snapped.

"How about a friend?"

All my adult relationships had been fake, to one degree or another. I wasn't sure I even knew what the word "friend" meant. I shrugged.

"Even if you don't want to talk, there are things I'd like to tell you. I think I could help you get some… closure."

A bitter, bark of a laugh escaped before I could swallow it. *Closure.* Damia, of all people, should know there was no such thing. "I already heard the whole story," I said. "I've got all the closure I'm going to get."

Janey didn't want to tell me what happened after I ran away. She released the details in pieces, reluctantly. I wished she'd just give me my phone so I could read about it myself, but they didn't trust me with information any more than they trusted me with sharp objects.

The short version—the one Janey gave me the first time I asked—is that Mallory and her team swarmed into ERC thirty minutes after I handed over the files. They had been planning and rehearsing the raid for so long that they could have done it blindfolded. If anything, they overestimated the fight they would encounter—most of the people in those buildings wanted to get out.

Researchers and employees calmly walked to busses that took them to a holding area. Agents in hazmat suits entered the buildings and the basements one at a time to assess their contents. Some creatures, like the elephants, required specialized handlers or equipment, and those evacuations took place over the next ten days. Dangerous substances and animals were secured. Steps were taken to maintain necessary support systems, and staff were assigned to areas that required supervision.

No one resisted. No one got hurt. Nothing spilled or escaped or got into the wrong hands.

It was as close to a miracle as anyone involved had ever seen.

But no one expected Johnathan Everett to miss the whole thing.

Mallory and her team ran hundreds of simulations of the raid, but it never occurred to them to wonder how it would go with Johnathan Everett locked in his darkened office with all communications silenced.

That's the detail Janey didn't want to share with me, and she talked around it for days. She told me about the chaos at the processing center. She told me about the very attractive agent who personally escorted her out of the building. She told me about the elephants.

But she tried not to tell me that Johnathan went quietly, without a fight, because of me.

They found him on his knees in a sea of bloodstained rose petals, the bouquet from his desk torn to shreds around him, his hands ripped raw by thorns.

He didn't yell or push the panic button or go for the gun in the top drawer of his desk because he was completely overcome with grief, not for his ruined organization, but for *me*.

"They're keeping him somewhere secret," Janey said, mournfully. "He has no access to anything. He doesn't even know you're *alive*."

Her sadness made me angrier than I had any right to be.

It was complicated for all of us, and I'm sure she saw me as one of the few who understood that. But I didn't *want* complicated. I wanted to remember Kit, and feel like justice had been served.

I didn't want to imagine the sound he made as the roses came apart.

"Did I miss anything?" I asked, summarizing for Damia. "Some magical detail that makes it all better?" I hated that she thought we could process past what happened. That there was such a thing as closure.

"That's not what I'm talking about." Damia waved the story away. "I don't expect that to make you feel better. I lived through it, and it didn't make me feel better."

Sometimes, I forgot that Damia carried the same trauma we all did—she just hid it well.

"Everyone thought the world would be right once they punished Jonathan, but that's not how it works, is it?" Damia asked.

I shook my head. I was starting to think that the past couldn't be healed. Maybe it would fade, after a while, and that's the best we could hope for.

"It's more complicated for us," she said. "We were inside. ERC was home, whether we liked it or not. The only way to survive was to make the best of it. You know how I felt, putting that file together for Mallory? I felt guilty. I felt like I was betraying a *friend*."

She dropped the admission like a baited hook and left it, but I didn't want to discuss my mixed-up feelings with anyone. How could I say that part of me wished Johnathan would walk into my hospital room with a stack of books he couldn't wait for me to read, or a wig so I could sneak out to lunch with him, or a hundred questions about what the pain felt like, because he'd be so curious about something like that?

"He won't spend his life in a cell," she said. "They'll let us think so, but it would be a waste of his mind. They'll give him a new name and a new nose and he'll land on his feet somewhere, as someone else." She smiled. "Funny, to think he'll have to do that. To be reinvented, the way you were."

I shrugged like it didn't matter to me. Like I wasn't already thinking about my next birthday, and half hoping for a bouquet of flowers and a cryptic note with no return address.

"They're going to start distributing the files," she said, choosing a different direction when I didn't respond. "Did Janey tell you that? People can pick up their own paperwork, or whatever belongings were left by loved ones who… didn't make it. It's quite an operation. They put Janey in charge."

I imagined Janey back at her desk, handing those pointlessly filed yellow folders to their rightful owners. There was something poetic about it, although I already knew I couldn't face it personally. The idea of touching that folder—my life at ERC, distilled onto paper—made me feel sick. "Maybe it will help people," I said. I didn't think so. But I was grateful to put the conversation back on neutral territory.

"Maybe. Maybe not." Damia closed her eyes briefly, like it hurt to think about it. "That's not the point. The point is that people are doing what they can to set this right. To put things back together."

I waited for the next part, where she encouraged me to get involved or go to a support group, but she just stared at her hands and pushed out a long sigh. Then, with the posture of a person preparing to drop through a hole in ice, she said, "There's something I want to talk to you about."

Damia sucked a breath in, slowly, the way she taught me to do when I was scared.

I held mine. I couldn't take any more revelations.

"I've been waiting for the right time," she said. "For you to be well enough." She touched my knee. "I don't want to cause you more pain."

So don't, I thought, but I was frozen.

"I don't think there's ever a right time, though, is there?" She stopped, hands shaking, face crunched with concern, and I thought she might decide not to go on. I would have gladly let her change the subject—anything that made calm, level-headed Damia shake would feel like a bomb going off to me—but her eyes turned hard and determined and I braced myself as she pushed the rest of the thought out. "I want to talk to you about Bobby."

Bobby. His name doubled me over. For a moment, I was lost inside the memory—the rattle of David's hospital bed as Bobby shook it, the anguish in his voice as he blamed me—and it took all my strength to come back to my grown-up body on the bench in the sunny courtyard. "That's... not easy for me to talk about," I said, hoping Damia wouldn't try to be my therapist again. "It's definitely not something I want to talk about now."

"I'm not asking you to talk about it," she said. "I'm only asking you to listen. There are things you don't know about him. Things you should know. For both of your sakes."

She could have just talked—I was too shocked to stop her—but Damia needed permission. She waited while I sat in stunned silence. The idea that she would do anything for Bobby's sake made my stomach hurt—she was *my* friend. He *abandoned* me.

Me. Before I became someone else.

Damia put her hand on my upper arm in a silent request to continue.

"No," I said, my head shaking all by itself, making me dizzy. "Why would you even…? *No.*"

"Please," she begged. "Just listen. This is… my way of putting something back together."

Damia looked at me with such earnestness—she wanted to help, and she thought this was the way—but she was trying to help *him*. The betrayal burned a hole right through me. "Absolutely not," I said. I tried to remember how far it was from the bench to my room. Could I do it on my own?

"Give me five minutes," she said, fast and all-business now. She knew she didn't have much more time to convince me. "Just one quick story. If you don't want to talk to him after that…"

"Talk *to* him?" I stood, clenching my teeth against another spin. "Are you serious?"

"Just hear me out, Grace, please…"

"No. Not a chance." I stepped away from the bench, not sure if I'd fall and not caring. "I can't believe you'd even suggest that." She reached out but I shrugged her off, sending my head into a sickening new roll. "I'm going in. And I don't want your help."

Or your friendship, I thought, and she flinched like I said it out loud.

I did want her friendship—desperately. But I didn't believe in it anymore.

I'm sure Damia expected me to sulk for a few hours, get a good night's sleep, and be calm enough to talk at noon the next day. But, as much as I didn't want to face my future, I wanted to face my past even less. None of it was real—my friendships, my hair, my music, my fame. It was all an illusion built by Johnathan Everett, and now it was crashing down.

I checked out against doctor's orders with Bobby behind me like a vengeful spirit chasing me out of a haunted house.

25

NIC

"You won't find it."

I was sneaking like a kid out past curfew, and Bobby's voice scared the hell out of me. He was on the couch, waiting up, when I returned from another long day searching for the lake house.

I tried to look casual. "Find what?" I asked, like we always met like this in the middle of the night.

"The lake."

He dropped the word between us and waited. I went to the sink. Filled a glass with water, even though I wasn't thirsty.

"I know you're looking for it." He started making up the couch with my sheets. "You should stop."

I abandoned the water on the counter. "I'm not looking for anything," I said. "I was just out for a drive."

Bobby sighed. "We both know that's not true." He handed me a folded blanket. "That lake house... it isn't a normal place. I don't know how to explain it. It can get... lost." He paused, looking sad and far away.

There was no point lying to him. He *knew*. I didn't like being so transparent. "How did you know I was going there?" I asked, shaking out the blanket. I focused on it instead of him. I hoped he and Thomas hadn't been sitting around together, worrying about me.

He fluffed a pillow and dropped it on the couch. "You were happy there," he said, avoiding my eyes. "Inspired. And you haven't been happy or inspired in a long time." He picked up the pillow and examined it, like it might help him explain. "And your mother is there."

The room seemed to shrink—I felt understood and violated as I smoothed my blanket over the hard couch cushions. Bobby was there the day we buried my mother. He helped me dig the hole. But that memory was mine, and I didn't like having it introduced as evidence against me.

"I know what it's like to leave someone behind," he said.

Heat rose into my cheeks—I wasn't just a boy who missed his mommy. "I'm just curious about it," I lied. "That's all."

He shook his head. He could always see through me, and my lies were an insult to both of us. But he didn't argue. He didn't have to—we both knew he was right.

"A place can't just disappear," I said.

"That place can." He tossed my pillow onto the couch, hard. "I can't explain it. But I know." He hesitated. He was struggling with himself, and I held my breath, hoping for more information about the lost lake. "It's not normal," he said, giving the pillow one last smack and heading to the bedroom. "You need to leave it alone."

He said it like a parent warning me not to touch the hot stove. But I was always the kind of kid who had to learn things for myself. I tossed and turned on the couch that night, waiting for the sun to come up so I could go back out and try again.

The next morning, over cups of black coffee because I forgot to buy milk, Bobby took a deep breath and said what he had probably been thinking for weeks. "You can't keep sleeping on my couch." His voice was firm, but his eyes stayed in his cup. "It isn't healthy for you. You need your own space. Your own life."

I nodded into my own cup. I knew this day was coming. It was probably a good sign that Bobby wanted to be rid of me. He sounded like the old Bobby—calm, sure of himself, in charge—and that eased a knot I'd had in my stomach since I got the call from the hospital. But it also put an uncomfortable spotlight on my own situation. If Bobby didn't need me, what was I doing?

"You need to move forward," he said, like he heard the question I was asking myself. "You'll figure it out, I know you will." He raised his eyes, and the intensity of his stare startled me. "But you need to stop looking for that lake. Trust me. Chasing ghosts... it doesn't get you anywhere."

He said it like he knew something about chasing ghosts, and I wanted to listen to him. But the car keys were burning a hole in my pocket, and my mother's ghost was blowing rings in my coffee. The lake was out there, somewhere. A place can't just disappear.

"I'm not kicking you out," he said. "You can visit any time. I hope you do. You know that. But you need to live your life, and your life isn't here." Then, ominously, "or at that lake."

He was wrong about the lake, but I didn't argue with him. We both needed our privacy. That couch was killing my back. And living on my own meant I didn't have to explain myself to anyone.

My own space ended up being the next room over from Thomas at the motel. It wasn't particularly nice or comfortable, but the price was right and I didn't trust Bobby's recovery enough to go farther away.

Moving my things, which consisted of a carry-on suitcase full of hastily chosen clothes and a plastic bag of toothpaste, soap, and other odds and ends, didn't require two people, but Thomas helped anyway. "We need to go shopping," he said, folding my meagre wardrobe into a drawer even though I told him to leave everything in the suitcase. "It looks like you packed this stuff in the dark." He held up a particularly worn-out shirt to make his point, and I snatched it back.

He wanted to look for a real apartment, but I didn't trust myself to do anything that required more than a one-week commitment. I didn't know what to do next, and every other time I'd found myself in this position, I'd made the wrong decision. This time, I wouldn't act until I was *sure*. And the only thing I was sure of, at that point, was the lake house.

I needed to find it.

"Where are you going every day?" Thomas asked, the third time I rolled in after midnight, and I realized I never even bothered to think up a cover story. I just assumed he wouldn't notice, which was stupid, because Thomas noticed everything.

Maybe, I wanted him to ask. The lake was an obsession at that point, and obsessions get lonely.

He lit up like we were kids on a treasure hunt when I told him the truth. "You should have said something before! I have the map." It was just like sentimental Thomas to keep the torn, coffee-stained map that the psychiatrist discarded after our last attempt to find the place. He pulled it out of an old photo album and presented it like a gift.

The last time I saw it, it was in a puddle.

"I'll help you look. It'll be fun."

Thomas always loved to be included, even in lost causes.

We took turns driving. When Thomas drove, he took crazy detours to see interesting sights, stopped at every gas station for snacks, and pulled over more than once to carry a turtle across the road. When I drove, Thomas kept up a constant, entertaining commentary while carefully curating the music and handing me pieces of candy.

It was less efficient than searching alone, but more fun. We made no progress.

After two weeks, he sat me down on the scratchy couch in my room. "We've covered the whole area three times," he said. "And we haven't found it. I think we remember it wrong." He sighed, sad about the situation and about his role as bearer of bad news. "I'm so sorry, man, but I've gotta tell it like it is. It's for your own good. We're going in circles, and we have to stop."

"We," not "you." I appreciated the solidarity.

"I'm bummed, too," he said, "I wish we could've found it. It would have been so cool, to go back…" He trailed off, probably imagining a happy reunion—all four of us at the lake house together, like old times. I knew how much it must hurt him to give a dream like that up.

I wasn't giving up.

I actually expected Thomas to get to this point much sooner. It was a relief, in a way. He was slowing me down. "So don't come with me," I said, crossing the room to the window that overlooked the parking lot. My car was right there. If I left now, I'd have a few good hours of driving before it got dark. "I'm grateful for your help, and I totally understand why you don't want to keep doing it, but I have to try." I wasn't going to stop. Not when I felt so close.

"At least take a break," he begged. "Get out. Meet some people."

Rent an apartment. Buy new shirts. Get a real life. Thomas could be very demanding, in his understated way. I opened my mouth, excuses ready, but he shook his head.

"No. We can keep looking for the place if you really want to, but driving around every day isn't the way to do it. We'll do some research. A whole lake doesn't just disappear." He slapped his thighs decisively. "But in the meantime, I'm going to a party tonight and you're coming with me."

I started to refuse. There was nothing I felt less like doing than drifting around a room, making conversation with strangers.

"No excuses," he said, holding up a hand.

I had so many excuses.

"I'm serious." He cut me off before I could say a word. "Get dressed. Now. You need to go out and be a normal person."

Thomas took me to a party at a lawyer's house, and for the life of me I can't imagine how he got invited. We didn't know anyone, although I recognized a face here and there. Nobody really famous, but a few people well-known enough to cause a buzz of excitement among the "regular" guests. I couldn't quite tell which group we fit into. I accepted a cup of punch that wasn't anywhere near strong enough for small talk, and followed Thomas into the crowd.

A group collected around Thomas, who attracted friends everywhere, and I found a quiet corner to hide in. The party wasn't so bad once I didn't have to talk to anyone. I leaned, breathing in the dusty books in the bookcase, mentally playing "famous or not" as people drifted by—a white-haired lady in a purple fur coat, a kid who couldn't have been more than twenty smoking a pipe. It was soothing—like watching a fish tank.

There was something nice about being in a home, among people, and not in a car examining trees for familiarity.

I watched a man in an expensive suit try, and fail, to impress a group of young women in tight dresses. He was a little too old, a little too short, and nowhere near rich enough to keep their attention, but I rooted for him.

He gestured expansively, almost spilling his drink. I wanted to pull him aside and tell him to stop trying so hard. But there was something about the way he threw every bit of himself into it that kept my attention. He was losing the game, but still the star.

Someone with the bearing of a C-list celebrity came in, trailed by admirers, and the girls left like a school of fish heading to a better food source.

"Well," the unsuccessful Casanova said, opening his arms like a magician about to take a bow. "That was embarrassing." He grinned sheepishly. "Entertaining, though, I hope?"

I was not as well camouflaged as I thought.

The man stuck out his hand. "Brad."

"Nic." I shook his hand and scanned the room for Thomas, who could always be counted on for a rescue. I didn't see him.

"I know who you are. Nicholas Bell. I'm a big fan." Brad grinned, genuine and disarming. "I always wondered why you didn't take off in the US," he said.

I shrugged. I stopped wondering about the limits of my own popularity a long time ago. I wanted to go back to the part where he was a little bit starstruck—I'd forgotten how good it felt to be admired.

"I have some ideas." Brad squinted at me, like a collector evaluating an interesting new object. "Come to my office, we'll talk. Tomorrow." He handed me a business card. "I'm serious," he insisted, when I didn't take it.

"Yeah, I appreciate the offer, but I'm not looking for a manager."

Brad studied me for a minute. "You're looking for something, though, aren't you?" His eyes, bright behind a pair of wire rimmed glasses, looked *into* me in a way that reminded me, oddly, of my mother.

I nodded.

"I think I can help." He gave me another long, probing look. "I don't know why. It's just... a feeling." He raised his glass. "It's probably the punch. But it feels like destiny. Come to my office tomorrow. You don't have anywhere else to be."

"How do you know that?" I asked, offended.

"You're at this party, aren't you?" He waved one hand in a circle over his head, as if our surroundings spoke for themselves. Another group of giggling young women spilled through the door, and he leaned toward them as if pulled. "I have to go. But I'll see you tomorrow."

"I didn't say I'd come," I reminded him.

"You didn't have to. Destiny, remember?" He raised his glass again, in a one-sided toast, and headed for the women.

"Back on the trail?" Thomas asked, wearily, when he caught me on my way out the next morning. I said yes, even though it disappointed him, because telling him the truth would have gotten his hopes up. But I went to Brad's office, instead.

I couldn't help it. My mother's ghost would never forgive me if I walked away from someone who offered "destiny."

Brad overflowed with ideas, and he shared them over coffee, then lunch, then drinks at the bar on the ground floor of his office building. He dragged me on a double-date with two of the girls from the party—single at fifty, he was searching for true love with teenage optimism—and even though it was a disaster, I didn't regret going. Brad's cringeworthy karaoke performance might have chased the girls off, but it made me laugh harder than I'd laughed in years.

After a few weeks, Brad convinced me to invite Thomas to his office "just to talk." But, of course, it was more than that. Brad presented his ideas. Thomas loved them. I stood near the door, a spectator in my own life. Coat on. Feet shuffling. But god, did I wish I could make myself sit down.

By the time I was pretty sure Brad couldn't help me, we were friends, and Thomas's hopes were up—I didn't have the heart to let either one of them down.

"Just give me a chance," Brad said. "You're too talented not to do *something*. And, from a purely practical perspective, the money's not going to last forever. I can help."

I only wanted two things at that point—to find the lake house, an obsession that had grown beyond all logic, and to somehow make up for how crappy I'd been to Thomas, James, and Ben. Brad couldn't help me with the first thing, but there was a small chance he could help me with the second.

"Give me six months," he proposed. "I'm not even asking for a year."

I wanted to ask Brad why he'd waste his time on a reluctant has-been like me, but I didn't. Based on the lack of traffic in and out of his office, I thought I might be the best he could do, and I didn't want to make him admit it. "Fine," I agreed. "But I'm not promising anything."

"You promise to seriously consider whatever I propose?"

"Sure, I guess. But I still might not do any of it."

"Fair enough. It's really all anyone can promise." We shook hands, and it didn't feel like as much of a mistake as I expected it to. *Even if it is a mistake,* I told myself, *it's just six months. How much damage can he do?*

James and Ben flew back to sign the papers. Thomas bounced, too excited to contain his energy. James insisted on a group photo—proof that it happened, I thought, more than a souvenir. Ben drummed the table, his eyes darting to me, asking, silently, if I meant it.

I don't know if I did. But everyone else in that room was so happy that I thought I might finally be doing something right. I wasn't sure, but they were. We were moving forward, together, and maybe that was what I needed.

26

CHARLOTTE

David's voice echoed in my ears as I fled the hospital. *If you're ever in trouble, go to Sky Lake.*

Maybe I would have tried, if Damia still had the map. But the map was gone. And failing to find Sky Lake would only prove the magic was gone, too—my ties to home cut for good.

I couldn't face that. It was easier to stay away, and keep the possibility.

I told the driver that I wanted to go to a hotel as far away as possible. I could feel the exhaustion in my eyes and the sharpness of my ribs even though I avoided my own reflection, and I half expected him to send me back to my bed. I clearly belonged there. But, unlike most ERC refugees, I still had a valid identity—Charlotte London, superstar—and the driver didn't argue with my credit card.

"I'll go out the back way," he said. "Avoid the press."

I could have kissed him, even though I know he was only after a good tip.

I wanted distance, but my body refused to cooperate. Less than an hour from the hospital, it started fighting. My muscles braced against every bump and turn. The smell of the vanilla air freshener hanging from the rearview mirror made me so queasy that I wanted to grab it and throw it out the window. Pain burned through my shoulder and up the side of my neck.

The car felt like a boat in a choppy sea. I hugged myself, skin clammy, teeth chattering in the ice-cold air conditioning. I needed to stop and lie still.

"Just leave me at the next place," I choked. I didn't care where I ended up, as long as I didn't have to move once I got there.

My phone rang constantly during those first few days. Janey—shrill and worried. Damia—understanding and full of apologies. The doctors—cold and clinical and interested only in my body, because I was still a medical mystery and they wanted to solve me. I listened to their voicemails from the safety of a king-sized bed just as white and clean as the one at the hospital, but soft. Comfortable. A bed to sink into and disappear.

They were right—I wasn't well enough to be on my own. In the hospital, I had clean air, clean water, nutritionally balanced food at regular intervals and people to make sure I ate it. Out in the world, I had to take care of myself, and there was no reason to think I'd be any good at it, under the circumstances.

I'd never had to do it before.

But nothing they said could make me go back.

I'd been Johnathan's prisoner—and his puzzle—for more than a decade. I had no intention of sticking around to be someone else's.

"I'm in a nice hotel," I argued, when Janey tried, for the third time in one day, to persuade me to return. "It's just like a hospital room, with better food and a nicer view." I was at the window, the city so far below that the cars looked like bright plastic toys. "I didn't even go far—I can be back in the hospital in less than an hour. Or at a different hospital even faster than that."

I did not tell Janey that I went as far as I physically could, and would be across the country if my broken body had been able to tolerate the ride. Or that I hadn't eaten anything more substantial than toast in days.

"That's not the point. No one is *monitoring* you." She was practically growling—a mother who has lost control over her unruly teenager but not accepted it yet.

Exactly, I wanted to say. *That's why I like it here.* I was anonymous in the hotel. I didn't have to put on a happy face, because the press hadn't found me yet and the room service guy didn't care how I felt as long as I gave him a decent tip. But I remembered how Janey massaged lavender oil into my feet every day for months, and swallowed my annoyance.

"What happens if you have a relapse and you're all alone?" she asked.

I don't care, I thought, but I knew better than to say it. "I feel great," I lied. "No pain at all. But I promise to report anything worse than a minor headache, ok?"

The truth would only wind her up. And I didn't have the energy—or will—to untangle her feelings.

I never told anyone when the pain came back. They would have tied me to a bed, and I wouldn't go through that again. I'd get better, or I wouldn't, and if I sat down and made a pro/con list at that point, the columns would have been pretty even.

But the pain *did* come back. I'd fall asleep feeling achy, and wake up with screams tearing through me like a fire. I'd start the day feeling almost normal, and the pain would prod me back to bed with its pointy fingers by noon. One second, I could stand up in the shower. The next, I was huddled on the floor, water going cold, no idea when I'd be released.

The pain still owned me, and anything could set it off—heat, cold, food, dreams. I had no control over my own body.

I can't live like this, I thought, every time it reduced my word to a pulsing red tunnel, but I *could* live like that. My body could, at least. And I couldn't kill myself, no matter how sweetly my balcony called. Too many people would feel responsible.

At first, I tried to escape from it—back to Sky Lake, for a few minutes of relief. But I couldn't. Even the false Sky Lake was closed to me. Nicolas Bell's voice brought me comfort, distraction, and the occasional whiff of roses, but didn't pull me out of my body anymore.

I tried to shut the pain out myself. I closed my eyes and slowed my breathing. Crossed my arms over my chest and imagined myself floating, or flying, or underground. Anywhere except inside my body. But the pain came with me, every time.

With no other options, the pain and I got to know each other. I observed its patterns, searching for meaning as it took me apart. Anything—a nightmare, a knock on the door, a hangnail—could trigger it. In the hospital, these things were prevented and managed. Outside the hospital, where stress came without warning, it brought me to my knees several times a day.

A bite of spicy food left me in agony for an entire night. A tense conversation took my breath for so long that I almost passed out. Once, in an especially self-destructive moment, I read the comments under an article about my escape and spent the next two days in bed, listening to old Light/Black albums while bruises bloomed all over my body. Not even Nicolas Bell could cut through it—compared to those venomous strangers, his beautiful voice felt small and far away. Not meant for me at all.

It was unbearable.

I pushed chairs in front of the balcony door. And then I pushed them away, because what was the point of keeping myself alive?

I was on the edge again. Ready to tip. And then, I had a breakthrough.

The pain controlled me. But it still followed *rules.*

Physical discomfort, like hunger or exhaustion, caused pain in my hip and shoulder, where the pellets went in. Pain from an emotional cause, like fear, radiated out from my chest. Both left bruises that hurt for days, proving that the whole thing wasn't in my head, and that's what I seized on. If it was real, then it was something I could beat. I just had to figure out what made it tick. Find the weak spot.

And I found it, after a while.

The first time I experienced a stress, it hurt a lot. The next time, it hurt less. After a while, it didn't hurt at all.

I could play this game, and I could win.

I started a list. First, I listed things that didn't hurt anymore, like too much caffeine, very hot showers, and the hotel fire alarm. I checked them off, which felt satisfying. I added things I hadn't experienced yet—fear, physical exertion, a papercut.

I rented horror movies to make myself afraid, and sad ones to make myself cry. I went to the hotel gym and walked, then ran, on a treadmill until I could go a mile without pain, then two miles, then three. I made myself stay up all night. I fasted for half a day, a full day, two full days. Every miserable second was a triumph, because it was slightly less miserable than the one before it.

I put aspirational items on the list—rollercoaster, fender-bender, broken heart. *Someday.* It was the closest I came to thinking about my future.

My life expanded, an inch at a time. Mornings on the treadmill became sessions with a personal trainer who taught me a hundred different ways to hit the big punching bag in the corner of the gym. He encouraged me to do yoga, which I hated but grudgingly embraced as my weak, tense muscles strengthened and relaxed.

Movies turned into an escape—it was a relief to lose myself inside other people's stories. As my head got better, I devoured books—cheesy romance novels, suspenseful mysteries, thick, immersive historical fiction.

Anything to win a few hours of distraction. The list itself, with its growing column of check marks, felt like an accomplishment.

But I knew real life would be harder and more unpredictable than any experiment I ran in my hotel room. I could put a book down any time. The treadmill had a big red STOP button. Punching bags don't punch back.

I had to consider the possibility that after everything, I'd still never be well enough for the world.

I wouldn't admit that fear to anyone, but Janey must have sensed it, because at some point she stopped saying I needed to go back to the hospital and started telling me to get out of bed and do something.

She called every day, trying to lure me into her empty spare room. "It's your room," she'd say. "I decorated it specifically for you." Trust Janey to try to make things better with a floral comforter and nice curtains. "You can't stay in a hotel forever," she would scold, but I could—Charlie London's money never went directly to ERC, so the shutdown didn't affect my access to it—I could live in the hotel as long as I wanted to.

More importantly, I couldn't live with Janey. Just thinking about how she betrayed me felt like an explosion inside my battered body. I avoided as many of her calls as I could. I begged her not to visit. I cut myself off from her just like I cut myself off from Damia. I had to—it hurt too much to face them.

But Janey wasn't entirely wrong. It was clear, by then, that I wasn't going to die. Which meant I needed to figure out what living looked like.

I measured my life in firsts. First time walking out of the hotel by myself. First time ordering coffee by myself. First time eating at a restaurant by myself. First time picking out a pair of jeans and buying them for myself.

It was easier than I expected it to be. For all anyone knew, Charlie London was still in that hospital. No one was looking for her. And I wasn't Charlie London anymore, with her piercing eyes and long red hair.

My hair was short, tucked into a cap more often than not. My eyes were brown. I didn't sparkle unless I chose to, and I didn't. It wasn't safe.

Charlie London couldn't go anywhere without attracting a screaming mob, but I was invisible. Free. I could go anywhere. Do anything.

And yet, I didn't.

It was scary, living inside a body that might betray me at any moment. I never walked too far from the hotel, or stayed out long. I worried about loud noises, extreme temperatures, conversations. Anything new had the potential to light a fuse under the pain, and I lived in fear of becoming helpless in public. So, I spent a lot of time in my room. Thinking. Or trying not to.

But my voice wouldn't let me rest. It kicked and turned and swelled against my ribs. A baby waiting to be born. A monster ready to be unleashed. Mine. Or Charlie's. Or Johnathan Everett's, since he was the one who made Charlie London.

My hands woke me up in the night, twitching with lyrics, and my lips formed around them even though I refused to write them down. But the lingering pain in my throat made me afraid to sing. I couldn't bear to hear my ruined voice any more than I could bear to drive to Sky Lake and find nothing but roads going nowhere through the forest.

My voice was Charlie's, I decided, and I wasn't Charlie anymore. No one wanted to hear from me. It was safer to stay in my hotel room, avoiding any conversation more complicated than a food order.

I might have continued that way forever if not for the hearing.

The hearings began as a chaotic attempt to sort victims from villains in the aftermath of the ERC shutdown. They continued as a televised spectacle. People were glued to them, but the organizers didn't have any more major players to drag in by the time I woke up. Ratings were dropping, they needed someone big, and I was the only big someone left. It was only a matter of time.

Mallory called personally to tell me my number was up. "It won't be a public session," she said, and I knew how hard she must have fought for that concession. "But it will be recorded and I'm sure clips will be everywhere by the end of the day. You won't be in hiding anymore. I'm so sorry. I tried to hold them off."

I think she expected me to argue about it, but I didn't feel entitled to special treatment. I owed my testimony as much as—maybe more than—anyone else. I only worried about my body. I hadn't asked it to do anything that stressful, and I didn't like the idea of doing the experiment in front of strangers. But I didn't have a choice.

"I understand," I said, and asked for the time and place. I didn't let myself think about the unfriendly people who would sit around the table judging me, or the crowd that would gather outside. When you have no control over your own life, you get good at living in the moment.

"You can bring someone—an attorney if you have one?—to advocate for you. They only have four hours, so wasting time will work to your advantage."

I couldn't imagine what Mallory traded for a four-hour time limit. They must have wanted to keep me for days.

"Should I let Janey know?" she asked, hopefully.

Mallory felt responsible for me, and she wanted to hand that responsibility over to Janey. I didn't blame her. But Janey already went through her own three days of testimony at a public hearing. She paid her dues. And, selfishly, I didn't want to manage her feelings on top of my own. I asked Mallory not to tell anyone. "I'll be fine," I promised.

"You'll bring someone, though, won't you? I could refer you to an attorney."

I promised I wouldn't go alone, and it was true. I was never really alone, because I always had Charlie.

I hadn't called on Charlie since *before*, and I worried that she might refuse to come out after lying dormant for so long. When the mirror reflected my own eyes back at me, even after I put Charlie's contacts in, pain flared in my throat. I thought *this is going to be a disaster.* But I was due at the hearing at nine, whether or not Charlie decided to join me.

My nerves calmed slightly when I didn't find a crowd outside the building. Mallory promised no publicity, but I still expected a leak, and the empty sidewalk seemed like a good omen. As long as I kept my head down, no one would pay any attention to me.

I squared my shoulders and pushed through a revolving door, fighting the panic that tried to grab me in the enclosed space—the hospital restraints left me with a persistent fear of being trapped. I hugged my purse against my belly and walked slowly to the elevator, praying the long ride up to the thirtieth floor wouldn't start my head spinning.

A solemn woman in a black suit took my coat and led me to a conference room. I followed two steps behind, taking in my surroundings with a level of interest they probably didn't deserve. Everything felt big and bright and new to me then, even the fake marble hallways and glass walled offices of a law firm.

In the background, I evaluated myself. My legs felt weak, but strong enough to keep up. My head hurt, but no more than usual. My stomach was unsettled, but I hadn't eaten anything, so that might not be a symptom at all. I was going to be *fine.*

You don't know that, the pain whispered, and it was right—I never knew. But I only had to get through four hours. After that, I could collapse.

We stopped outside a conference room full of serious people with notebooks and paper cups of coffee. Their conversation broke apart as I entered. The woman led me to my chair and offered me coffee—it reminded me so much of my first meeting with Johnathan's team that it felt like falling back in time. I was still Grace, then, and I hoped the memory wouldn't make it harder to become Charlie.

I needed Charlie, if I was going to get through this. I wrapped my hands around the hot paper cup and prayed.

"Ms. London," the lawyer in charge of the hearing said, his voice falling like I'd done something disappointing already. "Are you ready to get started?"

Sun glared through big windows, setting off fireworks in my eyes. I closed them, wondering if Charlie London was still a big enough star to get away with sunglasses indoors.

"Ms. London?" the lawyer prompted.

I was not ready, but that didn't seem like an acceptable answer, so I nodded.

"Verbally, please, so the court reporter can record your response."

"Yes," I lied. "I'm ready." But inside, I was still praying for Charlie. Summoning her. And she wasn't answering. My palms were sweaty, sliding against the cup. I could feel the first warning twinges of pain in my hip. I knew I looked like someone with something to hide.

Charlie materialized at the last possible second, like a train speeding through a tunnel, and the cold, breathless rush of her took me by surprise. There she was, reflected in the window with her big smile and good posture and confident hands that rested peacefully on the table until a point required a graceful wave or a big gesture.

Charlie, who always knew how to look and what to say.

Before my body had time to fully relax into its alter ego, the committee demanded everything I knew about Johnathan Everett. It seemed unnecessary—he was in custody and whoever controlled the hearings presumably had access to him. But they wanted my perspective, and when I spoke in generalities, they asked for more.

They wanted to know what motivated him. What he cared about. What he loved and hated and who he trusted and who he didn't. They asked me to tell them his favorite foods and books and movies and places—all the things you can't really force a person to be honest about. They asked me how his private persona differed from his public one.

And I sat there, somewhere underneath Charlie, holding the information tight because it wasn't their business.

It belonged to *me*.

I remembered Damia, telling me how conflicted she felt as she prepared to betray him. I wished I had explored my feelings with her, instead of facing them alone in the middle of an interrogation. But it was too late for that. They wanted to know everything.

Johnathan trusted Damia. And Chris. And maybe me. He loved chocolate. Fast food hamburgers. Good wine. In private, he was fully present in a way I had never experienced with anyone else. He cared about knowledge, for its own sake.

The pain in my hip spread, filling my pelvis with fire.

Could they possibly want to know all that?

"It's natural to feel misplaced loyalty," a woman with a tight white crown of curls said, leaning toward me. "But we need to know everything. Something that seems insignificant to you could be important."

She had intelligent eyes. A sympathetic smile. Hands that might have reached for mine, in a less formal environment. She really wanted to *know*. And the words were bubbling up, too much for my body to hold in the condition I was in. It would be a relief, I thought, to share them.

So, I told them about the butterflies.

I described the fear and excitement of visiting the basements that first time, when I was a child and Johnathan an all-powerful monster. *Are you afraid to follow me into the basement*, he asked, eyes dancing with mischief, and I thought *this can't be the same man who made the lady in the white room kill herself.* I described his unexpected enthusiasm for bomb shelters and cauliflower ice cream and my education, which he devoted himself to although he gained nothing from it. I painted the best picture I could of all those colorful wings in the air, and Johnathan next to me, awestruck.

In the end, I don't think I succeeded. I couldn't. You had to be there.

And they didn't want to be there. I heard it—the cold, metallic slam of every mind in the room closing against me.

They asked for the truth, but they didn't mean it. They only wanted the monster. I was alone with my contradictions.

I made eye contact with the white-haired woman, desperate for someone to understand. But she was a wall, just like the others. "You know he never told you anything that wasn't a manipulation," she said. There was pity in her voice, and I hated it, but the chill in the room made me nervous. I wasn't in charge here. They were. Charlie had nothing going for her but charm. "He only ever sought to control you."

I nodded even though I didn't—and still don't—think it was that simple.

And then Charlie took charge, moving the conversation into safer territory with her usual grace.

The group softened as Charlie described the most sympathetic version of my life. At one point, the attorney stopped me and clarified, for the record, that I was only eleven years old when I entered ERC. Whatever culpability they assigned to me before the interview evaporated as Charlie spun her tale. She was a beautiful, manipulative spider.

By the end of my four hours, I felt like a rag doll, but they weren't done with me. "Thank you, Ms. London," the attorney said as I stood to leave. He shook my hand with both of his. "We appreciate your time today, and we all have deep admiration for what you did. You are a hero."

I allowed the handshake to go on too long while someone snapped photo after photo. I didn't like being called a hero, but I'd read enough internet comments to know that I liked the alternatives a lot less. And even if I didn't, I had no energy left for argument. I was achy and feverish and seeing double.

Freed from the serious business of questioning me, everyone lined up for pictures. Even the assistant who delivered me to the conference room came back and lurked shyly in the doorway until I waved her over. It was strange to be *that* Charlie London again. The one people adored for no reason. I posed, calibrating my smiles to match the occasion, floating a few feet outside my miserable body.

"What's next for you?" the lawyer asked as he walked me out to the waiting car. "You must be eager to make up for lost time."

For ten terrible seconds I groped for an answer. Nothing was next. I didn't feel eager about anything. I couldn't imagine what would make up for the time I lost. But Charlie rushed in like a parent grabbing a toddler who's about to run into traffic. She sparkled mysteriously through my eyes. "I guess we'll just have to see."

The perfect answer. All magic, no information.

I smiled at the lawyer and he glowed back, years melting from his face under the full force of Charlie's uncomplicated charm. He wished me luck, and I thanked him, even though I was pretty sure I'd already used all my luck up.

I went back to the hotel and slept for fifteen hours straight, sprawled on top of the comforter because I didn't have the energy to crawl underneath it.

Janey didn't take the news well.

"You didn't even call!" she shouted, fists clenched like a baby on the verge of a tantrum outside my door the next day. It reminded me of our early days at ERC, when she'd show up at my room full of drama. "What is wrong with you?" she asked. "I wouldn't mind if it was just me you're keeping out of the loop, but you didn't call anyone. A lawyer, even! Or your publicist! You don't just go waltzing into an interrogation alone. They could have put you in *jail.*"

"Jail? Geez, Janey, I thought I was a hero, is there something you're not telling me?" I backed up, allowing her to plow into my room. I looked down at myself, regretting the pajamas I was still wearing at one in the afternoon. Janey would have opinions about that.

She rolled her eyes. "Fine, not jail. But do you have any idea how much damage you could have done to your reputation? Those hearings have *ruined* people."

I almost laughed. "Do you mean Charlie's reputation?" The bitterness in my voice startled me. Charlie got me through that hearing—I owed her. But I hated depending on her.

Janey's lips pinched but she didn't take the bait. "You can't keep living like this." She dropped her purse on my unmade bed and faced me like a soldier ready for battle. "Hiding in this room. Avoiding everyone who cares about you. If you can come out for the hearing, all by yourself, you're well enough to start moving forward."

"Moving forward?" I asked. "Where, exactly, should I be going?"

My bitterness grew into anger as we faced off. Janey reveled in her role as Keeper of the Files, handing out yellow folders from the same desk she'd been working at since she was a kid. She'd been complicit in everything Johnathan did, and part of me thought she'd be just as happy if we were all still doing it. She had no right to tell me to move forward, while she was still at that desk.

She glared at the floor. The toe of one shoe—a pink high heeled sandal that reminded me of Candy—poked the pattern on the rug like the solution to all my problems hid underneath it.

"I'm serious. What do you think I should do? Come back to the ERC building and work at the desk next to yours? Go out and be Charlie London?"

Janey winced. "I wouldn't ask you to come back there," she said, quietly.

"So, it's Charlie, then, huh?" I spun away from Janey, toward the window, where I could watch the matchbox cars drive by instead of staring holes into Janey. "I'm not sure you've noticed, but she's an imaginary person. Johnathan made her. She's not me." I sounded like a child, even to myself, but my identity crisis was, in some respects, harder to cope with than the pain. At least the pain didn't expect me to get up and get dressed and do something with my life.

"You made Charlie London," Janey said, sliding in next to me at the window. "Not Johnathan."

She leaned against me. Strawberries and bubble gum and the sticky, stinging smell of hairspray. Like old times.

Old times. When I was a prisoner, and she was helping Johnathan keep me that way. "Don't give me that empowerment bullshit," I snapped. "Johnathan named me. Decided what color my eyes would be. Changed every word I wrote." I could feel Charlie in my sulky expression, in the way I flounced to the bed and threw myself down. I had been Charlie for so long that I couldn't pry her mannerisms apart from my own, which made the situation even more depressing.

She wasn't real, and I wasn't real, either.

"Do you have any idea how lucky you are?" Janey asked. She sounded sad, but I still took it as an accusation. "How lucky we both are? We came out with options. You, more than anyone. Some people had nothing." Her voice broke. "The stories I see every day in those files…" she said, eyes swimming with tears, "would make you grateful for all this."

Her tears made me uncomfortable, but Charlie forced me to look her in the eye. Make her feel seen, even though I didn't want to see her. "I guess the grass is always greener," I said, finally. "I'm sure a lot of people think they'd like to be Charlie London. They can have her, for all I care."

Janey blinked and swallowed hard. "Fine. Whatever. Feel sorry for yourself. I can't make you feel different… Maybe you can't, either. But *do something.* You have a great team. They can get you into the recording studio or schedule some interviews or book you a show. Something to get you back out there. *You*, not Charlie."

Me, not Charlie. Like anybody wanted me. Pain throbbed around my heart.

"You don't think it'll make you feel better, but it will," she said.

Janey made it sound so simple. Make a list. Pick something. Put one foot in front of the other. She didn't understand.

"You loved music before you ever met Johnathan Everett," she said. "Your talent and work and voice made Charlie London. And they can make something else, if that's what you want. But you have to take a step. It doesn't have to be a big step. But you need to *start*. Sing something. Write something. Schedule something."

I couldn't imagine writing anything new and I never wanted to sing another Charlie London song as long as I lived, but Janey still gave me a good idea.

All those people—the ones Johnathan hired, who worked for him, and the ones they hired, who technically worked for me but were perfectly happy not to notice all the things that were wrong with my life—were still exactly where I left them. On my payroll. Absorbing my money.

I didn't know how to move forward, but I could stop *them* with the click of a button. I could sever the last strings holding me to ERC.

The realization flowed down like a gift from the gods, cool and soothing. And then, when I thought it was over, hot and alive with energy.

I couldn't even find the pain underneath it.

"You're right," I said, feeling almost joyful. My legs were strong, my head clear. My body, a burden for so long, practically floated—finally, I'd found something I could *do*. Something to check off in the *real world*. "Exactly right, actually." Purpose straightened my slumped shoulders. "I'll get in touch with my team this afternoon."

Janey hugged me tight and made me promise to call her later. "You won't regret this," she promised, squeezing, and I squeezed her back, agreeing completely.

As soon as she left, I made the call. Pressed the button.

Fired every last one of them.

I glowed with triumph, even though I knew I'd just set myself adrift. It was the first thing in years that felt *right*.

27

CHARLOTTE

I don't know what I thought would happen after I smashed what was left of Charlie London's life into little pieces. But Fate was coming for me, and it found me in the coffee shop across from the hotel the very next morning. I was sipping a latte, and Fate, in the form of a tall, skinny young man at the next table, was trying to talk a client out of a paying project that would, in his words, *suck out her soul.*

I didn't know I was in one of those moments, when life goes one way instead of the other. But people-watching—the real-life version of a movie—was one of my few pleasures, and I became engrossed in their scene.

He gave it everything he had. The girl didn't take his advice. I finished two cups of coffee, lost in the drama. When the girl started to cry, I casually moved to another seat for a better view.

The man hunched, too tall for the small table. His elbows, knees, and oversized hands competed for control of the space. I felt jittery from the coffee—a nagging voice reminded me that caffeine could set the pain off, and I should go back to my room—but I needed to see the end of the story.

The man patted his pockets for a tissue and held it out awkwardly. He mumbled an apology, eyes darting around, cheeks reddening. He was not accustomed to making women cry. The girl blotted her eyes so gracefully that I questioned the authenticity of the tears. "Thank you, Henry," she said, in a breathy, practiced voice.

Henry fussed, digging for more tissues before running to the counter to get a cup of water and some napkins. He wore a wrinkled pinstriped suit. His yellow socks, on full view due to his too-short pants, were printed with smiling green frogs. I found myself smiling back at them—a real smile, that I felt in my eyes.

The girl recovered, thanked Henry for his concern, told him she didn't think he was the right fit for her anymore, and swished out of the coffee shop, stopping at the door to see how many heads turned to follow her. I didn't like her, but I admired her dramatic exit.

Back at the table, Henry rested his chin in his hands. He clearly wanted what was best for this girl, even if it cost him money, and she didn't appreciate it. She didn't know how good she had it. No one ever encouraged me to do anything that wasn't good for their own bottom line.

Sympathy gripped me—for Henry, but also for the girl I used to be. The one no one looked out for. I was half the age of the woman who just swept out of the coffee shop when I became Charlotte London.

I should have had a Henry.

My chest hurt, and I braced myself. But the pain faded. Normal. *Healthy.* I held my breath, waiting for it to come back.

At the next table, Henry sighed. He looked so sad. So *deflated.* Like nothing he did was ever going to get him where he wanted to go. I knew that feeling, and it made me restless. I wanted to help.

Bad idea, the pain warned. It was right. I should go back to the hotel, before I passed out and humiliated myself. Henry was none of my business. But then he shifted, and I got another glimpse of the frogs. At the very least, he was harmless. And the pain didn't feel like it was coming back.

Henry pulled out his phone, started to type something, and pushed it away in frustration. I wondered who he wanted to reach out to, and why he decided not to. *Maybe,* I thought, *Henry doesn't have anyone looking out for him, either.* He slumped a little lower.

I couldn't just walk away, like his client did.

You can walk away, the pain said. *That is exactly the thing to do in this situation.*

I pushed it down. I wasn't trying to run a marathon. I got up and walked around my table. To his table. Without a plan.

"Hello," I said, and regretted my bravery immediately. I did not start conversations with strangers in coffee shops.

Henry looked up, blotchy and sniffling but trying to hide it.

Charlie hung back. Laughing, probably, at the mess I was in. Henry was staring up at me. I had to say something. "Can I sit here?" I asked, lamely. There were plenty of extra tables, but Henry was too polite to say no, and I took the chair across from him. "I overheard some of that. You were her manager? Agent?"

"Manager." He squinted and tipped his head to one side, like he almost recognized me, and I slipped my sunglasses on. "I mean, I'm trying to be one," he said. "Not exactly killing it, as I'm sure you noticed." He gestured at the door the girl just walked out of. "She was my only client."

"She didn't deserve you," I said, and another pang of sympathy came and went. How different my life would have been if I had a Henry, instead of Johnathan Everett.

He rubbed his face aggressively. "I screw everything up. I don't know how to talk to people..." He was fighting tears and out of tissues because he gave them all to the girl. "I'm basically out of business. I won't be able to pay my part of the office rent." He sighed so deeply that the petals of the fake daisies on the table trembled.

I tried to imagine anyone who ever worked for me risking their ability to pay rent for my sake, and couldn't find a single one. Henry sacrificed himself for that entitled brat. And I could fix it, with nothing more than my signature.

A rush of excitement tingled through me, followed by that nagging voice again. *What do you think you're doing?*

I stomped it down. I was doing something good, for once.

"I'm sorry," he said. "I shouldn't dump all this on you. Can I buy you a coffee? To make up for it?"

I fiddled with my sunglasses, considering. I wanted to help Henry. And Charlie *could* help him. I took a deep breath and ripped the glasses off fast, before the pain could whisper another warning. I prayed he wouldn't make a scene.

Henry's eyes widened as I revealed mine.

"Are you...?" he asked.

My heart stuttered, the way it used to in the hospital, and I thought *mistake mistake mistake.* But it was done. He recognized me. "Yes," I said, feeling the weight of the admission in my stomach. "Charlotte London." *No going back now.* I forced her confidence into my voice. "But don't say it too loud, or we'll be mobbed."

My new friend didn't know what to do with this information. Maybe, he didn't believe me. I was too thin. My eyes were the wrong color. My hair hadn't grown out yet. I felt self-conscious—like a not-very-good impersonator.

Henry just sat there, looking like he had a mouthful of live goldfish.

"And you are?" I asked, finally.

"Oh! Sorry." He offered his hand. It was cold and damp. "I'm Henry."

"Nice to meet you, Henry." I looked him in the eye like Charlie would. Charlie, who had no secrets because she lived an imaginary life. "How old are you?"

"Twenty-two." He winced, like he realized a second too late that he should have added a few years.

I tried to remember being twenty-two. The first time, when I was actually seventeen, and the second time, when I was twenty-two but Charlie was twenty-seven. *Young.* But Henry was honest. It radiated off him. He could be trusted. I pulled a fabric daisy out of the vase on the table and spun it between my fingers. Hiring Henry was no more impulsive than firing everyone else. And it was *good*.

I jabbed the daisy back into the vase decisively. "I fired everyone who works for me," I said. "Yesterday. There were a lot of them and they were in charge of complicated things and I don't have any idea how to sort it out."

Henry's eyes widened again, turning him into a cartoon. He clearly didn't know how to sort it out, either. "Everyone?" he squeaked, openly horrified.

"Yes. Everyone." I paused, hoping to see a spark of interest, but Henry kept staring at me like I was on fire. *Maybe he doesn't want to work with me*, I thought, and that little ache flitted through my chest like a cloud. "It was impulsive. Not like me at all. But there were… circumstances. Anyway, I'd like to hire you. Today. Right now, if possible."

Equally impulsive. But I couldn't be any worse off with Henry than I was with the vampires who worked with me before.

"You fired everyone?" he asked again, voice rising an octave. His reaction was making me nervous—how dire was my situation? Maybe I really *did* need a Henry. And I couldn't imagine going out into the world and looking for one.

"Everyone," I confirmed.

"I don't know… That sounds like… maybe you need someone… I'm not very…"

"I need your help," I said, and watched goodness fight with fear, right there on his face.

Henry was a helper. Goodness won. It always did, with Henry, whether I wanted it to or not.

Henry was not the kind of person who carried contracts on the off chance that a big star might materialize in a coffee shop and demand to hire him on the spot. "I can give you the address of the office," he said. "Or you can just come with me? My car's outside. I mean, you don't have to get in my car, obviously you don't know me and…"

"Thank you." I led the way out of the coffee shop, telling myself that I couldn't be making my situation any worse. "A ride would be great."

Henry pushed a stack of mail off the passenger seat and apologized for the mess. A sweatshirt, a toppled stack of books, and a laptop that looked like it had been dropped a few times littered the back seat. "I'm really not this disorganized," he said, as papers blew around us, contradicting him.

A playlist composed entirely of showtunes blared from the speakers. "I can change that," he offered, when he realized what we were listening to, but I liked the way the music shifted from one world to another, the stories impossible to follow.

I liked Henry. I felt, for the first time since I woke up, like it might actually be safe to move forward a little.

We parked at a building with a security desk downstairs and a huge bank of elevators. Henry pushed the button over and over until one stopped, and then ushered me in ahead of him. As we went up, he proudly rattled off a list of the firms on each floor, and I couldn't help remembering the first time Johnathan took me to the basement. Except that we were going up today, not down. And Henry's pride felt innocent and humble—he was just proud to be in this space.

The reception area in Henry's suite, which he shared with a partner, had white rugs and a leather couch and an enormous piece of abstract art on one wall. Fancier than I expected, which made me feel both better and worse about my decision. Maybe Henry could handle this mess. And maybe I was wrong to trust him. I caught a glimpse of myself in a mirror—skinny, worried, tired. What was I doing?

"Brad!" Henry called, as we walked in, and I tried to look like the prize he thought I was. But my hip was starting to hurt, and I could feel a headache brewing behind my right eye. "Brad, I want you to meet someone."

Brad burst out of his office, full of energy. He was a foot shorter than Henry, in a suit that must have been tailored for his fit, compact body. He wore wire rimmed glasses and expensive shoes and swept his hair into a stylish shape with a little too much product. A streak of gray hinted at the experience Henry lacked, but kind eyes framed by laugh lines told me that he, also, could be trusted. Relief flowed through me, but it didn't do anything for my hip. I needed to sit down.

"This is Charlie London!"

Brad gave me a long, critical look, like Henry brought imposters home sometimes and they couldn't be too careful.

"She fired everyone who works for her and she needs our help."

She needs our help. Not *she's going to hire us* or *get a contract quick before she comes to her senses.* To Henry, all that mattered is that I needed help.

I offered Brad the best smile I could manage. "I know I don't look like… myself," I said. "I haven't been out in public much, since…" The sentence abandoned me. I didn't have the words to talk about what I'd been through.

Brad nodded slowly, assessing me, and then reached for my hand. He held it gently in both of his. Not squeezing or shaking. Careful. My initial instinct—to pull away, or yank Charlie to the surface—faded. "We can sort that out," he said, as if similar requests came in every day. "Henry will have it under control by the end of the week."

Henry gulped audibly.

"I'll help," Brad added, and asked for the name and number of the person I called to fire everyone. "I'll start there," he announced, confidently. "And you will sit down and rest while Henry makes tea."

Henry looked relieved, then half-heartedly offered to make the call. "You leave that to me," Brad said. "Take care of our guest." I swallowed a laugh. Boy, would we both have been in trouble if there was no Brad in this office.

Twenty minutes later, I was curled up on the worn-out brown sofa in Henry's decidedly less chic office, enjoying a cup of cloyingly sweet apple-cinnamon tea while Henry asked about my hopes and dreams. "If you could be doing anything a year from now, what would you choose?"

Thinking that far ahead—a full year—made me feel panicky and sick, but I took slow breaths and pretended to consider his question.

"Stop that," Brad ordered, when he joined us. "She's not some 16-year-old who wants to be a big star. She's already made it. No interview questions."

I shot Brad a grateful look, because I didn't have an answer. But I loved Henry for asking. I wished someone bothered asking when I *was* sixteen.

"Everything's in order," Brad told me, calm and reassuring in spite of the mess I handed to him. "Your mail will come here from now on, and we'll get you set up with everything you need. We'll need to get some signatures from you later this week, but I can send a courier to you if that's better?"

"No," I said, surprising myself. My hip hurt and my head hurt and it would definitely be easier to sign papers from my hotel bed and let Brad and Henry take care of everything. But when I imagined that, I felt like I was losing something. "I think I'd like to come in, if it's ok with you."

Even then, Henry and Brad felt like home.

I told Henry I hired him because he tried so hard to save that girl.

It was true, in the sense that I never would have noticed him otherwise. But I really hired him because he was young and desperate and not very sure of himself, and I knew he wouldn't make me do anything more with my life than I was already doing.

I needed someone to manage my money and deal with the press. I needed someone to figure out how to get me a driver's license and all the other things a normal almost-thirty-two-year-old woman has. I didn't need—or want—anything more.

I trusted him to take care of my life without insisting that I live it.

But Henry wasn't as satisfied with his limited role as I expected him to be. He backed off when I said no to his suggestions, but he didn't stop suggesting things. And he pushed hard for my friendship, wearing me down one cup of coffee at a time. By the time I realized what he was doing, it was too late to step back without hurting him. And I didn't want to hurt him—I'd already let myself get attached.

Henry's boyfriend, Greg, took me on as a project. I resisted it, at first—I didn't want more people in my life—but he was as persistent as Henry. He dragged me out shopping—"all your clothes are from *before*, you need clothes for *now*." He wouldn't let me get away with quick, simple choices, either. We had to go to three stores. Try things on. Buy accessories. He threw away all my baseball caps.

He made me go see live music, even though I didn't want to. Watching music pour out of other people, while I kept mine balled up in my throat, was hard. Sometimes, it felt like my body would tear itself in two—half running bloody into the street, the other throwing itself on stage. "It's good for you," he'd say, when I couldn't hide my discomfort. "Just because you aren't ready to make music doesn't mean you don't need to hear it."

Greg was a chef, and often called me during off hours to try experimental new menu items. "Another bite," he would say, "and pay attention this time," like I was a bad student and not a friend he was trying to trick into eating a whole meal. Initially, it embarrassed me—we both knew he was the one doing me a favor—but the restlessness that made it hard to sit down for a meal on my own dissolved in the shiny restaurant kitchen. I didn't have any bad memories attached to a place like that. My body got stronger, all by itself, as I ate my way through Greg's menu. I tried everything except his famous chocolate cake, which still reminded me so much of Johnathan that I couldn't swallow it.

I stayed for hours sometimes, washing dishes. Grace and Charlotte and Charlie disappeared in the soapy water, leaving nothing but hands and arms and the endless parade of pots and pans and plates.

Greg and I went on long walks, dipping in and out of shops and noticing interesting places to bring Henry back to. We spent a perfect day going from a hat store (finding him the perfect one) to a used book store (finding me the perfect one) to a custom suit store, armed with Henry's measurements and my credit card. Eventually I wore him down, and we spent several white-knuckled mornings in an empty parking lot and one very long day at the

DMV before I triumphantly handed my brand-new license over to Henry, who got me a terrible deal on my very first car.

Freedom. Except that I still couldn't make myself drive to Sky Lake. I was too afraid. It was the only place I wanted to go, but I didn't think I'd ever get there.

I met with Henry once a week. We'd developed a real friendship—the only one I had that truly felt mutual—and I treasured my time with him. I needed him to help me limp back into the world. He needed me to listen to his worries and convince him to buy longer pants. It felt good to be an equal—not a star, and not a victim. I worked hard to pull my weight.

Henry always started with a ten-minute presentation of things I should do, followed by papers I needed to sign and decisions I needed to make. I refused his suggestions as kindly as I could and handed all my financial decisions over to Brad. And then, we got to the good part—lunch and ice cream.

I looked forward to my ice cream date with Henry all week. They were the one thing I never cancelled, even when I woke up full of excuses. He tried ten flavors before ordering his usual vanilla, and I ordered something new each time without testing it first, and we walked and ate and it felt like a little sip of the childhood I didn't get to finish.

It was so simple. Not what I would have dreamed about, if you asked me to imagine freedom. But it felt like all I could want in the world—choosing any flavor I liked and then wandering aimlessly with a real friend.

And yet, the past hung on my shoulders. Damia called and left messages. My doctors begged me to come in for scans. I woke up in a cold sweat sometimes, sure I dreamed it all and would open my eyes to the dreary walls of my ERC dorm room. I still spent days at a time in my fluffy white bed, hurting inside and out.

The only person I saw from before was Janey, who refused to let me go no matter how badly I treated her. She called constantly, even though I rarely answered, and considered my presence at her Friday dinner parties mandatory. I smiled and ate and put on my best Charlie London act while Janey filled my wine glass reluctantly and worried so hard it stung my eyes. I hated it. Her friends looked at me like an animal at the zoo—something they paid money to see, but were a little bit afraid of.

We reached a balance. At least, I did. Janey always wanted more, and I wouldn't give it to her. *Move in with me, start singing again, pick up your file, go to Sky Lake*—she was never satisfied.

I wanted to go to Sky Lake.

But I didn't.

I couldn't. Or I wouldn't. After a while, it didn't really matter. I had the license and the car and no more excuses, and I still didn't press the gas and go.

I'd sit in the car, hands tight on the steering wheel, heart aching, thinking this might be the day. But my fingers always let go. I'd get out of the car, stiff with tension and disappointed in myself and no closer to home.

I was afraid I wouldn't find it. Or that I would, but it would be old and abandoned and nothing like I remembered. Or exactly like I remembered, and disappointed in me.

In my dreams, though, I searched for it.

I drove the familiar route a thousand times, under a dark, threatening blanket of clouds that would bury me if I didn't get there soon. Fog clouded the path ahead. The forest was thick and dark on both sides of the road. All I could see in the rearview mirror were faces, twisted in agony or screaming.

Panic gripped my throat and branches reached for the car and although I was moving, nothing changed but the clouds. Lowering. So solid I could feel them, pressing down on me.

I woke up choking on wet, inky smoke every time.

I emerged from those dreams coughing and confused, my throat raw and my soul still somewhere else, and I could feel it. Sky Lake was slipping away.

And something inside me was slipping with it—my voice, a little rougher every time I woke up with that bitter darkness in my lungs. My soul, more and more reluctant to return.

As if he sensed my complicated homesickness, Henry started urging me to find a more permanent place to live. "You've been in that hotel for a *year*, Charlie." We were in his office, at the end of another unproductive meeting, and all I wanted was lunch and ice cream. But Henry wouldn't let it go. "A year," he repeated. His eyes were big and worried, like I'd done something truly insane. It must have seemed that way to Henry, who turned every space he occupied for more than an hour into a cozy little home. He pushed a stack of condo listings toward me, like I might find them more compelling up close.

"So what? I could live in a hotel for the rest of my life and not make a dent in those accounts you're always talking about." I flipped through the printouts. He worked hard to find places I would like. He'd already visited the top three. I felt guilty.

"I'm not worried about your finances. I'm worried about your..." He looked me up and down like he couldn't quite define the problem but it had to be there somewhere. "Your mental health, I guess. It's not *healthy* to live in a hotel. You don't really live there, because any time you leave for a few hours someone comes in and resets the whole thing to brand new."

It was interesting to see my situation from Henry's perspective. I had always lived in temporary places. Even in Los Angeles, where I played house with Chris, I didn't choose my own wallpaper or clean my own bathroom or feel any kind of permanence. The furniture was there when I arrived and when I left. A decorator chose the art with no regard for my taste. The laundry disappeared dirty and came back clean and someone else made the beds.

"Wouldn't it be nice to sleep in a bed you picked out? Hang pictures you love on your walls?" Henry dangled these things like prizes, and I didn't know how to explain that it would be like furnishing a house for a stranger.

"You could invite me over for dinner sometimes," he said. "It would be nice."

"It would be," I agreed, because it was true—I would have loved to be a person who invited Henry over for dinner.

"I just want you to have a home," he said.

The word hit me hard. *Home.* I saw trees flying by without changing. Felt the clouds drowning me from above. I shivered.

"I want you to feel like you belong somewhere," he said, and I thought *me too, but you can't always get what you want.*

"A condo is a good investment," Henry prodded, nudging the listings. "I think we should go ahead. You don't have to live in if you don't want to. You can rent it out. But it would be a step."

A step. Toward a home that wasn't mine. "No," I said, with more force than the suggestion warranted. He was only trying to do his job. "I don't want to buy a condo." Henry opened his mouth to overrule me—I always let Henry and Brad make the money decisions—and I tasted the dark, bitter smoke from my dreams. "I have a house," I said. The words pushed themselves up my throat and through my lips with the force of Sky Lake itself, refusing to be denied.

Calling itself a house, when it was more like an open wound.

Henry tipped his head, interested. Relieved, probably. He'd be buying moving boxes by the end of the day if I didn't do something to slow him down. "It's been empty for a long time and it's going to be a project," I said, quickly. "I don't have it in me yet."

"Well, that's a different thing." Henry pulled the condo listings back to his side of the desk. "A remodel is a big job, but Brad and I can manage everything. As soon as you're ready." He tapped the desk with the tips of his fingers, thinking. "We could go soon. To check it out."

"Soon," I agreed. I wasn't lying. The word didn't mean anything. "It's... very emotional for me." I allowed Charlie to come to the surface. "The idea of going back. I still need some time."

"You just let me know when you're ready." Sympathy shined out of Henry. He was so good to me, and I was playing him like an audience. "But in the meantime, how about if you start coming to my place for dinner on Sundays? You know Greg's a great cook and you need to get out of that hotel more."

Guilt made me accept Henry's invitation, and I tried to back out the day of the dinner. But he wouldn't answer my calls, and responded to each of my text messages with "be here at six." I had no choice.

At Henry's door, I heard the cheerful commotion of music playing, pans clanking, and a dog barking. "I owe you ten bucks," Greg announced, when he let me in.

Henry laughed from somewhere inside before appearing with a wiry brown dog in his arms. "This is Newt," he said, bouncing the dog, whose face was nothing but eyes and teeth. Newt's tongue lolled and Henry grabbed his little paw to make him wave hello. "And you owe me twenty, because she's on time *and* she brought wine."

Greg laughed and pulled me into the kitchen. "You can cut the carrots," he offered, as if cutting the carrots was a great honor. He directed me to a cutting board and shooed Henry away. "And then the celery. And then I need you to zest those lemons." When I looked at him blankly, he assured me he would explain zesting once I got there. "You'll get the hang of it," he promised, as the carrots rolled away.

I didn't believe him, but I would have done anything to deserve a spot in that warm kitchen, feeling useful.

We cooked and talked as the apartment filled with more people than I thought it could hold. Greg and Henry and I took turns choosing music. Henry picked his usual showtunes. Greg tried to educate me about jazz. And I shyly contributed my favorite Light/Black songs, which were a surprise hit.

At some point, I realized I didn't want Nicolas Bell's voice to transport me anywhere. For once, I felt perfectly happy exactly where I was—home, or something like home, anyway. And then I remembered Los Angeles, and

Chris, and pulled myself back. Happy was a dangerous way to feel. It could be taken away.

But Henry said "Same time next week," as I left that night, and I agreed. I wanted to be part of their family just a little bit more than I wanted to protect myself.

I *was* part of their family. Me, not Charlie.

Greg insisted that he needed my help in the kitchen, even though I was all thumbs and spills and clumsy injuries that never quite required stitches. Henry pretended that Newt loved me, even though Newt's bulging eyes never left Henry. And Brad, who usually joined us, along with a rotating cast of friends and neighbors, made me sit next to him because I laughed at his jokes.

No one treated me like Charlie London, but, somehow, I was still important.

I started looking forward to Sunday night as much as I looked forward to ice cream with Henry. But I couldn't shake the voice warning me to be careful. It whispered in my ears as I chopped vegetables for Greg and tugged my sleeves as I sipped coffee at the candlelit table crammed into Henry's tiny living room. *You don't really belong here*, it said. But I wanted to, so I turned the music up and ignored it.

Part of me must have known I was making myself another in-between place—warm and cozy but not somewhere I could stay. I could almost see the truth, shimmering over the table like heat rising from pavement. But I told myself it was just the candles.

We weren't allowed to talk about work at Sunday dinner, which was one of my favorite things about it. But Brad didn't like that rule. "I have someone," he whispered to me as Greg and Henry cleared the dishes one rainy Sunday night, leaning close so Henry wouldn't hear, "I want to introduce you to."

It was harmless. Just Brad, being a romantic. Nothing I couldn't avoid with a smile and an excuse. But the words felt like a threat dropped in my plate. Just sitting there, waiting to see what I'd do next.

Before and after words, I thought, flashing back to that day in the courtyard with Damia although this moment and that one didn't have anything in common. The candles flickered and a creeping sensation worked its way down my neck, like fingernails. I sipped my wine to steady myself, but it didn't taste good anymore.

Brad's offer felt like something that would tip my life upside down.

"She doesn't need you setting her up on dates," Henry scolded, reaching over me to grab my plate. This earned him a withering look from Brad, who had endured a terrible blind-date that very week courtesy of Henry's matchmaking.

I should have laughed at their exchange, but the air felt too thin for laughing. *Not the air*, I thought. *Time*. Our table was a bubble, and the outside world pressed against it—past and future snapping for bites of me. One wrong move, I knew, and this life I treasured would pop. I gripped my seat for balance. Whatever Brad was offering me, I didn't want it.

My heart slammed against my ribs, disagreeing.

"It's not a date," Brad insisted. "I wouldn't do that to her. He's a client of mine, and a big fan of hers, and he's kind of... stuck. He's searching for something. Going in circles. I think meeting her would shake him out of it. This is an entirely self-interested request."

Brad turned back to me, twinkling optimistically. Henry rolled his eyes and replaced my wine glass with a coffee cup. Outside, a form emerged from the rain battering the window—a stranger in the dark. Lost and longing for something. So familiar that it took my breath away.

Not real, I thought, remembering the ghosts around my bed at the hospital. But my heart reached for him. Vines. Strong and tangled and willing to drag me if that's what it took. I felt the fingers again, icy on my neck.

"I don't think so," I whispered, my voice scratchy and painful.

Brad's face fell but his eyes stayed hopeful—he would keep trying, and I would keep refusing, and my seat would move a little farther away from the table every time I said no. But I didn't have another answer. I only had my heart pounding yes and my throat full of black clouds and a ghost outside in the rain, trying to take me somewhere I wasn't ready to go.

"I really can't," I said, and poured his coffee, a silent apology for being uncooperative. A plea—*let me stay here a little bit longer.*

Greg brought out dessert—a berries and cream cake, because he knew I wouldn't eat chocolate—and the conversation moved on. But I couldn't get a single bite past my heart. It was rattling its cage, reaching between my ribs, trying to get at something *out there* when I just wanted to be safe and happy *in here.*

I crushed a berry with my fork. My heart wanted me to make a different decision. But it wanted all kinds of things it couldn't have.

Things you won't give it, the voice said, and I wished somebody would turn the music up.

28

CHARLOTTE

Sunday dinners and vague promises could only hold Henry off for so long, and I felt my time ticking like it did when Johnathan stopped putting the guard on my balcony, or when my heart stopped being able to bear the pain in the hospital. No matter how much I wanted to keep my world exactly as it was, that's not a state that things like to stay in.

Henry's suggestions, which used to float away on a breath, became solid things with grabbing hands and heavy feet. He waited in his office every week with research, numbers, and reasoning.

If I didn't want to start working on the house, how about renting an apartment?

If I wouldn't consider a show, how about some voice lessons, or a writing class—something to get my creativity flowing?

No matter what I refused, he waited persistently with an alternative.

He started asking me, at the end of our meetings, what I wanted to do with my life. When I finally admitted that I didn't want to do anything, he rubbed his temples like a tired old man with a headache. "You're not even trying," he complained, and he wasn't just talking about my failure to answer his question.

I knew his steady pressure would wear one of us out, eventually.

It happened on a Wednesday. We were at our regular lunch spot, and I could see his patience thinning—a sweater going bald at the elbows. I tried to divert him with a funny story about someone in the hotel elevator. When that didn't work, I presented menu ideas for Sunday night. But he wanted to have a serious conversation, and my attempts to lighten the mood only irritated him.

"Ok," I surrendered, when I ran out of distractions. "I'm listening. Just say it." I did not want to listen. I did not want him to say it. I wanted lunch and ice cream to be *enough*.

But it was not enough. In his slow, thoughtful way, Henry explained that there was a fine line between taking time to get your feet under you, and letting them fuse themselves to the pavement, and I was doing the second thing. "You have to pick a direction and start moving."

He sounded like Janey.

I fiddled with the thick cloth napkin. It was unsatisfying—I wanted something that would come apart in my hands. "I'm still adjusting to life… after," I said, trying for the sad look that always shifted him into sympathy mode.

"That's exactly what I'm worried about. You're adjusting. To this." He gestured at the restaurant, like it held all my problems in its dining room. "You need to get out of your comfort zone."

I wanted to tell him that not long ago, my comfort zone was the bed in my hotel room, and I'd come pretty far from there. But he wouldn't like that answer. "I'm working on it," I said, instead, and he shook his head, disapproval pulling his eyebrows down.

"Don't lie to me."

I flinched. Henry never spoke harshly to me. And I didn't *want* to lie to him. But he already rejected the truth, so what else could I do? I bit my lip to keep myself from crying.

"This is about your future," he said. "No, not your future. Your *happiness.*"

Your happiness. Like a thing that already belonged to me, just waiting to be claimed. I wanted to explain that I was happy on our ice cream walks. At Sunday dinner. Letting Greg talk me into unreasonable shoes. And I was terrified I'd lose all that, just because I couldn't sing or buy a condo or drive to Sky Lake.

"I'm not ready," I said. "But I will be. Soon." Soon, I reminded myself, could mean anything. An hour, a day, a decade. "I promise, Henry. Soon." *Don't give up on me.* I clutched the napkin and waited, terrified of losing him. And with him, everything else.

Henry sighed. A vase of flowers trembled between us, and I hoped I was not as disappointing as the girl at the coffee shop, the day we met. "I just want what's best for you," he said.

The argument loosened. Fell on the table. Started to melt into the tablecloth. "I know," I said. "And I'm grateful for it." I was. More than I could possibly express.

"Soon," he said, and when he said it, the word meant something. But I nodded, blinking back tears, willing to say anything to keep us at the table.

Henry apologized as we walked to the ice cream shop. "I shouldn't have been so pushy," he said, handing me a tissue. Poor Henry, making another client cry. "I didn't mean it."

Henry was as transparent as a pane of glass, and I knew he was mainly sorry that his tough love didn't get through to me. But we could go back to normal, at least for now, and my relief almost set the tears free. "You're the least pushy person I know." I leaned against him. "I know you're just looking out for me."

"Think about it, though, ok? Even if you sing something into your phone and send it to me. Just something. A start, you know?"

We walked, arm in arm, our feet following the familiar path. I would think about it, and I would decide not to do it, and Henry and I would have this conversation again and again until he gave up on me. I could see it in front of me like a highway, wide and straight and easy to follow.

My phone rang just after we selected our ice cream—vanilla for him, as always, and black raspberry with chocolate chips and rainbow sprinkles for me. On a normal day, I wouldn't have answered it, but the lingering tension made me jump at the distraction.

Janey's voice blared for the whole shop to hear, and I wished I let it go to voicemail. "So, I was wondering if we could move our Friday dinner to Sunday this week because work is crazy?" she asked, without saying hello. I heard busy office sounds behind her, and tried not to picture her old desk piled with yellow folders. "I know it's short notice but you skipped last week and I really want to see you this week, so please?"

For one, beautiful moment, I stood there with an ice cream cone and a bulletproof excuse. Sunday dinner with Henry. And then Henry leaned into the phone.

I could smell the cologne Greg and I chose for him on one of our shopping trips. I could see an idea brightening in his eyes. I could feel my world starting to tip. *Before and after*, I thought, and gripped the cone so hard that it cracked. Ice cream oozed out, cold and sticky.

"She's coming to my place Sunday," he said, and I dared to hope he was rescuing me. "But we'd love it if you joined us." My heart sank. "The more the merrier!"

"Perfect," Janey chirped, and panic surged through me. Janey could not come to Sunday dinner. Sunday dinner was *mine*. "I'll bring wine. See you then!"

She hung up before I could pull the invitation back.

Henry smiled innocently, pretending not to notice the ice cream leaking between my fingers. "We'll have Brad, too," he offered, even though Brad usually came to Sunday dinner and it wasn't any kind of concession. "It'll be a nice party." He took a bite of my ice cream and made a face. "I've been wanting to meet her."

Henry might not have been able to make me sing, but he could make a crack in the wall I built between my new life and my old one. And cracks have a way of widening.

I spent Sunday hoping for a last-minute reprieve—for Janey to get a cold, or a power outage at Henry's place. Anything to stop the collision. I jumped every time my phone pinged. Once, I saw Greg's name and thought *this has to be it*. But dinner was going on as planned. And I couldn't even get out of this with an excuse—even if I stayed in the hotel, Janey would be there, inserting herself into my new life.

Contaminating it with my old one. Or pushing me out, into a future I didn't want.

I cringed every time I thought about Janey in the same room with Henry, Brad, and Greg. I'd never get away from her if she wormed her way into their lives. And, in the back of my mind, I wondered if meeting her would break whatever wall of denial let someone as good as Henry be friends with someone like me.

A woman who worked for a monster.

Janey arrived that night with two bottles of wine and a big smile, but we'd known each other too long for secrets and I could see her nerves. The wine was too expensive, the smile forced. She hugged me so hard that it hurt, and I extracted myself from the embrace as quickly as I could.

Henry shook her hand so hard that her whole body shook with it. Greg hugged her hello like an old friend. Janey gushed greetings and compliments as jealousy blazed through me. If Greg had given her something to do in the kitchen, I might have burst into tears right in the middle of the party. But Greg pulled me into the kitchen, giving me a tight squeeze before pointing me toward the salad bowl.

I strained to hear the conversation in the other room. "So, you're Charlie's other friend," Brad exclaimed, and I peeked around the corner. He was taking Janey in like a great work of art that deserves to be admired slowly. "It is so nice to meet you."

I abandoned the lettuce I was washing—wrong, apparently, because Greg kept taking my pieces and rinsing them again—and hurried over. I didn't want them talking about me, and couldn't imagine what else they'd have to talk about. "I was starting to think she invented you," Brad teased.

I pushed between them, smiling too hard. Brad stared at Janey, stars in his eyes. Janey blushed and giggled and appeared to age backwards. They were too caught up in each other to even notice me standing there.

He's always a flirt, I told myself, but it was more than that. I could feel it on my skin—love at first sight—the closest thing ordinary people have to magic. I brushed it off like something dirty.

I don't want to be this person, I thought, but I wasn't happy for them. Only sad for myself.

Greg took my elbow and led me back to the kitchen.

Brad and Janey spent the evening in their own personal party, new love so thick I swear I could see it around them, shiny and impenetrable. I poked at my plate, feeling sorry for myself as they shot sparks across the table at each other. The candles were dimmer, the food less delicious, the conversation dull. Even the wine didn't smooth the edges of my dark mood.

The past squatted at my feet, scratching my ankles raw, and the future tapped insistently on the windows. *Time's up*. But I clung to the table. I wasn't ready.

Newt climbed into my lap, and I focused on his rough fur against my fingers as everything changed around me again.

Brad and Janey met for brunch the next morning, and dinner the night after that, and soon I was a reluctant audience to their blossoming relationship. "What kind of flowers will she like?" Brad asked me, before their third date. "What's his favorite food?" Janey demanded, before he went to her place for dinner.

When they had their first fight, they both called me. I didn't answer the phone—I couldn't imagine a less qualified relationship counselor. And I probably would have pushed them both to break it off. I worried about Brad. He was such a romantic, and Janey was a tornado.

A tornado I couldn't hide from anymore. She thought she knew what was best for me, and with Brad under her thumb, she had backup.

And she was up to something. I could feel it.

I cancelled our standing Friday night dinners when she started being cagey about who else she invited. I lied when she interrogated me about my plans, so she went around me to Henry, and I had to start lying to him, too. She was scheming. I just couldn't figure out the trick. So, I avoided her, and she chased me, and neither one of us got what we wanted.

Me—to feel safe in my new life. Her—to be part of my life.

Or, maybe, just to make me live it.

"She needs to get moving," Brad said, in Janey's voice, when I sneaked in to see Henry one morning. His impression was so good that I almost spit out a mouthful of coffee. "She's wasting her talent. Wasting her life. And forget about all that, she's just plain shirking her responsibilities. You know she has stuff to pick up at ERC? She'll never have closure until she does that. And she has to do an interview at some point—people are waiting to hear from her. And I don't know why she's living in that hotel, she has a *house*."

He repeated this with humor, but anxiety made his hands a little too expressive.

"I'm actually serious," he said, dropping the impression and deflating into a chair. "She thinks I have some kind of influence over you. She won't let it go. Help me out, Charlie, please. It's not like she's asking you to do something that isn't good for you. Henry's been bugging you to do this stuff for months."

Brad looked nervous. Henry looked interested in what would happen next.

I put my coffee down a little too hard, and it sloshed onto Henry's desk.

"Just pick one thing," Brad begged. "One thing from her list. That's all I need."

I grabbed a handful of tissues to mop up the coffee. "Buy her flowers," I said. "She'll forget about it."

"She won't," he groaned. "She cares about you too much."

She cared about me so much that she pretended to be afraid of Johnathan, knowing he'd never hurt her, in order to win a few more months, a few more weeks, a few more days of my cooperation. The angry words were in the back of my throat—I could feel their sharp edges, cutting me from the inside—but unleashing them would be wrong. Janey and Brad were happy, and no matter how I felt, they didn't steal that happiness from me.

"I'll pick up my things," I offered. I would put it off, and Janey would forget about it. But, for now, it would give Brad a win. "Soon. How's that? You can tell her you really wore me down."

Brad bounced to his feet and startled me with a tight, grateful hug. "You are making me look like the best boyfriend on earth. *Thank* you."

"She's going to eat you alive," I warned, and he just laughed.

"How about that client of mine?" he asked. "Meet us for a drink tonight?"

Brad quirked an eyebrow. Playful. Hopeful. I hated to disappoint him. But his question made the floor tremble underneath my feet. "Sorry," I said, swallowing a wave of longing that didn't feel like it belonged to me. "No."

I fled to the hollow safety of the hotel before anyone could ask me for anything else.

29

CHARLOTTE

I didn't pick up my file. I ignored the interview requests that piled up on Henry's desk. It wasn't hard to avoid those things, because I didn't want to do them. But my voice burned in my chest, and it hurt more and more to hold it there. It kept me up at night, rattling my ribs like prison bars. When you're only good at one thing, and you choose not to do it, it leaves a hole—a deep, painful hole. And Henry wouldn't leave it alone.

He suggested voice lessons—just for fun. He made an appointment with a doctor to evaluate my claim that my vocal cords were damaged. He bought me books on songwriting, sent links to vocal exercise videos, left biographies of famous singers lying around his office, hoping I'd pick one up and be inspired.

When none of that worked, he got sneaky. He sang along with the radio extravagantly every time I got in his car—I laughed but didn't take the bait. He bribed Brad's toddler niece to ask me for a lullaby when she and her mother visited the office one day—I distracted her with chocolate from Henry's secret stash. He intentionally got the most annoying songs he could think of stuck in my head, and I'd retaliate with something worse, but I wouldn't hum along.

I told myself that we were having fun, but I knew better. Henry was dead serious.

I didn't know how serious, though, until he scheduled his twenty-third birthday party at Brad's favorite karaoke bar and requested a song from each guest as his present. "This has absolutely nothing to do with you," he insisted, but he wasn't even trying to hide his triumph.

Henry thought it was funny—a surprise move in the game we were both playing—but he had backed me into a corner. It was such a simple request. I couldn't deny it without hurting him. And I couldn't grant it without hurting myself.

And, maybe, everyone else in the room. I hadn't let my voice out in so long that I was terrified of it. Every time I woke up from one of my nightmares with that black smoke in my lungs, I felt a little more rotten inside. How could I let that out in front of Henry and all of his friends?

I told him I could go to the party, but I couldn't sing. I felt it, sharp and final—another checkmark in the wrong column of our friendship.

Henry and Greg showed up at my hotel an hour before the party. "Come on," Henry teased. "It'll be fun." He jiggled a wig and hat like the sight of hair wagging in my face might be enticing, and I batted it away. I told him that I would go, but I wouldn't sing, and he seemed to accept that. But here he was, at my door an hour before the party with a disguise, acting like we never agreed to anything.

"You're the star of the show, Henry," I said. "Focus on being the birthday guy. I'll sit with you and enjoy the party, ok? It'll be fun." I wanted, desperately, for it to be fun. For what I could give him to be *enough*.

Henry shook his head firmly. "Nope. One song from everyone. That's the price of admission, and you are not an exception."

Guilt threatened to outweigh common sense as he pushed the wig into my hands. I said no to Henry so often. I desperately wanted, for once, to say yes. It swelled in my chest—the now-familiar desire to be a better person than I was.

"No one will know you. I promise," he said.

It did not seem like a promise he could make.

"One song, for me, and then you can lurk in the back of the room with Brad and Janey all night. It's my birthday, Charlie, please?"

The "please," combined with the saddest look I had ever seen, sealed my fate. He only wanted one song. Three or four minutes of my life. There was a time when I wanted to sing so badly that I made a deal with the devil for it. How could I say no to Henry? I wasn't Charlie London anymore. I wasn't a prisoner. There was no reason to think my voice would be anything more than a sound in that room.

"Fine," I agreed. "But if it's a disaster and I ruin your party, I'm not sorry." I grabbed the wig and went into the bathroom to figure out my face. Avoiding detection on stage required a different level of makeup than hiding at a table in a dark bar.

I walked in with Greg's arm clamped firmly around my shoulders, not sure if he was offering moral support or preventing me from running away. Pink lights streamed over the crowd, bouncing off disco balls hanging from the ceiling. A gold crown encrusted with plastic jewels waited for Henry. He plopped it on his head with childlike glee and insisted on taking a picture with me. "We'll have to get another one," he said, scrunching his nose as he reviewed it. "After the party. When you look like yourself."

Greg ordered me a drink and told me to relax, but I couldn't. My stomach was a hard little ball and my hands wouldn't stop shaking. Part of me wanted to get it over with, and part of me wanted the bar to fall into the earth before they called me up.

"Where's Brad?" I asked, when he hadn't arrived an hour into the party. Janey would come with Brad, and I needed her to be there before I went on stage. As much as her overprotectiveness annoyed me, she would know if I needed help before I did, and making a scene didn't bother her a bit. She'd drag me out if she thought I needed a rescue.

"Relax." Henry had already performed his ear-splitting rendition of "Sweet Caroline," and Greg was theatrically butchering "Let it Be." His gestures—hands over his heart, arms outstretched, one hand reaching for the sky—had clearly been practiced, and the crowd loved it.

Under other circumstances, I would have loved it, but I couldn't relax. Not with that stage looming over me. I didn't know if I could control my voice in this tiny room, wide awake, feeling everything. It was nothing like the drugged, impersonal performances of my last few years as Charlie London. And I couldn't even numb myself with the drink—my stomach was churning.

"He's stuck at the office," Henry said, when I wouldn't let it go. "I'm sure they'll be here soon."

Greg finished his song with a dramatic bow, drawing a chorus of claps and whistles out of the crowd before they good naturedly shouted him off the stage. He returned to our table, getting high-fives and pats on the back all the way. Henry jumped up and hugged him, and I wondered what I'd have to do to get a life like this. Fun. Friends. *Love.*

As Henry and Greg settled back down at the table, hands clasped, I wondered if it might be worth it. And then someone called me to the stage, and I knew it wasn't. What I had was enough, and now I was going to go up on that stage and ruin it.

I was about to show everyone the monster.

Fear reddened my cheeks, tightened my chest, and sloshed in my stomach. Excitement followed it, cold and energizing.

I didn't want to do this.

And I'd never wanted to do anything as much as I wanted to do this.

The feelings fought, competing for control of my body, as I headed away from the warm safety of the table. Henry reached for my hand as I left him.

"Thank you," he said, squeezing, and I knew I was doing the right thing just as clearly as I knew I was making a big mistake.

My hands shook as I adjusted the microphone. The pink lights turned in sickening circles above me. My face felt hot and sweaty—I prayed Charlie London wasn't shining through my makeup. And then it hit me. I was about to unleash Charlie's *voice*. I could be outed the minute I made a sound.

Or, I might not be. I might open my mouth and release an ugly yowl or a little squeak or a puff of dust. Fear overtook excitement, rippling through my belly.

I widened my stance, pushing my energy down through my feet, through the stage, and into the earth, the way one of my old teachers told me to. I pushed my shoulders back, tipped my chin up, and swept my attention through my chest, neck, and head, trying to remember all the good advice I never needed before. I took a slow breath, dreading and longing for the release of that first note.

I wished they'd hurry up with the music.

I wished the power would go out.

When I was thirteen years old, Johnathan Everett made me admit that I wanted to sing more than I wanted my freedom. Standing on that stage, shaking with fear, I felt the echo of that moment. I wanted to sing, even though I knew there would be consequences.

Even though I wasn't sure I would survive it.

My voice blazed out of me like fire—hot and cleansing. I thought I'd been seeing and hearing and feeling and breathing since I left the hospital, but I might as well have been buried underground. That first note left me naked and blinking in the light. Amazed by the big bright world outside.

How did I live without this? I wondered.

I caught a glimpse of Brad and Janey in the back of the room. Brad gave me a thumbs up while Janey jumped and waved. The audience leaned toward me, then toward each other, as the love in the song swirled through the room.

Not too much. Just enough.

Charlie London still had it.

But something felt off. I searched for Janey again, but as my eyes scanned the back of the room, my heart lurched. I hadn't been on stage in so long that I hardly remembered what it was supposed to feel like, but I knew it shouldn't feel like glass being pulled through my veins. I clutched the microphone and pressed myself into the floor and braced myself against the pain. But it grew, strong and insistent. My heart hammered and my muscles quivered from the effort of remaining attached to the stage.

This isn't right, I thought, and then my thoughts flew away, mixing with the music until I couldn't tell where I ended and it began.

I was losing control, and if I lost control, the whole room would go with me.

Heat flared under my wig, making sweat drip down my forehead, but my voice was barreling forward, tearing itself out of me. The air crackled with electricity, and this time, I didn't have Chris in the back of the room to blame it on.

Something was back there, though. I could feel it, pulling me.

The crowd glowed pink under the lights—rosy with love. *They're ok*, I thought, comforted by this, at least. And then the music surged again, hot and blinding. A memory came with it, so vivid that I almost fell inside, of David's troubled expression when he told me it would be different to sing away from Sky Lake. Was he afraid of this?

A sudden crack, like lightening splitting clouds, cut through the room. The forest swirled around me. I smelled roses. I felt pine needles under my feet and the breeze off the lake. But the trees hung too low, reaching with bony fingers. Something wet and rotten lurked underneath the roses. The clouds were black and I could smell them—dark, smoky, bitter.

It was home, but not—like the place I escaped to in the hospital, without the glossy exterior. It was corrupted. Ugly. Dangerous.

This isn't Sky Lake, I thought, *this is me.* And then, even more horrifying—
maybe it is Sky Lake, and I'm destroying it.

Despair pulled me down. My voice pushed me up. My heart reached
into the room, and something reached back—a hand in the whirlpool, warm
and familiar and trying to save me as I wrestled with the music. But my voice
was a creature bending the bars of the prison I kept it in, and I couldn't
control it.

The clouds rumbled warnings. If I stayed too long, they'd drown me—I
knew that much, from my dreams. But if I pushed my voice down again, I
knew it would leave me. Sky Lake would leave me. I wouldn't get another
chance if I didn't take this one. I stood on that stage with one foot in a
nightmare, and thought *only bad options.*

I sank my feet into the rotten pine needles, took a deep breath of sickly-
sweet air, and welcomed the black, threatening clouds. I didn't want this
dark, rotting version of home, but I couldn't bear to lose it. I let the
nightmare have its way with me.

Somewhere far away, I felt my heart wrapping around something solid.
Holding on.

I stumbled off stage as soon as the song ended, drained and trembling
and not sure how much damage I'd done. People were smiling, saying things,
holding hands up for high fives. *They're all ok*, I thought, relieved, but the
room felt wrong. Murky, spinning, one breath away from skidding off a cliff.

At the table, Henry waited with a huge grin on his face. Around him, the
bar pulsed pink, my headache come to life. "You were amazing!" he shouted.
"Amazing amazing amazing! I knew you would be! I *knew* it!" His smile
faded as I got closer. "You hated it," he said, drooping like a thirsty plant.

I forced myself to smile through the seasick feeling that throbbed in my
stomach, keeping time with the lights. "No," I said. "I didn't. It was just…
overwhelming." I didn't know how to explain that the song was still pulling
me, a riptide no one else could feel.

"You didn't *sound* overwhelmed. You sounded incredible." Henry dropped back into his chair, the plastic crown crooked on his head. "I wish you felt that way."

I had ruined his birthday. I could see it in his face and his posture and the disapproving look on Greg's face. The whole point of this party was to put me on stage. That's what Henry wanted for his birthday—for me to sing a song and to love it. And I let him down.

I wished I could go back in time, but I couldn't decide where I'd go. Back five minutes, so I could walk off stage happy? Back two hours so I could fake food poisoning and avoid the party altogether? I thought it might be more honest to go back to that day in the coffee shop and never approach Henry at all.

Greg put another drink in Henry's hand, and I took advantage of the distraction. "I'm going to say hi to Brad," I lied, each word a knife in my raw throat. "I'll be back."

Henry reached for me, but I shrugged him off. I couldn't talk to him. Not now, with the music still inside me.

I pushed myself toward the exit, struggling as the floor slid and rolled. I heard Janey, calling for me. I felt the pull of the music, trying to keep me in the room. But I flew out into the dark without slowing down. My heart was trying to sink roots into the sidewalk outside the bar, but I just wanted to get away.

It was still reaching for something. And I was still running away from it.

My voice didn't leave me that night, and I was grateful. But it stole all the strength from my body. I slid down the door as it closed behind me and sleep sucked me down in one gulp.

I woke late the next morning, neck screaming from the angle I kept it in all night, body heavy and sore. I'd only managed a few sips of my drink, but my stomach lurched every time I turned my head. And my phone was blinking with messages.

Henry. Greg. Brad. Janey.

I couldn't face any of them. I stumbled to bed and passed out again. But my life was right there waiting when my exhaustion let me go.

I had to see Henry. Face the music.

I put on a brave face as I walked into his office, even though I still felt fragile from my performance. I expected one of Charlie's smiles to smooth it over, but something had changed. I felt it as soon as I stepped out of the elevator. Like the walls were waiting for us to have a fight.

Henry presented his ideas one by one, as always, and I rejected them one by one, as always, and then we went to lunch. But it felt like the moment right before a dream turns into a nightmare. "Let's not talk business," I suggested rearranging my silverware at our usual table.

I knew I couldn't squirm out of it again—it was all over Henry's face. My time was up. I'd been hearing it for weeks, tapping the windows at Sunday dinner, ticking along with the clock in his office. But I still pushed for another week, another day, another few hours. A little more time, before I lost everything.

Henry didn't send food back at a restaurant, no matter how wrong they got his order. He didn't complain when someone cut him in line. He never left a bad review or insisted that he was right. How could he give me an ultimatum? But he would do anything for someone he cared about if he thought they needed help. And he thought I needed help.

"It's not business," he said, "it's your life. You can't go on like this."

He sat up straight, hands clasped, eyes locked on mine, miles away from the Henry I met in that coffee shop. I wanted to show him this confident version of himself. He'd be amazed.

"You need to sing. I don't care where you do it. In the shower. In the car. Write something and tear it up. Record something that you're not going to let anyone but me hear. But do something. Start somewhere."

I could see it in his posture and the set of his jaw—he wasn't going to take no for an answer. And I didn't have another answer. I picked up my fork and squeezed it, letting the edge of the metal bite into my hand. The world was tilting. Tipping me off the edge. And without Henry, I had nothing to hold onto.

Anger rose like bile—this was Janey's fault. She put these ideas in Henry's head. If only I'd been able to keep her out of my life. But how could I wish that, when she and Brad were clearly meant for each other?

Maybe, I thought, *I'm meant to lose Henry.* I could already feel the loss, heavy and inevitable, like the air right before it rains.

"Come on," he said, as desperate as I was to pull this conversation out of its skid. "You have a gift. Something to share. You can't just bottle it up because your life didn't go the way it should have." He leaned toward me, like he could give the words more impact with physical proximity. "You have a lot of life ahead of you."

He meant to be encouraging, but it felt like a threat.

I held Henry's gaze for a long time, knowing I might never see this look of kind concern on his face again. "What if I sing and no one likes it?" I asked, finally, even though I knew we were past gentle questions and tearful confessions of insecurity. I missed my chance. "I'm not Charlie London. And that's who everybody loves. I might not be... anything special." *Or I might be something very dangerous,* I thought, but didn't say, because it sounded crazy. "I didn't make myself famous. Johnathan did it. I'm... a fraud."

If only he knew how it hurt to say this.

But Henry was tired of my excuses. He threw himself back in his chair and slapped the table hard enough to make water jump out of my glass. "Who the hell cares?" He stood up. I hardly recognized him, looming over me in a suit that didn't expose his wrists and ankles, making a spectacle of himself on purpose, saying "hell" like it was just a thing he said.

Pride and grief drew tears into my eyes. He was growing up. And I was losing him.

"Johnathan made you pretend to be someone you weren't, right? To make you popular?"

I nodded reluctantly.

"And you'd rather waste the rest of your life than risk a real rejection." He threw his napkin down theatrically, and a pair of old ladies at the next table tipped toward us, not wanting to miss anything. "You can't blame someone else now, this is a choice *you're* making. *You're* choosing to give up, be a victim, not try. And I don't want to be part of that."

I said nothing while he waited for me to give him a reason to sit back down. He was right, and I respected him too much to argue. It *was* a choice, and I didn't know how to make a different one. He shook his head sadly. "If you want someone to absorb your money while you feel sorry for yourself, that's fine, but it's not me. Your call, Charlie."

He left me there, alone at the table. And I stayed, because the alternative—to chase him, when he wanted me to move forward—would have been an insult to the strong, honorable man walking away.

As much as it hurt, I had to give him credit for a perfect dramatic exit.

30

CHARLOTTE

Sulking in a hotel is a comfortable but unsatisfying experience. No one hears your heavy sighs, or encourages you to eat a little, or kicks you in the ass and tells you to get over it already. The curtains are thick, blending day and night together. Someone changes the sheets and cleans the bathroom. Everything you need is delivered by people who are paid not to notice what you're doing.

A sulk can last weeks in a hotel, and no one even knows it's happening.

Greg checked on me two days after the fight. He had the day off and wanted to go for a walk. "We don't even have to talk about it," he said. "Although if you ask me, it wouldn't take much to resolve this. Any little thing would be enough. Send him a recording, or let him book those singing lessons he won't shut up about. Or ask him to help you with your house! He can't resist a project."

They were all such reasonable suggestions, but it felt dishonest to do some halfway thing just to buy time. Henry wanted me to make a real change in my life, not pick the least painful item from a list. "Does he know you're calling me?" I asked, and when Greg said no, I declined the walk. I didn't want to be a secret in their relationship. Or worse, a disagreement. It would have been a betrayal of all those Sundays when I let them treat me like family, even though I knew it couldn't last.

I turned down Janey's invitations to dinner, and she accepted with guilty relief. "You know I love you, right?" she said, instead of arguing, when I suggested that my presence might put Brad in an awkward position.

It stung, but I knew she should put her relationship with him before our dysfunctional friendship, and I forced a smile into my voice. "Of course I know. I'll see you soon." And then, I sent her to voicemail along with everybody else.

A week went by, and then two, and I didn't see anyone who didn't work for the hotel. The little life I built for myself, so inadequate by Henry and Janey's standards but so precious to me, faded until I thought I might have imagined it.

I would have given anything to be back in Henry and Greg's kitchen, tripping over the dog while Greg patiently instructed me, for the third time, on the proper way to cut an onion. I would have loved to spend an hour evading Janey's nosy questions at one of those fancy brunch places she loved. I would have said yes to every single suggestion Henry presented, just for the pleasure of lunch and ice cream afterwards.

But my bed might as well have been coated in glue. I could hardly make myself get up and take a shower.

When Brad called, late in my second week of wallowing, his voice was the most beautiful thing I'd ever heard.

"Janey's really worried about you," he said. "She thought this would all blow over in a few days, and it hasn't, and she doesn't know what to do. She feels like she's in the middle, and I'm running out of comforting things to say." He sounded helpless and desperate, like Janey's unhappiness caused him physical pain. "Can you call her and tell her you're ok? Maybe let her take you out to lunch?" Then, like he wasn't sure he wanted the answer, "You *are* ok, right?"

"I'm fine." My voice, which hadn't done more than order room service in days, felt creaky and a little too loud.

"That," Brad said, "is not convincing."

He was tense. Worried about me, and about Janey. It was just like the day I promised to pick up my file from ERC, except this time, I didn't want to lie to him.

"No," I said. "I'm not ok." I walked to the window and pulled the curtains open, flooding my room with light. "I'm really sorry, actually. I let all of you down."

Brad started to argue with me.

"That is not convincing," I said, and he almost laughed. "Tell Janey I'll see her today." The light hurt my eyes, but I didn't shut it out. "Say you called and gave me a long lecture and I totally agree that I need to pick up my file and get some... closure. I'll be in her office at one." I couldn't go back in time and be a better friend, but I could keep my promise.

Brad stumbled through a thank you, clearly caught between gratitude and concern. "Are you sure?" he asked.

"Yes. I'll get my file, and you'll be boyfriend of the year."

"Thank you." He sounded like he wanted to climb through the phone and check me for a head injury. "That's more than I would ever have asked you to do. Are you really sure?"

"I'm sure." It was too little, too late, but it was *something*.

"We miss you around here, I hope you know that."

"We?" I asked, hopefully.

"He's haunting the office. It's pitiful. Please call him and put him out of his misery."

I called the minute I hung up with Brad, thinking maybe this was the call he would answer, but I only got voicemail, and then the usual text—*have you reconsidered?*

Henry and I could both be extremely stubborn.

"I'm going to pick up my file today," I wrote back. "I know that's not what you want me to do, but it's something. I miss you."

I would go straight to Henry's office afterwards, I decided. I'd show it to him. I'd find a way to make him understand that I was stuck, but I didn't *want* to be stuck anymore.

I kept waiting to feel something as I drove to ERC, but I was alone with the dull pain that throbbed in my chest since Henry and I had our fight. It was emotional pain, but also physical, because the poison left my body permanently unable to tell the difference. It felt like company in the hotel, but behind the wheel it became a dangerous distraction and I took careful, shallow breaths to avoid irritating it.

I parked my car in the empty lot. The sprinklers must have been on, because the big green lawn glistened. There was no evidence of my desperate run. I stood there for a long time, looking for it—it seemed like my path should be burned through the grass.

I walked up to the familiar door. For a second, I searched for my long-gone keycard, then pressed the buzzer. It was strange to ring the buzzer, strange to tell someone my name, strange to walk in and not know the woman who opened the door or the one who sat at the front desk.

I tried not to think about Johnathan's empty office. In my mind he still sat there with a thick, marked-up book, his notes waiting for mine.

"I know where I'm going," I told the receptionist. She hesitated, weighing the rules against the expression on my face. She let me go.

I walked without thinking to the North Tower dorms and stopped outside my own door. The bland, institutional hallway, with its permanent smell of microwaved meals and eerie quiet, felt exactly like it did when I lived there. A faded Easter wreath made out of construction paper eggs hung limply on my door—something Janey made to cheer me up a very long time ago. It fluttered to the floor as I turned the doorknob, the last scrap of brittle tape crumbling, and I gently pushed it to the side with one foot. Stepping on it wouldn't be right, but I couldn't quite bring myself to touch it.

Inside the room, my neatly made bed sat in the corner, like it expected me back at any moment, but a thick blanket of dust told the truth. A book and some papers littered my desk. The fluffy pink rug Janey insisted on when we were teenagers covered the floor. A magazine lay on the bedside table, open to an interview I didn't even remember sitting for. My own face smiled mysteriously up at me.

Charlie's face.

I couldn't tell the difference anymore.

Revulsion gripped me as I looked around the little time capsule. I didn't want to salvage anything from my past—I would have set it on fire if I could have. But my feet shuffled me across the rug anyway. My hands reached for the desk drawers. Maybe I'd find something—a treasure or an answer. A book of matches.

I went to the closet last. Turned the knob. Creaked it open, knowing, before I saw it, what I came back for.

The old cardboard box, gone soft and round at the edges, squatted on the floor, surrounded by mismatched shoes, exactly where I left it. Goosebumps rose on my arms.

My songs—every single one I wrote—were there, waiting patiently for me. I fell to my knees and pulled the box out of the dark.

I reached for a thick journal in a rich shade of red with a bird embossed on the cover. Johnathan gave it to me. I remembered writing in this book on an airplane, in a limousine, in a public bathroom, in the corner at a loud party. For a moment, I was back there—at the party, overflowing with inspiration. I ran my hands over the smooth leather, trying, and failing, to untangle my feelings. The girl in the memory was trapped. Pretending. But the inspiration was real. The words in the book, untouched by Johnathan Everett, were real.

They were *mine*.

Flipping through, I recognized the vibrant purple of a marker, the scribble of a dull pencil I had to borrow, the elegant flow of a good, inky pen Johnathan gave me as a gift. Every page brimming with words that I dug out of my soul.

I pulled out a blue one with flowers on the cover. I poured my feelings into it after my breakup with Chris, and I could feel them, humming a sad song in my hands.

Another, plain brown and worn from use, was full of songs I wrote after I first heard Nicolas Bell. They were all about Sky Lake, and I desperately wanted to share them with him. I flipped it open to the first page. *Sky Lake Lost*, it said, as if I ever would have been allowed to name anything myself.

This might be too much, I thought, pressing my hand against the spot right over my heart, where a poetic bruise had darkened my skin since the fight with Henry. I couldn't face all those feelings. I'd be overwhelmed, like I was when I tried to sing at Henry's birthday party. Like I was at that little show in Los Angeles. It wasn't safe for me to feel so much.

I replaced the journals, but hoisted the box into my arms. I couldn't leave it behind. It would have been like crawling away without my legs.

By the time I reached Janey's office with the heavy box, I was exhausted. The ache in my chest felt more like a heart attack with every step, radiating down my arms and numbing my fingers. I wanted to put the box down—I needed to put it down—but I couldn't make myself let the journals go. I was holding my music, preserved in that closet like a bug in amber. Waiting for me to be ready for them.

"Hey, let me get that." A man in a baseball cap grabbed the box like it weighed nothing, and it took a minute for me to recognize him as one of the guards who used to patrol the halls. Back then, he never smiled. "I'll get a cart for you." He swung the box casually under one arm and I winced, afraid a journal might fall out. They were precious. Important. I needed to keep them safe.